Praise for *Rolling Fields*
A book of the year for *El Pais*, *El Periodico* and *ABC*

'Effortlessly readable and fizzing with energy, this novel is by turns quirky, funny and thoughtful'  *Mail on Sunday*

'Incisive and bittersweet'  *Independent*

'Breezy, bittersweet and tangential, Trueba's prose captures the rueful regrets of a man who's searching for meaning and redemption in a life that's short on both'  *Daily Mail*

'What holds the attention is the evocation of a culture trying to break free of rural, religious and Franco-ist ties. Dani's wistful search for validation – from music, sex, or his father – adds a thoughtful dimension'  *Evening Standard*

'David Trueba's skilfully crafted novel is fast-moving and full of sparkle, but with a deeper pull beneath the surface . . . It is a novel that tackles the chaos of life nakedly and nobly'
Michael Eaude, *Literary Review*

'Funny, poignant, full of honesty and warmth'  *Sun*

'A redemptive epic . . . Leaves us readers try to figure out how is it possible that his experience of life looks so much like ours'
Carlos Zanón, *El País*

'An effortless, fast-paced and light-hearted yet tremendously good piece of fiction'  *Qué Leer*

# ROLLING FIELDS

David Trueba is a writer and film director. He is the author of many bestselling, prize-winning novels, all widely translated. His latest film, *Vivir es fácil con los ojos cerrados*, which he wrote and directed, was a smash hit with audiences, longlisted for the Academy Awards 2015 in the Best Foreign Film category and won Goya Awards (the Spanish Oscars) for Best Film, Best Director and Best Original Screenplay.

Rahul Bery translates from Spanish and Portuguese and is based in Cardiff. His translations have appeared in *Granta*, *The White Review*, *Words Without Borders*, *The Yale Review* and the *TLS*, and he was the British Library's Translator in Residence from 2018 to 2019. *Rolling Fields* is his first full-length translation.

# ROLLING FIELDS

## David Trueba

Translated from the Spanish
by Rahul Bery

W&N
WEIDENFELD & NICOLSON

First published in Great Britain in 2020 by Weidenfeld & Nicolson
This paperback edition published in 2021 by Weidenfeld & Nicolson
an imprint of The Orion Publishing Group Ltd, Carmelite House, 50 Victoria
Embankment, London EC4Y 0DZ

An Hachette UK Company

10 9 8 7 6 5 4 3 2 1

Copyright © David Trueba 2020
This English language edition is published by arrangement with David Trueba c/o
MB Agencia Literaria S.L
English translation © Rahul Bery 2020

Support for the translation of this book was provided by Acción Cultural Española, AC/E.

This book has been selected to receive financial assistance from English PEN's "PEN
Translates!" programme, supported by Arts Council England. English PEN exists to
promote literature and our understanding of it, to uphold writers' freedoms around the
world, to campaign against the persecution and imprisonment of writers for stating their
views, and to promote the friendly cooperation of writers and the free exchange of ideas.
www.englishpen.org

  Supported using public funding by
**ARTS COUNCIL
ENGLAND**

The moral right of David Trueba to be identified as the author of this work has been
asserted in accordance with the Copyright, Designs and Patents Act of 1988.

Rahul Bery has asserted his right to be identified as the author of the English language
translation of this work.

A CIP catalogue record for this book is available from the British Library.

ISBN (Paperback) 978 1 4746 1288 3
ISBN (eBook) 978 1 4746 1289 0

Typeset by Input Data Services Ltd, Somerset
Printed and bound in Great Britain by Clays Ltd, Elcograf S.p.A.

MIX
Paper from
responsible sources
FSC
www.fsc.org   FSC® C104740

www.weidenfeldandnicolson.co.uk
www.orionbooks.co.uk

For my brother, Fernando, who never follows
the roads that lead to Rome.

# SIDE A

*we all know how it ends*

We all know how it ends and it doesn't end happily. It's a funny story, this one, because we all know the outcome but not the plot. We're both all-seeing and blind, wise and ignorant. This is at the root of that melancholy we all share, the vague feeling that makes us weep on overcast days, that keeps us awake in the middle of the night and unsettles us when we have to wait too long for a loved one to return. It's at the root of excessive human cruelty and unexpected human kindness. In a way, it's at the root of everything: knowing the ending but not how we get there. This game has strange rules, rules no child would ever accept, because children don't want you to tell them how the story ends: they don't yet realise that knowing the ending is the only way to enjoy what comes before.

There's a death car outside the house.

'Papá.' The word echoed deep inside the cave of my memories. 'Papá.' It was my voice. 'Papá, wake up.' And then it was my kids' voices. '*Oto*, come on, wake up.'

I was asleep. And when you sleep you sink into a deep, dark well in which time is all time accumulated – you're both child and adult, a complete and timeless self, and I become the pure essence of Dani Mosca. To wake up is to take your allotted place on the calendar, to return to your assigned position: no more hugging ghosts and speeding down the invisible motorway of your dreams.

On my cheek, my son's kisses. Ryo still gave me kisses, despite his age. He was nine and his kisses were those of all nine-year-olds: soft, sloppy, long. Maya sat down on the mattress; I could feel her weight by my feet. She rarely kissed me anymore – kisses had started to seem like kids' stuff to her. And there's nothing a twelve-year-old girl loathes more than kids' stuff.

Why is it always this way, that when you're a child you're in such a hurry to grow up? Last summer I watched my children playing happily in the sand on the beach and I thought: *when do we stop making castles by the sea?* When do we make that mistake? When do we accept that this is something meant only for kids? But maybe we never stop making sandcastles by the sea, we just call it something else. Like how becoming a parent doesn't mean you stop being someone else's child.

It must have been 7.30 a.m. when I climbed into bed, making it abundantly clear that this morning and I weren't meant for each other. And then, just moments after I'd shut my eyes, my children's voices came into my ears. *Oto, Oto.* When they're feeling affectionate they call me 'Oto', which is Japanese for 'Daddy'.

They sleep on the far side of the garden, in what is now Kei's house and theirs, and which was once ours. I ended up living in the studio, separated from them, on the other side of the overgrown patio, like a lodger. 'That's the way you bohemian types do divorce,' says Petru, the pure-blooded, tattooed Romanian we call whenever we need a handyman. He'd installed a shower and a tiny kitchen in the studio, and created a more intimate sleeping area, cut off from the rest of the equipment: the mixing desk, the computer, the keyboard, the guitars, the cables. This is where I live now.

Bohemian is a word no one uses any more, but it's a perfect way of describing a person who comes home after seven in the morning and goes to sleep in a music studio, on a futon that's barely a foot off the floor. During the school holidays Ludivina,

2

who's every bit as Romanian as Petru, never let the children come over to my studio before I'd shown any sign of being awake. She never called me a bohemian. She made excuses for me. She knew that a single man is like a football no one kicks around any more.

Kei was away doing concerts and she wouldn't be back until Tuesday. But what day was it today? That was the question. Definitely late July. Definitely the summer holidays, because when the children have school, Ludivina makes their breakfast first, then sends them in to wake me up. And in August they'd be off to Japan with their mother, to spend three weeks with their grandparents in Okinawa, on the beaches of Motobu; with the prospect of their absence not far off, I wanted to enjoy their company as much as possible. Yes, it was definitely late July.

Ludivina has been helping us with the kids for years; she shares her secrets with me and insists that one day Kei will forgive me for everything and I'll be able to cross back over the garden and live in our home again. Nacho, who plays the sax and does most of the brass arrangements on our recordings, says that anyone who takes their kids to school in the morning is a fucking slave. But he's wrong. Children in the morning are like freshly watered plants. Kei dreads early rising and prefers it when I take them. She knows I get up at dawn, that I no longer sleep like I used to. I'm afraid of sleeping too much, too deep.

For my daughter, Maya, arriving at school late is a total disaster, so we sometimes get a taxi for a journey that takes no more than fifteen minutes on foot. Ryo likes taxis, especially when they have a Spanish flag hanging from the rear-view mirror; every time Ryo sees a taxi driver with the flag he likes me to tell him the same story.

It's the tale of a taxi driver who spends so many hours behind the wheel he suddenly forgets where he is, what city he's in, and

3

even who he is and what he does for a living. Then he looks at the passenger seat and sees them, Maya and Ryo, two Japanese children. Alarmed, he becomes convinced he's in Japan and has no idea how to say a single word in Japanese. He becomes overwhelmed, because nothing is more overwhelming to a Spaniard than ceasing to be one entirely. Then all of a sudden – *bam!* – he sees the red-and-yellow flag hanging from the rear-view mirror and he says to himself, 'Oh yeah, I'm Spanish. Phew! what a relief.'

Ryo had to be told this story every single time. He only had to point at the flag for me to kick into action: 'Look, Papá, the mini Spanish flag.' I'd speak in a very low voice so that the drivers couldn't hear, though sometimes they'd notice my son's laughter and try to figure out what we were talking about.

I like imagining my children when they're older. Here's hoping the child never disappears from their faces completely. It's sad when you look at a person's face and can't see the child they once were, and sadder still to see children who already possess the face of the adult they will become. My son, Ryo, has a classmate with the face of a stockbroker; he even charges kids twenty cents to borrow his mobile. 'Don't even think about getting any bigger.' That's what I tell my daughter, Maya, every day at the school gates. 'No matter what anyone says, don't even think about getting bigger.' I repeat it every time until she stares back at me with that forced look of reproach – Oh, Papá, you're such a bore – before she gets swallowed up into the school.

Now, when they launch themselves onto my bed, they know full well that I don't even open my eyes until I've had four kisses. It's a security protocol to avoid being duped by children who aren't mine, the combination to my safe. They still tolerate my games. Through clenched teeth, my daughter asks me, 'When will you grow up, Papá?'

4

One, two, three and four – four kisses, there we have it.

'Oto, wake up. Open your eyes. Papá, there's a death car outside the house!'

## a taste of old rags

Kisses after lovemaking leave a taste of old rags on the lips. That's why I always get dressed and leave. After sex, every position is a compromising one: my arm under her head, her cheek on my chest, our backs turned away from each other. And these days I don't want to spend the whole night sleeping next to anyone. Because the night belongs to those who love. And I don't love. I prefer to be put through the ordeal of them watching me as I dress, exposing the skin that now lacks the weightlessness of desire as I search for a sock or for the underwear I abandoned on the floor, or put on the trainers with laces tied the previous morning.

'Are you going?' Carmela had asked, with her customary resentful sweetness.

It's so nice when they're still asleep and you can get dressed and then blow them a kiss, with one foot already out the door. But Carmela sat up to set the alarm on her phone, so the farewell was more laboured. Sitting up on the mattress, she moved like a cat, with that dishevelled hair that looks so good on women. They should pay hairdressers to mess it up like that. We kissed twice more, each kiss as dry and raspy as the hangover.

Carmela was a waitress at Bar de Quique and that was the seventh time we'd slept together. Such accuracy was entirely down to her.

'It's the seventh time we've slept together in four months,' she told me. 'We're in danger of this becoming a chronic attachment.' I just coughed.

'I know your game, you only come here when you want to fuck,' she'd said as I walked up to the bar the night before.

She was thirty-one, almost fifteen years younger than me, but she talked about her age as if it were an ailment she'd decided to get treatment for.

'I need to do something,' she always moaned. 'I have to do something with my life. I have to find something different.'

I've heard this lament too many times and I always tended to dodge the issue to avoid getting caught up in the project myself.

'It's not what you think; I hardly ever go out at night. I can't with the kids.'

I was telling her the truth. But I didn't mention that I avoided Quique, my local, whenever I didn't want to end the night with her.

'You've gained a lover but lost a bar,' Animal reprimanded me when I suggested we go elsewhere. 'That's serious. Lovers come and go, but a good bar is for life. Being in love means not being able to have another drink when you want to.' These were the words of Animal, a man who'd lost all the bars in his life forever.

Animal says I'm impatient. He's always available; he has loads of time for everything. I don't; I'm anxious. They say the best test of your anxiety is if you flush the toilet before you've even finished pissing. That's me. I'm always impatient with soundchecks. Even encores lose their appeal when they go on too long. Carmela would undress me in three strokes, in her ugly flat in Ventas, before taking off her own clothes like a man, not caring what she revealed. The first time I spoke to her, attracted by the pale eyes and fair skin underneath that black hair, she stopped me in my tracks.

'I saw you once when I was at university in Clamores. My boyfriend took me; he loved your songs. He was an arsehole. His favourite one was "I'm Leaving".'

6

That song was actually a description of orgasm:

*I'm leaving*
*Tomorrow is here.*
*I was in, now I'm out*
*I'm not who I was*
*I'm leaving.*

Many people, though, interpret it as a break-up song and I liked the ambiguity, which may well have been intentional, since I've always associated the erotic climax, the spilling of seed, with escape. When satiated, pleasure kicks open the door to the next bedroom, one of the many paradoxes that make living a truly dizzying experience.

Over the course of two or three nights at Quique, Carmela lowered her defences, so I invited her to have one for the road before closing time and she accepted.

'You're going to fuck a waitress. It's such a classic rock 'n' roll cliche, doesn't it make you sick?' she said as we stumbled, kissing, into her place that first night. 'The musician who hooks up with the waitress.'

'I have nothing but respect for the classics,' I replied.

I walked from Carmela's flat to my house. That morning, I was the guy caught by the dawn doing jobs that should have been done under cover of darkness. Red-handed. The sun was like the lamp glaring in my face in a police interrogation scene from a movie. My only response was to whistle. I like to whistle as I walk. There are certain places where songs are born. On the street, on the way home in the early hours, in bed before fully waking up, on aeroplanes. And in the shower.

The shower is an expensive and not very eco-friendly place to be inspired, but the songs it produces taste like rain. Besides, it's a way of rebelling against my father's stinginess. When I was

7

living with him, he'd start banging on the bathroom door the moment he heard me turn on the shower.

'You don't need to use so much water for a shower! Turn the tap off when you're putting on the soap!'

If you blew your nose under the stream of water he'd get really mad.

'Man alive, do you know how much water you're wasting?' he'd reprimand me from behind the door. 'You think your snot's more important than water?'

Using water unnecessarily, leaving the lights on, keeping the fridge door open because you weren't sure what to eat, not drawing the curtains when the heating was on at night, throwing away a jam jar unless it was completely spotless: these were all forms of wastefulness my father couldn't tolerate. His favourite music was the rhythmic sound of a spoon hitting against the sides of an empty yoghurt pot as he went after every last bit. Scrape, scrape, clunk, scrape, scrape, clunk.

I wanted to finish the new album, so I enjoyed walking that morning, searching for a new melody. This one will be album number ten, not counting two greatest hits compilations. Ten albums in what's approaching thirty years in the business is, I think, a reflection of my eagerness not to bore people too much with my presence. And not to bore myself in the process.

*recently I've been thinking a lot about death*

Recently, I've been thinking a lot about death. Still, it's a big leap to go from that to literally waking up with a hearse outside your front door. Once my kids had managed to wake me, I looked out of the window. The driver had rung the bell several times, Ludivina explained.

'But I refused to open it,' she said. 'It brings bad luck.'

When he saw me, the driver sounded his horn, with all the ease of a friend swinging by to pick you up. An ease you'd never expect from a hearse driver.

Sooner or later,' Gus used to say, 'all cars become hearses.'

OK, Gus, but this one here really *is* a hearse. With its tinted windows and spacious, box-shaped boot for transporting coffins, it was, unmistakably, the final limousine.

I don't know why I'd been thinking about death so much recently. They say it's age, the awareness that you and those around you have entered its zone of influence, its orbit. But in this instance it wasn't so much a case of me thinking about death as it was death thinking about me. At various moments I've thought a great deal about sex, success, love, money, without ever waking up to find them parked outside my house. Maybe death is more powerful than any other idea: it always has the last laugh.

Seeing the hearse double-parked outside my house that morning made a great impression on me. It was summer, it was early, and luckily there were hardly any neighbours out and about, wondering who'd died, jumping to conclusions.

'Gosh, he's dead. Daniel, the singer. Or maybe someone in his family, or perhaps that Japanese woman who was living with him.'

I don't believe there's a soul on earth who doesn't see a hearse and think, 'it's come for me'. Even if only for a split second. It's like when someone opens a bottle of champagne and we're always afraid the cork, however random its trajectory, will end up hitting us in the eye. Or is that just me?

'Miss Raquel tried to find you,' the driver screeched, popping his enormous skull out of the window. His head was so big it seemed impossible he'd managed to get it back inside the car.

Raquel's my guardian angel. She's the one who organises our diary. I always introduce her in the same way: 'This is Raquel.

9

She keeps my career afloat.' She likes to say she's not so much my guardian angel as my security guard. Raquel doesn't have kids and so has made me into a kind of son, despite the fact I'm almost ten years older than her. She honours my commitments and her painstaking dedication to my schedule is proof – if proof were needed – that a mother really can be younger than her children.

Raquel didn't mind dealing with my furniture deliveries, absurd bureaucratic tasks, my ever-increasing pile of paperwork, malfunctioning domestic items. 'Speak to Raquel,' I tell everyone. I feel much more confident with people speaking to Raquel than I would if they spoke with me.

Sometimes I tell Raquel about my personal problems, to see if she can resolve them in the same diligent way she deals with the rest of my day-to-day affairs. She always picks up the phone, whereas I forget it, put it away somewhere, ignore it, because there are times in my life when I need to exist without that thing nearby. I haven't quite yet followed Animal's extreme example of saving all of his contacts as simply No or Yes, so he knows whether or not to answer the call. But Raquel picks up every call and can even keep several conversations going at once.

I have friends who say that Raquel is actually in love with me, which is why she criticises every move I make on other women: 'Since when do you like bimbos?'; 'Are you sure you want this woman to have your number?'; 'They're getting younger and younger. Soon you'll be asking your daughter for her contacts.'

When we first met I was drawn to how she dealt with a group we were playing a show with. We began working together and at one of our first concerts I drank enough to pluck up the courage to flirt with her. After my third raunchy look, she leant into my ear to restrain me.

'Just so you know, I like girls, and you're an inch away from making a fool of yourself.'

'It's your father's . . .' Raquel's penetrating voice cut into me, despite how far away she was.

'Of course. My father. Sorry.' I sensed a slight delay as my voice travelled to her ear in Rio de Janeiro. 'What time is it in Brazil?'

Raquel was on holiday there with a journalist she'd met at a gig we'd played in Montevideo a year back.

'Don't tell me you'd forgotten?' she asked me. 'Were you asleep? What day is it today, Dani?'

I felt the spurs of her caustic wit digging into my back.

'Day? It can't even be nine yet!' I answered.

'Are you with the driver? Is everything OK?' she asked. 'Tell me you can deal with it alone.'

'Of course I can,' I told Raquel. 'It's all good, I'm on it. I'll deal with it.'


## the first time I wanted to die

The first time I wanted to die – I mean really wanted to die, not just pretend I did because I was feeling sorry for myself – was when Oliva and I stopped being together. I hesitated there. I was going to write when she left me, or when we broke up, but with the passing of time the action itself becomes less significant than its consequence. We stopped being together. When that happened it felt, in a very cold and clinical way, as if dying wouldn't be all that bad. You die and that's the end of all the fear, the insecurity, the pain, all the cuts and scratches you carry inside. I felt it again sometime later, during another one of those unhappy moments when sadness wakes you in the night and digs its nails into your heart.

But that was different. All the subsequent times were different. I was older then, whereas I was only twenty-five the time Oliva cried as I stroked her hair and told her I'd always be by her side. Or perhaps it was she who said it to me, though both of us knew we'd never be by each other's side again. And then, for the first time, in my life, I wanted to die, because death at least had an undeniable value: the gift of opportunity.

The end of love is the closest thing there is to death unless you've actually experienced death, which is of course the actual closest thing to death. Just before they die, the dead probably think, 'Oh, right, so that's what it's like.' But when love comes to an end, no one understands a thing and we ask 'What's going on? No one told me anything about this,' because we can't see that death has just delivered one of its instalments.

My father upped and died just after Kei and I decided to separate. My second, immense separation. Sometimes you turn on the bathroom light and see cockroaches scuttling to safety; well, one day we turned the light on in our relationship and saw a clear line leading to abject misery. As I put it in a song I wrote for her that I've hardly ever played to anyone: 'Sometimes goodbye is a way of saying I love you.' Being in love isn't as perfect as we make out. There's no shortage of murderers who claim to be acting out of love for someone or other. The difficult thing about love is defining exactly what it is that you love. Not how much, or how, or how long, but what: when you say you love someone, what exactly is it that you love?

My father's eyes would light up whenever he saw Kei and Oliva. He had good taste in women. Can you inherit something like that? I suspect the fact that these two women not only went out with me, but also actually *lived* with me, was the only reason my father didn't consider his son to be a complete waste of space.

It hurts to think that he died just after Kei and I separated. For my father, marriage was the holy grail, yet there I was, clumsily spilling its contents everywhere. When I was a child my father would always say, 'Why do you have to be so clumsy?' whenever I knocked over my milk, or spilt soup from my bowl while placing it down on the tablecloth. I spilt my marriage everywhere too, and he barely got the chance to harangue me for it, because he died.

He called me from the hospital. 'It's Dad. I'm in the hospital.' I later found out that he'd had to rush back home from his morning walk because he'd shat himself. 'I shat myself,' he announced when I saw him in the hospital corridor. Maybe shitting himself was my father's natural reaction to death coming to find him: his intestine recognised death before he did. Even on the day he died, he still insisted that the doctors couldn't discover what was wrong with him. 'They're useless. All they do is mess around with these tests and they still can't find a thing.'

It wasn't surprising that death met him while he was out walking. My father was always going for walks. He walked in the mornings, in the afternoons and sometimes at night, too. He walked at home, up and down the corridor. He even walked in bed. If I ever got to his house so late that he'd already gone to bed, it wasn't at all uncommon to find him doing bicycle kicks on the mattress, or shaking out his legs as he talked to me. 'You'll go stiff if you don't move,' he'd say by way of explanation.

My father walked to escape death and old age. My father walked for the same reason I tour: to keep all of our plates spinning. Old age was hot on his heels and he kept on walking, but death sought him out intentionally, studied his routine and caught up with him on the allotted day. The pancreatic infection was so fierce that in just ten days it did away with this healthy, sinewy man, who was more rock than bone, tough in the way only country people are. A man who'd gone to A & E by himself, after taking a shower and changing – 'I shat myself in broad daylight' – taking two buses because he refused to pay for a taxi no matter how weak he felt: paying for a taxi was one affront too many. My father wasn't going to take a taxi to his own death. He took not one, but two buses. That was his way.

I didn't cry when my father died. I was with him in the room and the doctor warned me that the end was near. It was seven in the evening. My father was gasping for air, like a fish out of water, and I took his hand, which was constructed from the material hands used to be made from many years ago, when we were all peasants. A hand so firm and strong it was almost as if my own limp hand was the one being consoled. My father's hand had spent its first twenty years labouring in the fields and then at war; mine had spent that same period wanking and playing the guitar.

My father didn't realise that it was death tugging at him and I wanted him to know.

'You should be happy, Dad, you've had a full life. Be at peace.'

'Don't say that,' he quietly scolded me.

Those were his last words. He never spoke again; he died arguing with me, which had always been our habitual mode of communication. 'Don't say that.'

He'd already stopped speaking by the time the hospital chaplain slipped into the room to pray for him. A few days earlier, when he'd first come into the room to start his nonsense about preparing to leave this world, my father had told him, 'I'm as clean as a whistle.' The priest went to work on him quickly, with the skill and speed of a true professional. He applied the holy oils like a mechanic checking a car's tyre pressure.

I didn't cry as I watched my father die. In fact, I started laughing because a relative from his village, Aunt Dorina, showed up. She popped her head through the door in a way that was both funny and ridiculous. 'May I?'

Aunt Dorina came to Madrid often to see her daughter, Dori, a dermatologist in that same hospital. My cousin, Dori, had filled her mother in as to the severity of my father's condition after she'd come up from her consulting room one day, all smiles, to see how he was. While there, she'd offered to remove a mole from my neck.

'I'll remove it for you, if you want. Moles after forty . . .' And she stopped there.

*Stop being decorative and become signs of death*, I thought.

'And I know you're forty-four, because my mother told me we were born the same year,' Dori added.

I laughed because, just moments after my father had died, Aunt Dori had popped in to ask, from the door, if she'd come at a bad time. I gave her the same look I'd give to a supermarket delivery driver asking where to leave the shopping while the house is burning down. I laughed because I couldn't cry, and because her ill-timed visit jump-started all that morbid machinery, the endless phone calls and formalities. The whole process that means a man can't abandon protocols even after leaving life itself behind. My friend Vicente always used to warn me: 'You know what happens after death?' he'd say, 'Paperwork.'

I was flooded with responsibilities. Suddenly, I had lots of things to do, and you can't cry when you've got things to do. Many years ago, I'd written in a song:

*The day you went away*
*I couldn't die, though I was willing*
*I had to see the dentist*
*For a filling.*

But back then everything was light-hearted, or at least I had the energy to make it into something funny, or to make it into a song, which is basically the same thing. I closed my father's eyes, those beautiful honey-coloured eyes I'd been lucky enough to inherit. His mouth was hanging wide open in what was obviously life's final cruel trick, or death's first. I tried to close it so that no one would notice the lack of false teeth, his last flirtation with vanity.

As with witnessing the birth of my kids, being present at my father's death helped me to get rid of any mystical inclinations: dying, like being born, is just an arduous, messy physiological process. If, as he firmly believed, my father was going to be travelling straight from that place to the Kingdom of the Just, then that was no longer any of my business.

## *but I shed deferred tears*

But I shed deferred tears for my father's death. It happened three months later, in Barajas airport. I was taking my kids to spend a long weekend in Mallorca, at the seaside house where Bocanegra, my protector at the label for many years, always let me stay. It was the holiday weekend in May and the check-in queue had trumped even my worst expectations. The machines were all broken and we ended up missing our flight.

The attendant told me to try to change the tickets at the customer service desk, which was also flooded with passengers in similarly tight spots. I decided to join the queue in an attempt to avoid completely ruining the plans I'd made for my children. It was our first trip together since the split with their mother and I wanted it to have that foundational value that even small details have when you're entering a new era.

'I don't think there are any spaces left on the flight that leaves in a few hours,' the attendant said. She stared at her computer without looking up. 'I'm sorry; it's fully booked because of the holiday.'

The look of disappointment on the face of my daughter, Maya, who was fully tuned in to all the complications, infected her brother, Ryo, who had up to that point been finding the whole thing rather amusing.

'Does this mean we can't go, Dad?' she asked.

'Will the plane leave without us?' he added.

'I don't know, kids, I don't know.'

The attendant looked up from behind the desk, already seeking out the next person in line. For the first time, she looked straight at me, somewhat surprised.

'You're the singer, right? Dani Mosca?'

I nodded. Sometimes being moderately well known can bring moderate advantages. Would this be one of those occasions? Her body language changed and she seemed much warmer now as she went back to fiddling with her keyboard.

'There just aren't any seats; it's a really difficult situation,' she said again. 'Guess what! I know your father. My mother was one of his clients. She used to buy watches and jewellery from him, and kitchen furniture. He's such a great guy, your father . . . How is he?'

I stayed silent for a moment before telling her that my father had died three months earlier. Then without moving, I burst into tears, right there at the customer service desk, as if I'd just heard the news for the first time. The attendant apologised, without taking her eyes off me. She was attractive, thanks to her audacious nose, a bit older than me, with reddish streaks in her hair. I bit my lip to stop the flow of tears.

'The thing is, today was my father's birthday and I only noticed when I got the tickets out. He was so proud of being born on May Day. He was such a hard-working man and he loved celebrating this holiday on his birthday.'

The attendant looked at me with a tenderness that's so often missing from the daily grind.

'He was really special,' she said. 'Your father was a wonderful man, so kind. I'm deeply sorry.'

She sorted out our tickets and put us straight on the flight which, just minutes before, had been fully booked.

'I'm very sorry for reminding you of your loss,' the attendant repeated as we left.

'No, quite the opposite. I'm the one who should be saying sorry. I don't know what came over me.'

I cried profusely – barely able to speak – all the way to the boarding gate.

'In life, you only reap what you sow,' my father used to announce in his typically grandiose way. 'Treat people well and one day they'll return the favour.'

I could have shouted, 'You were right, Dad, you were right!'

He always maintained that life didn't follow complicated mathematical formulas: the more you give, the more you take, as simple as that. 'It's like working the land: it's hard, it's tough, but it brings rewards to those who cultivate it daily.'

When we got to our seats, my daughter asked me discreetly, 'Dad, why were you crying so much back there? Was it about the tickets?'

'Well, actually, I was crying because I wanted to thank your grandfather for helping us to get on this flight . . .' I stopped, not knowing how to continue.

'Right, and you couldn't, because he's dead,' Ryo added.

'Exactly.'

Life is so hard to organise and yet sometimes it can diligently organise itself, so logical it's unsettling, so perfect it's genuinely exciting. That's why it took me so long to cry for my father's death, in an overcrowded airport instead of the more intimate setting of a hospital room. And that's why I continued to cry

18

over a good few months at random intervals, whenever something reminded me how much I missed him. The delightful Señor Campos.

In Mallorca, Bocanegra had left us his whole house and swimming pool to enjoy, allowing us to have a taste of the riches he'd accumulated over the course of his seven lives. His professional biography could be summed up as follows: 'I've died every time there was a big technological change, every time two companies merged, every time some other son of a bitch was appointed or promoted above me, and yet here I am.' His nickname – Blackmouth – couldn't have been more appropriate for a man who always terrified my children with the unstoppable stream of swear words that flowed out of his mouth.

'Your kids are the fuckin' shit,' he told me once in an eruption of sentimentality that was overheard by my distressed children. 'What you gotta do, right, is to enjoy them now before they get big and life turns them into miserable bastards.'

Us music people all called Bocanegra *Whatyougottado*, because he started all of his sentences like that. 'What you gotta do is record another album,' he told me, 'and stop fucking around.'

At the time my head was already completely enmeshed in another album, so there was no need for him to make that demand. I was completely preoccupied the whole time.

A few weeks later I was helping Maya to get a costume ready for an English performance at school. We were alone in her mother's house, on the other side of the garden, when someone rang on the intercom. The noise, loud and persistent, rang out like one, two, three slaps to the face, that annoying, ugly, anti-musical sound intercoms always have. Only one person in the world rang the bell like that: my father. So I got up off the floor and said 'It's your grandfather.'

19

As I approached the door to let him in, with my daughter watching on expectantly, I suddenly realised that it couldn't be: that mad, assertive, intrusive, delirious way he used to ring the bell no longer existed. He'd never again make the intercom sound three, four, five times in a row, his finger on the button the whole time. He was dead. And his absence, suddenly irremediable, hit me all over again.

That was when I decided to carry out his last wish.

'It's Ryo, he always rings the door like that now. You have to say something. He won't listen to Mum,' Maya protested.

My son had unknowingly inherited my father's habit. Can you inherit that?

When I opened the door, I asked him why he was ringing the door like that. I scolded him: 'You just press once and then wait.'

'OK, Papá. But if you ring loud enough, someone will definitely hear you.'


*if you ring loud enough, someone will definitely hear you*


'Are you Mr Daniel Campos, sir?' the hearse driver shouted. He had a booming voice, or perhaps his giant head worked like a bell, making the sound resonate.

'Yep, I'll be out in a minute,' I said. I wanted to shower and get dressed.

'I'll go around the block, then; I can't stop here.'

I watched him moving off inside the car.

'Are you going, Dad?' my daughter asked.

'I have to. I'd completely forgotten.'

'Who called the death car? What's it for?' Her brother, staring intently at me, was waiting for an explanation.

'Well, it's actually for your granddad. We're going to take

20

him back to his village, to the cemetery. Don't you remember me telling you both?'

'Granddad's inside?'

'Well, his corpse is,' I replied.

'Really?' Ryo asked. 'Can I see it?'

'Of course you can't see it, you idiot,' his sister cut in. 'Don't you know he died months ago? He'll have rotted by now. Has Granddad rotted yet, Papá?'

Years before, I'd had one of these pointless discussions with my father, the same kind I now have with my kids, about the advantages of cremation.

'Now look here, son, you can do whatever you like with your own corpse,' he snapped, 'but I want to be in one piece for the resurrection of the dead.'

'The resurrection of the dead? Come on, Papá, the planet's overcrowded as it is and you're still banging on about that?'

He tilted his head to one side, paused, and said, 'What I'd really like is for you to bury me in my village, but I won't hear anything about ashes. I'm not a cigarette. If you want to end up in an ashtray, that's up to you.'

It was something like a last wish, despite the fact that he hadn't been planning on dying any time soon. The last two nights, during one of the morphine-induced hallucinations that made him stretch his arm out to touch a horse, or a vase full of flowers or a wall, he swore he could see right in front of him.

'It's there, son, right there.'

He'd torn off all of his drips and when the nurses arrived to put them back in place, he'd shouted, 'Get out! You disgust me. Leave me in peace. Get lost! You're all a bloody nuisance.'

Then he'd come to his senses immediately and apologised.

'I'm not myself, miss, please forgive me.'

What he found most inconvenient about being in hospital was not being able to do things for himself, being forced to rely on others, without his smooth-talking, elegant elderly gentle-man persona. That, and not being able to go and see my mother at the home, which he did once at the start of each day and again just before visiting hours ended.

When my father died, I let other people deal with the for-malities. Aunt Dorina, with her chubby cheeks that trembled with each syllable, asked me if we had insurance. I remem-bered Señor Marciano from Ocaso Insurance. 'Marciano from Ocaso,' he'd announce over the intercom. Every Christmas he used to bring my father a cigar, which they'd smoke in front of each other in the living room, like a synchronised swimming exercise. That was until my father decided to quit smoking and so the following Christmas he broke his Havana in a rage, then took Don Marciano's from his hands and tossed it into a gera-nium pot by the window.

'I've given up, and so should you! This stuff is poison.'

After my mother got sick, an interest in health erupted into my father's life. And it wasn't just a pastime but an obsession, which altered all of his habits and turned him into a new man. He performed unnecessarily strenuous exercises and prepared foul-smelling cocktails of garlic and onion, which he kept in the cupboard at the end of the corridor. He began reading, or rather, skimming through books about alternative remedies produced by disreputable publishers. He was so convinced by their diatribes about healthy living that everyone who visited our flat – from the encyclopaedia salesman to the *Reader's Digest* guy, and even the people who came to read the electricity and gas meters – would leave with their breath smelling suspiciously of garlic and onion.

Raquel took charge of the situation and busied herself with arranging the mechanical part of the burial. It was a quick, un-inspiring ceremony in Carabanchel, led by a priest who got my father's name wrong. The two wreaths included in the insurance payout – with ribbons spelling out two unarguable truths: Rest in Peace and Your Son Will Not Forget You – ended up getting squashed inside my father's vault. Before the coffin was sealed inside the cemetery wall, they asked me if I wanted the flowers to be placed inside the vault or left out.

'I don't know,' I said. 'What do people usually do?'

'I'll be straight with you,' the funeral director informed me. 'If you leave them outside they often get stolen.'

And so, without a great deal of conviction, I told him he should place the garlands inside since, after all, the flowers were for him. The man took the flowers and, in an act so idiotic as to be almost moving, crushed them together so they could be pushed next to the coffin. The floor was covered in fallen petals.

I don't remember inviting anyone to the funeral other than Animal.

'My father died,' I told him.

'Fuck,' he replied, 'and he was always so strong.'

Animal visited us at the hospital a couple of times and my father had given him a quick dressing-down in the corridors.

'You're too fat,' he told him.

My father, in his abundantly healthy old age, always liked to humiliate fat people.

'You should only eat what's strictly necessary,' he advised him, 'and not a single mouthful more.'

For Animal, whose life was all about the pleasures of excess, this was impossible.

I also called Martán.

'You have my deepest symphonies,' he told me in his habitual free take on our language.

'It's sympathies,' I corrected him.

Between the two of them, as well as Raquel, Kei and Aunt Dorina – who after twenty years without any meaningful contact with our family had become worryingly important in my life – we ensured that the attendance at the interment was more than acceptable and that my father could say his goodbyes before a decent crowd, which included many of my fellow artists. I was very grateful for the presence of my music friends, though surprised to see them at this kind of ceremony.

Victor, Serrat's bass player, said, 'I'm sorry, man.'

But the only response I could offer was, 'You mean, you actually go to funerals?'

Before either of us had ever attended a funeral, Gus and I wrote a song called 'Señor Martínez', about a chap who attends funerals the way other people go to the theatre. He was based on my father, who loved all things ceremonial. And what could be more pompous than funeral rites? He enjoyed the funeral rites, the chapel of rest, the mortuary, the Mass, as if they were all part of some captivating theatrical spectacle. Weddings were marvellous, but a funeral gave its attendees more interesting roles to play.

Perhaps people of his generation liked to give their all to such events as there were so few others to attend. Of course, he wasn't interested in concerts or travelling for pleasure, or going out with friends. He never took a flight or visited a museum, he went to bed at eleven on New Year's Eve and he never set foot inside a bar. Once he stopped smoking Mr Marciano's cigars, the only thing he had left to toast with was one of his paramedical concoctions.

By the end, his most joyous occasions for celebration were his bowel movements. Habitually constipated, he always used to share the ins and outs of his defecation, both bitter and sweet, with my mother and I. Later, it wasn't at all surprising to find him engaging the ladies who came by our house to look after my mother in highly detailed conversations.

'I had to sweat blood to get my bowels moving this morning,' he'd explain, 'but the stuff itself, when it came out, had a stupendous consistency. Textbook, I tell you.'

I occasionally walked in to find him having very intimate chats with both Oliva and Kei but, they'd always assure me, 'He's just telling us about his morning poo.'

Once I'd taught him to use his mobile phone with a certain level of proficiency and he'd stopped placing his fingers on three keys at a time, my father would take advantage of the long periods he spent straining his bowels to make calls.

'Son, you're not going to believe me, but I've been sitting on the can for ten minutes now and I don't know what to do. And this is after having half a pot of plum jam. Anyway, tell me, how are the kids?'

Knowing how allergic he was to speaking on the phone, I often associated his calls and his eagerness to have a conversation with the *Via Crucis* of his guts.

'How are you, Dani? How are things going? We haven't spoken for days!'

'Dad, are you taking a shit?' I'd ask him.

He'd deny it, but his syllables were elongated by the painful rhythms of constipation, and then he'd say goodbye in a real hurry and I could always hear the toilet flushing as he hung up on me.

His actual ability to use new technology didn't match his enthusiasm for it, but he seemed truly devastated when I told him that the fax machine, which fascinated him, had no future.

'What would you know?' he said.

On other occasions, he proudly boasted of his unrefined country ways. Faced with any kind of admin task, his excuse was always 'What can I do? I'm just a simple peasant.'

He criticised my children for playing with their contraptions, remembering in contrast how the children in his village used to entertain themselves by cutting off bits of rubber from the tyres of their first lorries and chewing them like gum while they wrapped their scarves around stones and then aimed them at each other's heads.

'That's how you have fun,' he announced, 'not with these blasted contraptions. I tell you, I pity the young people of today with their computers. You'll all end up like idiots.'

He became convinced that the past was better, which implied a sense of superiority over me, one he exercised at every opportunity. He associated the countryside with purity and cities with everything that was rotten in life. And so I felt it was only right to return him to the place he always visited, whether in reality or in his imagination, to reaffirm the strength of his roots. That's why I belatedly decided to transport the coffin containing his corpse to the village where he was born, Garrafal de Campos, a year after his first drab and drizzly burial.


## i make songs

'I make songs,' I replied to the hearse driver when, only seconds after we'd set off, he'd got straight to the point and asked, 'And what do you do, sir?'

My father found it laughable when he heard me say I made a living from writing songs.

'Come, son, go and get yourself a job, and stop fooling around.'

But I can't think of a better way to explain what I do to people.

Once, I caught an Argentinian singer attempting a better explanation on the radio.

'A song,' he said, 'is a comet that you grab in mid-air and either you hold it there for a while, or you never let go.'

This positively saccharine explanation made me blush, though

I had to admit the image worked. It must have convinced the girl presenting the show, whose defences were lowered after breaking up with her boyfriend of several years, because she ended up having a child with him – that was until he let go of the comet he'd been holding on to and went off with another woman. The next time I was at the radio station the same presenter said something that pained me.

'You know what, Dani, I'd rather have a piano land on my head than ever fall in love with a musician again.'

I've never met a woman who didn't regret falling in love with a musician, and that includes the ones who've fallen in love with me, even when we've managed to remain friends. The thing is, we just make songs, we don't actually live in them; at best, I fear, we live *off* them. We don't even stop to think about how they get made. I hate it when plumbers, mechanics or IT technicians tell me all about how they fixed something I paid them to fix and keep quiet about. I loathe telling people what I do, when they ask. Saying 'I'm a singer' or 'I make songs' just sounds so bad. It's ridiculous, and I know it. It sounded ridiculous to my father, and with good reason. Really what I do is I ring on doorbells, once, twice, twenty times and if I'm lucky, someone will hear and open the door for me. I could say that, but no one would understand.

The hearse driver introduced himself. 'My name's Jairo. I'm from Ecuador.'

I found it quite miraculous that his shoulders were capable of supporting such an enormous head, no matter how well built he was. It reminded me of one of those giant baby head sculptures that António Lopez did at the Atocha train station.

The hearse driver weighed up my answer with some scepticism.

'So you're a musician, then?'

*I can't keep my eyes open,* I thought to myself. The early

morning summer sun pounded my face through the glass. I lowered the window slightly.

'Shall I turn up the AC?' Jairo asked.

'No, no, I can't stand air conditioning.'

Oncoming cars let us through, half respectful, half suspicious. At a traffic light, a driver in his thirties recognised me and shouted through the window.

'You're Dani Mosca, right?'

I nodded.

'Somebody die?' he asked.

'My father.'

'Wow, I'm so sorry.'

'It's fine,' I said, 'it happened nearly a year ago.'

'Oh, right.'

Confronted with the look of shock on his face, I almost added that we'd been driving around non-stop since he died, looking for somewhere to bury him. But perhaps there was more truth in the joke than even I realised.

Once we got moving again, Jairo glanced sideways at me numerous times.

'Forgive me, sir, I see you really are famous. I didn't know, but then again, I spend all my free time watching Real Madrid. What kind of musician are you then? A singer?'

'That's right, a singer.'

'Oh yeah? And what kind of songs do you sing?'

'I don't know. Regular songs,' I said.

'Ballads, boleros, *vallenato*, a bit of *salsa*?'

'No, definitely not salsa.'

'OK, so rock, pop, that kind of thing?'

'That's right.'

A strange expression, showing something between satisfaction at his powers of deduction and pride at carrying an important person in his car, settled on Jairo's face.

'I just love dancing. Feeling your bodies so close together, it really lights my fire. I—'

'Right, yeah . . .'

I don't actually dance, not me. But we've always enjoyed that moment at our shows when people start dancing, jumping, moving around. I couldn't claim that any of my repertoire is particularly danceable. Oliva loved dancing and I'd sometimes dance with her to make her happy, but really it was more like clowning around.

'A musician who doesn't dance,' Oliva used to harangue me, 'is like a dentist who doesn't brush their teeth.'

I'd promised to take the kids to the Parque de Atracciones in Madrid and they'd protested when I told them it couldn't happen. I kissed them both as they ate cereal out of their *wankos*, their enamelled bowls covered with images of manga characters. Ludivina offered to make me something, but I wasn't hungry. I saw the looks of unease on my children's faces as I got into the death car. I'd shouted out of the window at them.

'We'll go to the amusement park tomorrow, I promise.'

'I should eat something. I didn't have breakfast,' I said once we were out of the city.

Jairo told me he knew the perfect place for a coffee and a bite. An endless stream of words continued to gush from his mouth when we reached the counter as he told me all about his business.

'Coffins and suits are ten a penny, but you have to find the one that matches your client, the one that represents them best.'

Kei's mother shoos away butterflies, because she says she can see dead people she's known in them. The Japanese are always warding off the spirits of the dead, and when they've been near a dead person, they have to waft away the air, which they consider to be contaminated. The affable driver was more concerned with the commercial aspects of death. To me, all the funeral paraphernalia was like a corset worn around some-thing completely intangible, no less grotesque than if love were simply a matter of talking about condoms.

'What's up? Heavy night?' Jairo asked when he spotted me jolting my shoulders in an attempt to shake myself out of my stupor. 'Must be a lot of parties in the music world, am I right?'

'There is a fair bit of action,' I conceded.

The waiter had given him a plate of olives with his second non-alcoholic beer.

'Would you like an olive?' Jairo asked, possibly feeling guilty about already having wolfed down four without offering.

'I don't like olives,' I confessed.

I didn't explain that I'd stopped eating olives when my rela-tionship with Oliva had come to an end. The association be-tween Oliva and olives wasn't purely fanciful, for I'd spent many a night riffing on her name, Oliva, and the shape of her arse, or the way her skin felt or the colour she turned in summer. Oliva was my olive, until one day I was left standing with the stone in my hand and nothing to put in my mouth.

I also refused to ever go to Boston. Never ever. Olives and Boston were off limits. That's just how I am. Oliva had moved there after we separated. When anyone said the word Boston or presented me with a plate of olives, the same thing happened: I was overcome by a nostalgia tinged with humiliation. My friend Nacho, who studied composition at an elite school in Boston, once invited me to come and stay.

'No, thanks. Too cold.'

'Come in the summer, then,' he suggested.

It made no difference; I would never go to Boston. I could live without olives or Boston, but living without Oliva was more of a challenge.

Jairo yanked me out of the whirlwinds of memory. We went back to the hearse. He'd parked it round the back, out of sight of the cars driving down the motorway. He told me that the bar owner had asked him to do it.

'I'm fine with you coming here, but I'll lose customers if you leave it out the front. Who wants to sit down and eat next to a dead person?'

I nodded sympathetically, but Jairo went on.

'In this profession, you learn how wary people are around the dead. Sometimes I get home and I smell. You know what I mean. That strange smell. It's nothing really, but still you ask yourself, what if I smell of dead people? So I take a shower and freshen up. I'll say no more.'

But he did say more. He always said more.

'Every profession has its quirks,' he added. 'How did you become a musician, then, sir? Does it run in the family?' Jairo started the hearse and stuck his head out of the window as he merged onto the motorway.

'No,' I replied, 'there aren't any musicians in my family.'


## we're normal people

We're normal people. That was the absurd way my father used to define us. I fought against it, quietly wishing not to be normal, to be special. But I could never shake off the stigma of being normal.

'We're just regular, normal people, Dani, my boy.'

Because in my profession the exact opposite is what's required. It's the only job where trashing your CV increases your chances of getting to the top. We once met Antonio Flores at the fiestas in Peniscola, where we played just before him. He was so friendly that we instantly became his confidants, despite not knowing him at all.

From a distance, it always looked as if Antonio was trying

hard to act out the most sacred rituals of musical self-destruction. When Animal and I went back to the hotel with him, the three of us all extremely drunk, we decided to invade the kitchen and eat all the food left out for breakfast the next day. Then we mixed up the room numbers, which were displayed with interchangeable tags, over two floors.

For once in my life, I actually felt like a proper rock star. As we headed back to our beds, I remember him saying to us, 'Bah, that's nothing. On the last tour we set fire to our mattresses and threw them out of the window into the swimming pool. Then we ripped the TVs off the walls and tossed them out as well.'

I felt a sense of unease: I was too polite, I'd never be a true artist. Sometime later, maybe the year he died, I met him in a train dining car. He'd just sold some rather pathetic, semi-naked photos of himself to *Interviú* and many people were predicting an ugly end. When I got there, he was singing to the waitress and accompanying himself with rhythmical thumps on the counter: 'You're the most beautiful thing on the railway network.' He didn't remember me, but I got to spend another stupendous afternoon in his company, displaying the hushed admiration of someone who could never dare to scale such heights of depravity. He died a fortnight later.

I lugged this 'nice boy' complex around with me for years; it may well have lasted the entire time I worked with Gus. Eventually, I shook it off. I accepted that I was the polite guy my parents had taught me to be: in a world where insolence and belligerence are the norm, I've never stopped saying thank you, good morning and please. For me, good manners have become an outward expression of physical cowardice. Galder, the singer from Bronkitis, a radical Basque rock group, once asked if he could break a beer bottle over my head, insisting that an ugly scar would suit me.

'It'll stop you looking like a character from some teen drama.

Come on, man, let me smash it over you. You can choose which side. I'll be gentle, I promise.'

He wouldn't stop going on about it, so Animal decided to make him leave me alone. He told him that if he touched so much as a hair on my body he'd tear one of his nuts off and give him a nice new singing voice. The moment he said it, Galder moved both hands over to the part of his leather trousers that shielded his genitals. Luckily, nothing happened and Galder, ever the punk rocker, is now the chairperson of the Spanish Society of Authors.

I was never a bad student, but the year my mother got sick my grades were truly excellent. It was my small, childish way of paying tribute to her. We lived on a dead-end street, Calle Paravicinos, which came to a stop at an enormous wall, the physical manifestation of my confinement. The other cage was my sick mother. I thought good grades would be a way of soaring above and out of those confines. My father read them to her out loud, one by one. 'Mathematics – outstanding. Spanish – outstanding.' This time he didn't stop, as he usually did, to reprimand me for a subpar grade or a comment from one of my teachers regarding my behaviour or lack of effort, generally along the lines of 'gets the grades, does very little'. When he'd finished reading them it was clear that, in his own way, he was proud of me.

'We expected nothing less from you,' he confessed.

My mother smiled; save the occasional absurd comment, she no longer took part in our conversations. Her only comment was 'Mathematics is so lovely.'

When my mother's illness first struck it took away the thing I loved the most: the goodnight kiss. I thought it was just one more thing you lose with age, like praying together before bed, one of the many catastrophes of growing up. Just like when she stopped buying me clothes, hiding the chocolate milk or asking me if I had lots of homework when I got back from school. One day mothers just stop coming up to give you a goodnight kiss:

> No more goodnight kisses
> Just car insurance
> And mortgages.

In my case, one night the kiss never came and I waited in silence. The darkness became hostile, gloomy, unwelcoming. I'd called her on several occasions, but eventually the night comes when you don't feel entitled to shout 'Mum, are you coming?' And so nobody comes.

When you wake up the following morning you may well be more grown up, more independent, but the night before all you are is sad. On the second consecutive night without a kiss, I cried to myself in silence. It felt as if something inside me had been amputated. I don't think losing an arm can hurt as much as losing that kiss.

But I've always believed it was the illness that made my mother forget our ritual. Just as one day she forgot to turn off the gas and I had to do it for her.

'Mum, you've left the hob burning.'

'I'm such a fool. Could you turn it off, please?'

Once, I got back from school to find her waiting for me on the street, outside the entrance to our building.

'I left my keys at home.'

Another time, she forgot to put her shoes on before leaving the house.

One day I watched my father cry after she came into the living room to ask us if we were planning on eating anything or not. Barely a moment earlier she'd been clearing up the plates from the dinner we'd just shared together. A few nights before, my father and I had assumed she was joking when she'd casually remarked, 'This programme's quite good. Is it new?' as the three of us watched *Un, dos, tres,* the most watched and longest-running show on TV at the time.

The tears my father cried that night were silent ones, but I noticed all the same. Never again did he tell her to 'pay attention' or say 'you're away with the fairies today' or 'give me strength, woman'. I'm sure the reason he cried was because he'd been asking around among people he knew, and they'd told him about the illness. Maybe he had a client who lived with a senile mother, or he'd visited houses in which Granddad had been plonked down by the window, where he endlessly repeated the same childhood anecdote. But my mother wasn't even fifty at the time and he wasn't willing to accept that these were clearly the first signs of a rapid decline.

The illness advanced relentlessly over the following years. My mother forgot who my father was and then she forgot who I was. And one day she stopped recognising herself in the mirror. She departed for an unknown land. A place I imagined as being completely unblemished, not dark but rather filled with an electric light, to judge by the almost permanent smile on her face.

The doctors had told my father a horror story, which became a reality before we'd even had time to come up with a survival strategy. We reinvented our day-to-day existence from scratch. A neighbour would come up to the flat when my father was out. He came to an agreement with her and she noted down the hours spent there in a little notebook hanging from the fridge, like a prisoner crossing off the remaining days of their sentence. And every Friday my father would tear out the sheet and pay her for her time.

When we got home my mother would greet us with a 'Now then, what did you forget this time?' And little by little, my father and I grew more and more angry at the way my mother's head was being emptied of her memories and her capacity for reasoning. Eventually a glass wall was erected, and we collided with it every day, every time we caught ourselves believing that things could go back to the way they used to be. But though he lost heart, though it forced him to push his working hours and, most of all, his patience to the limit, my father didn't let it defeat him. And my father was the king of impatience. Can you inherit that? My father became strong and supple, because physical exercise was his only salvation from this disaster.

I later realised that one way it affected me was by forcing me to look back over my life prematurely. In order to protect myself against the pain of having an inaccessible mother, I became a memoirist at fifteen. I had to recreate the past far too early, the past with her, our shared history. I carved those memories into myself so they couldn't be erased or become embittered. And I fought to preserve the wonderful image of what my mother had been as a defence against the crushing awareness of the mother she'd become against her will. Every time I felt low I'd take out the accordion of memories and play it.

Over and over again, my mother would tell me things like how 'Rosario, you know, the one from the tailor's shop, she's got a new floor. She swapped tiles for parquet and oh my, it looks lovely!' or that 'Those new shoes really suit you,' even though they were the same shoes I always wore. Whenever this happened I'd remind myself that this was the same woman who'd taught me to read, to speak, to have a firm grip on the kitchen knife, to fold a T-shirt, cover a book. To write my name – the d, the a, the n. 'The n's really hard, but the i's easy-peasy, isn't it?' The same woman who helped me to fold the pastry for apple tarts by placing her hands upon mine, who moved my arm to help me beat the egg whites more quickly so that the meringues would rise properly, who used to straighten my shirt collar with a light tug to my shoulders. 'Now look at you, aren't you so handsome when you're dressed up all smart?'

Once the extent of my mother's illness had become plain for all to see, the news reached the ears of the teachers and priests at my school, giving me a veneer of respectability. Now, I hardly ever got swatted or cuffed on the head just because one of them was in a foul mood; instead, I'd get chosen to mind the class in their absence or sent to the secretary to fetch some spare chalk or paper.

My rise to the top was gentle and understated, but nevertheless I sometimes felt uncomfortable about being a good student, the nice kid, anything that could provoke the resentment of the others. But they also respected the special circumstances behind my sudden rise. 'His mother's gone crazy,' I heard one of my classmates saying. When friends came over to my house, they could look into her eyes and see something that was no longer so clear to me, that my mother had become indecipherable and intimidating.

The exact opposite of what she once was.


## the exact opposite of what she once was

My mother was so serene. Her Catholicism was a calm and quiet devotion, whereas for the priests at my school it was always something threatening: probing, fierce and repressive. She always prayed to herself, at different moments during the day. At school we'd pray at the beginning and at the end of each day, led by a camouflage-coloured loudspeaker situated above the blackboard in each classroom. We prayed with military levels of discipline. Afternoon prayer always coincided with an urgent need to visit the toilet. Some of us would place our hands between our legs and hop about on the spot to calm our bladders, stop them from exploding. This was how we learnt that the needs of the body eventually win out against those of the soul.

My mother liked us to pray before eating and wouldn't let my father have his first spoonful until we'd finished the Our Father and the Hail Mary. Occasionally, she'd add a dedicatory prayer for some sick or recently deceased relative, for Mummy's family, for the naturalist Félix Rodríguez de la Fuente, for cousin Lurditas, for Fofó the clown.

At night, she'd sit at the end of my bed and we'd intone together: 'Gentle Jesus, meek and mild, look upon a little child.' But she was sharp enough to realise when it stopped being so natural, sometime between nine and ten years of age, a little after my first Communion. By then I'd lost my faith over the course of many Sunday school lessons, utterly convinced after hearing the obtuse reasoning and total lack of intellectual capacity of the school priests. If God really existed, there's no way he'd have chosen such brutish, twisted people to transmit his message of peace.

'Me, I never miss a chance to go out and groove to some reggaeton on a Saturday night, even when I don't feel like it. Do you know Azúcar, by Atocha station?' Jairo asked me. 'Well, that's where I head, to dance till the sun comes up.'

I couldn't help but imagine his gigantic head and his dark hair bobbing around on the dance floor, in direct competition with the glitter ball.

'You don't know what it's like to spend the whole day with dead people,' he continued. 'Forgive me, ach, but it really is tough, you know. And the families are the worst of all, because you have to be with them in their suffering, even if it only means wearing your condolences face, and you feel like crap all day long . . .'

I liked that expression, condolences face. I'd have to use it in a song.

'But I will admit that, even though it goes against the company's guidelines, every now and then I like to get a few laughs out of them, to ease the tension. Sometimes the families really appreciate it. At one funeral last month the ribbon hadn't been placed properly around the wreath. It was meant to say "Your family will never forget you," but you couldn't really make out the "never", so it looked like it said "Your family will forget you". And the priest is standing there waffling on, and so when there's a pause I go up to it and move the letters around in the ribbon so you can read the whole thing. And I say to the family, "Best make sure it stays like that, because now's no time for honesty, you know!" You should have seen how they laughed!

'Of course, if my boss had heard me I'd have been in for it. I got into this business by accident, you know. A close friend of mine died in Madrid. He'd been working on a construction site. It's a bit of a long story. It happened at the house of some very rich people, but the building works were illegal and so these folks, in order to get the dead man off their backs – I mean literally get him off their backs – agreed to pay for the burial. So of course that meant repatriating the body to Ecuador and a dead man can't travel alone. He has to be put in a box with a holy sculpture of Our Lady of El Cisne on it. Then there's all the faff of the funeral arrangements.

'So what happened was I offered to do the journey and organise everything over there so as not to stir anything up with the family. And it was all plain sailing, so much so that when I got back, the boss at the undertaker's told me that he had a position for me if I wanted it.

'Of course he did warn me that the job's not for everyone, it takes balls and guts. And look, I'm not going to lie, it's tough, but it's not as tough as being a drug dealer, or laying bricks in 40-degree heat.'

## no artist ever came from Estrecho

'No artist ever came from Estrecho.' My father would hack away at my artistic pretensions, my entirely unsubtle flourishes through which I announced to the world that I was going to be special. I may have been born on a dead-end street, but conventional working environments − offices, companies, workshops − never appealed to me and I had no interest in cars, mechanics, physical strength or being brainy.

He struggled to recognise it, but my father too had fled from old-fashioned jobs dictated by set times, bosses and strict discipline. He roamed the streets as a door-to-door salesman and became his own boss. He was independent − can you inherit that? − always on the lookout for new clients, armed only with his charisma and his gift for instantly relating to people.

Although Estrecho never produced any artists, as my father insisted, it did have a music shop with an enormous window display by the Calle Navarra exit of the metro station. It sold simple instruments, arranged neatly and impersonally. A keyboard with folding legs over here, two vulgar upright pianos over there, two guitars at the back, hanging down from the ceiling like legs of ham. And in a crib made up of cushions and bits of fabric, a polished clarinet and a saxophone, standing upright in its stand.

It was in this music shop one afternoon that I saw a sign in the window offering three free guitar lessons, with no further commitment. I went inside to inquire. The manager, Mendi, would shoo us out every time we showed up, like someone waving flies away in summer. He was the ideal salesman for a shop that wasn't interested in selling anything, but we'd still infuriate him by brushing our fingers over the strings of each guitar as we walked past, or by playing a few keys on the display piano. 'Listen, boy, why don't you shove that little finger up your arse, where it belongs?' People said he'd once been a musician, but he looked more like a claustrophobic lift attendant.

When I got home I told my mother about the advert I'd seen at the shop.

'Don't let them fool you; they'll get money out of you one way or another.'

She tried to get the idea out of my head, but by then I'd already fixed a date for my first lesson with Mendi. Nothing suggested it was a scam. In the shop, I'd asked him, 'Why are you giving away free lessons?'

'It's a promotion, see? One of you brats is bound to get a taste for music,' Mendi explained.

There were warts on his neck, like he'd had skin pellets rain down on him, and it was impossible to talk to him without looking at them. Sometimes, when he kicked us out for poking around too much, Animal would laugh and shout 'Nice wart!'

'So, shall I sign you up, then? Guitar or piano?' he asked. 'I do piano, the guitar lessons are done by a teacher who lives close by, on Calle Lérida.'

I looked at his warts; children are always so sensitive to physical defects. I remember how when she was little, my daughter had stopped saying hello to Animal, whom she'd always adored, because he'd had an accident and there were some stitches above his eyebrow. In reality, it was what Animal always called a workplace accident: he'd fallen over during a post-gig bender and cut his head open on the corner of a sink.

'Well,' Mendi demanded, 'which is it to be?'

I chose guitar to avoid going with him. And my first lesson was scheduled for the following Thursday, at six thirty. I told my mother I was going over to Villacañas's house to do my homework; she was fond of Villacañas because he said words wrong — aminals instead of animals — and got his verb endings mixed up, too — I losed a tooth, I've aten already, thanks. My mother liked to think I was helping him to become a more civilised person, but it was impossible to civilise Villacañas. I stopped hanging out with him two years later when he started sniffing wood glue in the school toilets.

I arrived at the guitar teacher's flat to hear an ominous-sounding chord being played by the student before me. He was a fat boy, my age. I knew him from the neighbourhood but he went to a different school, with a blue uniform that made him look like a sausage dog attending an English boarding school.

I poked my head through the door and saw the old teacher, half bent over, almost defeated by those clumsy hot-dog fingers, which made the guitar sound like a harp being plucked by a pair of elbows. I've often thought that maybe I benefited from having someone like that go before me. It's the same thought that pops into my head whenever I win any kind of musical award, which are always given in exchange for favours to a magazine or radio station: if you win, it's simply because you're less awful than everyone else.

The guitar teacher greeted me unenthusiastically. He asked how old I was and when I replied that I was twelve, he seemed sceptical.

'Really?'

The offer was only for those aged twelve and above. Mendi had already made this clear, even telling me to bring some form of ID. I took out my school library card, which displayed the year of my birth, 1970, but the teacher wouldn't even glance at it.

'Leave it, leave it. Ever played the guitar before?'

'No, never,' I confessed somewhat remorsefully.

'Good, it's better that way.'

Don Aniceto turned out to be gentle and patient. He'd explain each position as he sat in front of me, moving my fingers into the correct places. I realised he was a good guy towards the end of that first lesson, when he took the guitar in his hands and played three chords which, after my first clumsy attempts, sounded like they'd come down from on high.

'Guitars are like people: after three hours of being punished, they like a bit of affection.'

He let a goofy smile escape as he played another chord with his arthritic fingers.

'One never stops learning to play the guitar. Today you've begun learning, but if you really like it, you'll never stop. Even Andrés Segovia still learns new things about the guitar. You do know who Andrés Segovia is?'

I shook my head.

'Well, you should. But then again, all of your brains are stewing in that ghastly stuff you hear on the radio these days.'

I had my next lessons on the Tuesday and Thursday of the following week. By then I'd found out who Andrés Segovia was. His life, which I read about in the school Larousse, matched up with mine in interesting ways. My father was fifty-one when I was born, which meant that whenever my schoolmates saw him they'd always say 'Look, your granddad's come to collect you,' and I'd have to tell them 'No, that's my dad, not my granddad.' Andrés Segovia's youngest son was born the same year I was, only he wasn't fifty-one then, like my father, but seventy-seven. His sperm can't so much have swum as crawled towards that egg.

At the end of my last free lesson I told Don Aniceto, who hadn't asked whether or not he'd be seeing me again, that I knew who Andrés Segovia was now. He got up from his seat, went over to the record player and played me the second movement of Joaquín Rodrigo's Fantasia for a Gentleman, as played by Segovia.

Before it had finished, he said, over the music, 'If you apply yourself, you could end up being a great player.'

'Didn't I tell you it was a con?' That was my mother's response when I asked her if she could buy me a guitar.

I explained that no one had tricked me, the classes really had been free, as promised in the advert.

'Of course they were, but they're still taking advantage of kids, planting fanciful ideas in your head.'

'But I want to play. I want to learn how to play.'

'This is the last time you do this kind of thing without my permission,' she said, ruffling my hair.

I nodded. Then the look on her face relaxed and she went back to her chores.

'We'll talk about it with Dad when he gets home.'

But my father responded with smug laughter. Perhaps that's when he said the thing about no artist ever having been born in Estrecho. What I do remember for certain is him pointing at me and reining in my arrogance.

'You really want to learn something useful? Study typing. That will always come in handy.'

My mother came along with me to my first paid lesson with Don Aniceto. Maybe she wanted to see the face of the old man whose flat I was going to and his unobtrusive wife, who I barely ever saw. No one talked about child abuse back then. Some of the priests at our school used to come up and whisper into your ear, stroke your forearm to get a feel of your muscles, or invite you to drink wine with them alone in their office. And if one of them did football training he'd often stick around and watch the boys showering naked behind the partition, with a look of appraisal on his face. People said that one in particular had been sent back to Bolivia after a scandal involving a child, but what really struck us about him had been the brutality of his physical punishments. None of the other teachers could match the sheer intensity of his punches and slaps, surely the result of years of practice on the quivering faces of young Bolivian boys.

The guitar eventually came in the Christmas holidays, after a long month of my parents going to great pains to convince me I'd never have one.

'Forget about the guitar. Keep dreaming.'

I was grateful for their cruelty, because a few years before, during the saddest Christmas holidays of my life, my mother had taken me to a toyshop and just said, 'Go on, choose whatever you like.'

And whatever I chose would instantly be robbed of its magic. But that year, stumbling upon an unexpected guitar next to the tree, I got to relive the excitement of waking up on the morning of January the sixth, when we exchanged our gifts − a feeling which would soon fade away for good with my mother's illness.

Don Aniceto was authoritarian, inflexible and punctilious, and would get annoyed with me whenever I was too keen to learn a new chord or played a song by ear, riddled with mistakes, for haste was the arch-nemesis of his rigorous lack of urgency. But such was the passion he put into each lesson, the devotion with which he spoke about the instrument, that we always went to great lengths to please him.

For three years we saw each other every Tuesday and Thursday during the school term, in a class of three students, with all of us kept in a constant state of activity. He was effusive in his criticisms, seemingly wounded by our clumsy attempts, as if we'd just spat in his face. His spirit was so strong that when he became ill it was painful to watch just how quickly he fell apart. He faded away while waiting for a healthy kidney that never came, undergoing dialysis sessions that left him skinny and sickly green. Until one day he announced to us without ceremony that that afternoon's lesson, which took place three years after we first met, would be our last one with him.

I went to visit him twice and the second time he didn't let me come up after his wife had consulted him as I waited downstairs at the intercom. The previous time, he'd taken me by the hands and stroked my fingertips, as he used to do whenever I came back after the holidays, to see if I'd been practising.

'All right,' he said, 'you keep on playing.'

He didn't come out with some comforting aphorism, which is what he usually did during lessons – stuff like how a guitar was a man's best friend. If you ever knocked it when you were taking it out of the case or placing it on the ground, he'd scold you.

'Look here! every friendship has its limits, you know.'

His hands, with those rigid fingers that caressed the strings and crept up and down the neck of the guitar like the twisting branches of a vine, were the inspiration for my song 'Old Man's Hands'. So were my father's hands, with that war wound that came either from gangrene caused by a splinter from a pickaxe he was using to dig a trench in Tremp (the vulgar version), or shrapnel from the discharge of an anti-tank gun (the epic version):

*One day I'll have old man's hands*
*They'll show you who I really am.*

In the second year, Almudena, who'd been going to the earlier class, joined our group. When she sat down, the pleated skirt that was part of her convent school's uniform exposed her thighs and her bare knees all the way down to the coarse green socks she used to pull down, like the flashier footballers did at the time. She later told me that people at her school called her

Gordillo, because of the footballer who played with his socks pulled down and 'Not because my arse is fat, OK?'

She had lips as soft as cotton and smooth brown skin, although the body part I visualised most clearly, during the many frenzied wanks she inspired, were her thighs. Some of my nocturnal emissions, which I tried to remove from the sheets with a hairdryer before the cleaning lady arrived, resulted from dreams she'd appeared in, almost always submerged in a swimming pool, in which I was being kept prisoner between her thighs.

Don Aniceto would insist during his lessons that to play well we needed to achieve a harmony like water, submerge ourselves. But my erections were always provoked by noticing Almudena's white inner thigh just touching the edge of the guitar, a gently rhythmic accompaniment to her musical efforts. At fourteen, these were the first sparks that lit up my sexual awareness. It was something that had until then been dulled by the shadow of a boys school, where the only erotic possibility lay in the tawdry adverts for nude films published in *Pueblo*, my father's evening paper.

Don Aniceto didn't know how to talk to Almudena; her presence made him uncomfortable. One day, after he'd corrected her in a pretty heavy-handed manner, Almudena said to me on the stairs, 'I'm going to stop coming. I'm fed up.'

I felt terrible.

'Please don't, he's a good teacher, even if he can be tough sometimes.'

By then my mother had started getting sick, which meant I was always on the lookout for new places to call home. That class, her included, fitted into this category. The fear of not seeing her again led me to follow her home in secret and hang about outside the gates of her school, on Calle Villaamil, in case we bumped into each other. Whenever she noticed me, she'd nod in my direction from the pavement opposite.

Villacañas told me that the most effective thing to do was just lay it out straight.

'If you like her, then I think you just need to say: hey, wanna be my girlfriend?'

But that wasn't how I talked and simply to declare my affection, even with a more appropriate formula, was well beyond me. I didn't even dare to call her Almu, like everyone else did. For me she was always Almudena, because she inspired the same sense of awe I'd have felt in a cathedral.

When we stopped having lessons with Don Aniceto, I set up another fake chance meeting with her on the way to school. Standing there on the street, I asked Almudena if she was going to get another teacher. She shrugged her shoulders and said nothing, but I noticed she'd drawn a heart on her forearm with a biro next to two initials that didn't match my name. I don't think I ever saw Almudena again, but those thighs, strengthened from skipping and other playground games, stayed with me for many years.

It's a cruel thing to say, but disappearances also have something liberating about them. Almudena disappeared from my life and though I continued locking myself away in the bathroom with the most pornographic images I could lay my hands on, I no longer associated them with the desire for any specific person. It was more advantageous to masturbate in the abstract, without imagining any real object of desire.

In any case, the danger had greatly increased after my father removed the bolt to stop my mother from getting locked in again, which meant there was no time to get carried away. I had to ejaculate without letting my guard down, always alert, because anyone could suddenly open the door. And then I'd end up like my schoolmate who, when his mother had discovered him jerking off, tried to explain himself with a pathetic 'But, Mum, everyone in my class is doing it.' Which in turn was enough to get us all a telling off from our teacher.

I already knew, as we'd been told at school, that I was going to end up blind from wanking, but it was a price I was willing to pay. Ray Charles was proof that blind people are particularly sensitive to music. But once I was no longer able to see the number on an approaching bus or read from the board in class, I had to tell my father, who took me to an optician friend of his where I was prescribed my first pair of glasses. I was fifteen. Sometime later my friend Fran, who knew a fair bit about doctors and medicine, put me at ease: my wanking had nothing to do with my poor eyesight.

Almudena was still a presence, albeit a fleeting one; she fed my fascination for missed opportunities, failed meetings, exchanged glances, unfinished lines. She laid the foundation for other fleeting presences to come. The girl with wet hair who came to say hi after a show at Complutense University. A photographer from a newspaper in Logroño. The young woman at the chemist's in Aoyama where I'd bought Maya a new dummy the day she chucked the old one into the river, initially convinced she was too big for it before promptly bursting into tears and begging to have it back. The Dutch woman at the bike hire place in Amsterdam who put down her book, which it just so happened I'd also read in Spanish, to talk to me. The Mexican singer Valeria, who smiled at me after we sang two songs together at Bocanegra's daughter's wedding, the last wedding I chose to attend. The stunningly beautiful woman who worked at a motorway tollbooth in Behobia. And the waitress in Ibiza who gave me the three beers I'd drunk on the house because she said that one of my songs had saved her life; though I no longer remember whether it was 'For the Light' or 'Happy Harry'. These women, along with a few others created by my imagination, all starred in the song 'Fleeting':

*Fleeting*
*And your whole life changes, though nothing has changed*
*And everything happens, though nothing has happened.*

But cruellest of all was the way I felt that Don Aniceto's death also liberated me from his discipline and the precise hierarchy of his incremental techniques. I promised my father I'd keep having lessons at school, but I found the idea of signing up for lessons with the onion-faced, pot-bellied music teacher, who'd already managed to make us hate the recorder, Bach and Mozart, too depressing.

My mother liked me practising next to her and I'd spend my afternoons in front of the sheet music for songs I liked, which I'd managed to pick up cheap at a market stall in Marqués de Viana. I wanted to play the electric guitar, but I didn't dare suggest it while Don Aniceto was alive. Curiously, it was during another Christmas holiday that my father, perhaps more generous than ever only because he was incapable of thinking of what to buy me, left enough money in my shoes for me to finish saving and convince Mendi to give me a half-price Series E Fender Strato-caster, made in Japan, along with a tiny amplifier. The very first time that guitar rang out in the solitude of my bedroom, I realised that the walls were crumbling down – not the actual walls, but the ones still separating me from that other world I wanted to join.

## don't go around with that one, he's no good

'Don't go around with that one, he's no good,' Don Luis told me when he first noticed I was spending every break glued to Gus's side. Don Luis had stopped hitting us – the law no longer allowed it – but in the first half-hour of every lesson he'd bombard us with gentle slaps and tug at our hair. Then he'd dedicate the second half to make it clear he was doing it for our own good, telling us not to say a word to our parents.

For me, that was the democratic transition in a nutshell. Every twentieth of November Don Luis would take out his Spanish flag with the Francoist eagle on it and lead a group of loyal pupils down the Plaza de Oriente. He also dusted it off to celebrate the 12–1 win against Malta, but otherwise – whack – his history lessons continued to be punctuated by regular slaps. 'Don't go around with that one,' he told me; but I did, because Gus shone bright, even though he dressed like a vampire, all in black and with the collars on his shirts or jackets always turned up. 'Ávila's full of vampires,' he'd tell me when he described his city of origin.

'Ah, the new one. Let's see, then, what's your name?' Don Abdón spat.

'Gus,' said Gus.

'First of all,' the priest laid out, 'you stand when you're asked to speak. What did you say your name was?'

'Gus.'

'Gus, Gus, Gus, Gus,' the class echoed sarcastically, taking care to imitate the effeminate way Gus pronounced words ending in s. 'Gus, Gus-Gus, oh Gush, Gush,' we all jeered, me included, for it took me a while to dissent from group jibes of this kind.

'That's not a name I've ever come across,' said Don Abdón in an attempt to entertain the other pupils. 'What's Gus short for? Dis-Gusting?'

The whole class received the teacher's cruel joke with thunderous applause. This always happened: whenever a teacher said something that was intended to be funny we'd celebrate it wildly, as a way of escaping from silence and discipline.

'Quiet. Now then, new boy, explain yourself.'

Up until then we'd all called him New Boy. In our school, that name could last for years until someone newer arrived. In fact, the day Gus arrived, Loni, short for loner, stopped being New Boy and gained his new name. The custom of calling every new boy New Boy did cause a few mix-ups. One night after finishing a gig in Siroco a guy my age came up to me and said, 'Remember me? I was in your class for two years; you used to call me New Boy.'

'My name is Gus, sir, and I want people to call me Gus.'

Don Abdón smiled, shuffled around the paperwork on his desk, glanced at the list of pupil names and said, 'All right, Agustín, you may sit down. But remember,' he insisted, 'Agustín is a wonderful name. I don't think Saint Augustine would have achieved sainthood if he'd insisted on people calling him Saint Gus.'

Once again, there was widespread, rapturous laughter. Don Abdón could be very witty, just so long as the wit was being employed in the service of evil. I looked into Gus's sparkling eyes and, though he managed not to laugh, I knew that the situation amused him. Gus hated the name Agustín, I later found out. I called him Agustín when I was angry with him, or rather, when I wanted him to think I was about to get angry with him. 'Don't fuck with me, Agustín.' Professionally, everyone, including the press, always thought that Gus was short for Gustavo and he did nothing to dispel such rumours. But really it was short for Agustín – Saint Gus, as he'd occasionally say to me, winking at the reference to our schooldays.

Lots of people used to call Gus Dis-Gusting, especially at the start, in the playground, when other pupils always used to take the piss out of him before he eventually emerged victorious. His aunt used to call him Agus. And he tolerated it, but only from her. We loved Aunt Milagros. One of the things that made Gus unique was that he didn't live with his parents in

Ávila but had moved to Madrid to live with his aunt.

'It was quite a struggle for my parents to find a school as horrible as this one,' Gus used to joke, 'but in the end they managed and so they sent me to Madrid to enjoy it.'

Aunt Milagros ran a guest house on Calle de los Artistas, next to the Cuatro Caminos roundabout, when it still had those flyovers we all used to call Scalextric. Gus lived in a room in his aunt's guest house which, at least to my eyes, gave him a veneer of intrigue. There were six other rooms, usually taken by university students and people from the provinces going for job interviews in Madrid. Aunt Milagros used to cook for everyone, wash their clothes, do their shopping, but above all she looked after them and smothered them in kisses. She always gave me affectionate kisses once I'd become a regular fixture in her domain. She'd have me stand next to Gus and measure us by sight.

'You see how much taller Dani is than you, Gus? You must drink a lot of milk, surely?' she asked me, affronted by Gus's hatred of dairy products.

The guest house had a communal room, which Aunt Milagros had intended as a place of study. She even called it the study room, and it was watched over by a photo of her idol and fellow Ávila native, Adolfo Suárez, whose political career was already in decline by then.

When we wanted to cheer her up, Gus and I would sing, 'A vote for CDS is a vote for liberty, vote Suárez for democracy and society.'

And she'd smack us jokingly and say, 'Don't laugh! No one listens to him now, but history will put each of us in our rightful place.'

While history was putting him in his place, the best place in her little room was always reserved for that man and his wonderful cheekbones.

Gus avoided going back to Ávila even on bank holidays. His aunt insisted, 'Your parents miss you,' but he preferred to stay in Madrid and come over to my house. Ávila seemed ancient to him, old-worldy, all pasty like Saint Teresa's fingertips. Gus loved exuberance. He used to spike up his blond hair with gel and score his eyebrows. He only refrained from wearing make-up because the school's aesthetic norms prohibited its students from being contaminated by the trends that could be seen on every street back then, in 1984, the year Gus joined our class.

The two or three punks in our school had to flatten their mohawks a little as they crossed the playground, use their sports jackets to cover up the safety pins that pierced their arms and turn their Dead Kennedys T-shirts – Gus used to call them Los Kennedys Muertos – inside out. He was fascinated by artists I avoided, people like Elton John, Freddie Mercury, The Velvet Underground, Motown girl groups and David Bowie, whom I detested simply because one of the school Nazis, two years above us, adored him. He'd fight with me over every single artist I admired, waging war until one of us surrendered.

'I'll take your Bob Dylan with his ridiculous harmonica if you take my Stevie Wonder. At least he can play his.'

He liked provoking me, saying for example that Yoko Ono was his favourite Beatle, or that Van Morrison, whom I worshipped, was just an Irish version of Raphael Martos Sánchez. He took the piss out of me for the number of times I'd watched *The Last Waltz*, which he saw as little more than a reunion of bearded trappers, like Robert Redford in *Jeremiah Johnson*. His musical knowledge was disarming. He made me see that I was a prejudiced fool because I loved Cyndi Lauper but hated Whitney Houston, ignorant of the fact that 'True Colors' was written by the same guys who wrote 'So Emotional', a song he'd often belt out whenever he was in the mood.

★

If one thing characterised Gus, it was his desire for people's attention. He envied women for the way they could play with their hairstyles and their outfits, make-up, bold colours, high-heeled shoes, in stark contrast to boys with their uniform of jeans, T-shirt and trainers. He used to say we all looked like soldiers in some secret army. Anything went when it came to grabbing people's attention, and when a girl walked past him on the street he'd say things like, 'Just look at those shoes! Wouldn't you like to be elevated like that? One day men will be able to wear heels just like women. Anyway, what's the difference? We all shit and eat.'

My eyes would be glued to the guitarist's hands whenever we went to watch a band together, but his mind would be elsewhere.

'Wouldn't you love to be one of the chorus girls?'

He'd claimed that ever since he was small, whenever anyone had asked him what he wanted to be when he grew up, he always answered either a chorus girl or a hostess on *Un, dos, tres*.

'But,' he clarified, 'this is Ávila, right, and being a boy in Ávila and saying stuff like that is rather different from doing it in San Francisco.'

His eruption into the school caused a scandal, which he used as a catwalk. Rather than withdrawing into his shell during those early days, he simply accepted his punishment, all the insults. Armed with witty retorts for each and every provocation, he patiently won over almost everyone.

The tough kids in the class called him faggot, little queer, poofter, pansy. Taking this risk, in that densely packed, grimy space, full of violent, sweaty, brawny students, was the ultimate demonstration of his strength of character.

'One day,' he boasted to me in class, 'the only thing you'll remember about secondary school will be that it was where you met me.'

I soon realised he wasn't exaggerating. Whenever a teacher called him to the blackboard, the whole class would begin to make jokes and catcall him, cruelly mimicking his movements as he walked to the front. But when he got to the front of the classroom, he'd respond with a cheerful tap dance. I remember our Latin teacher, Don Ángel, stopping the class because he was so alarmed by the jokes he was hearing.

With the best teacherly intentions, he asked Gus, who was standing there on the parquet floor, 'Why do you think your classmates create such a commotion whenever it's your turn to come up to the board?'

'Honestly . . .' said Gus, savouring the pause before he finished his sentence. 'I think it's because they love me.'

His hands flapped around whenever he was explaining something, but he never lost his nerve when he was scolded, or when someone mocked him for being camp. Many preferred to leave him in peace rather than become a target for one of his poisoned darts. Whenever someone shoved or hit him – we were fourteen, when shoving is simply a mode of communication – they knew they'd have to deal with Gus's always unpredictable, never physical retort.

When the two class bullies tossed his sandwich out of the window one breaktime, he merely responded, 'One day, I shall let you both tie my shoelaces.'

I found it hard to stand by him every time, but once I finally did, we became inseparable. Animal, who by then had already become my main ally, was puzzled by my new friendship.

'Why do you like this dude so much?' he asked me when he saw us chatting between lessons, surprised that I wasn't ignoring him like everyone else.

'Why?' I answered. 'Just look at him. Look at him and then look at everyone else.'

Gus wasn't playing at being the class pansy but rather the

class artist, the special being, the extraterrestrial. He could draw beautifully and did effortlessly well in his studies, but he never took part in PE lessons. He always faked a limp or a pulled muscle. He drew an A for anarchy on the church wall, though he only confessed this to me once we were long out of school. We were on our way back from a gig in Seville and I was comforting him because he was upset after hearing about the death of Tino Casal in a car accident.

'It was me who drew that thing in the church,' he told me. 'I just wanted you to know. It's a stain I can never remove.'

He challenged the teachers with questions that made us all laugh and won concessions that benefitted the whole group.

'Don't you think it might be too hot for lessons?'

Or when the physics teacher threatened us with a group suspension, he sighed and said, 'That's good, at least that way I'll have company.'

One time our Spanish teacher complained about the odour wafting around the classroom and asked, rhetorically, 'Can anyone explain to me what that smell is?'

Gus gave his dry retort: 'It smells of school, sir. Maybe you've chosen the wrong profession for someone with such high olfactory sensitivity.'

When the music teacher asked us what song we wanted to rehearse to perform in church on the twenty-fourth of May, for the feast day of Mary Help of Christians, he suggested 'Like a Virgin', in all seriousness. He loved that song and in the gaps between classes he'd sit at his desk showing off his blond ambition, swaying his head and shoulders and pouting as he sang like a teenage Spanish Madonna.

We all had a soft spot for one particular teacher. His priest name was Neila but we all called him Niebla, Misty, because one of his spectacle lenses was opaque. Sometimes he covered sex education in his RE lessons and one afternoon he was talking about contraceptive methods. He went to great lengths to explain what IUDs were – repeatedly saying the word intrauterine device, which sounded to us like some kind of intergalactic barrier – when Gus raised his hand, seeking permission to ask a question.

'Of course you can. What is it?'

'What I'm wondering, sir, is how exactly you know all this, as a priest?'

Even better was another memorable afternoon when he got angry with Gus for talking too much in class.

'You know what, Gus,' which is what every teacher was calling him by then, 'let me tell you what I thought about you the first day you came to this school – and I can assure you that my judgement was spot on.'

'There's no need for you to tell me,' Gus interrupted. 'I know perfectly well what came into your mind the moment you saw me.'

'You do? Then please, tell me,' he invited.

Gus stood up, with the theatrical air he reserved for such occasions. 'You thought to yourself, A Star is Born.'

One day when Gus was asked to stand up and talk about the assassination that kicked off the First World War, he gave a measured response.

'You must understand that no world war ever began for a single reason. There are always many causes—'

'Stop beating around the bush, Gus, and answer the question. What was the name of the Austro-Hungarian archduke who was assassinated in Sarajevo?'

And as he searched for the answer, the pupil sitting behind him murmured, 'Faggot, cocksucker.'

And Gus, rising up to the occasion, answered, 'I think his name was Faggot Cocksucker, though in the interests of full disclosure, I must confess that Ventura whispered the answer to me.'

Our fondest memories of school often involved him making the bunch of morons that comprised our class and the usually distant, scornful teachers laugh as one. He soon gained a mythical status within the school, with everyone continually repeating Gus-related anecdotes and his legendary put-downs. The teachers would have preferred to suppress them, but resorting to Francoist authoritarianism was looked down upon at the time and their ensuing sense of guilt became the closest thing to freedom we'd ever known.

Eventually, the rest of the boys left him alone and we could spend our breaks walking around in peace, far away from the criss-crossing football games on the sloping sports pitch, where at any given moment one team would be playing uphill and the other downhill.

'The fool never dies,' he sometimes explained. 'In a tragedy, the fool is always spared.'

He was without a doubt the student we learnt the most from. He helped us to understand how unjust our mistreatment, which we had all accepted as natural, really was. Over the years, his uninhibited, leading-lady posturing confused many. He was neither handsome nor feminine. He had very visible stubble, which looked good on him, big ears and pale, acne-marked skin that dried up easily, leaving flakes of skin between his eyebrows, or in the folds of his nose.

Amused by his theatrical gestures, my father used to call him La Majorette. He wasn't bothered by the amount of time I spent with him, probably because Animal was always there as well, and the contrast between the two of them was stark. He won over my father because of the way he clowned around in front of my mother, singing 'Ojos Verdes' to her with his hand on his hips, the exact same way Miguel de Molina sang it.

Gus's name for the country we inhabited, caught somewhere between the drawn-out end of an authoritarian Catholic regime and the new morality of mass consumption, was Villastupid.

'First we take Villastupid, then the world.'

He'd often surprise me in interviews, saying, for example, that his favourite childhood toys had been his sisters' Señorita Pepis make-up boxes. Or that the greatest advances in women's rights in Spain had come about owing to female folk singers like Rocío Jurado, Lola Flores, Marifé de Triana, María Jiménez. Because when they sang they addressed the macho Spanish male and told him, 'You can fuck me, but for fuck's sake, fuck me good and proper.'

'That's all they sang about,' he said, 'and they got the female orgasm to be viewed with the same importance as the male one.'

He never told me who'd beaten him up in the alley by the Europa cinema, the night he showed up at my house with his face all smashed up, saying, 'Come down, Dani, I don't want to scare Aunt Milagros.' And I had to treat his wounds out on the street with hydrogen peroxide and cotton-wool buds so that my father wouldn't see, while begging him to go and get an X-ray. But he kept on telling me it wasn't serious, that getting a beating was good for your reputation.

'Hollywood actors make the screenwriters put it in. Haven't you ever seen a Marlon Brando movie? *The Chase*, *On the Waterfront*; if there isn't at least once scene where he gets hit, he doesn't do the movie. James Dean was the same. It's such a shame you weren't there, Dani,' he told me with a half-smile as I cleaned away the blood from one of his eyebrows. 'You would have been proud of me.'

And though I tapped him on the shoulder and told him to be quiet, I already did feel proud of him, every day, and I felt proud of myself for having dared to be his friend.

'It's so nice to be able to fulfil a promise,' said Jairo, the hearse driver. 'I'm guessing this is a promise you made to your father, am I right? Taking his body back to his birth village.'

I shrugged. I wasn't sure it had been a promise. I remembered having sat down in front of my mother a few days after to tell her Dad had died and her looking at me, trying to express something. 'My, my,' was all she came up with, because news no longer mattered to her. I stroked her hands; perhaps to her we were all dead and nothing really existed: there's no existence without emotions.

It was several months later when I went back to tell her that perhaps it was a good idea to bury him in the cemetery in his village. I told her that I felt like he was all alone and abandoned up there in Carabanchel with no one to visit him, with no relatives to wipe his headstone clean or lay fresh flowers on All Souls' Day.

'Do you think it's a good idea?' I asked my mother, not expecting a response but wanting to ask myself the question out loud. 'I think he'd like it, Mum, don't you?'

No, I didn't promise him anything. Whatever I did was only to make myself feel better, to do something to rectify his mediocre funeral, the lacklustre, unremarkable nature of his farewell. To experience my father's death for the second time after coming to terms with how important he'd been to me and to give him just a taste of the kind of epic occasion that used to make him so happy.

Jairo had put the air conditioning back on.

'You don't mind if I have it on low, do you? Is it because of your voice?' he asked.

I nodded. Air conditioning and cold water are my worst enemies, so much so that I usually wear a horrendous neckerchief. I tried to sleep, but Jairo insisted on talking to me.

'It's strange. I can't imagine how someone ends up being a singer. Please forgive my curiosity,' the driver said apologetically, shaking his staggeringly large head. 'I understand how you become an engineer, or a teacher, or a builder, but a singer . . . Can you study it? Is there a degree you can do in it? Anything?'

## it all started in a toilet

It all started in a toilet, a school toilet. We called them the pissers, and they stank of urine, damp and disinfectant. The stoners would leave banana skins to dry on the outside awning in preparation for smoking and we'd hide in one of the cubicles during PE lessons. On the ceiling in the urinals, somebody had used a lighter to write 'The end of the world awaits you', followed by a long-expired date. Perhaps the world really had ended then and we were none the wiser. Or as Don Eulalio, our Spanish teacher, used to say, 'The world may well have ended by tomorrow, but I still expect you to have learnt how to conjugate the pluperfect tense.'

I liked that teacher, also a priest, who taught me how to read sonnets out loud and the savage, metred humour of *La Celestina*. One month I even won the class literary prize, which wasn't particularly prestigious or noteworthy; it consisted solely of having your poem displayed on a noticeboard in the corridor and your test score going up by one point.

Soon after that our PE teacher Don Dionisio took me to one side. I thought he was going to congratulate me for the poem, as other teachers had done, but it was the exact opposite.

'What have you got against the Spanish flag?'

'Nothing,' I said.

The poem was called 'The Flag' and it was a hymn against wars and patriotism, against the urgent need to spill blood in the name of a glorified dishcloth. It was a pacifist allegory, inspired by the intense debate about Spain joining NATO.

'That poem is a piece of shit, and the best thing you can do now is tear it off that wall and feel ashamed about what you have done.'

'Don Eulalio liked it,' I reasoned.

'Don Eulalio is a moron, and what you deserve is for the Moors or the French to come and invade us and rape your mother and sisters.'

'I don't have any sisters,' I retaliated.

He waved me off with the military demeanour I associated with his lessons.

'Off you go, run back to your friends. But just so you know, you've failed this term's assignment.'

'What if we started our own group?' Gus suggested to me one morning, hiding in the toilet while Don Dionisio outran the rest of the class.

'A group?'

'Yeah, for the competition.'

Towards the end of every May, Don Jesús – the coolest priest, the one who ran the students' centre and all the youth activities, wore jeans and untucked shirts, and actually tried to make a difference – would organise a battle of the bands. It was always won by his folk Mass group – four lads who livened up the Eucharist with versions of Simon and Garfunkel's 'The Sound of Silence' transformed into the Lord's Prayer. Or Dylan's 'Blowin' in the Wind' but with the lyrics changed to 'We know you will come / We know you will be there / Breaking your bread with the poor'. Which Gus and I changed to 'We know you will come / We know you will be there / I can't take this shit any more' when we had to sing it in the compulsory Mass that took place every Thursday. Everyone called the contest Monkey's festival, owing to Don Jesús' strong resemblance to a little monkey who starred on a popular TV show at the time: same expansive forehead and same long arms shooting out from overburdened shoulders.

I responded to Gus's question with scepticism.

'What would we do up there?'

But Gus was already sold on the idea.

'We *have* to start a group.'

One door was already open to us: Animal played drums for the folk Mass group. Monkey had managed to domesticate him and although he'd got carried away a couple of times with his drum solos, sparking protests from some of the older, hearing-aid-wearing parishioners, Monkey always stood up for Animal.

'Brothers and sisters, this is not noise but the rage of youth. The rage Our Lord Jesus Christ felt when he expelled the merchants from the temple. If Jesus came back to Earth, he'd be playing in a rock band,' he'd once claimed during Mass, to widespread scepticism.

Gus had it all laid out; we just had to convince Animal to leave the official Mass band and join up with us. Animal had his doubts.

'I can't just leave the group; I've been playing with them for two years.'

Gus had asked me to convince him and I pleaded with him.

'The stuff you play with that lot is a heap of shit. We're going to make music we actually like. Come on, for fuck's sake, don't tell me you aren't interested.'

And so Animal agreed. It was me who'd given him the nickname Animal because of the drummer in the Muppets' band. His father ran the mattress shop my father had bought my mother's special bed from when they'd had to stop sleeping together, because she had to be tied down with straps at night.

'But what's Gus going to play?' he asked me.

Animal had spent many an afternoon at my house, helping me to figure out the chords for songs by The Kinks, The Beatles, Buddy Holly and Eddie Cochran as he ate up tins of foie gras, licking it off his fingers.

At our first meeting, when the band was officially formed, Gus said, 'Well, I could play bass, that's not so difficult, and I can sing as well. The things band leaders always do,' he added, completely unfazed.

Monkey was visibly surprised to discover we were thinking of taking part in the contest.

'You lot, start a group? This I have to hear!'

He told us that when we were ready we'd have to get through the auditions at the school's rehearsal rooms. It had to be an original song, covers didn't count, although he was flexible enough with the rules to allow Animal to play with the folk Mass group as well, rather than having to quit.

'I'm not going to give you our drummer just like that,' he said.

Writing the song became a form of torture. We went over to Aunt Milagro's to vomit out some rhymes.

'Wouldn't it be better to write the music first?' Animal suggested. 'That's what we do in the other group.'

But Gus cut him off. He pointed at me. 'You won the poetry competition last year, didn't you? Write something, then.'

A melody came to me one breaktime in the pissers as I drew circles on the urinal with my wee. I used the physics lesson to come up with some lyrics to fit the music. I tapped out the rhythm on a sheet of paper with my pen. Gus looked at me from a distance; he'd understood what was happening and I gave him an optimistic thumbs up. He'd managed to convince a medical student called Fran, who lived in his aunt's guest house, to teach him to play the bass, or at the very least to hold it upright and extract some kind of rhythm from it. When I showed Animal the lyrics he began whispering the words to himself as he slapped his thigh in time:

*The janitor's daughter is thinking about it*
*The judge's nephew is thinking about it.*

'Cool,' Animal said when he'd finished. 'What does Gus think?'

But I still hadn't dared to show it to him. I needed the approval of someone with some level of musical expertise and Animal was miles ahead of us in this category. At least he knew how to play.

'I'd put loads of drums at the end bit, when you repeat the chorus. Loads of drums,' he concluded.

*The girl in detention is thinking about it*
*The museum guide is thinking about it.*

But Gus read it very differently from Animal. He immediately began singing the words, without even knowing what the melody was meant to be, though it wasn't difficult to guess given how repetitive it was.

*The newlywed bride is thinking about it*
*Her shy brother-in-law is thinking about it.*

He sang the words, nodding his head in approval. When he'd finished reading it, his eyes met mine and he held out his fist for me to bump. Then he made the same gesture to Animal and their knuckles collided.

'How does the last bit go? What happens in it?'

'I dunno,' I replied, 'crazy, superfast?'

'Yeah, yeah. I like it. I really like it. I'd put in a few more lines, something like "The English teacher is thinking about it.

As she's walking her dog she's thinking about it." And we'd actually sing the last bit in English,' he added.

'Amazing,' Animal said.

It was probably the best idea in the whole song. When we got up from the bench at the junction by Franco Rodríguez metro station, we all filed off towards our own homes.

But from a distance Gus said, 'Boys, we have our first song. And I know what our name's going to be, too. Las Moscas – the flies.'

After all, didn't it all start in a toilet?


## come on, let's do it

The chorus was an eruption, intended to bring together Animal's thunderous drumming and all the noise we could make on the guitar and bass, and we spent half an afternoon practising in a basement beneath the school:

*Come on, let's do it*
*Thinking about it all day, just can't be OK*
*Come on, let's do it now.*

At the time I was spending every evening listening to Bob Marley's *Legend*, so I came up with a reggae rhythm for the repetitive part of the song. Animal hammered out the rhythms and showed Gus what he needed do with his bass for most of the song.

'Look, man, it's just two strings and two changes. You can't go wrong.'

I was free to add whatever improvisations I wanted during each bridge section. During our first practice Gus and I began splitting the vocals quite naturally.

'You take one line, I'll take the next.'

Animal approved. 'It works.'

And that was it: we remained a vocal duo for the rest of our career together. There was nothing more to it. Singing hadn't crossed my mind, but it didn't seem to bother Gus and the song was picking up speed. It was still painfully monotonous, something I tried to change with my guitar part, while Gus, always fascinated by James Brown and Fats Domino, made rhythmic yelps and shouts with his voice, something that would end up becoming his unmistakeable trademark.

The practice room had a drum kit and three small amplifiers, but it was really a workshop and a storage cupboard, with piles of surplus desks and several plaster figures of saints and martyrs that were either being repaired or hadn't found an appropriate place to go in the school. Monkey stuck his head in to see if we were ready. So as not to give away a single detail, I began to play the guitar intro to a Stones song.

'Wow! You really can play. What a surprise,' said Monkey admiringly.

When Gus had heard me letting it rip on the guitar, he said, 'Dude, you can really fucking play.'

'Nah, I can get by, that's all.'

But I could see the admiration shining in his eyes and I was overcome with a euphoria that lasted for that whole practice session, right up until the magical moment of our first performance to our first lone spectator.

I'll never forget the look on Monkey's face when Gus and I began to sing our lines. Animal's playing was solid and he battered away at his kit. Monkey's expression betrayed a mixture of pain and embarrassment, which caused his cheeks and bald patch to break into a sweat before the heat of the chorus:

*Come on, let's do it*
*Thinking about it all day, just can't be OK.*

He gestured for us to stop, but we extended the chorus into an intense set of variations. Animal finished with an incredible drum roll, for which he stood up in order to enjoy the feeling of unloading every last bit of his body's energy. This was followed by a tense silence and then suddenly, at the back, where the alabaster and plaster figures were all bunched together, the raised arm of Saint Dominic Savio dropped off from his sculpture. It hit the floor and shattered into pieces. Saint Dominic was meant to be our academic role model, St John Bosco's student who died when he was only fifteen, after a life devoted to faith. Someone whose motto — death rather than sin — denounced our lack of scholarly dignity and devotion on a daily basis.

'You must be crazy if you think I'm going to let you sing this pornographic song at the festival.'

That was Monkey's reaction. I don't think I ever saw him looking so serious or disappointed. His favourite thing to say, in his haughty way, was, 'I'm not angry *with* you, I'm angry *for* you.'

We got embroiled in an interminable discussion about what the word pornographic actually meant, given that our song didn't contain a single rude word, or anything explicit. Monkey was outraged.

'*It*, thinking about *it*, everyone thinks about *it*. Do you think I'm a complete idiot, that I don't know that "it" means, what you mean to say when you say "it"?'

Gus tried to justify the words we were singing.

'"It" doesn't mean anything. It's abstract; it could mean whatever you want it to mean.'

'I wasn't born yesterday, you know. You won't get this one past me,' Monkey repeated. 'Leave the amps unplugged and go home, all right? My decision is final. Las Moscas will not play in the contest.' And with that he bade us farewell.

He'd found our name funny.

'What are you calling yourselves, then?' he asked before the rehearsal.

'Las Moscas,' we said and he laughed.

'The flies? Couldn't you have thought of something a little more unpleasant?'

Gus shook his head once Monkey had left the rehearsal room, having vowed to boycott our debut.

'I'm worried Las Moscas are going to shit.'

We didn't know then how many times we'd repeat that sentence over the years. Flies always go to shit.


## *flies always go to shit*

I never dreamt I'd be a singer. I hadn't ever sung at family celebrations; there were barely any celebrations at home once my mother got sick. It was me who convinced Gus we should get singing lessons, even though at that stage we'd already released our first album and had more than a hundred performances behind us. We were still as tone-deaf as ever and our voices got wrecked by the excess in those shabby dives that hosted our performances.

The idea of taking singing classes seemed ridiculous, surrounded as we were by groups made up of kids fresh out of school, all allergic to anything that made it look like they took their career seriously. Knowing how to play was frowned upon, looking after your voice a cause for embarrassment

Gus said, 'OK, if you insist, we'll do it. But we go to the best, not just any old duffer.'

Mr Robert Jeantal was a French singer who'd settled in Spain and did voice coaching for a few well-known artists. I don't know who put us in touch with him, but I do remember that when he received us at his home near Plaza de España, his hair was plastered down with gel and his fingers were twisted over with arthrosis. He was warm and charming but also serious.

He made us stand at each end of the corridor, placed himself in the middle and said, 'Sing. Something you know – one of your songs, perhaps.'

He made us squat. Gus started, I followed. I can't remember which of our songs we belted out in that place, crouched at each end of the corridor. The teacher put his hand out to stop us.

'Push your voice down, so that you can feel it coming from inside, from the deepest cavity. Your voice should be coming from your bottom, not from your throat.'

We looked like a pair of broody hens, and when we looked at each other, we burst into fits of uncontrollable, hysterical laughter that shook our bodies from head to toe. With exaggerated hand movements, Mr Robert told us to go on.

'Louder, louder! Come on, don't worry about the neighbours.'

But he wouldn't take us on.

'I have a lot of work at the moment, many students, serious people who hope to and – crucially – *can* make a living from singing. You have something wonderful; you're young, daring, smart. But you're terrible singers, with weak voices.

'And anyway, the one who holds himself well and has some charisma' – and he pointed to Gus – 'can't reach the high notes. And I fear that the one who could be a good singer' – and he pointed to me – 'lacks the essential qualities needed to succeed in this profession, with those glasses that make him look like an accountant. But keep going. You'll have fun for a few years – and you'll always remember it when you're both working in offices and only ever sing in the shower.'

In spite of this humiliating verdict, he gave us the number of one of his students, a woman who'd begun giving private lessons to make some money.

Elisa became our singing teacher. Gus took against her from the outset. He was annoyed that she didn't appreciate his voice, which he couldn't get to stand out or to comply with her tedious tuning exercises. For him, Elisa was still stuck in singing lessons from the previous century. But Elisa was friendly and didn't seem to get tired of correcting or chiding us.

She was slim, with a toothy smile. Gus called her Sunsilk, like the shampoo, because of her glossy, voluminous hair. She laughed at Gus's jokes. That always happened. Gus had this ability to insult people and still make a good impression on them: he was endearingly cruel. Elisa would sing Barbra Streisand songs at the piano in the flat where we had our lessons, highlighting the vocal flourishes in 'The Way We Were'.

She performed twice a week at a local nightspot whose carpets contained the personal details of its loyal, haggard clients – provincial types travelling through Madrid with their whore or their secretary lover. My lessons with Elisa went on for years. Gus avoided her. Maybe that's why I never told him that we also slept together, in the same informal way I attended the classes, in the gaps between gigs. But what really impressed me was the way she'd let out a piercingly high note when she reached orgasm, like a coloratura soprano.

Beginning to look after my voice and taking lessons was, at least for me, a way of making up for my early success. All those years at a Catholic school had made me believe that rewards could only be achieved through sacrifice, and since we were rewarded instantly, I devoted my life to looking for the sacrifice. Not Gus; no, for Gus a gift was a gift and the only thing to do was celebrate your luck.

Animal had had the good sense to record our audition

for Monkey on cassette, which our classmates found highly entertaining.

'Is it true he won't let you sing?' they all asked.

To add insult to injury, Monkey had decided to invite the girls from the Catholic school across the road to the contest. The idea that the school would be filled with girls caused feverish levels of excitement among the staff and students. We'd only ever seen the sixth-form girls who attended our school in the afternoon, all shocked by the lewd comments flung in their direction by a bunch of boys educated in a single-sex environment. We threw fistfuls of earth at them, splashed them with water from the fountain, hurled obscenities – and the more daring among us would even pinch their arses on the stairs, or fill their Tippex bottles with spunk when they weren't looking.

Gus let everyone in the whole school know that Monkey had censored us by stopping us from competing. Of the six groups that did take part – one of which was a girl group called Las Pumas (though they sounded more like hyenas) – the song performed by Animal and his folk Mass group ended up winning. And so they came back onstage to play their winning entry again, like in Eurovision. We called their lead singer Preppy, because he appeared to have emerged from a parallel universe, with his Californian fringe and boat shoes. But when Monkey got up on the stage in the sports hall to hand over the prize, something unexpected happened.

First of all, the boys in our class began to shout 'Censorship, censorship, censorship.'

A year earlier, the only palatable music programme on public TV had been cancelled because a Basque punk girl group had sung a Stooges cover. Niebla had tried without success to make us understand the difference between liberty and libertinism. Our classmates were shouting 'Las Moscas, Las Moscas, Las Moscas!' and 'Censorship, censorship, censorship!' while

Animal, still sitting onstage with the winning group, accompanied their chants with theatrical strikes of the drums.

Gus later called this our Spartacus moment. Perhaps all those boys who'd made Gus's early days at the school so difficult were now making it up to him. It was wonderful to think of all this as an act of reparation.

If there was one thing Monkey couldn't stand, it was being singled out by young people. This blot on his otherwise flawless record was ruining his reputation as someone who was open and sympathetic to the struggles of youth. So he took the mic and tried to quell the shouts.

'We don't do censorship here. Las Moscas simply didn't possess the level of skill that we expect from contestants.'

The boos were overwhelming. 'Censorship, censorship.' And the students were chanting name of our group, helping it to be born. 'Las Moscas, Las Moscas.'

Monkey admitted defeat and invited us onto the stage.

Perhaps, in different settings and with a higher level of skill, we've had more resounding successes since then. Perhaps, at the height of our popularity, we had nights of transcendental communion with the people who'd come to see us. But the atmosphere on that late afternoon of the twenty-fourth of May in the school sports hall was truly unforgettable.

We got off to a slow and uncertain start. I'd borrowed my guitar from Preppy and Gus had lost the strap for his bass, which he'd also been lent by a member of another band. Animal managed to disguise any slip-ups beneath the onslaught of his drumming and I added extra phrases to my guitar part, spurred on by the overwhelming response from the audience. Even the girls were jumping and the bolder boys, hungry for feminine contact, used the chaotic mosh pit as a chance to touch, brush up against and push into them.

Downstage, Monkey shook his head disapprovingly along

with the other teachers, a patronising smile on his face the whole time. But we were setting the place alight. Gus let go of his bass to twist and turn all over the stage, dragging the microphone stand around as if it were his tango partner and dropping to his knees in front of the crowd. He'd just discovered his natural habitat; he'd endured his tough childhood to get to this place and he was never going back. He let loose the onstage monster who'd been hiding inside him his entire life. For the finale he simply grabbed his crotch with his hand and shook it, in a simultaneous gesture of appreciation and contempt.

'You must be a bit like the group Verde70,' the hearse driver suddenly commented, not caring one bit that I was sitting there with my eyes closed, trying for the umpteenth time to get some sleep. 'Know them? I'm a big fan myself.'

'No,' I confessed, 'I don't.'

'"Dying for Your Love", "Not So Easy", "Hopelessly Late"?' Jairo felt it was his duty to list the titles of their best-known songs and then to sing the last one.

In order to shut him up, I said, 'I'll listen to them as soon as I can, I promise.'

'And what's the name of your group?'

'Las Moscas. Well, it was.'

Jairo shook his head. 'Haven't heard of them.'

'Everyone calls me Dani Mosca because people still associate me with my former group.'

Jairo proceeded with his interrogation.

'You're not together any more? I guess you broke up for the usual reasons: fights, egos – that must happen a lot, right?'

I shrugged.

Some joker overtook the hearse at great speed but still took the time to let out a snarky whistle.

'Watch it, dickhead!' Jairo shouted then regained his composure. 'You're a good son, Dani – mind if I call you Dani?'

75

'Of course not.'

'You're a good son, Dani, and the exhumation and all the other stuff can't have come cheap. Can I ask you how much they charged you for the exhumation and transfer?'

Once she'd got over her surprise at my act of necrophilia, Raquel had dealt with all the formalities.

'You want to dig up your father almost a year after he died?' she asked almost mockingly. 'But you never go to funerals and you always insist that death is just an excuse to make money from people even when they've stopped existing.'

That was me in a nutshell: the most contradictory man in the world.

'It must have cost you a pretty penny.'

Jairo began breaking down the costs of transferring the body for me – the licenses that had to be granted, the exhumation techniques – in such a matter-of-fact, relaxed way that he could have been talking about any old job. I closed my eyes, but I couldn't sleep.

'When it comes to loved ones, you do what has to be done, full stop. I totally understand.'

I couldn't get comfortable in the ample space provided by the passenger seat. My head was flopping around all over the place, I was bothered by the sun shining through the window and most of all, the driver's conversation never let up.

'Hey, if you're really tired, you can have a siesta in the back.'

'In the back?'

'Yep, in the back.'

We entered the tunnel, another piece of infrastructure that had been paid for with European money, back when they'd scrambled up the map of my childhood movements, modernising the interminable stretches of elevated curves, the B roads with their roadside bars, petrol stations and first-aid posts.

'In the back?'

'Yes, yes, in the back. Get in the back.'

## *my first love song*

My first love song wrote itself. We'd got involved in the protests against joining NATO and our school folders were all
covered in 'Bases Out' stickers, to the horror of some of our
teachers. We only ever listened to North American music, and
watched American films and TV series, and yet we were swept
away by a ferocious anti-imperialism. We hung around with
Fran, who was still living at Aunt Milagros's guest house while
he prepared for his finals in medicine.

Fran had gone from giving Gus bass lessons to becoming our
main musical adviser. He spent every day revising for his exams,
but we discovered music by people we'd never even heard of
on his record player. He taught me how to play James Taylor
and Paul Simon songs on the guitar, which I'd practise every
day beside my mother, who'd say 'It's so lovely, the guitar, such
a beautiful instrument,' over and over. Occasionally, she'd stop
gazing into the distance and clap for me.

It was also Fran who took Gus, Animal and me to the protests,
where he'd point out who was who among all the politicians
and artists. Sometimes these events ended with concerts, and
this relationship between music and antimilitarism quite naturally led me to write 'I Was Looking for Love and I Found War',
which has the dubious honour of being my first romantic song.

Fran was from León and wanted to specialise in neurosurgery
because he was attracted by the challenge, the high level of
precision it required.

'One tiny slip-up,' he explained to us, 'and the patient is a
vegetable.'

He talked about going to the USA and leaving our country behind, because 'Over here the size of your balls will always be more important than the size of your brain.'

He was an attractive guy, who'd stroke his beard with the four fingers of his right hand, and his hair was parted in the centre in a perfect line, which he'd endlessly smooth over in a studied movement. He seemed so sure of himself that it sometimes came off as arrogance. He had a surgical sense of humour, which he employed with a double-edged scalpel – one side indifferent, the other downright scornful. He was six or seven years our senior but acted like he had fifty on us, both in terms of life and musical experience.

He had a friend who worked as a pilot and brought him records from the USA, The Grateful Dead and Alice Cooper, which we'd listen to in his room at the guest house. He smoked joints – said that every doctor did it to order to make them more emotionally detached before an operation – but he never offered us a single puff.

'The brain doesn't stop developing until you reach eighteen,' he told us. 'Until then, any psychotropic could damage your neurones. Look at what happens when people start smoking too early: their growth is stunted and then they age prematurely. It's like when people do too much sport or get too much sun.'

Animal wasn't all that impressed by Fran. He always said that a dude who blow-dries his hair every morning can't be trusted and he thought Fran had an excessive influence on us. Perhaps he was also annoyed by the devotion that Gus and I were beginning to display towards him.

When we accompanied him on demonstrations Animal would use his job at his father's mattress shop as an excuse.

'Really, though, what the fuck does the referendum matter to us if we still can't vote?' he argued.

But I knew that the reason he didn't want to come was

because he didn't want to be with Fran and because he felt betrayed by how close we were to him. And the disdain was mutual, as we discovered when Fran saw us with Animal.

'I get it. You hang out with someone like that so that you appear smarter, like girls who go out with an ugly friend to look more attractive.'

Sometimes Fran introduced us to his university friends. That's how I met Olga. She was one module away from finishing her degree at night school and in the mornings she worked as a receptionist in a dental surgery. She had blonde hair and her face was covered in freckles, which gave her a childlike aspect, and she had pearly white teeth that looked like they'd been aligned by some masterful hand. She had thin lips and giggled at the rhyming slogans I came up with during the demonstrations. 'Less cops, more ice pops,' was her favourite. Though she was also astonished at my success one Saturday morning when the entire crowd on the Paseo de la Castellana, all the way from Bernabeu to María de Molina, started singing my chant:

*Take your military budget*
*And shove it up your arse.*

According to Fran, Olga was involved with the dentist she worked for, but this information didn't stop me falling in love with her.

Sometimes Olga would sit and have beers with us. Fran made us drink beer interspersed with glasses of water.

'Beer has the perfect amount of amino acids,' he'd lecture us, 'but it's dehydrating, so it's good to combine it with water.'

My attempts to get close to Olga were fruitless and since I hadn't had a dentist's appointment in years, it seemed like a good idea for me to book one at her clinic. It was a way of seeing her alone at last, without Fran and his medical student friends. The dentist found three cavities, a cause for joyful celebration, as it meant two more appointments. My father paid for the work, but not before first insisting that he was going to make sure I brushed my teeth at least three or four times a day, 'Because these dentists charge a fortune, you know.'

As I left the final appointment, feeling deflated because my cavities had been fixed without any complications, Olga suggested we get a drink together.

'My classes don't start until later today.'

'How's your group going?' Olga asked once we'd sat down in the cafe opposite the clinic.

'It's going well. We've already got three or four songs,' I told her. 'We're playing in a bar and we want to take part in one of those competitions, to see if we can get some cash.'

I was trying to act grown-up with her, but even so the bar's owner, a rotund lady who brought us glasses of beer and some rather soft *patatas bravas*, asked Olga if I was her little brother.

'No,' she said, 'he's my boyfriend.'

'Ah! you like them young, I see,' the owner exclaimed. 'Good for you. Men don't stay fresh for long, you know.' And she pointed to her husband behind the bar. 'Look at that good-for-nothing I have to put up with now; in his younger days he was quite something.'

'My father's fourteen years older than my mother,' I told Olga in an attempt to make our age difference seem insignificant.

'Do they get on well, your parents?'

'My mum's sick.'

'Oh, my.'

I'd learnt from my father to take maximum advantage of our unfortunate situation with visitors and colleagues: 'You don't know how hard this is – my heart is split in two, but one has to keep going.'

I told Olga about our life, the problems we had at home.

My mother was still living in the house at the time. Suddenly, Olga's eyes seemed to well up as she listened to me telling her things about my mother's illness and life at home.

'It must be very hard for you.'

I shrugged. 'The worst thing is not knowing if she can really hear you or not, if she's aware of anything. If she feels anything at all,' I confessed.

She ordered a coffee. She had to leave soon for university, but I opted for another beer. As she was stirring the sugar into her cup, the dentist came in and looked over at us. He came to our table and kissed her on the lips.

'I'll have a coffee with you two,' he said.

*I was looking for love, and I found war*
*Seven light years apart.*

He sat down and though his conversation was entertaining, I couldn't really process his anecdotes about patients with manky teeth or the amusing effects of anaesthesia. Instead I just gazed at Olga, ever so distant: opposing NATO had been a necessary way of seeing her at the protests. The two of us with raised fists and me walking in the trail of her pale forearm, attempting to make her smile, make the freckles dance around on her face, with my stupid slogans. Conscious of my abject failure, all I could do now was sit down and write:

*There are no trenches*
*In the battles of the heart*
*I was looking for love, and I found war.*

And though Gus and Animal liked the song enough to go with it, I never told them where it had come from, or how Olga had shown me the corpse-strewn battlefield that love left in its wake. I feared that if I told my friends, I'd be met with sneering put-downs, or Fran's doctorly superiority.

Fran always seemed to be addressing you from on high; though in reality he was usually sprawled out on the sofa in Aunt Milagros's small lounge, puffing fag smoke out through a window that gave on to the lightless inner courtyard. We played him our first songs.

'Puerile but pretty good. You've got to start somewhere,' was his verdict.

He gave us advice, showed us examples of musicians he liked, gestured at me to pass him the guitar so he could show off a few chords. Although I was a better player, he recognised that I lacked musical taste and knowledge, because I'd never had anyone to guide me in the right direction, other than the music magazines, which I read like the gospel of my new church. I liked being with him, going out with him, accompanying him to cinemas and bars where I was treated like an adult.

Being with Gus and Animal was different. We'd talk about the group, about our plans. I managed to escape to a sixth-form college for the last two years before university; at the college there were girls, new friends, beers at the bar across the road, a far more diverse world than the one at school. Gus's idea of going out was different from ours and he kept to himself, away from my crowd. Quite often he'd come up to Animal and me with a beer in his hand, fed up of standing at the bar, and ask, 'Don't you get tired of this?'

Unlike us, he enjoyed dancing and going out to places that had a little more charm than the neighbourhood bars we frequented, with their wooden tables and olive stones and sawdust all over the floors. The second we hung up our instruments after practice, Gus would abandon us. He was our loyal and enthusiastic accomplice until that moment, then he'd disappear off into his own night.

We shared a space in a council-run building on Calle Tablada, and sometimes after practice we'd sit in the Dehesa de la Villa park with a guitar and mumble something that sounded like a song being born. Animal had a real knack for pinning down the rhythm. Gus was more creative. I remember how, on one of those afternoons, he convinced me that all of our compositions had to open with an ambitious and unpredictable guitar lick that would act as a declaration of intent.

'You have to show them you're not just any old idiot with a guitar, Dani. You have to show them you can really play.'

Even today, when I sit down to finish off a song, I insist on finding that opening lick, which Gus saw as our trademark.

We'd often relate episodes from our lives to each other and Animal amused us with anecdotes from the world of mattresses, or with details of new atrocities being carried out at the Catholic school. It was during one such moment that Gus finally told us the story of his escape from Ávila. Because that's what it was, an escape. Sometimes Gus, who usually filled the space around him with joyful noise, would spend long periods in silence, but that day he launched himself into relating the circumstances that had taken him away from the city of his birth.

'I went to a school run by priests,' he told us, 'in a city that many people believe is surrounded by walls so that no one can get in. But the truth is, the walls are there so that no one can get out. The boys at the school were mostly a bunch of wild, rustic savages. I had a friend called Moncho, who was the son of the province's military governor.

'Moncho loved being around me; he followed me everywhere and he used to give me his toys to keep. He was so fond of me and expressed it so often that I found it embarrassing. "Gus, you're my best friend and you always will be." He was a strange kid, suffocated by his father, and we'd do really gross things together. Like sometimes in class I'd sit behind him, he'd pull his trousers down and I'd shove my pen into his bumhole. The other kids would see this, but no one dared take the piss out of Moncho, because his father's authority spread all the way to the teachers.

'Sometimes he'd unzip his trousers and shoot his load into his hands. And when the teacher wasn't looking he'd chuck the spunk everywhere. It was a sick prank, halfway between erotic and disgusting.'

Stuff like that would have seemed unbelievable to anyone who was unfamiliar with schools like ours. People who've never seen another student holding a bottle and pissing into it, throwing bogies so that they stick to the ceiling, or masturbating in front of the class while the teacher writes on the blackboard.

'One day, during class, he passed me his pen and I shoved it in. And the cap – you know, the cap of a biro – it got stuck there by accident,' Gus continued as we stood there open-mouthed. 'And my mind went blank and I took out what was left of the pen and put it on his table. When I told him the top bit had got stuck inside, Moncho turned pale and tried to get the tip out of his arse. But when he couldn't he began shouting and stood up with his arse sticking out, to the great alarm of the priest, who shouted "What on earth is going on?"

'It was April and I wasn't allowed back to the school,' Gus continued. 'I was expelled on the hush. It was like I had measles or some other infectious disease, but I didn't care either way. I spent a few happy weeks at home, just listening to the radio with my mum and looking through my sisters' drawers while they were at school.

'I passed that year without having to take the exams, but they told my parents to find another school for me. My parents had the idea of sending me to Madrid for the next school year, as there was no way I could stay in Ávila; you have no idea how big a scandal I'd caused.

84

'Of course, Aunt Milagros was overjoyed and so was I, because I'd dreamt about Madrid my whole life. For a bumpkin from Ávila, Madrid was like New York.'

So Gus went to live in his aunt's guest house on the prophetically named Calle de los Artistas, as he used to say. He'd always wanted to witness all those repressed provincial types exploding into the frenzied modernity of Madrid, a city where they could all tear off their masks without their parents, relatives and neighbours being able to see or judge them.

'The anonymity of the big city allowed us to be free,' he explained once in a radio interview we did together.

But I understood that the sheer power he unleashed onto so many stages, no matter how grotty, was his way óf prolonging his adolescent flight, his hard-won freedom. And I always admired the lyrics he wrote – regardless of how simplistic, frivolous or just dumb they were – because each song contained the story of his life, the only revenge he was capable of.

## the only revenge he was capable of

He did it with every rousing call, every cry of encouragement, every let's go, every come on. With every party, every crazy act, every display of boundless enthusiasm or tomfoolery, Gus was carrying out the only revenge against his world he was capable of. 'You can stay put,' he seemed to be saying to those dark childhood years.

'I feel bad for Moncho,' he told me, remembering that boy from his school in Ávila. 'He stayed on, and I have no doubt he was beaten into conformity and can probably now be described as a normal member of society. That's probably the saddest thing that can happen to anyone.'

Once, my son, Ryo, noticed a photo hanging in my studio,

which shows Gus by my side during one of our early performances. The image of the two of us together piqued his curiosity.

'Papá, was the boy singing with you in the photo really your friend?' he asked.

'Yes, he was my best friend.'

'But why does his hair look like that and why is he wearing make-up?'

In the photo, Gus has his hair combed back and mascara around his eyes.

'Because he liked to go onstage looking like that,' I replied.

'But then why didn't you do your hair like that, if you were such good friends?'

'Because I liked him the way he was and he liked me the way I was.'

After hearing this answer, my son mulled it over for a while.

Finally, he asked, 'Would you like me better if I was more like you or more like him?'

I took my eyes away from the old photo of Gus and me for a second and smiled at my son.

'I'd like you to be like you.'

When I first met Gus's family they came across as cautious, considerate people.

'I've made them suffer so much,' Gus explained. 'I was like an accident of nature, bad luck.'

We'd go to his house to eat when we were playing in one of the two venues in Ávila that put on live music, or after playing at the summer fiestas in El Escorial, Arévalo or Las Navas del Marqués. Gus loved to show off about the group's success in front of them, despite his conventional, prudent family's perplexed reaction to his tales from the world of showbiz.

'Our secret,' he explained to them as his mother filled our plates with delicious food and his father sat there chewing in silence, 'is that Dani and I complement each other perfectly. Every successful partnership needs that contrast; it's just a shame you got me for a son when you'd have preferred to have a polite, demure one like Dani.' He pointed at me as he attempted to convince them of this argument. 'But there you go, it's just bad luck. You were unlucky.'

Gus's two older sisters adored him and would come out to see us wherever we played. Gus pointed them out to me.

'Those two, they were the ones who created this monster you call your friend. They dressed me up and played with me like I was their doll.'

Gus always included a version of 'Girls Just Want to Have Fun' in our set whenever they were present and he'd dedicate the song to them with a little introduction.

'For the two most important girls in my life.'

Whenever Gus's sisters had a moment alone with me, they'd ask me all about their brother.

'Has he got a girlfriend?'

And when I told them no, they'd ask, 'Boyfriend, then?'

'Nope.'

Gus's sexuality was a mystery. He looked so impeccable that he sometimes led you to believe that sex was something altogether too mucky for him to be sullied by. He picked and chose freely from both sides, as a way of satisfying his own eclectic taste, but as far as we knew – that is, Animal, me and everyone else involved with the group – he never actually ended up in anyone's bed.

Though the poses he struck and his wardrobe were very flamboyant, he never actually dressed as a woman; rather, as a kind of glamorous, baroque dandy – a look those in the know would describe as New Romantic. He liked to repeat something Boy George was meant to have said but which may actually have been him putting words into his hero's mouth: 'Having a cup of tea is more entertaining than having sex. The fun thing is always what's around you.'

Gus's eroticism was always shrouded in mystery – at least, that is, until Eva showed up.

When he showed me the lyrics of a song called 'Strike Me Off', I knew he was carrying out his idea of revenge. I simply added a bit of distorted guitar, asked Animal not to let his thunderous drumming let up even for a second and allowed the sound to envelop his voice as he sang:

> Strike me off your blacklist
> Strike me off your obituary.

I joined him for the chorus on backing vocals, with a higher-pitched harmony:

> Because I will be
> The only star you'll see
> In your boring, shitty life.


## every family has a secret

Every family has a secret, a secret that explains everything. Mine is no exception. I discovered it one day while I was helping my father to file his invoices. He used to send them to his clients every month. The sums were ridiculous, but they simply reflected the money he loaned to his clients so that they could buy clothes, kitchen furniture, watches, communion bracelets, typewriters and domestic appliances. I used to tell him his job was not all that different from that of a Jewish moneylender, which offended him.

'You don't know how much people love me,' he countered.

But I think the ironic reference to his Jewish origins was what most annoyed him. Though his physiognomy clearly betrayed a Jewish background, he'd lived for many years with the ubiquitous anti-Semitism of nationalist, Catholic Spain.

'Dad, your surname is Campos, which is one of the names adopted by Sephardic Jews in your area, you work as a door-to-door salesman and you have a nose worthy of a rabbi, which of course I've been lucky enough to inherit.'

He stopped me in my tracks.

'Stop spouting idiocies you've picked up from some rag. My family has been Christian since the day Noah built his ark.'

It was Christianity that had led him to take part in the war. The communist threat against the shrinking world of his father's home soil, the village church, prevailing law and order, had been enough to make him into a Falangist when the war broke out and he was sent to the Lérida front. One day he gave me his old military ID card with a note folded up inside: 'So that you may remember the mistakes I made in my youth.'

My father didn't like talking about the war, but on his way back from the front he witnessed horrific killings being carried out in the rearguard and felt that his values had been betrayed. He'd get annoyed whenever the topic was brought up in conversation by some old friend from the front or the military hospital where he spent several months. I snatched these small anecdotes from discussions that were cut short.

I heard about the hunger, the cold, the cruelty, the innocence and the cowardice. The war allowed him to travel, to get to know places outside his village, and made him never want to go back there. It made him confront death in a brutal and shocking way.

One afternoon, a relative reminded him of something the officers used to do: if a soldier had attempted to desert from the front, the firing squad always had to be made up of his fellow villagers, his closest friends.

'Do you remember that morning?'

My father cut him off with a look and nodded in my direction.

'The walls have ears,' he responded, which was his way of saying there were children listening and that they should be spared from hearing about that hell.

My father also saw a naked woman for the first time in the war. And not as part of some cabaret but dead, in the pine wood where they'd set up the front. The corpse still looked fresh and one of his fellow soldiers had shouted, 'See, I told you these whores had nothing on underneath.' The soldier unzipped her overalls and exposed the white, bloodied, naked body of this girl who, according to my father, can't have been more than twenty, and was more beautiful than you could imagine. Her belly had been blown open by a bullet.

He must have got his end away in brothels, with wartime girlfriends, or the many women left lonely and miserable after the slaughter – the forgotten widows forced into hardship – until he met my mother. Every survivor of a war needs to be able to use love to reconstruct a long-gone, uncontaminated time. My mother was two years old when the war ended, but she'd still live to witness dramatic events after her parents and siblings died in a fire at the family home, from which she was spared only because she'd been out running errands. She was taken in by some kindly nuns in Valladolid and my father met her when she was working in a guest house.

I was always certain that in my mother's untainted youth my father had rediscovered something of the purity that had been forever corrupted by that brutal, dirty war, something that finally helped him to find some form of salvation. After a brief and intense courtship, my father ended up bringing her to Madrid, he in a hurry to get married and she to have a home again, even if it was a modest-sized flat in a building on a cul-de-sac.

Whenever I asked them why they hadn't had more children, they told me that my mother had gone through spells of depression, resulting from her traumatic past. A doctor had assured them they'd never be able to have children and my birth was a late, happy surprise; I felt so proud to hear that my existence was the result of a miracle of nature. This legend became intertwined with that of my mother's fragility and many of my relatives would remind me of it whenever they saw me. 'You didn't come easy, my child. What a surprise you were to us all!'

This early demonstration of my uniqueness, this heroic act of having been born through sheer grit and determination, did much to soften my displeasure at the lack of siblings or even grandparents. My father's parents had died shortly after my birth and all I remember is a crumbling adobe house my father pointed out to me in the village one day, saying, 'That's where I was born.'

I never held any suspicions regarding the official version, which was both epic and poignant, until that afternoon when we were sorting out my father's papers and he sent me into his bedroom to find a missing folder. I entertained myself by poking around in the bottom of his wardrobe, where he kept a small cash box and some files. That's where I discovered a folder with an official seal on it. Inside was an adoption certificate with a date that was very close to the date of my birth. Seeing the word 'ADOPTERS' in capitals, with my parents' names written in the space that followed, was too much of a shock, so I stopped sniffing around, closed the folder and tossed it back into its hiding place.

For two days I walked around in a daze, an eleven-year-old who suspected everything and everyone, sizing up his parents for the first time and studying his own face in the mirror in an attempt to make the shadows go away. Adopted? But how?

I was so like my father that sometimes complete strangers would greet me on the street and say, 'Send my best to your father. You two look exactly the same, like peas in a pod, identical twins.'

I studied childhood photos I'd seen thousands of times before, stuck onto walls or placed upon the cloth that covered the wooden sewing machine case. I examined them with fresh eyes, as if seeing them for the first time. Me in my mother's arms, me in the washbasin where they used to bathe me in the summer, me on my father's shoulders. In the one hanging in the living room next to my parents' wedding portrait I was only four or five months old, surrounded by the two of them. But what about before?

*I look at your face, compare it with my own.*
*But where did I come from? Where am I going?*

What if my parents weren't my real parents? I waited for them to leave the house one Sunday afternoon and went back to the wardrobe, to discover who I was, down there, under my father's clothes. I often read spy novels, but I always thought spying was something you could only do far away from Spain; here, the crimes committed always lacked any mystery or subtlety. It was always a case of so-and-so going at his neighbour or his wife with a hoe or an axe, or else another seemingly weekly terrorist incident.

I looked through the rest of the papers and there it was: the concise, blunt document granting them custody of a new-born male. And there was my exact date of birth, and after it a woman's name, Lourdes María, followed by her two surnames, one of which was also Campos, like my father. Further down in the document was another unsettling detail: father unknown. So maybe I was the biological son of a close relative, a child born in sin and adopted by generous parents, desperate to have a child. Now, I understood the truth behind the miracle of my arrival into the world, why my parents were so old, why I had no siblings.

From that day on, saying the words mum or dad, something I'd done hundreds of times a day, became a strange and painful experience – a moment of almost feverish significance. What about them? What did they feel when they heard it? Mum, Dad. I knew the idea of sitting down to discuss it with my parents was a fantasy: the longest conversations we ever had were about my grade cards, which they'd sit down and read in great detail.

'What's this here? "Gets the grades, does very little"?'

'Dad, they say that about everyone; it's just to annoy you.'

The sense of shame the two of them passed on to me extended to the physical. One morning I got up at dawn to pee and when I opened the bathroom door I discovered the two of them naked. The way they both screamed then slammed the door shut, their panic, their anguish – all of it meant that I was back in bed in no time. They were intimidated by everything to do with the body, though perhaps Mother managed to overcome her shame when we prayed together at night before she kissed me and tucked me in. But even then it was always done with a sort of clinical distance. They weren't the kind of people to whom physical demonstrations of affection came naturally: the verb 'to love' was conjugated in everything they did for me, but it was never spoken out loud.

'Mum, would you tell me if I was adopted?' I managed to squeak one day as my mother sprinkled cinnamon onto our three bowls of rice pudding.

I noticed I'd successfully managed to transmit my anguish to her, despite the fact that she'd replied, 'Of course, why do you ask?' without even looking up at me.

'No reason,' I said.

'There's nothing bad about being adopted, quite the opposite. Adoptive parents give a child what they wouldn't otherwise have. So I wouldn't hide it from you, of course I wouldn't,' my mother lied in her pious way.

Over time I've come to regret that moment, because her illness began soon after. Maybe the lie was tearing her apart from the inside and that's why she didn't say anything. After that day I often blamed myself for her condition and beat myself up for not keeping my mouth shut, not waiting:

> *Not telling her it didn't matter*
> *That life's like a cloud, and it soon passes over*
> *And that everything I ever had, I owed her.*

I'd write these lines twenty years later in a song for her – because songs are letters that never get sent but instead waste away in your pockets, just as the things you don't say waste away in your heart.

I soon embarked upon a discreet investigation into my case. It wasn't hard to trace Lourdes. The next time we visited the village, it only took three inquiries to discover that it was none other than Lurditas, the daughter of some relatives I knew well, someone we'd said prayers for at home. We'd said prayers for her because she'd died and details of what happened to her would occasionally slip out in stray conversations. It was always 'poor Lurditas'; 'when the thing with poor Lurditas happened, remember?'; 'that was the year of the drama with poor Lurditas'; 'an Our Father for Lurditas, yes, our cousin, the poor thing.'

When I accompanied my father on his trips to the village, I'd find the house where Lurditas's family lived and find any old excuse to sit in their living room, even though they had no children of my age. Her grandfather, Hermógenes, who was my father's uncle, would always be sitting by the door humming to himself. If I came into the house to ask for a glass of water, Lurditas's mother – whose name was either Jacinta or Juana, I could never remember – would point to the framed photo showing a beautiful, smiling girl in a nun's habit, her eyes wide open with enthusiasm.

'That's Lurditas. You never knew her. You know what happened, don't you? She died doing what she loved most, looking after the world's poorest children.'

'When did she become a nun?' I asked, trying to finish tracking her life story.

'Oh, young, very young. She was still a girl, really.'

One night, before my mother went into a home and after we'd put her to bed and gone back into the living room, I seized the opportunity to rid my father of that burden.

'I know you and Mum aren't my real parents,' I told him.

My father sat there in silence as we finished eating, his gaze firmly fixed on the TV, and we didn't exchange another word. I noticed his jaw twitching.

'Finish that croquette,' he said, pointing to the tray in the middle of the table, on which the last piece of our sad dinner was sitting.

I'd have been sixteen then and felt perfectly entitled to know the honest truth about my origin, in the same way that Gus had told me the story of his forced departure from Ávila a few weeks earlier.

'Your mother always wanted me to tell you, but I resisted,' my father began explaining. 'For her sake, and for yours.'

After dinner he entered my room and rambled on about my schoolbooks.

'You need to work on your writing. Calligraphy is the most valuable treasure you can take away from school.' He placed his hand on my shoulder, not daring to say anything.

For years he held on to the shame of locking himself in the bathroom to wash my mother, always warning me, 'Don't come in; I'm giving her a shower.' He clung onto that distance so that he'd never have to ask me how I was, how I felt about everything that was going on in our family, what I thought about the thing that was happening to us. 'Mum,' we'd say completely naturally when we referred to her.

Sometimes we only had to mention it in passing for his voice to start breaking and then he'd say, 'We can't support you as much as we used to, but don't think she isn't proud of what you've achieved.'

My father taught me that a father can cry in front of his son and that this gives crying a value unknown to children, who tend to cry whimsical, passing, opportunistic tears. But a father's tears fall like lead. And it was enough just to watch him from afar as he dried his eyes with his handkerchief or looked off into the distance, because that's all there was – there was never any explicit confession of pain or sadness. Never any outbursts of emotion, any opening up to share our wounds. Can you inherit that?

That evening I sat there in silence, not moving my eyes from my desk. My father spoke to my back, his eyes running over the objects hanging from the wall: three handball medals, the photo of Van Morrison, the one of Nastassja Kinski entwined in a boa constrictor, the *Planet of the Apes* poster, and the photo booth photos showing Animal and Gus in four equally idiotic poses.

'We all make mistakes in this life. You'll make them, too. The only important thing is to get up and put right whatever it is you messed up. No one is infallible,' he added.

I'd have liked to help my father, tell him it's not important, it doesn't matter if you don't tell me anything, it's fine the way it is, but curiosity trumps compassion. I didn't know how to interrupt him.

'Your mother showed me the error of my ways,' he continued. 'She helped me to put it right. You've heard of Lurditas, haven't you?'

'Of course,' I said.

He told me that our distant cousin from the village – distant being the adjective he always used to mitigate things – spent some time staying here 'in our house, when she was very young, eighteen, nineteen, and, well, sometimes things happen, and the flesh . . .'

I figured he wanted to say the flesh is weak, but he restrained himself.

'We fell in love, if you can put it that way, when you're incapable of controlling your own instincts, and you were born from that brief, misguided relationship.'

There I am, being born again in my father's confession. So I wasn't the adopted son I'd imagined myself to be, at least not completely. I was a son born of what Spanish soap operas dress up as sinful desire: incest. Each additional word, each detail visibly pained my father; his confession came out like a bread knife being slowly extracted from his throat.

Of course, their relationship could never be.

'Lurditas was studying to be a nun.'

My mind jumped to conclusions, my imagination unable to wait for the pieces of the puzzle to be put together.

'Your mother couldn't have children and we'd tried a thousand different things. We had our doctor look for a baby for us, some child with no parents to look after it, but the procedures were so complicated and all of a sudden we had one right here at home. And Lurditas agreed that you could be the son we wanted so badly, because she . . . she was an angel.'

My biological mother had handed the fruit of a secret and furtive pregnancy over to my parents, lived the whole thing out within the walls of our house in what must have been a heavy

97

atmosphere for the three of them. It was all done legally and behind the backs of family and acquaintances, that threatening entity we always referred to as 'the village' or 'people from the village'.

Lurditas told them she'd entered the convent and that it was impossible to leave, let alone travel, when actually she'd postponed her training and told the people from the congregation that she had to look after a sick relative. And so, amid all the lies and dissimulation, I was carried to term with the three protagonists all in agreement, all committed to the same blood pact.

I'll never find out what rough edges of his conscience my father had to file down to make this all sound so upright and pleasant, barely more than a funny story, a small hiccup along the way. I could never know the version of the story the two women would have told, because one of them was dead and the other had no memories left. For years I'd seen the tenderness in which my father had enveloped my mother. It was only in that confession that I was able to see the glimmer in his eyes when he spoke about the other mother, Lurditas. That stupid name that reduced her true personality to a vulgar and grotesque diminutive.

'And she left,' my father added, 'and she was always rooting for you. And she was so grateful for everything your mother did for us, for everyone, because it was your mother who saved us all, who put us back on the straight path from which we'd strayed. It was she who was able to forgive, to forgive me, because I was the one to blame for everything that had happened, I was the one who'd put the family in danger.'

'And what about her? She was killed?' I couldn't say her name out loud.

'Yes, she was killed in Africa, where she went to work as a missionary.'

My father was welling up, trying not to cry.

'Dad, how old was I when she was killed?'

'Three, give or take. It happened in Zaire, which is what they used to call the Congo. I don't want you to think the decision we took was forced, or that there was something dirty about it. Your childhood was wonderful. Your mother has always adored you and still does. To us, you were always . . .'

But I interrupted him again.

'Did she ever see me? Did she meet me?'

My father took a deep, slow breath and suddenly he seemed relaxed, as if liberated from something that had been pushing down on him, stopping him from breathing.

'She always carried your photo and she wrote to us. It was our secret, the three of us. The four of us now,' my father told me in my darkened bedroom, lit only by the adjustable lamp on my desk.

I knew he wanted to let me in on the secret so that I wouldn't stir things up or say anything, so that I wouldn't think to go to the village and get involved in those people's lives, with all the grace of a sentimental elephant.

'But she did see me? Did she ever see me after the birth?' I asked, growing restless.

'Yes, once, before you could walk. She spent an afternoon with you, in our house.'

'And what did she say? What did she say about me? What did she say to you?'

My father gave me a piercing look, which seemed to take him through my eyes and into a far-off place, one that belonged only to him. He answered me from that place.

'She said you seemed like a very happy boy. That's what she said.'

'I'll die like a bird,' my father used to announce to anyone listening, 'without so much as a peep.'

And so he did. Lying down by his side, separated from him only by the wood of the coffin, I was a kind of vampire, menaced by the light of day. Jairo had insisted I lie down in the back.

'I've had many a siesta there,' he said.

He pulled into a petrol station by the motorway, and next to the air and water pumps, just out of sight of the attendants, he showed me how to position myself, my body fully stretched out next to the coffin. Then he tossed me two ornamental cushions, which made me look a bit like Bela Lugosi. I stared at the curtains on the windows and at the limousine's cushioned ceiling. There haven't been all that many limousines in my life, just that stupid thing at the Latin Grammys in Las Vegas and the night we played at a disco in Pozuelo. I think that's it. Oh no, there was the time we were invited to the music market in Los Angeles. I remember the stunned look on Animal's face and his comment, 'It's like a fucking brothel on wheels.'

A duo from Compostela were riding with us, and while the woman took off her shoes and rested her legs on the leather seat, the man, a very socially conscious type, shuffled around uncomfortably. He spent the whole time asking if there'd be photographers at the Greek amphitheatre in Griffith Park, where the concert was taking place. He didn't want to be photographed enjoying the delights of a limousine.

But Animal just gave him a friendly slap on the thigh and said, 'I can already hear your next song: "Fuck the Poor".'

Now that I was lying down, it was easy to be lulled away into sleep. Back in the world of dreams again, different points in time became jumbled together. I remembered my longest stay in the village, over the summer when I was thirteen. My father didn't send me there for the whole month of August simply because he wanted me to put down roots in the village. No, that wasn't really it. My mother was about to undergo further, more serious tests to find out how far the illness had spread and I'd only get in the way if I stayed at home.

It was the woman from the grocery shop at the end of the street, Doña Manolita, who best described the effect that long stay in the village had had on me.

'He's become a bumpkin,' she told my father, noticing that the volume of my voice had gone up by several decibels.

I was carrying a slingshot and bounded all the way up the stairs of our building. My memories of the village were pleasant ones and I was unaware that everyone could see just how far I'd descended into rustic savagery. I remember the affectionate aunts and uncles whose family links to you were never entirely clear, greeting everyone you met, all the people saying, 'You look just like your father.' I was related to everyone I met there: cousin, nephew, godson. I liked how close everything was, the freedom, riding bikes, nature, the absence of any real danger beyond the main road. Mornings on the tractor, harvesting the grain, hauling bags to the granary in the afternoon, fried sausages for breakfast.

'Another banger?'

'Yes, please!'

Bottles of Mirinda orange with a layer of rust left around the rim of the neck after the lid was removed by the man at the clubhouse, which wasn't so much a club as a soulless room with two tables and a bar.

During the endless rosaries and Masses, the priest would share political slogans, speak out against the socialists and insist people vote for Blas Piñar. It was quite normal for him to interrupt his reading of one of St Paul's letters to the Thessalonians in order to rail against Carrillo. Although by then political debate was starting to die down and the jumble of acronyms you could cast your vote for had shrunk, the priest was still longing for a lost order.

He'd shout at the fifteen pensioners who made up the congregation to abstain from using contraception, 'for the condom is a tool of Satan and He will destroy you if you let Him enter your house.'

The oldies, huddled together on the seats at the back of the church clutching their berets, would mutter loudly, 'What use have I got for condoms?' making me laugh with their comically bemused looks.

Some of the kids in the village had such a good sense of fun, were so full of life, that they helped me to stop worrying about my mother so much. One of my distant cousins was called Alejandro, though everyone called him Jandrón. He was sturdy and strong and insisted that only pansies used the brakes on their bikes, which meant that when he wanted to stop he had to do a huge skid, throwing up a cloud of rust-coloured dust in the air and flinging him to the ground. His elbows and knees were always red raw as a result.

Jandrón took me under his wing. One night we got drunk together on a bottle of *anis* he'd sneaked out of the club and he took me to the yard round the back of his house so we could show each other our dicks. His was bright red, with a flat, round head, and he tugged his foreskin back with all the delicacy of a bear. He insisted that wanking made you go blind and that babies came out of their mother's arses.

'When you're born, you're getting shat out by your mum,' he explained.

These nuggets of physiological knowledge plunged me into a deep confusion.

That morning, feeling closer to each other than ever after our piss-up, we sat for a while on two planks of wood with our stiff dicks out while Jandrón spat onto his hands and polished his foreskin until the hens came along and started to bother us. This also happened whenever we took a crap in the yard. They'd come over to peck at the shit we'd expelled on the dry straw, which is why we always kept a stick to push them away while we did our business, next to the torn-up strips of the local newspaper, *Ya*.

Jandrón deftly grabbed one of the hens, immobilising it with his huge hand, and inserted his penis into its rear end. The hen, which was brown and white with an orange beak, kept curiously silent as it was sodomised.

'Look how quiet it is. It likes it,' Jandrón commented as he moved it back and forth. 'I'm not going to come today because I don't feel like it, but this is how I practise fucking,' he informed me. 'It's just like with a girl.'

His T-shirt only covered the top half his bum and the image of him with the hen squashed between his thighs is one I'll never be able to erase from my head.

'I'll tell Luci to show you her tits tonight,' Jandrón promised me. 'She lets me touch them and her nipples go hard like chickpeas.'

But cousin Luci, who was our age and already boasted well-developed breasts, wasn't on board. She was solidly built and completely straight-up.

'I'm not going to show my tits to some guy from Madrid just so he can go around laughing at country people and looking down on us. In your dreams!'

To be the only boy Luci wouldn't show her tits to was truly traumatic. I reserved my passion for cousin Ignacia, Jandrón's little sister. I was attracted by her green eyes and her bone-dry curly black hair; she really was beautiful. Her eyes shone when she laughed and one day, when we were all sat in a circle playing truth or dare, she let me kiss her. It was a short kiss, though Jandrón made it longer by pushing our heads together so that our mouths remained touching. But all the magic was lost by then, amid everyone's roars. That's where I had my first kiss, in the village. A moment many associate with childish feelings of tenderness and embarrassment but which for me is hard to separate from the horror of the group with their jeering smiles as Jandrón bashed our heads together.

For another dare I had to sing in front of everyone, so I stood up and sang the most popular song of that summer, 'Escuela de Calor', all the way through. As I sang, my face burnt with embarrassment and my eyes were glued to Ignacia and her straw-like hair. Everyone whistled and jeered, but afterwards Ignacia told me that I was a good singer.

This happened that same afternoon, when the others weren't watching, and as she said it she placed a note inside my hand, written on a scrap of graph paper. It just said 'Ouy Evol I'. When I managed to get her alone, she explained that the message was written backwards and all I had to do to read it was put it in front of a mirror.

'It's so that no one can figure out what you've written. Me and my friends all do it at school in Valladolid.'

She'd taken me to a hiding spot behind the house, beyond the backyard. A cat was feeding her five tiny kittens, taking shelter under the straw in the loft. They'd been born that very morning.

Before we went back to the house where Jandrón and the others were waiting, she said, 'I've shown you my secret, now you have to show me something back.'

'What do you want me to show you?'

As I pulled the elastic of my boxers away, she took a peek for less than a second before she burst out laughing and then backed away from me in shock, whispering to herself, 'It's so ugly, it looks like an old radish.'

Before long, Jandrón's father discovered the kittens. He frightened the mother away with a stick and dragged Jandrón and me up to the loft. He accused us of having taken a saucer of milk to feed them.

'What were you planning? To fill the yard up with cats?' he said as he shoved the kittens into a sack of grain.

Then he threw two heavy stones inside and tied the sack up with a rope. I knew that it was Ignacia who'd taken them the bowl of milk, but I said nothing.

'Now, get down to the river and toss the sack in,' Jandrón's father ordered. 'And if I find out you let them go, I'll tear your bloody arms off.'

Jandrón and I carried the sack down to the riverbank. The kittens were mewing away inside, but the heaviest thing was the stones. I burst into tears and Jandrón made fun of me.

'Don't be such a girl.'

He smashed the sack three or four times against a rock on the riverbank and then tossed it into the water.

'This way, they won't suffer. If we let them out my father will kill us.'

But he must have told cousin Luci about the crime, because the following day she called me a cat killer in front of everyone. From that moment on, Ignacia stopped talking to me and avoided my company. She believed it was me who'd told about the cat giving birth and her hiding place, and the looks she gave me were ones of open contempt. Since then, I've noticed that every cat I walk past seems to regard me with fear and mistrust, as if it knows all about me.

That was the only bit of shade in an otherwise bright and sunny summer in which my time might have been spent repairing an adobe house or shooing flies away from a cured sausage left out to dry. The same sausage that would leave a ring of blood-red fat on the bread and stay tasty for the entire week.

The day my father came to pick me up I said goodbye to everyone, including Ignacia, who pulled her face away when I went to kiss her. On the way back, the car broke down on the hills outside Guadarrama, so we had to wait for a mechanic friend of my father's to come.

'Did you like my village?' my father asked as we waited. 'There's nothing more wonderful than growing up in a village.'

'Then why did you leave?' I asked him.

He shrugged. 'I wanted to see the world, but now I've seen some of it I wonder if I'd have been better off staying put,' he said with a hint of fatalism.

I may have believed him at that precise moment, but he wasn't being serious. He, too, had needed to escape from that fenced enclosure and find his own path, at a time when he was desperate to be independent, autonomous, the master of his own destiny. Can you inherit that?

That was the last time I had such a long stay in the village. I'd go with my father for the summer fiestas, just for a few days, but as soon as I was old enough I chose to stay in Madrid on my own rather than go there with them. Jandrón continued to lead the pack, Luci ignored me or called me the young gentleman from Madrid, and if I ever saw Ignacia we'd just greet each other with a nod. Anyway, she was completely unattainable, having ascended to her rightful position as the most beautiful girl in the village. People literally called her The Beauty.

I woke up when the car began to gradually slow down. We were entering some town in order to get on the country road. Maybe we were already in Medina de Rioseco. I sat up, opened the curtains and looked out of the rear window. The car following us nearly crashed into a street light when its driver saw my face emerging from among the dead.

'Well? Doesn't it feel good to have a little kip?' Jairo asked, as enthusiastic as ever. 'We'll stop now for a coffee and you can get back in the front.'

I yawned unselfconsciously.

'You know what we say to kids in my village when they yawn like that? We say, you must have been a lion in a previous life.'

## you need to know how to get in and out

'Being onstage is like life – you need to know how to get in and out,' Sergio told us after deciding to look after us, get us from one place to the next, book our shows.

He'd seen us play at a venue underneath the Plaza de España and asked us when we were playing next. We weren't. He bought us some beers.

'I don't do contracts. We do everything by handshakes.'

We later found out that people called Sergio 'Bellend'. Preppy had got us our second show, a concert at the Catholic school in Atocha to celebrate the end of the academic year. He was taking part with his group and invited us to play three or four songs. The rivalry between our two schools was ferocious and it wasn't unusual for volleyball finals to end in blows: the concert was expected to be heated.

I remember us trashing the dressing room because the jeering from the students was so overwhelmingly loud. Animal hung down from the clothes racks and yanked the taps off the sinks. The pupils spat on us as we played and Gus responded by clutching his groin. The sound was appalling, the guitar was giving off loads of feedback and by the second song I'd already given up. We had four songs, and we played them all, with the same outcome each time; the only redeeming part was the end of each song, when Animal went into a fit of ecstasy, leaving everyone open-mouthed as he laid into the drums. We were listening to The Doors and wanted to sound like that, but our lyrics were still a hotchpotch of pretentious nonsense.

The booing at the Atocha concert was thunderous, even when some of the crowd sang along to the cover of Bowie's 'Heroes' Gus made us play. Even Preppy was unable to spare us his withering verdict.

'It's kind of different when you don't have the whole school on your side, isn't it?'

But still they invited us to play at the school on the Paseo de Extremadura at another celebration organised by the boys in the youth club. So in five days we'd written a new song and rectified a few of our more embarrassing defects. We had to make a huge racket, so that the boos were completely engulfed by the noise.

Ever since then I've always liked the first song I play to be angry, like a child having a tantrum, something to open up your lungs. I'm always nervous at the beginning – nervous about the crowd, the atmosphere, the sound, the lights, everything around me – so the more furious the take-off, the easier it is for me to keep going.

The dressing room is a strange, cold, insipid place. Most of the time it's little more than a grubby damp closet, piled with crates of drinks you share with another group. You leave your bags on the floor and, minutes before you go onstage, you feel deflated and demoralised because you know something that the audience doesn't: you're insignificant, you don't matter one bit. So you use the opening song to raise your spirits, to make you believe in what you're doing, to occupy the stage fully, regardless of your surroundings.

Some venues don't even have a dressing room. You just walk from the bar to the stage through the crowd. Those final few steps that take you up to the mic are always the worst, because they mark out where the transformation you don't always believe in is supposed to take place. And you go out there and play like a con man, like a child doing an exam they haven't studied for.

I like it when the room's well-lit and I can actually see the audience, not just a blinding stage light in my eye. It helps me to feel like I'm not just in a practice space but playing to real people; though in truth the view is often rather depressing, all half-empty pits and scattered groups of viewers having private drunken conversations. You often ask yourself, 'What am I doing here and how do I get out? How did any of this happen?' But before you can answer you're already playing – and when you're playing, everything works.

Jairo ordered a white coffee at the cafe on the main road in Medina. I hate the smell of *café con leche*, it makes me retch. I don't care if it is one of our national drinks: for me, it smells like being in an office. So I stood leaning against the door, far away from the stench of reheated milk. Jairo interpreted my posture as a sign of melancholy and came over with his mug in his hand.

'Did you spend all of your summers here as a boy?'

'No, not all of them. Actually, I only spent one summer here. But that was enough. My father's village was a strange place to spend the holidays in. There were no trees, no swimming pool, no football pitch. You'd bathe in the heat.'

'Hard soil. I come from a wetland area, where trees grow like buildings. Do you know it at all?' Jairo asked, referring to his country.

'A little, from travelling. I once played in Quito at a concert organised by the Ministry for Foreign Relations and I loved it.'

'Well, the whole country is beautiful. I recommend going back.' Then he launched into an uninterrupted speech about orchids and magnolia trees, carrots the size of cucumbers. 'They look like a giant's dick, pardon my French. Our region is so rich and our politicians loot it all. Just like here, I guess. No one gets spared. They're all a bunch of good-for-nothings.'

This comment made me feel lethargic again. Insulting politicians is like talking about the cold in December.

Instead, I went outside to phone my kids and let Jairo go back to his seat at the counter. There was a brothel at the end of the street, closed at the time, with a large red sign that read 'Borgia 2'. There may not have been a Borgia 1, but it gave the impression that this crumbling brick facade, which promised cheap whores to passing drivers, was part of a franchise.

When an unenthusiastic Maya answered the phone, I told her I was still travelling.

'Was Granddad born that far from Madrid?' she asked me with genuine curiosity.

'Well, it takes three hours. It's in an area called Tierra de Campos.'


*no more summers*

'No more summers,' my father announced when my mother's illness meant we couldn't leave the city any more.

We were condemned to spend every summer in Madrid, in our cul-de-sac which seemed to attract all of the city's heat. My father had a Madrid Transport Corporation card, which got me into the swimming pool near Plaza de Castilla. When he arrived in Madrid he'd spent a few years working for the bus company, but there was another name on his pass – Ricardo Morales Conde – and my father explained that if anyone asked, I should say I was Ricardo Morales.

'It's nothing illegal; I just haven't had time to renew mine and a friend has lent me his.'

You could take lessons at the pool, and there was a diving board, two similar-sized swimming pools and a cafe where I'd sometimes go to have a sandwich. I met a few different people in each of these places, boys who I'd play a bit of basketball with but who I never saw elsewhere. If I was walking down the street and someone called me Ricardo, I'd turn without thinking, knowing straight away that it must be someone from the pool.

In between taking dips we'd play table football in our swimming kits. A girl called Elena – who everyone called Rabbit because of her teeth, so big that you could have used them for an archaeological dig – followed me around, making it clear she really liked me. I told her I didn't want a girlfriend, though I was dying to have one – even more so after my failure with Almudena, my inconclusive flirtations with Ignacia and my rejection by Olga, which made up a pretty lamentable record for my sixteen years.

Elena ignored my fierce rebuttal. 'I love you and you know it. I love you, I love you.' She'd repeat it like that, three times, throwing me even further into a state of panic. She'd jump into the water and hold on to me as I swam, stubborn and insistent. And if I tried to free myself from her grip, she'd sit in front of me, furious, pull a threatening grimace, and say, 'You do what you like. I'm totally in love with you and you will be my sweetheart.'

Enrique, who was the son of a bus driver and my closest friend at the pool, said I should take her into the showers and see exactly how far she was willing to go.

'You'll see, she'll get scared off and then she'll leave you in peace. That's your best option with bold ones like that.'

This seemed like a pretty reasonable solution, so one day I decided to return her greeting. When she said, 'Well, well, light of my life, are you going to acknowledge my existence today?' I brought my mouth to her ear and whispered, 'Meet me in the shower at the back of the girls' changing rooms in five minutes.'

Nervously, I headed over there and managed to sneak in without being seen. Elena instantly disproved Enrique's theories when she hugged me fiercely and, instead of running away in terror, began to rub herself up against me. My erection was bursting out of my trunks, but she resisted when I tried to get my dick out or take off her clothes.

'No,' she'd say, 'leave them. I like it that way; it turns me on.'

I put my hands under the top half of her costume to stroke her adolescent breasts and watch her rub herself against me until I came in my trunks before turning on the shower, which soaked us both.

We repeated this groping ritual on two further occasions; she kissed me passionately, my teeth colliding with those protruding trowels of hers.

'Listen, Ricardo, are you doing this because you love me, or just because you're a dirty little boy?' she asked me on the second day.

That's how she actually spoke. She'd say light of my life, toodle-oo, scrumptious, lickety-split. But the worst thing was when, in the middle of our erotic frenzy, she'd bring those teeth right up to my ear and whisper, 'Put your hands on my botty. No, silly, not like that, under the cossie. That's it! Come on, pinch my botty. Yes, like that.'

After our third furtive encounter in the showers, Elena felt emboldened enough to wait for me by the swimming pool gates and take my hand.

'OK, Ricardo, we're sweethearts now,' she told me.

I freed my hand from her grip.

'I already told you, I don't want a girlfriend.'

She looked at me with the gravest of expressions, the tip of her chin quivering, on the brink of tears. It was one of those turgid summer evenings and she walked off down the street, greatly offended, her flip-flops crashing down ominously on the pavement. I was afraid she'd come back to find me or pursue me with her love over the days to come, but she never said another word to me. In fact, she actively avoided me, which was a tremendous relief, however much I missed our wet groping sessions.

My friend Enrique summed the whole situation up with succinct irony: 'You didn't get laid, then.'

Once we'd started the band I stopped going to the swimming pool every day. I preferred to hang out with Gus, who always managed to get out of going back to Ávila, and Animal, who'd pinch a few coins from the till in his father's shop so that we could drink in the evenings. Sometimes I chose to spend my time locked up at home in front of the fan, holding my guitar. My father was indignant.

'If you didn't have the swimming pass you'd be up in arms, but now that you have it, you couldn't care less. That's humanity in a nutshell,' he despaired. 'How tragic.'

He was right.

After those uncouth scenes with Elena in the shower, it was almost a year before I went with a girl again. It was the day we did an open-air concert at my new college, for the second of May celebrations. My new classmates found out I had a group and suggested we play a concert at the school to raise funds for the end-of-year trip. We now had almost ten songs, plus a few covers of songs we were bold enough to destroy, such as Elvis Costello's 'Alison', or 'My Generation', which Gus would sing, repeating every single detail and inflection from the Who concert film he'd seen a thousand times. This gave me space to shine on the guitar.

Perhaps seeing me play helped Sonia notice who I was. Until that moment she'd sat at the back of every class, gazing aimlessly out of the window. Whenever we went out for a drink she barely spoke, focusing all of her attention on rolling spliffs. And when we went out on demonstrations against student reforms, which were great fun and almost always ended in dispersal and destruction, she preferred to slink away with the more violent groups, the ones throwing the Molotov cocktails.

She had long fingers, and I liked watching her removing thick clumps of tobacco and deftly rolling the Rizla with a card-board filter she'd torn from a cigarette pack or a metro ticket. I smoked with her to make myself appear interesting; though it didn't really work for me and I had to pretend to inhale the smoke.

'You've got a nice face,' she told me.

She wanted to be known as the toughest girl in the school, but the night of the concert the two of us escaped to Parque del Oeste and flung ourselves onto the grass, where we had sex in a clumsy, uncomfortable and somewhat ridiculous manner.

'You're not very experienced, are you?' she asked me with a smile on her face and her trousers pulled down to her knees, the two of us soaked in my first-timer urgency.

Technically, I lost my virginity twenty minutes later, among the shrubs in the park. Sonia had bright pink lips but liked to look scruffy and sometimes wore a Che Guevara beret to class. We thought we were in love with each other and sometimes she'd come along to concerts with me. I was getting to know people at music venues and it was fairly common to be let in without paying or to be given free beers.

Sonia lived with her mother, who worked as a secretary for a socialist minister, and as we had free use of the empty flat, she invited me into her room and taught me how to fuck. Slowly but surely, I discovered we had nothing to talk about, that our tastes and personalities were, if not incompatible, completely unrelated, and our mutual attraction wasn't enough to keep us together. Gus's verdict after the first time I brought her along to practice for a few beers was far harsher.

'She's got lovely eyes, but she's like a house where the lights are on but no one's home. Knock, knock,' and he cruelly mimed himself knocking on her head.

Gus's pronouncements could be devastating. His dislike of Sonia influenced our decision to break it off at the end of the academic year.

In my final year of college, I tried out every possible variation of fully clothed sex with another girl from my class, Nuria. Every night we'd ended up drenched in the dark corner of the entrance hall to her block near the Quevedo roundabout. That was until I proposed booking a hotel room; this had been recommended by Fran, who was highly amused by my first sexual adventures or, as he liked to call them, 'the call of the gonads'. He suggested a specific room in Hotel Monaco, near the centre: number 12, which had a decorated bathroom and frescos painted on the ceilings and could be rented by the hour.

Despite the more favourable settings, Nuria couldn't get wet and we found ourselves in a somewhat absurd situation in which I was unable to get my penis more than a disheartening inch inside her. Overcome with guilt, she kept saying, 'I'm such a failure, I'm such a failure,' and I let her toss me off by way of compensation for the cost of the hotel room. Back then I was incapable of understanding a girl's needs, of helping and accommodating her. All I wanted was for my own desires to be sated as urgently and impersonally as possible.

The worst thing of all was discovering that satisfaction always remained out of reach. The hunger persisted; what you had to eat was never enough. You were always hungry for something else, no matter how much Gus insisted that I was to blame, that I was a romantic narcissist, that I was in love with love, that my idea of love was a mere dream. The number of times he told me 'Dani, dreams are for dreaming, not for living.' Maybe that's when my confusion between desire and reality was forged. The only certainty lay in the words to a song I liked so much during that period of emotional ups and downs: that we could cheat and lie and test, but failing was the one thing we never failed at.

## *failing was the one thing we never failed at*

My father took a while to recognise the sound of the amplifier and, after almost a year of me having an electric guitar in the house, he was still coming into my room to ask me if it was the same guitar. He moaned about the earful one of our neighbours was giving him on an almost daily basis and asked me to turn it down, reminding me that excessive noise would leave me deaf and dim-witted.

'You know what Napoleon said, don't you? That music is the art of making noise.'

My father was fond of that one. Sure, he may have been distorting it for his own ends, but doesn't everyone twist other people's words and historical events to suit their own agenda? My father didn't place much importance on our school perfor-mances, or the fact that I played in a group, mostly because the other two members were Gus and Animal, which made him think of it just as a hobby I did with my friends. Whenever he saw us, huddled around my guitar, he'd remind us of that Napoleon quote.

'And Napoleon was a smart chap, ask anyone.'

My father's oddities increased with his resolution to keep a sunny outlook despite the painful situation at home: he washed the dishes without any soap, insisting that they were hardly dirty in the first place; he used the same cloth to clean the toilet and the sink, in that order; he never used the remote control, because that way he could get some exercise by getting up and down, and what was worse, he wouldn't let me use it either, to stop me from getting stiff; he engaged in dialogue with TV presenters, including the parapsychologist Jiménez del Oso, whose stories about UFOs fascinated him so much that after going his whole life without reading a single book, he bought the entire series of the esoteric *Trojan Horse* novels; he watered the geraniums my mother had put on the windowsills, causing water to cascade onto the street and not sparing the papers I'd left on the table, which ended up getting soaked; he'd put his shoes on using the spatula we used for serving flan and then, without a second thought, put it back in the cutlery drawer; he'd fart in the corridor, then announce, in fits of giggles, that there were storms on the horizon; he decided that instead of ironing his clothes he could get away with leaving them stretched out underneath his mattress before he went to bed.

But his reaction to my mother's illness was physical in nature. You could see how fit he was just from watching how fast he walked. Can you inherit that? I like to walk at full speed. It sometimes helps me to get out of being stopped by people asking for autographs or photos: they see me walking like that and understand straight away that I must have some urgent appointment. For my father, however, walking quickly was a way of showing off.

When walking back home from a shopping trip he'd lift the bags up and down, like weights in a gym. He walked so fast it wasn't uncommon for him to collide with people in his way. One morning he trod on Doña Manolita's dog, which was lying down outside the shop, and another time he knocked down a schoolboy. On one of these glorious strolls I watched him knock down a bin with his shoulder and push over a ladder that a phone company repairman was using to scale a telegraph post. His cyclonic stride left so many victims in its wake that in the end he had to resort to walking on the road. When he had no option other than to use the pavement, he'd imitate a car horn and beep at pedestrians to let him through. 'Beep, beep, coming through.'

The way he walked was an act of defiance: he was in a race against the world. No one, not even a stranger, was allowed to overtake him, he had to beat everyone. All he had to do was choose a destination – that corner, the traffic light, the entrance to the metro – and reach it before everyone else.

The only prize he ever won in these secret races was a broken arm. Early one morning, he was trying hard to overtake a young woman who was hurrying along to university; perhaps she was already late, because she suddenly sped up and overtook my father, which he took as a personal affront. So, in order to get back to pole position, he pulled out all the stops, accelerating and managing to overtake the girl so authoritatively that he was even able to turn his head and flash her the triumphant grin of an Olympic medallist. But at that very moment, my father tripped on a loose paving stone and broke his arm. The girl was a good sport and stopped to help him, but my father concealed his pain, saying, 'It's nothing, my dear, just a stumble,' and it was only once she'd left that he went straight to hospital.

I'd just turned eighteen and my patience with him was

dissipating as fast as his walking pace. I was mortified by my father; I couldn't take any more. Our relationship was being pushed to the brink and the slightest thing would incite our anger. The amount he went on I'd have needed twelve brothers to share the burden.

By the time I started university the group was performing so often that I'd sometimes miss a class or go to bed at four in the morning without telling him.

'You'll end up in the gutter,' he'd chide when he burst in on me in bed at eleven or midday.

We'd already had a huge clash when I'd asked him for money to sign up for driving lessons and he'd refused to give me any. Ever enthusiastic, he took me to the university campus one day and assured me that in just three lessons he'd teach me to drive like a pro.

'Forty years I've had a licence and not a single scratch,' he kept on saying.

We put my mother in the back, with her belt on, and I sat in the driver's seat.

'Nice and gentle . . . Use the clutch . . . Come on, smooth. Now give it some welly . . . Easy does it. A car's like a horse, you know, you have to control the reins . . . Listen to the engine . . . It's a gear stick, not an egg whisk . . . Caress the wheel. Give it a bit more gas and put it into second. She's calling out for it but brake a little first . . . Watch the engine, listen to it.'

I quickly got tired of his instructions. I wanted to drive because it would free us up to take on gigs outside Madrid, but his lessons were insufferable.

Every now and then my mother would ask, 'Where did you say we were going?'

My father's attempts to correct my driving quickly descended into insult.

'You really are useless. There's no way you're my son, you're

119

a complete dullard. No, no, not like that. Is there anything going on in that head of yours? Look, some can and others just can't. Sweet Lord above, you really are a waste of space. All that music and yet you're incapable of listening to an engine. Can't you see you're burning the clutch? If ever you go to driving school you'll ruin us. What on earth are you doing? Absolutely useless, you are. Brake, can't you see the road?!'

When I couldn't take it any more, I stopped in the empty car park of the biology faculty, got out in a rage and started walking home. My father took the wheel, drove up to me and spoke to me through the window, driving all the while.

'If only you were as skilful as you are proud. You have to be humble if you want to learn.' When he saw that I was ignoring him, he eased off the chiding and tried being more loving. 'Come on, son, get back in. I'm sorry I acted that way; I'm just trying to teach you.'

'You know what, Dad? I'm never going to drive in my life.' Then, looking him in the eye, I said, 'I swear.'

'Well, well, look what's happened now, I've gone and put you off driving completely. It's all my fault, of course. What a monster I am. Some teacher.'

Now more hurt than I was, he drove off and left me behind.

I remember walking back to Calle Paravicinos alone that Sunday afternoon, in no hurry to get back to the house with my father in it. I whistled a melody to keep myself entertained and, little by little, it grew into a song. That's what happened every time: any heightened emotional state resulted in a new idea. Then I'd call Gus and Animal and we'd get together. Either we'd finish it off, or we'd scrap it if we couldn't get it to sound the way it did in our heads.

'I was surprised to see you doing this journey alone,' Jairo confessed, 'but Miss Raquel already warned me not to expect any other family.' The hearse was gliding through the first few tiny villages that announced the arrival of the wheat and barley fields. 'Usually, the whole family organises a convoy,' Jairo, who never shut up, continued, 'but I was told you don't drive.'

'No, I don't drive.'

'How do you do it? Cars are crucial in the modern world,' he announced.

'You think so?'

'Look, I guess you can live without a car, but you'll be worse off,' he backtracked.

'Well actually, I live a very full life,' I answered, a little wounded.

That very same year, Animal got his licence and became the group's official driver, even if his frequent benders occasionally complicated our travel plans somewhat. Though Aunt Milagros was eager to pay for his driving lessons, Gus considered driving to be the height of vulgarity.

'One minute you've got your licence, the next you're married with kids,' he announced.

Jairo was telling me about families at funerals, the convoys, how difficult it was to drive to the cemetery without losing one of the cars, how one time the deceased's children had crashed into him from behind.

'Can you imagine the paperwork! And all because they weren't keeping a safe distance. It's lucky it was a slow collision and they didn't break open the coffin. So you must take a lot of taxis, then?' Jairo asked, persisting in his mission to know everything there was to know about me.

'Yes, I take taxis.'

'You see, I don't. Never do. In my early days here in Spain I had to take a few and they'd never stop for me, because they saw I was foreign and assumed I had no money. And then there's the cost. I live in Mejorada del Campo, so go figure.'

'You think they didn't stop for you because you're a foreigner?' I asked, feigning interest.

I didn't tell him that sometimes they don't stop for me either, when I'm travelling with a particularly flamboyant gipsy musician or a very scruffy band member.

'Yes,' Jairo insisted, 'you Spaniards claim you're not racist, but you do it without noticing. Sometimes I'll go into a cafe and notice how the old ladies grip onto their handbags. It's really strange, I head for the counter and – *zap!* – suddenly you see every bag being clasped in its owner's hands. That's racism right there, my friend. It's not always about them calling you a dirty spic.

'And then there's my girlfriend, a pretty, attractive woman, if I say so myself, with great curves and a nice body. People are always assuming she's a prostitute. Tell me it's not racism when a Spaniard assumes a woman's a hooker just because she's Latina.'

Mariana was Latina, though no one used that word back then. She was the third woman my father hired to look after my mother at home. The second one had been the lady who used to clean the stairs in the building; he fired her when he caught her pulling my mother's hair. She made excuses, showing her the nail marks on her arm. 'She scratched me first.'

My mother was capable of violence on the rare occasions when her nerves were really frayed, but even so my father accompanied her to the door and told her, 'Don't come back tomorrow. You're not cut out for such delicate work.'

He heard about Mariana from Doña Manolita. Doña Manolita

was our great ally in the neighbourhood until she sold her grocery shop to some Chinese people who gave her a bin liner stuffed with 24 million pesetas in banknotes. I adored her because she used to give me sweets every day when I went down to buy bread. Doña Manolita had a granddaughter whom I was obsessed with for years. When she wasn't at school she used to help her grandmother, who'd make her pick out each piece of fruit for me as if it were a rare treasure. 'Take these pears today, don't bother with the peaches.' But I was only looking at her granddaughter's blossoming breasts as she leant over to handle the goods; those were the only fruits I wanted to enjoy.

One day Manolita asked me to tell my father that she knew a woman who could help us out at home. Mariana was Colombian and had a five-year-old girl. She came over one afternoon to chat to my father, with her black hair and shy demeanour. My father was seduced by the sweet tones she used when talking to my mother and decided to let her have a month's trial.

Mariana was gentle and meticulous, and possessed a natural patience that was ideal for coping with my mother's irrational, looping conversation. Life with Mum was getting increasingly difficult: her deterioration was evident, her moods had got worse and she was suffering from nocturnal hallucinations. On occasion, she'd be seized by a physical fury around small things such as shutting a box or a door, suddenly repeating the action thirty or forty times, quicker and more violent each time.

Mariana arrived early, at nine, and as she was doing the housework she'd sit my mother down in a chair so that she could always keep an eye on her. It was my father who occasionally took my mother outside, which could be dangerous. One time she saw her reflection in a shop window and suddenly ran off, crossing the busy road with no awareness of the risk, shouting in distress the whole time. I stopped taking her for walks because she'd try to direct traffic with her hand, 'Go on, that's it, straight ahead,' and I couldn't handle the embarrassment and despair it awoke in me.

'I'm sure your girlfriend loves it when you sing her those songs,' Mariana said one evening after popping her head into my room to discover me playing my guitar alone.

She'd probably been working at our house for a few months and our interactions had been limited to a few polite sentences. At the time I'd lock myself away in my room the moment I got home, to avoid any commotion with my father. I liked looking at her big, slanted eyes. Despite being in her forties, you could see the beautiful girl she must once have been, all the more surprising given the harsh facts of her life story.

The five-year-old girl wasn't her own but her daughter's daughter. Her mother had given birth when still a teenager, got involved with drugs along with the father and died a few years later. Perhaps the most visible mark of those tragic events was the serenity with which Mariana took on the work of looking after my mother.

'I don't have a girlfriend,' I replied. 'I've never had one.' I wasn't lying at all.

'They'll soon come,' she generously prophesied.

She wiped the dirt that had accumulated on the books and the VHS cases with the cloth. Two of the videos had strange titles displayed on the sleeves: 'Pre-Socratic Philosophy' and 'Parallelepipeds'. In reality they contained porn anthologies, a carefully chosen selection of great moments and top-class performances that Animal had compiled for me from his own collection. I'd written those ridiculous titles so that they wouldn't arouse anyone's suspicions, though they had the opposite effect. My father would stop and look at them, intrigued by the absurd titles.

'One day I'll have to sit down and watch one of these philosophical films of yours.'

'Pre-Socratic?' Mariana read. 'I've no idea what that is.'

'They're the philosophers who came before Socrates and that lot.'

'Oh, I didn't know,' she replied to my vague explanation. 'You like philosophy?'

I gulped. 'Sure do,' I said, blushing. 'It's fun.'

'Well then, perhaps I can borrow it one day, see if I understand any of it,' said Mariana, turning towards me to witness my deeply perturbed expression.

I was looking at her tight-fitting clothes and her bright, vivid eyes focused entirely on me.

'Pre-Socratic, is that how you say it?' she asked me casually after leaving the tape where it was and continuing with her cleaning.

'Yes, exactly.'

'Parallele . . .'

'Parallelepipeds,' I said, putting an end to her struggle.

'Why don't you make a song about that? What a strange word . . .'

'Actually, all of my songs are either about parallelepipeds or Pre-Socratics.'

I remembered the Les Luthiers song about Thales of Miletus and hummed it to her. Mariana laughed her easy laugh.

'You're quite something. Can I tidy up the papers on your desk, or would you prefer me not to move your stuff around?' She gestured towards the chaos in my room.

I was embarrassed by the clothes on the chair, a pair of dirty boxers poking out from among the T-shirts.

'You can move whatever you like,' I said, and we looked at each other again, or rather, brushed our eyes against each other like two arms touching as they pass.

I began lending her a hand with her work, entertaining my mother by saying silly things that made Mariana laugh as she was making the beds or mopping the bathroom floor. If she was in the kitchen I'd come in and nibble on a piece of fruit. And I'd help little Belinda with a drawing whenever Mariana had to bring her to the house because there was no school that day or because she had a fever.

The girl was always cold and her mother – her grandmother, really – would wrap her from head to toe in woollen shawls. She was a bright girl, with an answer ready for almost everything, and having never really interacted with little children before, I was unexpectedly delighted by her presence.

She'd point to her mother and say, 'Play a Julio Iglesias song, he's her favourite.'

And I'd put on a silly voice and sing 'Fuiste mía.'

Mariana would turn around and look at me with a beaming smile. Once she'd become more relaxed in my company, she'd throw the cloth at my face or slap the air while looking at me.

A sense of mutual challenge grew between us. She saw me as a kind of solitary orphan, misunderstood by an over-the-top, emotional father, a sensitive boy in the midst of the chaos of that house. She couldn't imagine, or perhaps she could, that I was letting myself be carried away by sexual fantasies, that I was secretly watching her arse under those tight clothes and that I was enthralled by her smooth grey skin. One day I put my hand on her shoulder, and she turned around to face me and we kissed. It happened by the entrance to the kitchen, in the corridor. Where my mother couldn't see. That was all we did, then I backed off and she kept working.

It wasn't just a fit of madness. We spent two or three weeks doing that, stealing a kiss whenever our paths crossed. The kisses grew in intensity and duration. She introduced her tongue and so did I, but then we'd move away and I'd go out or she'd go into the living room to say something nice to my mother.

'I'll be back in a minute, all right, is that OK?'

And she'd listen to my mother giving the same response she always did.

'Wonderful, yes, just wonderful.'

When we were in my room we'd move into the corner, our bodies close and our hands on each other's backs. Despite this outpouring of kisses, we never let ourselves get carried away.

In the afternoons, when my father got back, she'd come in to say 'Goodbye, I'm off,' and we'd kiss, in absolute silence, for fifteen seconds. I figured any longer and she might feel embarrassed. But in spite of the risk, the passion just intensified, and she began closing her eyes and relaxing her neck as we kissed. I'd put my hands on the nape of her neck, underneath that black hair, coarse and hardened by dyes.

'You won't believe it,' she told me one afternoon when she noticed my interest as I stroked her hair, 'but I've got grey hairs.'

One day, after my father had said, 'It's a shame to waste such a fine day,' and taken my mother out for a walk, I put my hands under her clothes and began removing them. I undid her bra, pulled her leggings down to her thighs and let my hands crawl under her T-shirt. She stopped me but still allowed me to rub up against her body.

I came noisily in her hand and instead of pulling it away, she continued to caress me though my trousers passionately and energetically. Despite my panic, the two of us stood there in the middle of my bedroom as I kissed every part of her body that had been exposed, her succulent breasts, the arse that jiggled beneath her hips, her ample thighs.

It was hard to find the ideal moment, but when my mother took a nap on the sofa I'd lead Mariana by the hand to my bedroom and we'd give ourselves over to our desire, pushed up together against the wall. Our hands discovered skin moist with passion beneath our clothing. These moments were always rushed, furtive, urgent, fully clothed but sparked up with kinetic energy.

The first time that I reached my hand over to the drawer to get out the pack of condoms, she shook her head and pushed me out of the room as she adjusted her clothing. Another time my mother opened the kitchen door to catch us in the middle of kissing. She just said, 'Excuse me, my mistake,' and Mariana looked at me reproachfully before going out into the corridor to find her.

We always had at least twenty minutes alone while my parents went out for a walk. One day I got Mariana completely naked and lowered her onto the sofa. We made love, though not quite slowly or gently. We always kept an eye on the clock, because one day we'd been surprised to hear the key in the door and had had to rush to get our clothes back on in a scene that was as comical as it was horrifying.

'I thought you'd already gone, Mariana,' my father said, surprised to see her.

'I took the opportunity to give your room a quick tidy, sir.'

Mariana always called my father sir.

'What we're doing is so bad,' she confessed to me one day, 'so bad. You know, sometimes when I get home I cry.'

I tried to convince her that I was an adult, responsible for my own actions, and that she shouldn't feel bad. Our conversation was interspersed with brief kisses. We couldn't see each other at hers because of the girl and anyway, she shared her flat in La Elipa with two other Colombian couples. Once I suggested we go to a nearby hotel, but she refused.

'A hotel? Are you crazy?'

There were two or three magical days when my parents had gone to hospital check-ups or to visit someone, when we had a few hours to ourselves.

'I've got the doctor tomorrow, so we won't be in all morning,' I heard my father say.

'Very good, sir,' Mariana replied, 'I'll use the opportunity to wax the floor.'

The next day I'd helped her to finish off her chores so that we could fall into my narrow bed together, where I could delight in her flesh and the frightened look on her face. She guided me through the process.

'Not so fast, go slowly. See that little bone there, just by the entrance . . . yes, that one. Stroke it gently, slowly. Put your hand here and say something nice. You need to learn not to be too rough, or to go at it too fast.'

Perhaps Mariana ruined me forever, turning me into a sweet-toothed glutton, as I was once called by a Catalan singer, comparing my sexual appetite to a boy left alone in a sweetshop for five minutes. But Mariana also gave me the self-confidence that's so important as you approach the final precipice of adolescence. She reaffirmed my belief that the intersections between generations are the most interesting kind, both in friendship and in life. And she taught me that the best way to complement one person's early passions is with another's final passions. That bringing the end of a journey together with its beginning helps you to take in the whole course, gives you a sense of the bigger picture.

'The thing about Colombian women is we like sex too much,' she told me one day as she was putting the sheets into the washing machine. 'It's a blessing and a curse.'

I tried to make our sexual encounters feel like something more than a mere exchange, a form of sexual first aid, but little by little both she and I realised they were merely a superficial utilitarian tool. I enjoyed her like a toy designed for a boy who doesn't play with toys any more.

She began to distance herself and eventually she said, 'Never again, got that? It will never happen again.'

But the next time round I overcame her defences with my jokes, my boldness, and my determination. Until one night, when my father told me over dinner that Mariana had resigned. I studied his face to see if he was insinuating anything beneath his actual words. But he just shook his head and got up from the sofa to change the channel.

'I tried to get her to stay, I even offered her more money, but she didn't want to. Said she needed a change of scenery – those were her exact words, a change of scenery. Clearly, the poor thing doesn't get much scenery in this place,' he added, and I lowered my head in shame. 'She told me she'll stay as long as it takes for us to find someone else.'

And he got up again to change to another channel. With the arrival of commercial TV channels, his trips from the sofa to the TV had become more frequent.

I spoke to her and insisted she didn't have to leave her job on my account, that our encounters weren't necessary. She kissed me tenderly on the cheek and stroked my hair.

'I'm not leaving for you, I'm leaving for me. You'll understand one day.'

My father found a woman from the neighbourhood who'd taken early retirement after working as a nurse, and the day Mariana left, I saw them saying goodbye to each other, my father giving her the money she was owed.

'And a little extra, for you to buy yourself something nice with.'

I think my father also liked Mariana; there was no way he could have been immune to her arousing scent or that look of hers, so full of longing. Maybe my father did suspect something, because the women who looked after my mother from that point on were all older and entirely lacking in sexual appeal.

Kei, too, only ever hired completely unattractive nannies for our kids, women who repelled lust.

'The only thing that matters is them doing the job well,' she'd respond to me, completely seriously.

'That's not true, my love, they're children,' I'd say back to her, 'and we need to familiarise them with beauty from an early age. Do it for them.'

Since then I've had affairs with work colleagues, with a sound engineer we used for our concerts, with a casual roadie on a tour, with Bocanegra's secretary. With the stage manager when I had a walk-on part as a guitarist in a performance of *The Cherry Orchard* at the María Guerrero theatre, directed by my friend Claudio. With our press manager, with one of Alejandro Sanz's bassists, with the hygienist from my dental surgery, with a mother from my daughter's school, with a handful of journalists who specialised in getting romantically entangled with their interviewees . . .

Though there were times when it was necessary to keep things hidden from view, that sense of clear urgency, of now or never, was always contaminated by my affair with Mariana. During the months I was with her I ended up so thin that my Latin teacher was genuinely shocked when he called me up to the board to analyse a sentence. 'Have you stopped eating?'

I caught up with Mariana on the landing on her last day working for us. I handed her my childhood guitar, the one I'd bought off Mendi when I was twelve, which was out of tune but still usable.

'Take it,' I said. 'For your daughter.'

The girl sat caressing it in my bedroom, and I moved her fingers to show her some basic chord patterns and the first bars of a kids' song.

'Maybe she'll learn how to play,' I told Mariana on the staircase that last day.

We kissed for a second, a chaste kiss that attempted to wipe away all the dirt from our rushed and unequal relationship. That moment, as she walked away down the stairs, her eyes full of tears, I wanted to erase the guilt and blame. To remember only the passion and our genuine affection for each other.

Losing her opened up a remorseful void inside me. I convinced Gus and Animal to let me try out a punky cover of Julio Iglesias's 'Lo Mejor De Tu Vida', which we played in the venue on Calle Libertad where we performed once a month. Our version was a success because it highlighted the song's bitter subtext. I still bring it out from time to time and once I played it on a late-night TV show, earning me a lovely affectionate postcard from its composer, Manuel Alejandro, which I still guard like a treasure.

Many years later, while waiting in the Atocha station for Animal and Martán to travel to a concert, I was approached by a young girl with a very slender face and an almost weightless chin.

'Thanks for the guitar,' she said.

I didn't understand straight away.

'What?'

'I'm Mariana's daughter, the one who used to work in your parents' house.'

'Right,' I said, taking in her whole appearance. 'Belinda,' I said, hugging her perhaps a little too forcefully.

She told me she'd graduated in law and was working for a German car company.

'Very boring, and I never learnt to play that guitar, unfortunately.'

'I see. And your mother?'

'She's getting on. She went back to Cali when the crisis started. She has early onset emphysema and it's better for her lungs over there.'

. I pursed my lips, calculated that she must be approaching seventy, and remembered her smoking a rushed cigarette at home, waving the smoke away so that my father wouldn't be able to smell it when he got back.

'Does she still like Julio Iglesias?'

Belinda looked at me with her eyes, which were neither as beautiful nor as huge as her mother's, or rather grandmother's.

'She likes you more. She's always asking me to buy your CDs. She owns all of them.'

## the song of your life is never the song of your life

The song of your life is never the song of your life, or at least it's never the song that makes the deepest impact on other people, the one they associate with their happiest memories, the one that communicates with their most private emotions through a secret tunnel. The song of a musician's life is the one that made them a musician. And for us, that song was 'The Dumbest Song in the World', which I came up with while I was entertaining Mariana as she worked and looked after my mother.

I remember the look on Gus's face when he heard it for the first time. I would later change some of the lyrics with him and add some backing vocals, and we'd eventually follow Animal's advice and truncate the rhythm in the final verse which, without a doubt, made it into a song by all three of us. But I still remember being in our rehearsal space, waiting for Animal, and me putting down my acoustic guitar after playing it to Gus for the first time. He looked straight at me, saying, 'Dude, now we really have a song.'

*The dumbest kid in the world*
*Became the dumbest man in the world*

*And he married the dumbest woman in the world*
*In the dumbest way in the world.*

Because it really was a proper song, one that went way beyond our pathetic variations on the same three chords. He wanted us to go over it together before Animal arrived.

'Even that brute will be dumbstruck. You'll see.'

*He wrote the dumbest song in the world*
*With the dumbest emotions in the world*
*From the deepest hole in the world*
*In the ugliest neighbourhood in the world.*

And when he did arrive and heard us singing it, he said, 'We have to play this at the contest, no fucking around!'

*With the dumbest beat in the world*
*And the dumbest chorus in the world*
*But one you'll never forget.*

At that point in the song Gus began to improvise with a doo-da, do-da, do-bee-dee doo-bee-da, which was what he'd always wanted to sing because – he believed – the most beautiful lyrics are those that mean nothing at all. He understood that humanity's most sublime poetry is expressed in the words doo-be-doo-be-doo or tra-la-la-la-la, and if you get there you're getting closer to the true essence of music. According to him, that's why I liked singing 'The Night They Drove Old Dixie Down' so much, because I got to let it all out at that na, na, na in the chorus.

'You don't understand more than a handful of the other lyrics, but that na, na, na says it all. The whole story is there.'

We already had enough experience of playing live to know

that, as far as our audiences was concerned, the less complex the better: Doo-da, doo-da, doo-be-dee doo-bee-da.

It makes it more like a circus performance and occasionally helps you to attain the highest level of recognition you can get from an audience, which generally involves simply seeing them move their feet perfectly in time with your onstage movements.

When we decided to take part in competitions and behave like a proper band, we recruited Bulldog, a bassist who was a few years older than us and had a background in metal groups. It was clear that Gus would never manage to wring the slightest harmony from the instrument. His singing was improving all the time, and his stage antics were more and more impressive, but Animal and I always shared glances when the bass disappeared in the middle of the song or went completely out of time.

Bulldog played in a state of electroshock and had spent a long time working with two sisters from Pamplona who'd started a group in Madrid. The fights between the two girls were brutal and legendary, even though they were almost identical with their hooked noses, ladle-shaped chins and fringes down to their eyebrows, which they cut for each other. We shared a practice space, and some evenings Bulldog would invite us to come and watch their scuffles. For years we shared concert and festival bills with the two sisters, and though they were always at each other's throats, they never begrudged us stealing their bassist.

Having a proper bassist gave us a greater musical wingspan. Bulldog wasn't creative but he certainly was muscular; although his presence made Gus even keener to avoid our company.

'I see Moron Night has started,' he'd shout at us as we sat round our table covered with beers before going off in search of more sophisticated forms of entertainment.

Bulldog told us that a friend of his – 'a fairy,' he said – had

135

bumped into Gus on several occasions at the Arlequín, a gay disco with a basement where big groups of men could fuck and suck each other off. But Animal and I didn't set too much store in what he was saying, making it clear to him that being in our group meant obeying Gus's instructions. Because although Gus knew nothing about music, and although he may have been little more than a tambourine-wielding back-up singer who leapt around onstage, as Bulldog saw it, his intuitions were always right: 'This bit needs to be slower'; 'now the rhythm needs to be a bit faster'; 'let's repeat this bit'; 'no, no, now let's just have the bass on its own'. Above all, he had a magnetic appeal. However much I sang and played the guitar, I always had my eyes fixed on him, awaiting the next set of instructions from our conductor.

When Fran came to watch us play with Bulldog for the first time, he toasted me with his beer after the show and said, 'Welcome to the first division. All bodies need some muscle to keep themselves upright.'

That was our big decision: not just to keep being a school band, a bit of fun, but to try to take a step forwards. That's why Gus was annoyed when I matriculated in history of art.

'Are we students or musicians?' he asked me, offended.

It's true that I didn't see how we could make a living from it, no matter how many local venues let us drink on the house by way of payment, or despite the fact that Sergio – we still didn't know that everyone else called him Bellend – was getting us into proper venues and festivals.

'I can't tell my father I'm only going to do music from now on,' I said in my defence.

'You can't? When are you going to stop being a scared little kid, Dani?' Gus spat back at me.

I didn't dare upset my father like that while he was struggling so much with my mother.

It seemed a good idea to sign up for a local talent show; it would be a good test, a way of discovering our true place. The prize for winning the contest was the chance to record four songs in a studio and release them as an EP. We sailed through the first round, which took the form of a performance by every band inside a big, soulless sports hall.

'We really liked "The Dumbest Song in the World",' said the presenter leading the panel of judges. 'That melody of yours is catchier than the flu.'

He was known as The Champ and despite his amusing *nom de guerre*, he had actually had huge success with radio-friendly music. He managed several groups and controlled the radio playlists with the record companies, exchanging advertising investment for weeks of airplay. We were aiming to make it big via less nefarious routes, but nevertheless, his praise gave us the confidence to take on the final round.

The problem was that we'd wasted our best piece of ammo to get to the final, while all the other finalists had saved their heavy artillery. We shut ourselves away inside Aunt Milagros's guest house to see if we could write another song.

'What if we write an anthem?' Gus suggested suddenly.

'What do you mean, an anthem?'

'A song that's not merely a song but something more: a declaration of principles,' Gus explained. 'A hymn to how we want the world to be, that kind of shit. The fucking lyrics to the national anthem of the country we'd like to live in.'

'I think you've lost it. How are we going to make an anthem?'

Gus, who was getting carried away, took the words right out of my mouth. He grabbed the recorder we'd place on the table in case we had any good ideas and began singing the song, which he did all at once, completely transported:

> *Be my home and my station*
> *My bar, my hospital*
> *Be my bed, be my fridge*
> *My favourite band, my banner of peace.*

He raised his voice as if the melody already existed underneath his words and stood up with the recorder by his mouth, like a microphone:

> *Be my voice and my speaker*
> *Be my first Communion*
> *But without the wine and wafer.*

He closed his eyes and smiled, which is how he said you always had to sing, with a smile.

> *No marches or parades, just fancy dress*
> *No fines for excess happiness.*

When he'd finished he passed me the recorder like a bullfighter folding his cape before handing it over and said, 'I'd call it "My Country", but I'm open to suggestions.'

It was simplistic and rushed and we could never have imagined that that song would be the one to put us on the map, even as we were recording it after winning the contest. That morning in the studio was a happy one for us, a morning where we wanted to try out everything, learn everything, play everything.

Sergio had reached an agreement with The Champ, an essential move if we wanted to emerge victorious from the contest, as it was the presenter himself who steered the panel's final decision. He went on to become our biggest evangelist among the greater public, that entity we'd never set out to conquer and that was suddenly making its presence known to us there, just in reach of radio play.

'Excess Happiness', which was what the song ended up being titled, was the opening track on the record we made after the contest. We played in bigger venues, to a more open and eager crowd, and then an important label expressed interest in getting us to make our first proper album.

We soon discovered that our name belonged to a company owned by The Champ, along with the publishing rights for the songs and the sole rights to our first two albums, as dictated by the contest's one-sided regulations. This incident inoculated us against future disappointments of the music world: the entire advance from the label was spent on buying our freedom and we never got back the rights for those two songs. We also had to pay The Champ compensation in order to keep our name, Las Moscas.

That was how Tony Bocanegra became our new professional guide. The name sounded like the moniker of an Italian Mafioso, but it belonged to a droll Andalusian who'd been recommended by several music veterans; though always with a caveat: 'Let's just say, better the devil you know.'

## the devil you know

The road stretched out ahead in an endless grey line that cut through the fields on both sides, fields that ran the whole gamut of shades of yellow and ochre. The landscape bore a certain familiarity, from trips taken with my father. That was his soul, perhaps. Far more meaningful than the corpse in the back of the hearse, inside that pine box. This was his soil. The grain was ready for the harvest that would arrive in few weeks' time, each ear overcome by the weight of its well-nourished head.

A vulture was devouring the innards of a bird that had been run over, only flying off once the approaching hearse had become a clear and present danger. My father used to have a joke about that infinite horizon line: he'd say that as a child the carts he saw approaching at dawn wouldn't arrive until mid-morning. The silhouette of the blacksmith or the honey or cheese seller in the distance would announce a new arrival to the village. Time passed slowly back then.

'The belly of the journey,' I said.

Jairo laughed.

We'd passed through one of those undulations in the road that used to make my stomach turn when I was a boy, with their sudden peaks and troughs, and that was when my father always used to say that we were in the belly of the journey.

Jairo hit the satnav with his hand.

'Oh, crap, we've lost the signal,' he complained.

I remembered my father always getting lost at this exact point. 'They've changed the roads again,' he'd despair. He'd say things like 'how the hell did they manage to make it so hard to find the diversion'; 'trust my luck – they've changed the name of the road again'; 'you used to turn right here'; 'it's like they're trying to annoy me' – because he was incapable of acknowledging he'd got lost again, in the same place he always got lost.

One day I told Gus and Animal that, during one of these incidents, my father had cried 'Fuck the MOPU' in desperation. At the time, MOPU was, the Ministry of Public Works. From that point on it became our trademark expletive. Animal would say 'Fuck the MOPU' in response to any kind of bad news.

When I was a boy my father would make me write down in a notebook all the villages we passed through from Madrid until we got to his one and have me memorise them all like an anatomy lesson. He knew some legend or folk ditty relating to every single village in the Tierra de Campos region and he'd recite each one on cue the moment he saw the name on a road sign: 'the people in that village were real savages'; 'that one made the best cheese'; 'someone in the next village sold his grandfather a blind donkey'. For him, the journey was a journey back to the past.

Life was still just as it had been for the previous six-hundred years when my father was born and yet when he died the world was completely unrecognisable to him. Ox-drawn ploughs, a complete absence of telephones or electricity, having to draw your water from wells, doing your business in the yard, pigsties built onto the house, washboards in the river, carbide lamps and packhorses. Modernity had stolen his skin, and men, unlike snakes, can't regenerate.

Whenever I thought to ask my father how he'd lived through such profound transformations, he'd just shrug and say, 'You stop whining. Take what you can and move on.'

I was born as man was setting foot on the moon. My father had been born while Europeans were killing each other in trenches, back when world wars didn't even have numbers. The challenge for me was to find a professional route that satisfied my youthful vocation; for my father, born in the Middle Ages, to dream big was a sign of madness, of delirium. How could I judge him? How could I fail to understand his stinginess, his caution, his submissiveness, his certainty, his fears, his fatalism?

I inherited his ability to be friendly around people he didn't like.

'Never refuse to greet anyone,' he explained. 'Don't give them the advantage of knowing what you really think.'

I notice this trait in myself every time someone comes up to me blathering about how they like my older songs more than the new ones, or how the group just isn't the same without

Gus, or how our live shows aren't as good they used to be. They're always greeted with a smile and a polite response: 'could be'; 'perhaps'; 'so they say'; 'I'll look into it, thanks'. Reactions dictated by my father, a well-bred salesman, a man so certain he was right that sometimes he didn't even have to fight to get his way.

'The worse they treat you, the friendlier you are to them.'

I think that this somewhat zany piece of advice has helped me to deal with distrust, poor relationships and occasionally even allowed me to take pleasure in the discomfort of others. My father was his own best press secretary.

'My job is all politics,' he told me. 'I ring on people's doors. No one gives me anything for free.'

The only stumbling block on his route to being universally well-liked was situated in our own building: his tenure as president of the tenants' association left a trail of aggrieved neighbours in its wake. His insistence on fixing the leaks in the roof himself, or painting the staircase the way he liked it, frequently caused him to clash with the neighbours. He ended up calling the lady from 2A an impertinent witch, the man from 1B a gluttonous peasant and the couple at 1C glorified circus clowns.

One time he accidentally kicked the neighbour in flat 2C in the face while showing him how high he could raise his leg thanks to his daily trips to the gym. There was an opportunity to make new friends when the ancient couple at 1A were replaced by another family, but then my father spotted the new neighbour tossing a cigarette butt out the window, picked it up off the street and, after ringing their doorbell, placed it right back in his hand. His only words, delivered with his customary quixotic pride, were, 'I think you dropped this.'

My father wrote his own history book and it told a saccharine, idealised version of his life's journey. He didn't like arguing with me about things I'd read in books. 'I lived through that; I'm not going to let you tell me the way it was,' was how he'd always respond. I stopped getting annoyed by his attitude when I myself began being confronted with official versions of the history of Spanish music during my time. I'd read the simplistic narratives and think, *that's not how it was.*

We all like to adorn our lives with everything that was luminous about them, so that we can die surrounded by light rather than shrouded in the darkness of disappointment.

Whenever I asked him, 'Dad, how can you say you get along well with everyone if you don't even talk to people on the stairs of our building?' I'd always get the same blunt reply.

'You'll see. One day, you'll see. Sons only learn to be sons when they become fathers.'


## sons only learn to be sons when they become fathers

Perhaps I never understood my father better than I did during that fortnight spent sleeping by his side in the hospital room. I had to postpone everything in my diary. Raquel got me out of all of my commitments and even came to help sometimes, sitting with my father while I grabbed something to eat, dropping by the house or visiting my mother at the home. She told me that once, when they were alone together, my father had asked her about my life with Kei.

'I'm sure they're just having a rough patch. They'll get back together. They say Japanese women are very faithful, don't they?'

'To tell the truth, I don't know much about Japanese women,' Raquel replied, 'but I fear that your son isn't very faithful.'

'No,' she later told me he'd replied, 'my son has a problem. He's been a nonconformist ever since he was a boy.'

'That's not necessarily a defect, though, ' she told him, leaping to my defence.

'It absolutely is. In this world you must conform. You have to conform if you want to be happy,' my father assured her with his unshakeable self-belief.

The worst consequence of old age is everyone invading your privacy. People stop respecting your habits and hang-ups, your own way of doing things, from hygiene to the way you organise your day. Someone who only wants to help comes and takes charge of you. But taking charge of you means taking charge of your private territory. My father's lost independence turned him into a grumpy old man and his inability to take care of himself put him at loggerheads with everyone else.

One night he spoke to me about his work, how he'd left a steadier job behind to become a salesman.

'You should have seen me going from house to house. In my own modest opinion, I was good at what I did. I don't know if you see yourself as being good at what you do, but I certainly was good. Very good.'

I interrupted him. 'You don't need to tell me that. Don't you remember how I had to help you for a whole month that time your arm was in a sling?'

I'd been planning a very different kind of holiday when he broke his arm. In September we were going to be recording our first album and we wanted to be fully prepared. Bocanegra assured us he'd look out for us and find us a suitable producer, someone with good taste.

'Don't get the wrong idea,' he told us. 'I've signed you because I want you to be yourselves.'

We were desperate to be ourselves; free from Bellend and The Champ, we wanted to avoid getting trapped in the nets of other sharks. So Animal, Gus and I had planned a trip to London. For a whole month we'd try to listen to all the music we could, study how to make the best of professional production and then start working on the new album. Gus said we needed to anglicise ourselves, de-yokelise ourselves, shake the dirt off our bodies and get out of Villastupid.

'For once the flies will go to the honey instead of the shit,' he said encouragingly.

We booked tickets to leave on the seventh of July; according to Gus, it was important to leave Spain at the start of the feast of Saint Fermín, the country's most representative day. But when I had to help my father to get his pyjamas on the night he came back from hospital – his arm in a cast after his fall on the street – I suspected my plans might be in peril.

Opening his fly to go to the toilet had become a real hoo-ha.

'Just what exactly is it that you find so difficult about undoing four buttons, boy? I'm going to piss myself.'

'OK, OK, Dad.'

But it wasn't all that easy to undo his buttons, moving my fingers around barely an inch away from my father's dick.

I waited until he was in bed before I told him about my trip.

'Fine, off you go to London, don't worry about the rest of us. I know full well just how ungrateful and selfish you can be.'

I tried to convince him to take some holiday, spend more time with my mother. He threw it back in my face.

'Lovely idea, son. What a shame there's this thing called money that you use to eat, dress yourself and go off on your trips.'

'Dad, I'm going away with my own money.'

'Of course, I forget, you spend the little you have on these silly jaunts.'

When I told my father that we'd signed to a label, he smiled at me with disdain and said, 'Well, I wouldn't know about that business. You know what Napoleon said, don't you? That music is the art of making noise.'

When I placed the small trophy we'd won in the contest on the tiny desk in my mother's room, he sighed and said, 'You can't trick your mother into believing you've won the Nobel Prize.'

'If I don't get the money out of people before July, I might as well give up. In August they go on their holidays and, worse, in September they come back broke because they've spent all of their money. You don't understand what the summer holidays mean to these people. It's like a religion for them – they think the sky will fall on their heads if they don't take one. This is a country of carefree spendthrifts,' my father lamented.

I thought up a solution.

'Maybe you can find someone to help you for a small fee, a friend.'

But my father cut me off.

'Stop organising my life for me. Off you go and I'll get along as best I can for the six weeks I'm in plaster. I won't be able to drive, put things in my bags or cook. I won't even be able to undo my buttons to piss. I'm really looking forward to it.' Then he played his final victim card: 'But there you go, such are the trials sent to us by the good Lord.'

I spoke to Gus that evening.

'Your father can get fucked. Don't mess me around, this is London we're talking about.'

'Maybe we could postpone it until August,' I suggested.

'In August we need to practise for the recording session and the place will be full of tourists. I'm not going all the way to London just to bump into Miss Angelines taking snaps in Piccadilly.'

It was obvious that Gus wasn't going to change our travel dates and I decided I wouldn't let it upset me.

'All right, you two go. I have to stay here with my father.'

Gus and I were close, but our friendship had clear boundaries.

146

It made no demands: don't ask your friend for something they can't give you and you have a friend for life. We'd never exchanged a blood oath. I think Gus and I learnt to treat each other as professionals before we actually became professionals: we were united by a shared passion and that was enough.

When people congratulated us about 'Excess Happiness', they always wanted to know if it was my song or Gus's. But Gus would always parry the blow, saying, 'It's everyone's song. In this group we share everything, except, of course, the glamour. That's all mine.'

When Gus left us I spent years tangled in regrets. I was convinced that if I'd imposed a more stable form of coexistence, a deeper connection, then none of it would have happened. For years I persisted in the belief that I should not only have rejected the line of coke that The Champ offered us to celebrate our victory myself, but also insisted the Animal and Gus do the same. Maybe then none of it would have happened. But instead I just said 'These guys are up for anything,' and washed my hands of it all.

I might have tried to exercise more control over his surroundings, his feelings, instead of that easy mutual respect. That discreet distance defined our relationship and that's why he slipped away from me. I knew that a more intense and codependent friendship would have probably pushed us apart far earlier, caused a sudden rupture, but I still couldn't avoid feeling a sense of guilt. The same guilt I experienced when his sisters hugged me at the funeral and asked me if I knew about all the stuff he was involved in.

Or the look Aunt Milagros gave me at the undertaker's when she said, 'You were meant to look after him, Dani. You promised me you'd look after him.'

Gus and I admired each other. One night, following a pitiful performance at a concert we played a few days after wrapping up the recording sessions for our first album, Bocanegra subjected us to a curious test of faith by having private conversations with each of us. He told Gus that I lacked any charisma or showmanship, that I was boring onstage and that perhaps he'd do better on his own. And he told me that he'd known a great number of artists like Gus.

'They're fun, exuberant, good to be around, but they're empty and bring nothing to the music. He'll end up a strain on your career.'

We both gave him the same reply: that the two of us together was the only plan. Gus and I talked about it with each other, but rather than being angry with Bocanegra, we were amused by his trick.

'He's the bastard we need, isn't he?'

'Yes, he's the bastard we were waiting for.'

'Yes, he's that bastard who'll lead us to the promised land.'

I wasn't best pleased about Gus and Animal going to London without me. Years after, they'd still be coming out with anecdotes from the trip, that strange pair who were surprisingly able to get along without me, Animal happily occupied with pints of beer and drunk girls, and Gus fascinated by glam and all the hip venues. They never abandoned the musical influences they acquired on that trip: they always liked to tell a sound engineer that something didn't sound British enough.

'And what does that mean?' the technician in question would ask.

Gus would sum it up, 'Alcohol, squalor, grease, boys who were sexually abused by their fathers, getting the belt at school and warm, bitter beer.'

'And drunk girls,' Animal would add.

Their adventures formed a stark contrast to the *Via Crucis* I endured with my father. Seeing him work was a sight to behold. He never gave his name as he rang the intercom. Instead, he'd say something like 'a man of honour', or 'a man of peace', or 'a good Christian'. He'd be recognised immediately and the door would open.

He'd say yes to coffee or biscuits if offered, and sometimes he'd ask for a glass of water or to use the toilet. He'd give his opinion on the new curtains, the clock, the most practical way of keeping a house cool, the roadworks or the stupendous Mass the priest had given at Alfonso from the petrol station's funeral. He was talkative and trusting, and then he'd get out an invoice and proceed to take the payment, giving them the exact change without ever mentioning the ugly matter of money.

In that neighbourhood on the outskirts of town, my father acted as walking supermarket, loan shark and counsellor in one. In small instalments, they'd pay him back the total price of a blender, a watch, a couple of rings or an alarm clock. Those humble people were grateful for the service.

'Never work for rich people,' he warned me. 'They don't understand how much you struggle to earn money. Whereas humble folk will always pay you back on time; it's a matter of pride for them.'

My father's business was centred around such a philosophy and with time I realised his analysis was correct.

It took me a while to understand that my father's true merit didn't lie just in going into houses and signing people up despite having no legal contracts, or anything more binding than the buyer's word; nor did it lie only in the smart way he had of selling products. The true beauty of his work lay in the way in which he gained the confidence of strangers, his dedication to each and every client, however meagre a sum he stood to make. He offered luxury, privilege, the delight of having this cheerful, devoted man pay you a visit.

Years later, I realised that this was the only way to view a career in the music business: the privilege of people listening to you, letting you into their lives, their cars, their mornings at the gym, putting you on just before bed, was a favour that had to be returned with pure devotion. My own trade was an extension of my father's itinerant one. Can you inherit that?

His clients talked to him about problems with family, work, school. And my father never left a house without providing a well-thought-through, made-to-fit solution. He gave advice that was brimming over with common sense. He'd tell people what their daughter should study, which careers had the most openings; he'd go to nearby building sites or markets to ask if there was any work going for the son or daughter of a client who'd lost their job; he'd recommend someone to intervene in a family feud, make common cause with someone else who was suffering heartbreak, console people after a disappearance and establish truces between warring parties. He was the evangelist of a religion in which everything could be resolved with the good sense of a humble intelligence. He was both Don Quixote and Sancho Panza, the perfect blend of the two sides of the Spanish character, the perfect man, a mythical visitor: 'if only my husband was like you'; 'if only my parents thought the way you did'; 'if only my late husband had known what you know.'

All I got, on the other hand, was endless chiding whenever I had to open the portable sample jewellery case.

'No, not that one, for heaven's sake, the other bag.'

'He doesn't so much help me as slow me down,' he'd tell his clients.

'Even opening my fly takes twice the time with him. All that studying and yet when it comes to real life, he hasn't the foggiest.'

Some old dear would always leap to my defence: 'Oh but he's delightful, he's grown up to be a lovely boy.'

'I don't complain, not me, I never complain. But after all the work I've done to put him on the right track, you'd think he could get a haircut. But no, he won't give me the pleasure. If that's the way kids these days want to look, we'll just have to accept it.'

'Come and help put the mugs away,' he'd shout to embarrass me in front of a housewife who'd offered us some coffee.

'That's what happens when you become a father so late in life,' he explained on the fifth floor of a lift-free building I'd dragged my way up to after he'd bounded up the stairs in another display of his sheer physical strength, beating me to the top as if his life depended on it.

'This lad came out feeling tired.' Every morning, he'd plague me with this routine. 'Come on now, it's like you came out the womb exhausted.'

Around one o'clock we'd begin accepting the snacks that were lavished upon us in each house and then we'd go to a local restaurant, where my father would doze off as he leafed through *ABC*, its front pages expressing outrage at the decline of a country that now lacked the rudder of authoritarianism. They were unbearable working days, which my father sometimes prolonged until ten at night just to punish me, something I knew to be the case because when I wasn't with him he'd always come home earlier to take my mother out for a walk. There was an element of baptism by fire, of breaking me in like a wild horse.

'Now you know the work that goes into earning each peseta I give to you just so you can waste it,' he told me on our way home.

Used to working alone, he was incapable of being anything other than authoritarian, capricious and impertinent with me. Sometimes crossing at a red light was completely necessary: 'Look, no one's coming, what are you waiting for, chop-chop!' On other occasions it was a crime: 'What, you think the lights

151

are just there for decoration? If you don't respect traffic signals you're putting your life into your own hands. Do you know how many people are killed every month in collisions in Madrid?'

This all came to a head during a visit to the house of Concha, Consuelito Vargas the winemaker's wife's cousin. This approximate method of identification was the traditional way of referring to customers: Petra, the one who lives on the second floor above the grocery shop; the Arroyos, in the Gumersindo building; the innkeeper's wife with the limp from opposite the Corrochanos; the one-eyed woman from the haberdashery on the corner. No one just had a name. Even Clotaldo, from the cafe bar beneath our house where we often ate, was Clotaldo from the bar downstairs. It sounded better the way my father said it, *ClotaldofromtheBARdownstairs*. Sometimes I imagined him referring to me as 'the good-for-nothing from the room at the end of the corridor', or 'you know, the one who's always in a daze at the dinner table.'

Concha, Consuelito Vargas the winemaker's wife's cousin, was suffering from a summer cold when my father and I arrived at her flat. She received us wearing a rather frayed plush dressing gown.

'It's just a cold,' she claimed.

But visiting doctor was another one of my father's roles.

'Now, listen carefully. Put some water on to boil and bring me two cloves of garlic.'

'Please, it's fine, really,' the woman insisted. 'I don't even have any garlic; I haven't been able to do the shopping for two days now. And I'm taking my medicines.'

'Forget about medicine and all that nonsense,' my father responded, taking out a thousand-peseta note and ordering me to go to the supermarket to buy garlic and anything else the lady desperately needed.

'Well, if you insist, can you get me half a dozen eggs, three tomatoes, two red cucumbers and a lettuce,' said Concha, Consuelito Vargas the winemaker's wife's cousin.

'But, Dad,' I was about to complain before being instantly cut off.

'But nothing. Off you go this instant. Can't you see the state this poor woman's in? Her temperature must be pushing thirty-eight.'

The sun was punishingly hot and no one had gone to the bother of telling me where the market was, so I wandered the streets until I found someone to ask.

'There's no market round here; they may have meant the supermarket, but it's a little far to walk.'

I felt that as I'd let a decent amount of time pass I could go back to the building despite being empty-handed. My father was having none of it.

'Don't even think of coming unless either you've got the garlic or a far better excuse.'

'It's not that, the problem is I don't know where to go.'

My father's response was easily audible on the street, through the intercom.

'He's a real simpleton, this boy, he really is. And what's worse, with my fracture I have to put up with him for an entire month.'

Concha, Consuelito Vargas the winemaker's wife's cousin, spoke over my father to give me directions to a local corner shop. I made my way to the place she'd described under the unrelenting midday sun. I imagined Gus and Animal sitting in the cool shade of some dank London pit, drinking pints of beer as they chatted away to Elvis Costello, Joe Strummer and Nick Lowe, or ate spinach with Morrissey.

'You're a real dunce, aren't you?' my father greeted me as I handed over the string of garlic and the other things Concha,

Consuelito Vargas the winemaker's wife's cousin, had asked for. 'You numbskull, you've gone and bought the entire year's garlic harvest. I only asked for a pinch and look what you've brought me! And these are bad, they're worthless. Take a look, they're hollow inside. What a disaster! It's true what they say, do it well or not at all. If I'd have known, I'd have gone myself.'

'Well why the fuck didn't you? I'm sick to death of this shit!'

And I walked out of Concha, Consuelito Vargas the winemaker's wife's cousin's house, slamming the door in anger behind me. I waited for my father to come down after administering the miraculous potion to his poor client.

From there we were planning to visit the one-eyed woman by the haberdashery on the corner, an old bat with a glass eye. My father took his time coming down. He stepped onto the street with the box of samples, without turning to face me. So I got up and followed him.

'I'll carry those bags for you, Dad.'

'I suppose you think it's just peachy, don't you, humiliating me like that in front of people who know me.'

I gulped before I levelled my accusation.

'But it's OK to do it to me, isn't it? You're allowed to humiliate me whenever you feel like it.'

'I never humiliate you,' he replied, looking straight at me after he'd put the heavy bags containing the samples back onto my shoulders. 'But seeing how useless you are drives me to despair. You don't know how to conduct yourself or behave. I want you to actually learn something while you're working with me for these few weeks, but all I see is that sad, spiteful face of yours.'

'All right, Dad, leave it, it's fine.'

'You want me to leave it? You're the one who needs to leave it! You're good for nothing. A freeloading oaf, a lazy fraud, with your school band and your amateur ditties. I've had it up to here with you, you'd better believe it!'

'Dad, don't be a pain in the arse.'

My curt reply was enough to get me a slap in the face from my father's brick of a hand.

Being hit by my father wasn't what hurt the most. What hurt were the eighteen years I'd been putting up with him, forced to be there dying from the heat while my two best friends were in London. It hurt because I dreamt about being onstage. I was convinced that it was my destiny to stand before a devoted crowd as they sang along to my songs, not to be buying garlic and peppers for Concha, Consuelito Vargas the winemaker's wife's cousin.

It hurt because the slap was witnessed by three kids going past on their bikes, who responded to the sight by laughing and shouting 'What a wallop!' It hurt because it meant I had to get away from him, I just had to, so I ran off in the other direction after leaving the bags on the pavement. And what hurt the most was knowing that there would be no more rows between us, that that one had been the last.

## water, be a string to my guitar

'Water, be a string to my guitar' was a line from a Darwish poem we set to music that was given away free with some newspaper as part of a charity campaign in response to the umpteenth crisis in the Middle East. There was a time when I enjoyed collaborating with people, producing upcoming artists and lending myself to festivals and judging panels for the pure joy of meeting new talent, playing with strangers, raising funds or speaking up for lost causes.

Water is a natural feature of many of my songs and if I take a step back, I can see that it's a defining element in my whole life. It appeared very early on in my fantasies. Not just in Don Aniceto's insistence that we submerge ourselves in the study of the guitar like water, but also tied up with pleasure, eroticism, wisdom, the passing of time. They say that the amphibious experience of being in the womb is relived every time we come into contact with water. The womb is always referred to as a lost paradise and I believed it too, until my daughter was born with congenital muscular torticollis after being forced into an uncomfortable position inside her mother. I learnt that day that there are no ideal places for human beings – our fate is to adapt to our circumstances, however tricky they may be.

Oliva also emerged from the water. After the argument with my father I went to live with Fran. One of his flatmates was away all summer and I was able to stay in his room. I took a few clothes and snuck out the fake ID to get into the transport workers' swimming pool, so that I could escape there in the mid-afternoon on the days when the heat was suffocating. That year my swimming pool friend Enrique was away studying for a master's in engineering, though he ended up opening a bar. But I would grab my towel and trunks, sometimes my guitar, and go to the pool to be alone, passing the time in the water or sprawled out on the lawn, in the most secluded corner of the grounds. Elena had found another victim to pour her overflowing reserves of love onto and I watched her smooching her sweetheart from afar.

Oliva ran the kids' swimming lessons. Before discovering who she was I'd heard her name shouted by children's voices a thousand and one times every day. 'Oliva, Oliva, Oliva.' They went to her for everything and I looked for her among the bathers, in shallow end of the pool. When I first saw her she seemed so firm, so powerful, so sure of herself, that I preferred to keep my distance. She walked past me with her curly black hair tied up in a tight ponytail, wearing a swimming suit that allowed you to glimpse her athletic body, hardy shoulders and powerful arms.

She always walked barefoot, even on the grass or the terrace of the cafe, dragging the floats she needed for her classes behind her. Sometimes she saw me looking at her and she always reacted in the same way, with a cheerful smile, the same smile she gave to everyone else at the pool. She never flirted; her main focus was always the children she taught.

When she got out of the water she'd undo her ponytail and shake her hair, and in this simple movement, spring would erupt into midsummer. She always dried herself off in the sun, displaying her tan without the showiness of other women, and she'd glide around the sports centre with ease, like a colourful fish in its natural element.

Her lessons were so popular that she taught another group in the early evening as the sun was starting to go down; once she'd finished and got them all out of the water she'd have a final dip for leisure, as a reward for getting to the end of the day. I planned my afternoons to coincide with this final lesson.

One of the boys Oliva taught was a tubby loudmouth who everyone called Foskitos, after a popular brand of Swiss roll. One afternoon he slipped in front of me, injuring his knee. He'd been walking over to eat one of the buns he periodically wolfed down over the course of the day and began to squeal, frightened by the sight of blood. I got up to help, cleaning his wound with my water bottle as I consoled him.

'Look, it's nothing, see?'

'It hurts,' he shouted, 'it really hurts.'

As he cried, a big green blob of snot tumbled out of his nose in slow motion, making its way to the floor for what seemed like an eternity. Oliva came towards us. As she approached she took off her sunglasses and a shiver went down my spine. I was confronted with eyes so bright, so remarkable, that they seemed as if they'd been made not to look with but to be looked at. She inspected the kid's knee and soothed him before exhaling slowly.

'Back in a second,' she said and went off somewhere.

She came back with dressings and a bottle of ethanol, which left Foskitos's knee a browny-red colour.

'It's just a little scratch,' she told him. 'There, there, don't cry.'

She grabbed the enormous bogey with her own hands, which she then cleaned off using one of the dressings. How could she have done something like that so naturally?

'No more swimming until tomorrow, OK?'

We got up off the ground and she thanked me.

'No worries.'

The other kids were calling her from the pool, shouting at her to get back to them. I wanted to shout the exact opposite thing – 'Stay with me, don't go' – but there was no way I could compete with the racket they were making.

'It's just as well you have a nice name,' I said, 'because that lot will wear it out.'

It was true. All the time you could hear the children shouting, Oliva, Oliva, Oliva, Oliva this, Oliva that, Oliva told me, Oliva says, here comes Oliva – the last one being the best news I could hear of an afternoon. Oliva laughed and scratched the back of her neck beneath those curls.

'Don't you believe it! Everyone used to laugh at me in school.'

Then she went back to the children in the water.

When the lesson was over she came back towards me and smiled more expressively than usual. I noticed a slight gap between her upper incisors, a true work of art. Before she left, she squatted down in front of Foskitos and whispered something into his ear. She stood still and watched as the boy walked to-wards me and opened his mouth.

'Oliva says to tell you thanks a lot for helping me earlier.'

'Tell Oliva she's the most beautiful woman I've ever seen and would she please be so kind as to fall in love with me straight away.' That's what I wanted to tell him. But I didn't. I looked at her checking to see if the boy had carried out the task.

What I told him was, 'I'd like to have a swimming teacher like her, too.'

The boy ran back to her, shouting cheekily, 'He says he wants you to give him swimming lessons, too.'

'It was a joke,' I clarified, slowly and from a distance.

'Whenever suits you is good for me,' she shouted before leaving.

The next day she stayed after the class to swim alone. I was reading a book, though not a word was going in; each line took me back to Oliva with a furtive glance towards the trail she left in the water.

When she walked past me on the way to the changing room, she joked, 'So when are we going to have that swimming lesson?'

I sat there with my hand resting on the sole of my bare foot, a pose I thought made me look interesting.

'Don't worry about the lesson. We could have drink if you want, though.'

'If you don't mind waiting. I'll have a shower and then I'll be out.'

During those endless fifteen minutes all my future wishes paraded before my eyes. It was like experiencing death but in reverse; I guess it was like experiencing life – the intensity, the hopes and dreams, the fantasies, the desire, the different scen-arios. The atomic power of falling in love.

My seduction of Oliva, if you could call it a seduction, was slow and stately in its progression. I didn't even mention her to Gus and Animal when they got back from their trip to England. Oliva was another world I didn't wish them to be a part of – Animal always reduced everything to a lewd joke and Gus, ever the fierce critic, was capable of excoriating just about anyone. I didn't want to risk introducing them to Oliva just to have my illusions shattered. I mentioned her to Fran, however, the day I first saw her, and he laughed at my affliction.

'It's all dopamine,' he explained in his clinical, learned way. 'Don't look for any mystery in love. Your heart's just drugging your brain.'

But the only time I didn't go to the pool was on the weekend, when she had no classes and it was rammed full with people all garishly enjoying the summer. On the other days there'd be stolen moments when we'd sit together under the trees for a while or have a beer at the bar, and sometimes I'd go for a swim at the same time as she went in for her final dip. She corrected my movements in the water.

'Imagine it's a string. Imagine you're going up and down a string. That's all it is.'

She could make fun of you mere seconds after saying something completely lovely. She spoke with her whole body, from the tips of her mighty feet to her slightly gappy teeth, as if using language was just another part of an athletic display.

I began to use Foskitos for my own noble ends. I'd give him a piece of chewing gum and tell him to ask Oliva if she wanted one too.

'Tell Oliva that if she's got some time afterwards I'll stay and wait for her.'

Foskitos was my messenger, my annunciatory angel, my cuddly chubster. He was greedy, loud-mouthed and slow, and yet I became so fond of him that one day his mother, who was his spitting image, only thirty years older, came up and thanked me.

'The boy's become very attached to you.'

'The feeling's mutual, madam, the feeling's mutual.'

We were so close that when he brought along the harmonica he was trying to learn to play I'd let him drool all over me as he practised, just so that Oliva would come over and tell him, 'Foskitos, don't get distracted. We're having a lesson and you need to get back into the pool.'

'I'm off now'; 'I dislocated my shoulder today'; 'I can't stand up'; 'I've had it with these kids' – she only had to say a few words to me and her body would stretch out like a beautiful cat. Oliva had this habit, which I later recognised in some ballerinas, of talking to you while stretching. She'd push open the door to the bar, reach out for a beer, or walk around carrying her sports bag with an aerobic, feline grace. She'd say 'oh man', 'damn it', 'groovy' and 'righto' all the time, but I forgave her because sometimes she touched her upper lip with the tip of her tongue and I was overcome with an irresistible urge to kiss her.

She could click her finger joints and I'd say, 'Please, don't do that, it makes me shudder.'

But she'd just laugh at me before scratching the plaster wall with her nails, or running a fork around the rim of her beer glass. And if I ever criticised the way she spoke – 'groovy is such a lame word' – she'd take my hand in hers and squeeze until I was forced to apologise. At such moments, the physical distance was broken, but I was unable to comprehend anything that was happening between us. I was convinced she considered me unimportant, unthreatening, just someone to hang out with in the summer, a lad from the pool. She was only a year older than me, but after my experiences with Olga I knew how enormous such apparently small age gaps could be.

'Hey, Foskitos, do you know if Oliva has a boyfriend?' I plucked up the courage and asked the chubby blabbermouth one day as he scoffed down my packet of crisps in big handfuls.

'Boyfriend? She had one last year, a really cool guy. But he doesn't come here any more.' He fell silent, offering no further information. I got ready to shake him until he spat out everything he knew, but suddenly he flashed a sardonic childish smile my way and said, 'She likes you now.'

I choked on my own saliva. I took the packet of crisps off him and gripped him by the throat.

'Tell me everything you know right now.'

The kid answered back, 'She hasn't told me anything. I heard her talking to her friends.'

Her friends were a group of girls who sometimes came to the cafe. They were loud and pretty dull.

'One of them asked her,' the boy confessed. 'She made fun of her because she said she'd been talking to you a lot lately.'

I wanted him to recreate Oliva's conversation with her friend word for word.

'How would I know? I couldn't hear properly; I was drinking my chocolate milk.'

'But what did she say exactly? Please, Foskitos, try to remember.'

'What happened was the other girl asked if you'd made a move or hit on her yet, I think. Anyway, Oliva said you definitely had a girlfriend because you'd never asked her out or anything.'

I still waited a further two days before kissing her on the street. And I needed six beers to pluck up the courage. Before doing that I'd told her the following things: I didn't have a girlfriend; that I played in a band; that we were going to record our first album; that it had all started at school; that I'd left home because I couldn't deal with my father; that my mother was ill and had no memory; that I was staying in a friend's apartment; that I was thinking about renting a place for myself; that I had big plans for the future; that no one could stop me; that one day I'd play two consecutive sold-out shows at the Plaza de las Ventas; that I was turning nineteen in two weeks. I told her all of that, my entire life story, and when there was nothing left to say I added that she was the most beautiful woman I'd ever seen.

'I won't be for long,' she replied with a dazzling but sarcastic grin.

But she was.

### the chess-playing cat

'The chess-playing cat,' said Gus. 'That's what Oliva reminds me of.'

I'd introduced them months ago and they'd got on well with each other, but that was the first time he'd said anything about her to me.

'You know what I mean?' he asked. 'My sisters had a cat at home and what the cat liked most of all was jumping onto the chess board while they were playing. First it would walk carefully among the pieces, without knocking any of them over, as if it knew how to get to the secret of the game,' he explained. 'Until it had taken over the board, and then with a couple of paws and a tail swipe it would knock off every piece, and they'd have to stop playing.'

I shook my head, smiling. 'What do you mean, Gus?' I asked.

But I knew what he meant. I understood his own fear, which I shared: sooner rather than later Oliva, like the cat, would ruin our game, mess up our board and impose her own made-up rules. Love threatened the group. I never forgot Gus's image of the chess-playing cat.

Oliva came with me to pack my suitcase, so that I could move in with her.

'You live on a cul-de-sac?' she asked me in surprise as we approached the building. 'Now it all makes sense.'

We bumped into my father, who'd come home a little earlier to take my mother for her evening walk. Oliva and my mother glanced at each other, nothing more; I didn't know how to do introductions. It was the beginning of November and I'd made up with my father; though we kept a cautious distance from each other, like rival fans at a football match. By then I'd been with Oliva for four months and it was she who suggested we split the rent on her flat, since one of her housemates was leaving. I was earning money every now and then from playing live and she worked weekends as a waitress in a TGI Fridays. It was a small flat in Aluche, one we wouldn't stay in for long, but it would always be our first squalid, unforgettable home together.

'Dad, this is Oliva.'

'Do you study together?' my father asked, ignoring the fact that I barely ever set foot on campus.

'No, I'm his girlfriend,' she said, not mincing her words.

My father burst out laughing.

'His girlfriend? Don't you mean something else, special friend or, I don't know, is it hook-up you say these days?'

'No, I mean I'm his girlfriend.'

I'd told Oliva a lot about my father, about his personality and the fights I'd had with him, which is why she'd decided that the best form of defence would be a good attack.

My father adored her from that first meeting. This was hardly surprising, as she had everything he admired in a girl: she was cheerful, plucky, sporty and beautiful. What was surprising, on the other hand, was that Oliva found my father charming, warm and affable.

'You only have to listen to the way he talks to your mother,' she said. 'And it's plain to see he adores you. He's obviously jealous of me because he thinks I'm going to steal you away,' she said innocently.

I tilted my head to one side. 'Quite the opposite, from my perspective: he's jealous of me. Didn't you see he was hitting on you?'

'Don't be silly. He's a gem of a man.' Oliva would use old-fashioned expressions like that. 'And your mother is just beautiful, though you look more like your father.'

To some extent, Oliva and I used to compete as to whose family was worse. She was the only girl in a family of five boys who'd made her life rather uncomfortable but toughened her up in the process. She'd competed with them in every game and every childish tiff, and had grown stronger and stronger, thereby attaining that mixture of femininity and virility that made her irresistible.

'The only way of making them respect me,' she explained, 'was to beat them at everything: running, swimming, cycling. They went through every drawer in my room, scared off all the boys I liked, painted moustaches on my dolls and scratched my records because they weren't by AC/DC or Led Zeppelin, which was the only music allowed at home. You're an only child; you have no idea what it's like to grow up surrounded by brothers.'

Conversely, my parents for her were a shining example of love that remained steadfast in the face of time and sickness. Her parents couldn't stand each other.

'My mother calls my father "that man". I swear, she does! "Can you ask that man if he'd like some more lentils?"'

These were the whispered conversations Oliva and I would

have in our uncomfortable bed in that flat. It was blessed with one of the ugliest views in Madrid: one of the windows gave onto a dank, wet, foul-smelling courtyard where our neighbours would hang their clothes to dry in a space so small that one tenant's knickers would brush past the boxers of the dweller opposite if they raised them up too quickly. The drainpipes led into the courtyard and sometimes they were so loud it made conversation difficult and you'd have to stop talking while the guy on the third floor was flushing his toilet. The other windows afforded us a desolate view of the entrance to the Aluche metro station and the road, which was surrounded by dusty, arid land. I liked to joke that these views were merely the price one had to pay for the glorious experience of living somewhere with a view of Oliva.

One of her friends who studied with her at the National Institute of Physical Education moved into one of the free rooms after having a row with her boyfriend. Vera soon became a kind of chaperone to us. She'd played handball for years, was very short and sinewy, and wore the most horrible glasses, which gave the impression of someone who'd accepted being ugly without putting up a fight. She was friendly and chatty and had a long history of romantic misfortune, which she often joked about.

'Short of carving me into pieces, men have committed every atrocity imaginable against me.'

Oliva made love the same way she swam: with long, athletic strokes, sustained in the strength of her arms and legs. She was powerful even during intimate moments; sometimes she managed to immobilise me just with the strength of her thighs, so that I was unable to get out of bed to go to band practice or recording sessions. She could have robbed me of all of my energy and I'd have gladly let that happen. On the contrary, I felt far more energised: I achieved more with her at my side, and more quickly.

She wasn't the contemplative type and she didn't like to rest. She was always in motion, though I did teach her to tumble face down on the mattress and let me run my hands down every inch of her skin. Sometimes I'd pass my fingers over the curves of her body and whisper things I never thought I'd say out loud, until she mounted me and then soaked up all of my desire with the sheer force of her abdominals. If I had an erection she'd celebrate by taking control of it with her strong, steady fingers; ultimately, she could do whatever she liked with me.

She came to watch us play the launch shows for our first album, where we finally sounded like a proper band, thanks to Bulldog's contribution on the bass. While we played, she stood leaning against the bar, smiling back at me when my eyes met hers.

'You're so different onstage, you know?' she told me. 'You let Gus be the star, but you stay where you are, the solid pillar propping up the group.'

Oliva's verdict filled me with confidence. Even Gus began to like Oliva, surprised by her strength and the huge amount of independence she granted me.

'She's not boring and she doesn't stifle you. She's not clingy, she lets you live. And she's got a man's body! I think she brings out your gay side.'

I was shocked. 'A man's body?'

'Yep – muscles, big shoulders, legs of an athlete. She's a strong girl. There's nothing feminine about her.'

'Bollocks. You need to see her naked . . .' I responded, offended.

'Well, if you'd care to invite me,' he said before running over to Oliva. 'Your boyfriend's promised to invite me to a threesome with you two.'

She enjoyed the gigs, although she didn't like staying up all night. She was a morning person. When I took her to the cinema she'd fall asleep on my shoulder and excused herself by saying, 'You're the first intellectual boyfriend I've had. You take me to see concerts and to watch movies; with the others it was all about kayaking down wild rivers, climbing La Pedriza and planning hiking routes for the holidays.' Then I'd feel a pang of retrospective jealousy and I'd worry that I was boring her with my sedentary habits, because I'd never owned a track-suit or hiking boots and I never actually used my trainers for sports.

When Gus told me she was the kind of girl who could really make you suffer, I took it as the highest praise: we often said to each other that if a song didn't have the potential to turn into an embarrassing failure, then it wasn't worth starting. As with everything else in life, the only journeys worth embarking on are the ones that could end badly.

There was a mutual sense of allure between Gus and Oliva, a fight in which both sides were too strong to make a move, so instead they observed one another from a distance. Animal, on the other hand, clearly adored her. They even shared a passion for Bruce Lee and she stubbornly attempted to teach him to high-kick an imaginary enemy with his foot above his shoulders.

'She drinks like a man – no half measures,' was Animal's verdict.

With her next to me I began to attempt writing a different kind of song; I wanted to talk about my new feelings. My verses were so naive and inept that I began reading poetry in a chaotic and frenzied way, starting with anything that sounded modern and transgressive, from Rimbaud to Ginsberg. Later – having humbly accepted the fact that I was only trying to write songs, not win a Nobel – I set about scouring the archives of rhyming poetry, the old Spanish classics, to master that tough language.

I found lyrics and images that made lines of my own spring up in my head. It was with some embarrassment that I'd go into antiquarian bookshops and leaf through poetry collections to discover writers who might open up some new pathways, ones more interesting than our own cluster of songs about being young and having a good time. My woeful education had left me lacking in reference points and cultural knowledge, and when I sat down to write the words weighed down on me like lead.

My reading helped me to understand that the corset worn by each song – its rhymes and metre – wasn't a restriction but simply represented the boundaries of my battlefield. I chose to read the most beautiful fragments by other writers to Oliva, who barely read at all, while expressing to her my desperate need to be able to write decent lyrics.

'You have to find your own way of saying things,' she consoled me. 'At the end of the day, the way you talk is like the way you fuck. It doesn't matter how you do it as long as someone else is enjoying it.'

I couldn't say 'I love you' to Oliva because if I did, she'd make fun of me with a ditty from the soundtrack to some twee romantic film while frantically miming playing a violin. You'd tell her 'I love you' and she'd begin humming the tune from *Love Story*. I couldn't say 'I miss you' or 'I like looking at you' to Oliva because if you did, she'd place both hands over her heart, like a character from a Disney film. If I praised her extraordinary eyes, she'd laugh at me: 'Those are contact lenses, dummy.'

I couldn't caress Oliva without her throwing herself on me. Oliva liked to use arm-wrestling as a way of resolving arguments: 'Whoever wins is right'; 'whoever wins decides what we're doing tonight'; 'whoever wins chooses dessert'; 'whoever wins doesn't have to wash up'. She always won, every single time. She liked to bite my neck and arms and give me love bites, which she'd then pretend to discover when we were out with friends, shouting, 'Who gave you that?'

Oliva was a doer. She always had to be doing something. She was afraid the world would stop if we were inactive. I was the opposite, preferring to leave what could be done today for tomorrow. Oliva liked how I moaned loudly when I came, but she never shouted herself. When questioned, she'd say, 'Vera's next door and it's not kind to enjoy it too much when your friend is single.'

Oliva like to squeeze my balls as I came, extracting every last drop of semen.

'You're like a greedy sperm bank owner,' I told her.

Oliva didn't like oral sex.

'I don't know. I know you like it, but it's not for me. I hope you don't mind.'

I didn't mind at all, because I liked everything about her.

She was honoured when I first wrote a song about her:

*All the things you don't let me say*
*I say when you're not listening.*

But she couldn't help adding, with a sigh, 'That's not me.'

Perhaps she was annoyed by the way I'd invented this love in which she played a substantial part: she was so intelligent that she could see where my story was heading.

'The problem with idealising everything, Dani, is that one day you'll faint from all the effort.'

*All the things you won't let me do*
*I do them when you're dreaming.*

And though it was the first sincere song I'd written without fear of being laughed at when I played it in front of a crowd, she shook her head and joked, in that tough way she'd been taught to behave ever since she was a girl.

'Dani, you're impossibly twee.'

*You're everything*
*Everything that exists*
*And also the things no one sees.*

Gus added the backing vocals, clearly pronouncing and repeating all the 'you're everythings'.

'So, we're going soft then, are we?' Animal commented the first time we practised it, putting his sticks aside and picking up a pair of brushes, a really touching thing for him to do.

'I like it,' added Bulldog, who'd just got his girlfriend pregnant and was wavering between terror and ecstasy.

We were still tweaking songs in the studio and we treated 'Everything' like a dangerous, flammable material. Once we'd mixed it so it sounded just right, Gus turned to me from the mixing desk and said, 'Will your wild beast like it?' That's what he sometimes called Oliva: my wild beast.

## my wild beast

Jairo was enjoying the surrounding countryside.

'It's ugly but beautiful, if you get what I mean,' he said.

I definitely got what he meant: as we passed through a succession of dusty villages I'd thought to myself that with the advertising reach of Hollywood films, a landscape like this one would have reached mythical status by now. But there was only hard ground. No lone rangers, just tractors and trailers.

I looked out of the window. Derelict dovecotes and granaries, another ghost town and even the superb irony of two rivers whose names – Seco and Sequillo – both meant dry, their beds populated with wild reeds.

'Those are the most treacherous kinds of river,' my father would explain, remembering some past flood in the area, 'because the bends get blocked up and so when it rains, the water can't flow and the banks burst.'

Yet again, the past continues to flow beneath the surface.

My father eventually decided that the time had come to put my mother in a home, so she could be looked after by professionals, watched around the clock, protected from herself. Loving her wasn't enough any more. I wasn't living with them, nor did I fulfil my duties of visiting them once a week, embroiled as I was in gigs, travel, my life with Oliva. She was the one who most insisted that I go and visit my mother, but my selfishness was busy constructing its own cathedral and, having just turned twenty, I was riding on the highest wave of my own ego.

My father wanted to discuss the decision with me, though the conversation was really just an opportunity to castigate me for my lack of interest.

'A son abandoning his mother is just as bad as a mother abandoning her son. Dani, you will have to look after her when I'm no longer able to.'

I spent entire afternoons with my mother during the last days she spent living in her own house before we finalised the arrangements for her transfer to the home. I spoon-fed her her dinner and felt how strange it was for a son to be feeding his mother; I cleaned her and changed her before bed. Wasn't it meant to be the other way round? I took my guitar with me and whenever I saw that look of attentive distraction in her eyes, I'd start to play, as I'd done for so many hours as a teenager.

Almost intuitively, my mother still knew how to pretend

she was listening, give an appearance of normality. I put on music she liked, songs by Amália Rodrigues, Concha Piquer and María Dolores Pradera. That last afternoon, we played 'Estranha Forma de Vida', which may be one of the most beautiful songs ever written, and Oliva sat down next to us to listen to Amália Rodrigues's mighty, elegant voice for the first time.

Whenever my father visited me at the apartment by the Bilbao roundabout where I'd moved with Oliva, I'd shut myself away while she sat down to chat to him about life and the state of his business. They both agreed that the big shops would sink the lone trader, killing off a whole way of life. The big shops and the credit cards. My father hated credit cards, maintaining that if people couldn't physically see money, then they were condemned to spend it imprudently.

Oliva's hatred of big business came from the months she'd spent working in the Galerías Preciados department store, where her apparently very pious boss had harassed her. She'd also had to put up with an exhibitionist who used to call her over to the changing rooms before exposing himself.

'It wasn't so much disgusting as sad,' she remembered tenderly.

Oliva stopped studying PE and matriculated in special education, though she worked as a sports teacher throughout the year. She trained a girls' basketball team and often on Saturdays I'd go over to watch her standing on the court, directing the chaos. Before each game started all the girls would huddle around her and let out their battle cry: 'Win, win, win!' When she got home after a game I hadn't been present at and I asked her how they'd done, she'd give me a half-smile and say, 'Lose, lose, lose.'

Our band also used to shout something before going onstage: we'd place our hands on Gus's hand and he'd shout out a slogan, a different one each time. I got all the exercise I needed from having to follow Gus's movements while performing his star jumps among the smoke and heat, the celebratory carnivalesque part of the group. Sometimes he'd lose up to two kilos in a single concert, drenched in sweat and completely exhausted by the time it was over.

Our second record, *Strange Girls*, took its title from a song that Gus and I had written together, about how strange girls were becoming more and more normal. Bocanegra was convinced that our route to success lay in having a female audience.

'They actually buy stuff, they're loyal, they're not smartarses and they only offer advantages, whereas men are all treacherous brutes.'

He urged us to enjoy every last mouthful of our fandom and allow ourselves to be loved by our female followers. It was unlikely that someone as exuberant as Gus could satisfy what these girls were looking for, but our songs were light and fun and whenever we looked out from the stage we saw a mostly female crowd, all dancing happily. Gus wanted us to play every show in suits and ties, and he sometimes got his way. When this happened, we'd step onto the stage transformed into a scruffy version of Ultravox or Roxy Music.

But what Gus could do was confront Bocanegra and Renán, our manager. He'd insisted we wouldn't go on television, claiming that there was truth in the superstitious belief that when someone recorded your face they were stealing your soul.

'And also,' he said, 'you have to mime the song, so you're losing your soul and your dignity.'

We'd agreed to do it on several occasions and the stage set-up was always so ridiculous that on one kids' programme Animal decided to play with baguettes instead of drumsticks. Bocanegra didn't understand – for him being on TV was something too sweet to resist – but nonetheless he laid down the condition that if we were asked to play it had to be live and with the whole band.

We appeared on a programme called *Afternoon* and played 'The Dumbest Song in the World' at the channel's request, because they wanted a recognisable hit. Gus introduced the song after warning that five thirty in the afternoon was nowhere near rock o'clock, dedicating it to all the dumb people out there listening. I said nothing, frozen with panic.

The repercussions of going on live TV were immense: we started getting recognised in our apartment blocks and in bars, and Gus's sisters called him from Ávila, giddy with excitement. My father watched it sitting next to my mother and told me that he didn't really understand the words and the guitars were very loud. He also said, 'You sing too far away from the microphone and that hair of yours covers your whole face. But, to be fair, when it comes to the art of making noise, Napoleon would have been proud.'

The map of the cities we played in got bigger and we gained more loyal followers, fans who came to every one of our shows. Politics had taken a back seat to money and so our promotional appearances had to be fun and light-hearted. Still, Gus generated headlines, like that time he said that Spanish music had acted like an anti-dandruff shampoo for the nation.

'These songs have scrubbed the muck off our country's face,' the newspaper proclaimed, showing a photo beneath the headline of us all pretending to be relaxed as we jumped from the balustrade of a Valencia hotel terrace.

When Gus went on the radio and was asked about our influences, he replied that what mattered wasn't who influenced us but who *we* were going to influence. We appeared on the front cover of the youth pull-out of a national newspaper, with a light-hearted quote from Gus: 'Before we couldn't play. Now we're just better at pretending.'

I was annoyed at how the music was becoming less important as the marketing buzz grew around us. I tried hard to make the songs sound better, with more sophisticated arrangements, counting Animal as an ally in this effort, but Gus went the other way, inventing new moves, louder declarations, bigger postures. He understood the nature of the new country we now all belonged to far better than we did.

'Have a good time, snap out of it. We're not going to change the history of music, Dani,' he'd shout at me when he saw me shut away in the studio booth working on some little detail, re-recording a fragment or tweaking the mix. When I drew blank on a rhyme he'd make fun of me.

'Don't burst a brain cell, Dani. Even Bob Dylan rhymed fandango with Durango.'

Success had a strange effect on us: on the one hand it em-boldened us, reaffirmed our value, but at the same time it also led us in a different direction, gently pushing us towards a place far away from where we'd started. Bocanegra would talk about getting more people to our gigs, pressing more records, doing more shows, until one day, I spoke up.

'Maybe it's not so good always to be thinking about more, more, more.'

But Gus cut me off with one of his witty comebacks.

'When it comes to earning more money, we're all in agreement.'

Gus often repeated that we had to make the most of it before it came to a premature end, but I never believed that something to which I hoped to dedicate my life would just stop.

Bocanegra was adamant. 'What you gotta do is record a good video, something that grabs people's attention.'

We recorded one for our most popular song off the second album, and Bocanegra and three men from the label came to the shoot to make sure everything went according to their plan.

That moment in our careers felt like it was more important than any concert we'd played, a clear symptom of the problem.

The director was a boy who worked in advertising and used to shoot the label's bigger-budget videos; he made us get into four baths full of water, placed around the set. Our instruments mercifully unplugged, we obeyed, and over the course of the day we heard the song a thousand times over the loudspeakers. *Be careful what you record*, I thought to myself, *because you'll end up being completely sick of it.*

The guy in charge of costumes was a handsome, slender guy who, while we were in the water, made us wear elegant clothes loaned out by some expensive brand and helped us with the dressing gowns during breaks in filming. He was called Carlo, and he was Argentinian. He and Gus became close friends, often going out to bars together, and Carlo always took the time to dress him or accompany him on shopping trips for new looks to wear at our shows.

'Is he your boyfriend?' I asked him once when he brought Carlo over for dinner with Oliva.

'Yes, he is, but I'm not going to introduce him to my parents just yet, don't you agree?'

After our initial amusement on that shoot, when we watched Animal cause the water in his bath to overflow, or Bulldog all dripping wet like an abandoned pooch, the water in the baths went cold and it became really uncomfortable to stay lying there. Wearing drenched clothes was a real pain, and having to take them off and put them back on while other bits were being filmed or the water was being reheated became laborious. It was a pretty good metaphor for our career: nice when the water's hot. Perhaps it taught me a lesson about being prudent, about retaining a good dose of scepticism when surrounded by general euphoria.

Or perhaps it only taught me that hot water also gets cold.

Once Gus started dating Carlo, no one doubted his homosexuality any longer. Brutalised by years of single-sex schooling, homosexuals to us were a dark, mysterious sect whose members met up in secluded toilets and found each other via the classified sections of dirty magazines. Animal and I learnt to be respectful because Gus was so close to us, but Bulldog was more disdainful. On one occasion, using alcohol as an excuse, he showed clear disrespect towards Carlo. He was offering to change our appearance and dress us in a more striking fashion, something that didn't chime with Bulldog's rigid, tattooed ex-con look.

'No one's dressing me up like a faggot,' he shouted.

Gus waited until we were left alone in the new practice space before addressing Bulldog.

'I'm bored with you, I don't care about anything you say, you bring nothing to the group, you're vulgar and predictable. We're all up for having a good time, but we also want to play our songs onstage to the best of our abilities and no one here is better than anyone else. But you, you're no one, you're worse than no one, and I don't want you here. Grab your things and get out, and get fucked, because I can't put up with you for a moment longer.'

Animal and I maintained a cowardly silence, though we were also ready in case Bulldog decided to hit Gus, which wasn't entirely unlikely. Animal and I lowered our heads as he gathered his things. When he left, no one said a word for a good while. Animal, who had the strongest relationship with Bulldog, shoved his drumsticks down his trouser leg. Gus began whistling the melody to 'There's No Business Like Showbusiness'. I thought he'd done the right thing, but I said nothing. Animal always admired the forthright way Gus used to speak, and years later he'd still remind me of this whenever I needed to make some unpleasant decision or say what I was thinking out loud but lacked Gus's bravery.

'I miss Gus so much right now,' was all he'd say. 'He didn't care about telling anyone to get fucked,' he'd recall, 'like that time with Bulldog, remember?'

Gus was the first person I heard use the word vanilla to define me and others like me, people who weren't keen on having new adventures, be they sexual or psychedelic. Vanilla is the guy who goes into the ice-cream shop and always chooses the same predictable, safe flavour. That's what I was to Gus, vanilla, and he'd chide me for not going on a night out with him: I'd finish off my beer, always three or four too many, and go back home, where the peace of Oliva awaited me. Animal drank until he dropped, but Gus frequented other establishments until the small hours.

My dislike of cocaine had something of a class complex about it. In Estrecho we'd witnessed the decline of the junkies, local people who looked seriously worse for wear, the drug taxis that in exchange for a dose would take other addicts to the slums where you could buy for cheap. We'd all taken the sister of some friend to the suburbs to visit a dealer who'd fuck her in exchange for a hit, or known someone on the waiting list for some gleaming new rehab programme. We didn't belong to the previous generation, who'd been unaware of the consequences: we'd grown up with contraception campaigns and 'Mothers Against Drugs', with the effects always in full view.

I'd seen some of my father's friends battered and humiliated by their sons coming home and assaulting and robbing them in order to fund their heroin addictions. But what I hated even more was the sweat that exuded from coke-heads, who were always ambitious guys working in business – imposing, powerful and with strong opinions – and who'd nod at you in the direction of the bathroom or the glass table where they'd cut you a line. Gus, on the other hand, accepted any and all offers, whether they came from executives, salespeople, venue owners, music journalists, fans, friends, every walk of life.

I never even used alcohol to help me work; I always consumed it as a reward rather than a stimulus. When I taught Gus the song 'For the Camera', he thought it was a coded message to him:

Being bad makes you feel good
You know it, everyone does
But who are you trying to fool?
I know it's only for the camera.

And though he liked it and always sang it with gusto onstage, he never stopped calling it my moralistic song.

'We could even go back to school and sing it to the priests, and this time they'd definitely let us compete.'

I sensed the environment that awaited us all too early and Oliva, so sane and healthy, was the refuge I could always return to when I felt disgusted by the music scene. There was a good side: the boys and girls who made fanzines or set up venues so that their favourite groups could come and play in their one-horse town with a population of 3,000. Those who recorded their own CD compilations of their favourite tracks and spent their time photocopying concert posters to plaster around the city, or who sweated blood to attain a grant from the local councillor in charge of youth and culture. But there was also that endless parade of impostors, fake friends, fake fanatics, fake musicians, fake experts, even fake fakes, who were only interested in the scene, the surface level, the outer layer – and of course in scrounging a bit of cash.

Animal and I frequently embarked on monumental post-show

benders, when coming down from the adrenaline was impossible. One act in particular, which involved hopping from one parked car to another, always went down well. In Zaragoza I ended up sleeping with an obese, mouthy girl we'd met after playing at the Pilar fiestas, who swore she was getting married the next week: who could deny a quickie in a guest house to someone in that situation? But the guilt made me flee the crime scene in the early hours and go to sit in the old Portillo station, waiting for the first train to take me back to Madrid.

Animal reasoned in his oblique way that this couldn't be thought of as cheating on Oliva.

'What you've done is sacrificed yourself for the sake of humanity. Like people who leave behind successful lives to go and volunteer for Médecins Sans Frontières. You've done your good deed.'

Post-concert blackouts formed part of an established ritual. That's why I liked Oliva travelling with us, tagging along at each concert: I preferred it when she took me off to bed, or at least when she was there as a steady presence to witness the piss-ups. There's no doubt that the nights always offered attractions it was impossible to turn your back to. Encounters at ungodly hours, venues you needed a password to get into that served food at five or six in the morning, managers who'd lock the place from inside and offer you a final shot or place a bottle down on the table so that everyone could turn things up a notch. Other nights, though, were as empty and arduous as overcast skies.

We had a few fights. I saw Gus headbutt a guy in Requena and Animal get into a fist fight in Granada. In Andoain we were adopted by the local Basque musicians, but we had to make a dash for it when Animal tripped and broke the jar where people were leaving donations for ETA prisoners. In Llanes two guys got onstage to demand we say something in the local Asturian dialect and then tried to beat us up. They interrupted the concert and attempted to get Gus to learn it by heart, *barriga farta quier gaita*, but Gus went up to the mic and said, 'Now let's see, who can translate "go get fucked, you pieces of shit"?' At our first show in Santiago, someone threw a beer bottle at us that landed on the drum kit. We had to hold down Animal to stop him from launching himself into the crowd.

## that thing called success

That thing called success fell upon us when we weren't prepared for it – that is if anyone can consciously prepare for such an accident. Success for Animal meant never being short of beer money and Gus had fantasised in front of the mirror about being a star for so many years that he took to it effortlessly. It fell to me to carry the burden of common sense. I had to deal with all the boring stuff: contracts, agreements, gig dates, planning, promotion. 'You do it'; 'I'm not up to it'; 'Whatever you decide is fine by me.'

Renán was beginning to count us among his four or five most profitable bands. As he managed both our diary and 'the choppy waters of the industry' – an expression he liked to pull out with great ceremony – his dealings with us were becoming more attentive and careful. We treated him with the distain artists always have for money men and he quickly figured out that he had to discuss everything with me alone.

We hired a professional bass player for the tour, a guy called Ramiro who had a conventional, ordered life as a teacher and earnt a bit extra from taking part in mimed performances on TV. Between the keyboard player, Nacho's brass section and our technicians, we ended up with ten people onstage.

Our second record had been a mixture of love songs inspired

by my passion for Oliva, party songs meant to be played live and enjoyed, and the songs Gus and I had come up with over the course of an evening devoted to experimentation. We attempted to make things that came easy to us sound more complex. The third album tried to be too many things all at once. And it came out sounding as confused as we really were.

Unlike our first two recordings, where the producer had acted as little more than an efficient, speedy sound engineer, on the third album we were able to work seriously with him. We flipped around the songs and created interesting sounds, even when the erratic direction we were heading in was becoming more and more apparent.

Ramón was fairly experienced and had his own studio where we could spend as much time as we needed. Sometimes he brought his son, who had cerebral palsy, to the studio with him and Oliva would take him for walks around the Puerta del Ángel neighbourhood, where the studio was located. He was always smiling at us, with that contorted expression that hit us deep inside. Everyone called him Bambi, not because of the orphaned fawn in the Disney movie but because whenever you sang him 'Ay, Bambino Picolino,' he'd clap his hands and jiggle about in his seat.

In fact, the cover of our third effort was a photo Oliva had taken of Bambi at the top of Caramuel park, with a view of Madrid behind him. It was out of focus, but you could still see that childish face and that boundless, uninhibited smile. Bocanegra was annoyed by how much we all liked it.

'How are you going to sell any records with a mugshot of a boy with cerebral palsy on the cover? Are you crazy?'

But the album was called *Play for Me*, and the mixing up of the two concepts brought us a rare feeling of freedom and detachment. The battle raged on until someone in the office tossed the new Nirvana album, which had a baby in a swimming pool chasing a dollar bill on the cover, onto Bocanegra's desk. Suddenly, he had something to compare it to.

'Putting a child on the cover allows people to decontextualise the group,' the assistant continued. 'The amateurish photo – real life as opposed to something preconstructed. The home-made image that doesn't reek of some elaborate marketing scheme.'

And with that professional-sounding explanation we defeated the reticence of the executives.

*Don't give in, don't move aside*
*Don't disappear, don't run and hide*
*Play for me, play for me, play for me.*

Less than a month after its release we had a silver disc, or gold maybe, I forget which, and a women's magazine awarded us a prize on the condition that we played two songs at the awards ceremony at the Palace hotel. We agreed, and as we sat at the prizewinners' table, Gus was unable to take his eyes off the girl awarded best young model of the year, who couldn't have been more than seventeen.

She was called Eva, short for Genoveva, and she'd been born in Alicante to a Spanish father and a Belgian mother. As slender as a leaf blowing in the wind, she possessed that languid fragility some models have, with light eyes and a face whose lines looked like they'd been sketched on by a skilled architect. Gus pointed her out for me.

'Look, that's the kind of girl they stopped making in the seventies.'

He managed to approach her and they talked all night despite the strict vigilance of the two guys who were managing her interactions. Before long she was laughing at his jokes.

When I went over to be introduced, he just said, 'Dani, Eva.'

And she said, 'I love your song "Play for Me",' and laughed, flashing a row of baby teeth.

As I went to kiss her I touched her wrist, which was as thin as a twig.

Animal never liked models; he said he was only interested in women who smelt like Spanish omelettes. Gus loved that whole scene, trendy girls and good-looking young guys, sleek impresarios and journalists dressed head-to-toe in free clothing; a scene that would soon incorporate footballers, once they'd undergone the initiation ceremony of plucking their mono-brows. I went home with Oliva, a woman not built for fashion and advertising but mountain air, the hustle and bustle of daily life and wrestling matches with her brothers.

Animal and I had left Gus in Eva's company, and the follow-ing afternoon Animal blurted out, 'Well, did you fuck that girl from yesterday?'

Gus shook his head. 'Dude, you make it sound as if I'd raped an entire boy band.'

We'd all moved to places in the city centre and we only ever returned to Estrecho to visit our parents or Aunt Milagros, who celebrated our arrival with wonderful blowout meals of beans and lamb. We played almost one hundred concerts on the tour to promote the album and learnt to play properly just from having to do it so often. We also learnt to up our live game, listen to the crowd's every breath.

We took part in a festival in Split, playing on the beach sur-rounded by palm trees, and Renán got us a rare show in Bel-grade, which meant we spent a whole week without sleeping, in an atmosphere so celebratory that the subsequent war made us feel as if we were living in two parallel realities. We were so busy playing the same songs in different places that it felt like time had stopped, that it served only us: every night the same ritual, the same introductions, the same jokes, the same piss-ups, the same fans, the same company and the same encores. I think we even had the exact same conversations and mealtimes. And when one of us screwed someone – as I'd started to do on journeys far and wide, without the guilt of my initial infidelities – it was like we were all screwing the same girl. With a different face and a different voice, sure, but still always the same.

Gus changed his suit and shirts, but I didn't even bother with that, because I'd managed to hold on to my glasses from three years back, and no one was going to get me out of my plain dark T-Shirt and jeans or make me cut my long hair. Oliva liked to run her hand through my mane while pretending to be sick of her wild curls, but I always threatened to report her to environmental standards if she cut off so much as a single one.

Animal gorged on happiness, the most content man in the world. All he needed was his beers and the company of all those girls who for some reason found themselves attracted to the dude at the back of the stage; the guy who would shred the drum kit to pieces and then stop to piss into a plastic bottle mid-concert. As for Gus, his story with Carlo disintegrated into a stop–start friendship and his relationship with Eva grew platonic as she became a famous model and began travelling the world.

We played in Valencia so many times that we ended up establishing a colony of friends in the city. One day Gus introduced me to a clothes designer, only slightly older than us and with a name that really stuck: Marina Miralta. Marina would come to watch us play and, at Gus's request, she provided us with clothing. She even designed a bunch of suits that sort of became our official uniform. It was at a time when I dreamt of sounding like The Style Council and would even sing 'My Ever Changing Moods' onstage, real slow. Gus, meanwhile, wanted to be seen as a dandy.

Marina had been the first person to discover Eva. She'd

walked past her on the street when she was fifteen and suggested to her that she pose for a catalogue of her new designs. From there, Eva had made the leap to professional magazines. Marina always wore these big, spectacularly designed glasses that accentuated her Renaissance nose, rounding off a face you couldn't help but admire. She looked like a Valencian Anjelica Huston, only very thin, almost transparent, in fact.

After one of our concerts in Valencia, Marina threw a special late-night party for Gus and me at her studio, because we were staying on in the city for another day. The party turned out to be an intimate orgy, during which Gus and I were invited to intermingle with beautiful girls and boys. They looked like they'd been chosen according to rigid aesthetic standards and were paraded before us in a kind of decadent, sensual procession. It wasn't the first time we'd ended up at this kind of celebration, but it was by far the most sophisticated one.

Of all the acts of sexual excess we committed during those years, that night in Marina's atelier was perhaps the one that most closely resembled the mythical image of lust and depravity in the world of music. There were fountains of punch spiked with ecstasy and after half an hour I'd have got it on with Miss Angelines if she'd happened to show up.

Marina led us to the bubbling Jacuzzi on her terrace, which was protected from neighbours' prying eyes but open to the Valencia sky. Inside the Jacuzzi we took off our clothes and writhed around making love in all of its varieties until the sun came up.

'Now this is what I call success, am I right?' Gus called over from the other side of the pool.

I smiled at him. I liked Marina, who participated in the mass fondling in her own awkward way, with her wiry, flat-chested body, just two nipples that happily stood on end when caressed. The other girls were noisy and rather two-dimensional, all models and aspiring models, just like their male counterparts, who were Gus's main focus.

One of the girls, Marina explained, had been a boy only a year earlier and you could definitely make out traces of something masculine beneath that lovingly cultivated air of sophistication. Manuel was now Manuela. Just before dawn, as I lay on one of the comfy deckchairs laid out on the terrace, Gus came over towards me, accompanied by Manuela. Marina had fallen asleep by my side and I was unable to gather the necessary strength to get back to the hotel.

Gus and Manuela began caressing me and between the two of them, they removed the towel I'd had wrapped around my waist. They appeared to be enjoying themselves with a game they'd devised for me. A moment later they began taking turns to suck my dick. I was confused and my mind was racing. Seeing my friend right there, crouching down and licking my inner thighs with a smile on his face, interweaving his tongue with this girl's tongue, was something I found both exciting and unnerving at once. I pushed him away with my bare foot, kicking him on the shoulder. He fell to the floor in fits of laughter.

'Vanilla,' he said and walked off.

Manuela climbed onto my lap and pretty soon we were making love, or something similar, on the deckchair. In the distance Gus glanced occasionally in our direction, always with a smile on his face. I remember that night observing Gus's naked body in a way I never had before. Extremely thin, with fine, white, almost feminine skin, his hips and ribs clearly visible.

My mobile phone made a noise and Jairo looked at me. We continued to talk as he drove, but I'd stopped listening some time ago in order to focus on the memories the outside scenery was awakening in me. I took the phone from my pocket. It was a text message from Raquel.

How's it going. Are you nearly there? I'm sending you the
mayor's number. Remember, you need to call him when
you're five minutes away from the village so they can
guide you to the cemetery.

That was Raquel, all the way in Brazil and yet still attentive
enough to saddle me up and fill me in on the ins and outs of
my strange trip.

'How long until we get there?' I asked the driver.

'Just a moment, let me see what the box says.'

The driver pulled over to consult the satnav. I stuck my head
out of the window. All the turnings now led to villages whose
names all had 'de campos' at the end: Villamuriel de Campos,
Villamayor de Campos, Morales de Campos, Montealegre de
Campos, Boada de Campos, Celnos de Campos, Meneses de
Campos, Belmonte de Campos, Cuenca de Campos, Tamariz
de Campos, Gatón de Campos, Villafrades de Campos.

'The screen says we're fifteen minutes away, but if you're in
a hurry I can step on it and cut that in half.'

'No,' I said, 'there's no rush.'

With my mobile in my hand, I went over my most recent
emails. There were a few messages from Raquel's office with
the terms and conditions for a concert, along with a short email
Kei had sent from Germany, reminding me that this was the
morning I had to take my father's remains to his birth village.
*Don't forget, don't go to bed late.* She'd sent it the previous night.
*And don't get sad.* She was always so attentive, so concerned for
me. *Why don't you take the kids? They'd love to get to know the
village. Or perhaps you think there's something a bit sinister about
taking them to a burial?*

In her message, Kei was asking me the same questions I'd
asked myself that morning. The journey was too morbid and I
didn't want my children to inherit the stupid Spanish obsession

with all things death-related. I'd like death to mean to them exactly what it means to me: a trivial farewell at the end of an immeasurable adventure. I want them to learn to devote their best efforts to being alive.

## no one gets old in music

'No one gets old in music,' Vicente told me at his house one afternoon.

Vicente was a veteran presenter on Radio Nacional I'd met around the time our second album came out, during an interview in which Gus had landed his habitual, sardonic blows. I really liked what Gus said when he was asked if we represented the youth of today.

'When I look in the mirror I don't see the youth of today, I see me, only me, and unless all the youth of today are hiding directly behind me, I just can't spot them.'

But when the interview was over, Vicente said he'd found my presence intriguing, because unlike Gus I didn't seem so determined to play a role. From my perspective, it seemed that while Gus was witty and brilliant, all I did was blurt out the same old dreary soundbites. I confessed as much to Vicente, but he shook his head.

'Even champagne loses its bubbles.'

Vicente was the first person I spoke to, a good while later, about the possibility of parting ways with Gus. Every now and then I'd imagine a more solitary career, without always worrying about how each song would sound when we played it together. How to fit the backing vocals in, having to adjust myself to Gus's tastes and performance style, to the demands of the group and the admin involved in every gig. Gus had been offered work acting in a TV series, playing a variation on the character he played in real life. I told him to do whatever he wanted, although it seemed like an unnecessary risk when things were going so well with the group. He accepted the part, which only made him more popular.

I'd see Vicente from time to time. He put on a concert at the university to celebrate some anniversary of his programme and he convinced me to play as a duo with a female singer. He wanted all the performances to be new, unique. I said yes, though on the day of the rehearsal I felt the girl was too self-conscious, trying on and taking off the same top fifty times, searching for the perfect look.

The best thing about the collaboration was that it made Oliva jealous for the whole week.

'You'll fall in love with her. She's so beautiful, she has such a lovely voice.'

There was something unusual about Oliva and me as a couple: jealousy didn't exist between us except as a source for jokes, or for my lamentations about her previous boyfriends, men I hated despite never having met any of them. Oliva's jealousy of my duet partner revealed an unknown side to her, more insecure and fragile than she appeared. She felt affronted when she found out the girl was going to sing a version of 'Everything' with me.

'But you wrote that song for me!'

In spite of that she came to the concert anyway and when it was over she asked me, in her forthright way, 'Well? Did you fall in love with her?'

After Vicente was forced to take early retirement at the radio station, we'd hang out occasionally at his place in Tirso de Molina and he'd give me records from his immense collection that occupied every corner of the flat.

'The relationship between musicians and music critics isn't an easy one,' he told me. 'The only person with an ego bigger than a musician is someone who's paid to talk about music.'

Together with Fran, he was one of the few people with whom I could argue without it becoming a competition. He played me songs I'd never heard before and set me back on the right path when I was completely lost. It was Vicente who got me into T-Bone Walker, even giving me all of the records by that guitarist, happy that after so many years of living in ignorance he'd become one of my idols. I've since lost count of the number of times I've played my guitar over his in 'Mean Old World'.

When Animal came along with me all he'd ever talk about was the world's greatest drummers and he'd often be surprised when Vicente chose Art Blakey or Max Roach above Ginger Baker, John Bonham or Keith Moon. He opened up my ears to Brazilian music, which I'd hated up until then, bored to death by the obligatory festivities of samba and the ubiquitous bossa nova, or bossa antigua, as Gus used to say whenever he heard it in some restaurant or lift.

Vicente wasn't a musician, but he knew everything there was to know about music from his twin roles as frantic treasure hunter and considerate, thoughtful listener. Gus used to say that he was an old, solitary queen and I don't think Vicente would have been bothered by the description. He taught me to listen to strong women like Etta James, Nina Simone, La Lupe, Mina, Billie Holiday, Maria Bethânia, Elis Regina, Dinah Washington and Eartha Kitt, as well as fragile men like Roy Orbison, Sam Cooke, Nick Drake and Chet Baker. For him it was essential for people to create their own family, a family tree of influences and legacies that had to be accepted unconditionally.

Vicente was quite hard on me when I recorded my first solo record.

'It's not you, you're hiding yourself.'

He may well have been right, for Gus's departure was hovering over everything I did back then.

'Music's full of dead people, don't let yourself become another musician who spends his whole life carrying a corpse on his back.'

When Vicente took his own life I was overcome by sadness and guilt: I hadn't seen him for a while and I could have helped him. But I was living in Japan at the time.

'Getting old and sick is a stupendous way of ending up wanting to die instead of being afraid of it,' he used to say.

He donated his collection to the radio archive and, a few days later, jumped out of his window onto the square outside his flat. He'd lost all hope of beating the cancer that had spread through his body; he feared not being in control of the end of his life and so hopped out of it, like someone getting off a train before it comes to a complete halt.

'Some people have a strange relationship with death,' Jairo told me.

He must have noticed the serious expression on my face and was trying to pull me out of my thoughts, convinced as he was that one of the hearse driver's duties is to alleviate the suffering of the relatives of the deceased.

'You really see it a lot in my profession,' he said. 'And you know what? Usually it's to do with how familiar they are with death. You see, some people have lost many loved ones, while for others it's their first time, and the difference is really noticeable. As with all other walks of life, experience helps you to overcome things a little easier. Do you remember your first death, your first real death?' Jairo asked.

'Of course.' Of course I remember.

When that stray dog is you, when you see it there, abandoned, lost, scrawny and filthy, its snout worn away from sniffing around in rubbish and its hide wounded from sleeping out in the open, and you see yourself in it, all you can do is go up to it and run your hand over its neck. And you're unable to resist the way it rubs its head and ears against your leg, drops its tail and begs you to take it with you. It's then that you know that although two lonely souls may not be able to cure loneliness, they can help to alleviate it.

I saw that little mutt early one morning, on the Quevedo roundabout. I was coming from God knows where, from some unsuccessful attempt to rid myself of the dark pain that had been buried deep inside me since my break-up with Oliva, and I brought him back to the flat with me. He didn't take long to collapse onto the floor, on the image the sun was sketching out through the window. The same place Oliva had always chosen to sit down and revise when she had exams.

'And what am I going to call you?' I asked it.

'Clon. His name is Clon,' I said to my father a few days later.

But he was incapable of pronouncing it correctly. 'Clos? Col? Plon? What an ugly name you've given him, my boy.'

I took him with me whenever I visited my mother, who for many years had banned animals from the house. 'A flat's no place for an animal.' My father loved the dog and I always left him in his care when I was away playing shows. He'd take Clon to work with him in the car: the dog couldn't mess up the car because my father had already purposefully made it filthy. Another one of his quirks was having a veritable pigsty for a car: the seats were covered in bags and he left empty fruit crates in the back. For him it was the perfect cover, because no one would steal from a car that looks like that and it protected him from those who may expect a jeweller to carry valuable items in the car. It was his grubby pauper disguise, which rounded off the humble image he liked to present. Clon was happy to contribute to my father's car camouflage with his filthy paws and muddy fur.

'So then, I see you've swapped the girlfriend for the dog,' my father said cuttingly.

'Precisely.'

But however much he batted it off with his usual stinging comments, I knew that he was deeply affected by my break-up with Oliva. If he never tried to discover what exactly had happened, it was only because he was convinced his son wouldn't come out of it all that well. It was enough for him to see my face and how thin I was to get an idea of my deep pain.

'Let's go, Clon,' I'd say and the dog would wag his tail as I headed for the door.

'Lindo,' my father said, 'I'll call him Lindo. It suits him much better than Pon.'

And so my dog ended up with two names: Lindo Clon.

*Lindo Clon, my sad reflection on the street*
*Today you're barking with my voice*
*Where am I? Where am I going?*
*Who am I? Is it even worth knowing?*

I was used to people being fascinated by Oliva. She was attractive and extroverted, and possessed that social gift of emitting confidence without trying at all to make herself visible. She was the beach every wave wants to break onto and yet still she gave off a certain air of mystery; she could be both sarcastic and tender with complete spontaneity, but there was always something more distant and more profound there, something no one could reach. And it was something of a surprise to find myself next to her.

I was, she used to remind me, her least flattering trait, her bad side. I used to stay in bed and admire the way she got up so early to go running, or rose at dawn in winter to go and run a ski club for kids in Cotos.

'It's six in the morning, Oliva. There have to be less cruel ways of being happy.'

But there weren't.

She needed activity, to give herself to others, whereas I always came back from concerts and trips seeking peace and isolation. Barely a month passed between her finishing her course in special education and her getting a work placement in a centre for handicapped children. I didn't realise how much that first job would distance us from one another. Her day and my night. Making a living from music, going out and singing, having a good time so that others can have a good time, isolates you in an artificial, nocturnal paradise.

Oliva liked sacrifice: the more difficult the child at the school, the more burdened with problems they were, the more motivated she was and the more enthusiasm she gave off when she told you all about it at home.

'Today he spat at me. He hits and shouts, but I swear we'll get there in the end.'

I felt relaxed about her going into special education and joked with her about her new job.

'Now you'll be able to deal with someone like me. You'll learn how to meet the complex needs of a nutcase, a moron, a halfwit.'

When Fran met Oliva he exhibited the same delight and attraction she aroused in everyone. Of all of my friends, he was the one she most gelled with. Fran was a doctor reluctantly working at a private hospital, hoping to save enough money to be able to go to the United States to complete his studies. He was ambitious and stubborn; he got what he wanted.

Oliva liked us going to see him because she could talk about the challenges she faced at work, things she was hardly going to discuss with Animal and Gus. Normal people's trials and tribulations made them yawn with boredom – all their energy and attention were eaten up by music and our career. Fran was more mature and more stable, which was why he'd played a key part in my upbringing, as an adviser, as a friend, as a teacher.

I loved seeing them get along because I was the necessary link between them, my most mature friend and my most desired girlfriend. When Animal, Gus and I were together we were entirely cut off from the real world – even more so when we were on tour, where it was so easy to forget about the person sleeping in bed at home. It's very likely that I stopped giving Oliva the care and attention she deserved after the group came unstuck. With that, I became unstuck from the ground beneath my feet.

Oliva and I always struggled to communicate with each other. When we first fell in love we needed Foskitos to act as a go-between: we hadn't been able to get to the bottom of what we felt for each other during our walks, or when we went for a swim and had a drink together. The break-up was exactly the same: I was just as unable to interpret the signs of decay, our growing apart.

I found out it was over completely by accident. I'd returned from two concerts with a song bouncing around in my head and I needed to visit the studio owned by Ramón, our technician. I often recorded guitar demos at his place when he wasn't busy with some other job. He worked as an audio engineer for the Italian-style music productions that were hogging the charts at the time, puerile songs transformed by a few pompous arrangements, like women who are covered in make-up but have nothing to say. Sometimes Oliva would come along with me and then she'd spend the time entertaining Bambi, always taking care to bring him a T-shirt or the sweets he loved.

Ramón's son celebrated each of her visits with that happy smile he wore in his best moments. Sometimes she visited the studio without me just to see the boy and take him for a walk around the park or buy him an ice cream.

'I stopped by Ramón's studio today,' she'd say then tell me who was recording there, or that some well-known singer had tried to hit on her.

Ramón and Oliva were the only two people who knew that I was harbouring doubts, that I was tempted to try to record something solo, without the group.

With his habitual intelligence, Ramón told me that 'Until you hear yourself singing solo, you won't know if you can or if you want to do it.'

The very idea felt like a betrayal of Gus and Animal. But that day Ramón had said, 'Come to the studio and we'll try something. I'm free this afternoon.'

I sang him two parts of the unfinished song. He gave me a rhythm and I let myself go with the electric guitar while I finished improvising the rest of the lyrics. In hindsight, it's rather curious: I was playing around with a track called 'Days Without You' which, as sometimes happens with songs, wasn't so much premonition as anticipation. You don't write about something that happened to you, you write something and *then* it happens to you:

*Soon there will be days without you*
*The future, a sad calendar.*

It was a real surprise to hear my voice without Gus's beside it. It had a different pitch; it sounded more serious. Ramón

produced a rough mix, a basic recording with minimal adorn-
ments, and we waited for Oliva and Bambi to come back and
give us another opinion. She gave me a look of approval.

'It's good.'

If I sensed a deep sadness in her expression at that moment,
I must have assumed it was because of the song. Bambi entertained himself, ignoring us as we worked. At some point he
went over to the drinks machine, brought a bottle of water to
Oliva and handed me a can of Coke.

'Coke?' I asked, puzzled. 'You know I don't drink Coke.'

Everyone knew I never touched it; remnants of a hangover
from my adolescent anti-imperialism.

Ramón shook his head and explained that it was for Fran,
who sometimes came along with Oliva. I looked at Oliva's
expression and understood everything.

I sometimes ask myself if it wasn't some kind of payback for
the group's success, all the things we'd had to renounce or sacrifice. We'd become like big kids who got paid to play, totally
bewildered by all the sales, the fans. Maybe my father was right
when, seeing us burst into laughter at some idiotic joke, he'd
say, 'Enjoy it while it lasts. You'll pay for it someday.'

In that fraction of a second, I went back over the last few
months with Oliva and compared them with the happiest and
most intense times in our relationship: the slightest caress no
longer led inevitably to lovemaking; I didn't consult her about
every little thing; nor did she come to me with her work-related
worries; I no longer came back from late-night gigs in a hurry
just to be with her. I was spying on my own life, just like when
I discovered my adoption papers, trying to figure out who I
was through the behaviour of those around me. Faced with
a chaotic jigsaw puzzle, I was attempting to join together the
pieces that defined me. And what I found tore me apart.

Oliva burst into tears the moment we arrived home, saying,

'That's not it, that's not it,' without trying to explain exactly what it was she did feel for Fran.

I spent the following days consoling her, despite being inconsolable myself. If you haven't lost the one you love while telling them 'Everything's fine, everything's fine,' then you don't know what love is. I tried to retain some of the tenderness that had kept our relationship afloat as it came to its end and didn't worry about Fran, didn't call him, didn't even want to talk to him. What difference does the loss of a friend make when you've lost the one you love? That was my thinking.

I thought about the emptiness of life without Oliva and yet I couldn't adhere to those pathetic codes of possession that in other couples transform heartbreak into open animosity. Heartbreak gave me a sense of value: such was my passion for Oliva that losing her was just another way of loving her, enjoying her. It was a perversion of mine, a secret and unhealthy perversion that gave me a sense of satisfaction even in this most abject unhappiness.

It was another form of liberation. Now, I was just a guy who made songs and who knew that he could coexist with pain as long as he viewed it from the outside, saw it as being someone else's business. What's certain is that it was definitely happening and pretty soon it was all over.

We kissed on the day she left with all of her things and I changed the answerphone message we'd recorded together on that distant day when we'd moved into our flat. I shared the news with my closest friends, trying not to make it sound as monumental as it actually was. 'We're not together any more.' My broken heart made less noise than a smashed vase.

Gus was the first to gather information about her and Fran, after the first few months, during which I quarantined myself like an infectious patient. They went off to Boston together and Gus felt that he was to blame because Fran had come into our life through the guest house owned his aunt Milagros. But there were no hard feelings.

'It doesn't matter,' I told him. 'These things happen.'

I felt like being alone, bringing the story to an end in an orderly, peaceful way, without dressing it up in resentment. It was a kind of sorrowful seclusion. The concerts helped, having to put on a mask and go out onstage to entertain the crowd by singing them love songs, which had now become songs of pain. I was saved by the care shown to me by Gus and also, in his own crude way, by Animal, who'd said, 'Man, there sure are a lot of cunts in the world,' and left it at that.

They tried to get me out of my shell every night, suggesting new projects and saying 'Come on, man, we need to record soon. We need more songs. We're playing in Cartagena tomorrow, then it's Murcia.'

I discovered that friends are never entirely sad about your sorrows because it gives them the most wonderful opportunity to show you how much you matter, how much they care about you, how generous they're prepared to be.

And then I became a singer! Yes, that was when I really became a singer, perhaps because I had nothing else left. When I'd believed myself to be a broken person, when neither the circumstances nor the ideals that had been betrayed mattered much any more, when there were no dreams or fantasies left, the only thing left for me to do was to get up onstage, finish another song and answer the next interview question. No matter how big the hole was, you had to stay above ground: my career had ruined my life, maybe now it could save it, too.

Some people say that the fourth album contains a few of the best songs I've ever written; they were born out of that absence and then added to by Gus, who was on another completely different kind of decline, his fate similarly transformed. Together we wrote 'Lol-li-pops', exactly so, with each syllable spelt out, because Gus insisted it had to be sung like that. Though the song had a happy, upbeat rhythm, it was built upon the ruins of melancholy:

*Like a kid let loose in a sweet shop*
*That's me*
*When life gives you lol-li-pops.*

Cruising along in our van – our romantic VW that let us down on every journey – we'd laugh about our sleepless nights and share anecdotes about loony impresarios, friends who'd lost the plot, what happened at the show, the delusions of some female fan.

*Like a dog eating dirt, like a slob*
*That's me*
*When life gives you lol-li-pops.*

We laughed about the girl who'd slept with Animal the night before, the complete bollocks Gus had spouted to some prissy presenter on a local radio station. The time I tried to smash my electric guitar onstage but couldn't find a way to break it in two no matter how many times I hit it, when I felt like such a fool that I threw it into the crowd and split open the head of a boy from Logroño. It was all about keeping moving, going forwards, stepping on it.

*I ate my sweets up too quick*
*And all I can hope*
*Is that life gives me lol-li-pops.*
*Loads more lol-li-pops.*

It was all about being convinced that it was worth making

just one more song before we surrendered. And we never surrendered.

## 150,000 copies of my abject misery

We sold 150,000 copies of my abject misery in authorised outlets alone. 'Lol-li-pops' became our most famous, most loved, most listened-to, most celebrated song. 'Lol-li-pops' opened up doors into arenas that up until then had been inhabited only by huge groups. It brought us sponsorship from a fizzy drink brand I hated, showering us with levels of income I'd never have imagined people like us attaining.

I was fascinated by the idea that so many people had converted our private sorrows into shared sadness, our private hopes into communal dreams. We were an honest group, when we could easily have limited our goals just to staying solvent. Gus, Animal and I tried to sing about what we felt: losses, hopeful and pointless waiting, loneliness, the humour of survival. Pain acted like an engine for my music: I realised that people outside need to understand that you're talking to them about yourself, so that they can look in the mirror and find you in their reflection.

In a radio interview Gus said something I found really exciting, and he said it with his eyes fixed on me: 'We're the least cynical group in the world. We're transparent.'

We made songs to heal wounds, because we knew of no other medicine: we gave out lollipops because we needed them ourselves.

My father began taking my mother to the countryside, saying the air did her good. He'd sit her among all the bags and fruit crates in the car and drive to the mountains of El Escorial or the pine forests of Peguerinos. He'd walk with her along the footpaths and into the picnic areas. He got the cleaning lady – an evangelical Brazilian who said her country needed less singing and more military dictatorship – to buy her a tracksuit. My father would come to pick up the dog, parking the car on the pavement and ringing the intercom to my flat with his customary lack of restraint.

'Lindo loves walking in the mountains. He's sick of your neighbourhood and your apartment,' he'd say as we watched the dog leap into his car.

Occasionally, I'd accompany them and be entertained by my father's energy: he could throw the same stick for Clon a thousand times and then steal it from between his teeth with an authoritative jerk. All the while he never let go of my mother's arm as he pushed her along, forcing her to keep up with his ridiculous pace. He'd ask me if I was thinking of getting myself another girlfriend – that's how he said it, 'getting yourself another girlfriend' – with the secret hope, I think, that it would get Oliva out of my head. But Oliva wasn't going anywhere.

Once she was living in the United States she'd call me on my birthday without fail and also at Christmas if she was coming home to see her brothers; when mobile phones entered our lives, we swapped the painful timbre of her voice for an affectionate exchange of text messages. She never said Fran's name and I never asked about him. For all I knew he could have been hit by a train in Boston. I still didn't know that losing an enemy was far easier than losing a friend.

I went along to one of Eva's photo shoots with Gus. He wanted to convince me that the photographer was perfect for our fourth album cover, saying that I had to meet him. He was an excitable, over-the-top young guy, who pronounced the word England as *In-ger-land*, in a self-mocking and rather winning way. For Gus it was the perfect excuse to spend a day with Eva, who changed her clothes almost fifty times, not in the slightest bit bothered that we could see her body. It was skinny and scrawny but with tits that had been touched up in order to maintain that weightlessness we could admire when another T-shirt was put over her, or when she leapt onto a satin bedspread. Everything looked good on that clothes hanger of a body.

She chain-smoked, coquettishly, really just letting the cigarettes consume themselves between her fingers. Like Gus, she accepted every invitation to do coke from the photographer, the people from the magazine, and a whole host of salespeople and employees who swarmed around the place pretending to give advice or say something intelligent.

Wherever we went we'd see a half-naked Eva in advertising campaigns at bus stops or in magazines; they might have been advertising lingerie, a department store or a perfume. In Gijón, Gus kissed one of her posters in a phone box and some guy going past in car shouted 'Drunk!' at him, to which Gus replied, 'What do you know? She's my girlfriend!'

'So what have you got in mind for the *alabum* cover?' the photographer asked in a break at Eva's session.

We still didn't have a release date for the record and we wanted to call it *Weekday Diving Suit*, an image from a song that we liked, but the label, showing sounder judgement, made us agree to *Lol-li-pops*. Then the photographer came up with an idea. The three of us would have our backs turned, with only our necks visible, and we'd all be offering a light to a stunning woman with a cigarette in her mouth.

'I'll do it,' said Eva, excitedly. 'Can I be the girl?'

The instant she came on board, Gus, who hadn't been all that keen on it up to that point, thought it was a wonderful idea.

In the end, we decided we wouldn't be giving the girl a light. Instead, each of us would be handing her a lollipop.

An enthused Bocanegra kept saying that 'Each song on the album is a different lollipop and mark my words, lads, they'll stick to your teeth.'

I'll never forget Gus at the photo shoot for that album cover. At one point the photographer left his camera on the studio floor and came towards us as we posed against a white background.

'Lift your *cheeyin* up,' he said and raised Gus's jaw until it was in the perfect position with the light.

Gus mentioned to me that this had been a lifelong dream. And it was. He liked all things artificial, tacky even, anything that didn't resemble his repressed childhood; at times he even gave me the feeling that there was something ancient in his excessive desire to be modern.

Gus knew all of Eva's secrets and he once told me he'd accompanied her to get an abortion after a Dutch model had got her pregnant. The night we did a playthrough of the album for the media, she acted both as our godmother and our cover girl. The two of us were left alone for a moment as we were being served cocktails and I took the chance to talk to her.

'I don't think you'll find anyone in the world who loves you more than Gus,' I told her.

She showed me her splendid set of teeth and tucked one lock of her straight hair behind her ear.

'You bet. I think the same about him. He's magical.'

Gus had insisted we record our own version of Spinetta's 'Muchacha Ojos de Papel', so that we could dedicate it to her. He explained that he sang it to her some nights, like a lullaby. So they were sleeping together? In fact, it seemed that Eva called him sometimes when she was desperate and downcast, and that he would sing to her over the phone.

'Eva's not well,' Gus told me. 'She's surrounded by people, but deep down she's very lonely.'

That's why he'd sang to her:

*Girl with the paper eyes*
*Where are you going? Stay until dawn.*

## where are you going? stay until dawn

I think I was wrong to confuse Gus's fascination with Eva with something like fireworks. Gus engaged in more sexual activity with men than with women, so Eva couldn't have been more than an impulse, essentially aesthetic in nature; and likewise for her he was just a pet to snuggle up to in lonely moments. But imagining him next to her, in the urgency of those desolate nights, coming to her rescue to sing her tender lullabies, made me confuse his fits of madness with love.

There was something dangerous in Eva's beauty, her fragile jumpiness. She was the perfect example of a model who satisfies a commercial sexuality, one that insists you be both boy and girl at once. Gus enjoyed that gleaming, sparkling world, but my own ambitions had vanished after losing Oliva. I didn't want to admit it, but success suddenly made me uncomfortable. It felt insignificant, like an outer layer of clothing. I didn't want to be owned by the public, and Gus and I were engaged in an endless struggle not to repeat ourselves, to give each song brushstrokes that were free, anti-commercial and subversive.

Our desires ran counter to those of our fans. That was why I never reprimanded Gus for the disdainful way he used to grab his crotch before the crowd's applause, or call all our cheering spectators bastards. 'Goodnight, you bastards.' We didn't want devotion. We wanted to be free, hold the reins, be ourselves. As is always the case, this desire forced us to detest those who were most like us and we struggled to mix with other like-minded groups. It forced us to be uncomfortable, forever unsatisfied.

'And then you became forever future,' I wrote in a song about Gus. Because I remembered him always looking ahead, never to the past, maybe because of how much he'd struggled to get where he did, to be the way he was. Gus was always an optimist. In moments of anguish, of doubt, of not knowing which direction to go with our music, he'd always put his foot down.

'What matters is tomorrow.'

You had to think about the next concert, the next song. You had to make something that was the opposite of a museum, where everything is ordered and dated, and time has come to a halt. Gus's favourite move was the jump. He liked to do it in photos.

'Let's do it jumping,' he'd suggest.

Happiness for him was that moment when you're suspended in the air. Not the initial impulse, full of good intentions, or the landing, a lead weight of frustration: he wanted to be flight, perpetual motion, weightlessness. Gus loved photos that captured movement. He drove photographers to despair, always jumping the moment he saw them click. He was restless and intense, and no one could stop him.

That's why I turned down every tribute concert I was offered after he died, despite the fact that during the days of national mourning, his death resonated in a way he'd have loved. It made the TV news and several newspaper headlines: they all spoke of a life of excess, a problematic personality and many addictions. Several rather sordid stories came out, sinister obituaries that were embellished to make sense of a suicide that wasn't a suicide. Even The Champ jumped on the bandwagon, with a media appearance in which he assured people that he'd foreseen Gus's premature death just from looking at his face.

'When I discovered him, he reminded me of James Dean,' he blurted out shamelessly in one interview. 'You know, live fast and leave a pretty corpse.'

Through it all, I felt sick. I realised that when confronted with the premature death of someone they know, people always have to find some meaning in order to soothe their own perturbed spirit: 'Well, I always said it would happen'; 'It was inevitable'; 'I warned him'. Death has to submit to logic so that the living can rest easy, to keep them from stumbling upon the truth, that nothing is logical.

'Today you're alive, tomorrow you're dead,' Gus once said to the priest we called Niebla in the middle of an RE class. 'Explain to me how we're meant to live with that and not believe that God is a sadist?'

No explanation satisfied him.

'You know what I think, sir? Religion is wrong, heaven is this right here, being here now, in this moment.'

*Now*, that word he'd used so many times since he'd decided as a young child to live life to the full – and it always came across in his lyrics, that deep commitment to always appreciating the gift of life.

I was never convinced by the official version of Gus's death. But for Animal and Martán, our new bassist, my denial stemmed from nothing more than frustration.

'It will pass. You have to accept it,' said Bocanegra.

He took me to dinner to cheer me up and to try to find out what the future of the group looked like without Gus.

'There *is* no group,' I told him. 'Without Gus, there is no group.'

'Don't be silly. Think about it.'

But how would Las Moscas fly without Gus? Where to, where from? To comply with the cliche, the label released a greatest hits album, a selection of the best songs from the four albums, together with some rarities, demos and live recordings. It sold well. No one can deny that death is great publicity. But that only lasts a few weeks and then comes the void.

'Death is a con,' Gus often said.

It was a still photo, the thing he hated most in the world.

Gus died in the entrance hall of an apartment block on Calle Orellana, near Alonso Martínez. According to the police, he'd been taken there by someone whose identity would never be discovered. He'd lost a shoe along the way. Logic led them to believe he'd visited a nearby house or somewhere in the area where drugs were being sold and that perhaps a mixture of various substances had caused his cardiorespiratory arrest at around five in the morning. Pills, amphetamines and alcohol.

I asked the police officer leading the investigation if he believed it was an accidental death or a suicide.

'That I cannot say,' he replied.

When the report came out there was nothing to suggest a huge consumption, a voluntary self-poisoning, but by then it was almost a month after his death and no one was interested in refuting the story of another musician dying from an overdose. The death of Kurt Cobain a year earlier had brought the idea back into people's minds. In music, if you die young you're only fulfilling your own legend. I fought against this dumb, predictable version of events, which denied Gus's real personality, but you can't fight against myths. It's not a battle worth wasting your energy on.

Early one evening, still deeply upset by Gus's death, I walked over to those streets. I sneaked into the building where he'd died and waited for night to fall. I sat down near the exact place they'd found him, in the gloom under the stairs, near the gas and electricity meters. Anyone entering the building wouldn't have been able to see me. The police had questioned the residents but no one had seen or heard anything, and there was no evidence to suggest that they were lying or hiding something.

I looked at the names on the mailboxes. Where had they carried him from at five in the morning? A local venue, the street, a nearby flat? Where had he lost his shoe? The police weren't all that concerned with finding out. What more could you do? It was obvious no one had forced him to take those drugs.

I stood there for a while, leaning against the wall, facing the building's elegant facade. I watched people go by. There were still some flowers there, propped up against the wall by some of our biggest fans on the day after his death. Some passing boys kicked them out of the way. Gus would have done the same.

It was a dirty death that didn't fit him. I'd seen him taking drugs and, while it was a habit, it had always been done in moderation, without affecting the group and only when he was enjoying himself with his other friends. He wasn't an addict. Everyone close to Gus thought I'd taken my eye off him, let him fly too far, stopped worrying about him.

'He was your friend and you didn't know what he was involved in? Some friend you turned out to be,' was my father's verdict.

I didn't reply.

At the funeral home his mother took my hands and said, without taking her eyes off me, 'Gus loved you so much, the poor thing. He wasn't like you, he didn't know . . .'

She didn't finish her sentence. Didn't know? What did I know that he didn't? I thought for a long time about what his mother had said. He knew how to live, but perhaps I was more skilled in the art of survival.

I also saw Eva that day. She hugged me with her needle-like body, lovely even when crying inconsolably.

'We'd seen each other a few days earlier,' she told me between sobs.

I hadn't seen him in almost four days. We would have been going to play in Seville and Córdoba the following week, where we'd have talked about new songs, laughed together. Then after dinner we'd have gone our separate ways to catch up with our contacts in each city.

I looked at Eva as she walked away. The wind was blowing her hair in every direction and one of her companions placed her jacket over her shoulders. She looked like a worn-out aristocrat. Gus would have loved it.

Oliva had called me from Boston. We spoke on the phone; she felt sad for me.

'Do you need anything?'

I told her no, I didn't need anything. I still couldn't grasp that I was going to need a whole lifetime to get on with reconstruction, with rebuilding the columns that had once held me up.

'Will you do any kind of memorial for him?' she asked. 'Let me know if you do.'

I imagined a reunion of old friends, colleagues and former loves, all coming together to pay tribute to the deceased. Is there anything Gus would have hated more? What was the past now, when he was all future?

# SIDE B

## my father's village

My father's village spreads out from the edge of the main road. You take a hard turn to come off it, then you hit the course of the stream. Everything was born in that muddy pool, among the reeds. I'm sure it was inhabited by mosquitoes before any humans lived there and then later by flies. As a child I remember there being pesky, frantic flies on the tablecloths in every house I visited; I went after them in my spare time, squashing them under my palm, and sometimes I'd watch one drowning in the cream of the milk before someone removed it with their finger to have a glass.

I pointed out the sign for Garrafal de Campos to Jairo, with the rock symbol on the board, and then the main avenue, which was the Calle de las Escuelas; although to say the words 'avenue' and 'main' was to exaggerate grossly the actual size of the village. I didn't recall the trees planted along the pavement, or the allotments filled with sunflowers, but it had been so long since I'd last been here that everything was a surprise to me, including a few houses that had been refurbished, with bricks in the place of the original adobe. They'd also tarmacked the road, which used to throw up clouds of red dust whenever a car came around the bend.

The voice on the satnav announced confidently that we'd reached our destination, but the way it said it – 'You have reached your destination' – sounded more like an omen. I don't usually take notes, because I only believe in the ideas I don't forget, but I think that 'You Have Reached Your Destination' could be a good song title.

And then we were surrounded by people. An enormous man dressed in a beige suit and a bright red tie stepped in front of the car, and the driver braked to avoid running him over. He was wielding an ornate ceremonial mace; it looked like a toothpick in his enormous hands.

'You don't recognise me, do you?' The man who'd opened the door was now questioning me, his face a hair's breadth from my eyes. 'I'll give you a clue. We were great friends as kids . . . It's Jandrón. Remember?'

Jandrón was now the mayor. He'd turned into a respectable version of the boy I'd known all those years ago, back when we used to show each other our dicks. He was wearing an official-looking sash across his chest, but rather than giving him an air of authority, it made him look like a chicken wrapped in cling film on special offer at the supermarket.

Without asking, he grabbed me by the arm, pulled me out of the car and plunged me into reality. He crushed me into a massive hug and I remembered how he could bend horseshoes with his hands even as a child; though time had been cruel to both of us, something of that brute strength endured. Behind him came other people, mostly effusive older ladies, who gave me wet kisses on the cheek. I recognised some of their faces, like Aunt Dorina's, while others were vaguely familiar because most of them shared my father's nose – my nose, that is – as if they'd made a cast and handed out copies during a masked ball.

The joints in my hand, which suffer from the arthritis I've inherited from my father, were squeezed enthusiastically by the village's complete electoral register. The old ladies shouted things like 'don't you remember me?'; 'don't you remember who I am?'; 'you're the spitting image of your father – you have the same nose'. Another added, 'And the same eye colour,' as she whipped my sunglasses off with her hand. 'There's a lot of the mother in him, too.' And the different verdicts kept coming: 'You look younger on the telly'; 'on the telly you look taller'; 'you don't look like you do on the telly'.

Eventually the mayor imposed some order.

'Can't you see he's tired after his journey? Now come on into my living room.'

He led me to the gate of an old barn that had been painstakingly done up and featured the worst excesses of Spanish traditional construction: exposed bricks, an array of materials, imitation aluminium doors and window frames, terrazzo floors.

'What would you like to drink? We've got Coke, Fanta, Aquarius, everything.'

'Would you have a sparkling water, by any chance?'

'Hmm, no, we haven't got sparkling water,' he said apologetically.

We could hear the sharp tones of a woman's voice behind us: 'I knew it, these artists are all divas.'

Jandrón introduced me.

'This is my wife. I'm sure you remember Luci.'

And there she was, Luci. Still strong and robust, she wore glasses now but behind them were the same eyes she'd had as a child, always ready to challenge you. I brushed up against her breasts as she kissed me on both cheeks and I remembered the time she refused to show me her tits because she said I was a city boy who looked down on country people.

### allow me to introduce the musicians playing with me tonight

Allow me to introduce the musicians playing with me tonight. On bass, Martán, from Paris, 12th arrondissement, Ledru-Rollin metro station, met thanks to an interrail journey that brought him to Spain dehydrated and broken. My father had picked him up at a petrol station on Cuesta de las Perdices and offered him a room for a few days: 'I have a son like you who doesn't live with me any more.' It wasn't unusual for my father to take in people he'd just met. He liked to brag about his acts of kindness. 'Everything you give comes back to you.'

I met Martán one afternoon when dropping by to collect Lindo Clon, after a trip to New Orleans with Animal in the days when Gus was busy filming his TV series. Martán and I chatted for while in short broken sentences interspersed with English.

'Just broke up with my girlfriend,' I told him. 'Six years – boom – all to shit,' I said, miming a summary of the catastrophe with my fingers. '*À la merde.*'

'I'm sorry, *desolé*,' he replied.

I nodded, 'Yes, desolation.'

Perhaps that word came from the idea of having *sol* taken away: no sun, in the dark. Desolation, *desolé*, the opposite of the Spanish *olé!* – a state of no *olé!* No Spain, no fiestas, no bulls, no sun, no *sol*. My head was like a factory pumping out these absurd thoughts 24/7, which Martán listened to without understanding a word.

'Your father told me you're a musician.' He didn't actually say father, but farzer. Your farzer. '*Moi, je joue aussi, la basse electrique.*'

'Bass?'

We talked about music. He liked jazz.

'You know what they say?' he said, shrugging his shoulders bashfully. 'Ze jazz musicians enjoy playing much more than ze audience enjoys watching them play.'

Martán hadn't showered for ten days when my father picked him up. According to my father, his feet smelt so bad it scared away the ants. He'd showered the moment he'd got to the house, but it had been a short one, interrupted by my father's pounding at the door.

'Ah! That's because he doesn't like wasting water,' I explained.

My father took him to the Valley of the Fallen, Franco's tomb, his favourite monument in the region.

'Do you have anything this nice in Paris?' he'd asked.

He bought Martán a journal to note down his Spanish proverbs. My father loved popular sayings; it was a legacy of his rural childhood and he had one for every kind of situation. Proverbs are always ambiguous – one always entails its exact opposite – which is precisely what popular wisdom consists of: never being wrong.

Martán helped me to learn to live without Oliva. It did me good to talk to someone who hadn't known her, who didn't associate me with her. Gus felt that Martán – handsome and blond with bright eyes – would bring a touch of class to our group and insisted we give him a trial. That's how we discovered that he played better than all of us. Animal's sense of hospitality went into overdrive and within three days it was like he and Martán had known each other their whole lives.

When he later proved to be a magnet for attracting girls, Animal came to think of him as the best possible worm to go fishing with. 'Every hook needs a good worm,' he'd explain. Martán would repeat the proverbs my father had taught him, but riddled with hilarious mistakes, and had already heard my father cite Napoleon several times as he carried on disparaging our music.

Music for Martán wasn't something he'd ever planned on doing professionally. He was about to go and work for his father's company and the trip to Spain was his last taste of freedom, a freedom he'd used up going from beach to beach, living off a diet of churros and wine. After coming to a few practice sessions and familiarising himself with our songs, we invited him to join the group and the time came for him to make the most significant decision of his life. Go home or stay with us.

He became my friend exactly when I needed a new one the most. Shortly after we met he invited me to go to Paris with him. 'You need to get away,' he said. And he was right. He invited me to stay in his house and in the end I spent nearly a month there with him. I think I fell in love a good few times during that trip, though really I was still in love with someone who was no longer with me, which got me a ticking off from two Parisiennes.

The women of Paris give tickings-off like they've been practising their whole lives – it comes naturally to them. The first one was called Agnès and I liked everything about her, starting with her name. She'd been Martán's girlfriend when they were fourteen. 'She'll take your sorrows away,' Martán told me. But it wasn't so. My sorrows lingered in spite of her caresses.

I got involved with the second Parisienne because she was the granddaughter of Spanish republicans and she harboured a fantasy of coming to Spain with me.

'No, Anne, I need some time.'

She called me a coward, and she was right. She called me everything under the sun and she was almost always right.

'You'll never get Oliva out of your head,' she told me, 'because you don't want her out of your head.'

No, I didn't; why would I? Oliva was getting along just fine in my head. I told myself to stay away from broken hearts. Broken hearts are like bits of broken glass – they hurt when you tread on them by accident.

Martán became the bassist in Las Moscas just as were putting together our fourth album, our last album, our legendary album. I learnt about music from Martán, and ever since that first trip to Paris with him the records of John Coltrane and Miles Davis have been just as important as those of Trénet, Léo Ferré, Barbara and Françoise Hardy.

I still remember Gus's surprise when I told him about Henri

Salvador. 'That's how it's done,' he commented, reassured that someone could grow old like that. Martán remembers how I used to sing that song, 'La Folle Complainte', out loud, insisting on telling anyone who'd listen that this tune, about the dust resting on the furniture in an old mansion, was the best song ever written. I'll never be able to thank my father enough for his overflowing sense of hospitality, which brought me a new friend for life.

And on the drums, Animal. Animal is my heartbeat, always behind me, always keeping time. A percussive heart, fanatical and faithful: nothing about Animal has ever been orderly or predictable. He's my pillar, the spinal column of my music, the scaffolding supporting the story of my life, the story of my songs.

My songs only ever took off with his thunderous clobbering, even though they'd been composed alone with only a guitar. And yet, I've never thanked him, because he's not the sort to show or to seek gratitude. Forever onwards. Incapable of organising his own life the way he keeps mine together, he's been knocked down time and time again but has always got back up, content to eat the leftovers from other people's dinner, devouring it in his own feral way.

Of all my friends, he's the most damaged and the wisest. He's my favourite fuck-up, yet he possesses the nobility of a knight-at-arms. How many times can a person smash their head open? He alone has received all the stitches a band needs, so many that there's no way it can come apart now. He always believed in us more than we did. Walking onto the stage, I hear him pounding the kit. I step forwards, put my guitar around my neck, turn slightly towards him and then, yes, I'm ready. Let's go.

Sometimes Animal has these fits, these sudden revelations. They're like speeches that flow from his mouth uncut, un-edited, the precise moment they come to him. They're almost like epiphanies. Suddenly, he'll go all incandescent, turn off the music in the van and say something like: 'All of us must be against matrimony, against patrimony, against patriotism, for they are the enemies of freedom. The only institution a man should respect is fraternity, because fraternity comes from generosity. But the family, the family is all about possession, protection, division.' He'd go on like that, with all of us listening.

One day he told us that the only possible title for any song is 'Life Goes On'.

'All songs should be called that, because it's the only possible title: "Life Goes On". Even the Bible should just be called "Life Goes On".'

One day, on noticing the depths of my sorrow and despair after Gus's death, he gripped me firmly by the shoulders and told me, 'We all have to die, it's our duty. If we didn't die it would be horrible; we'd have to kill each other. Dying is our only hope. Dying is the meaning of life, Dani, and don't you forget it.'

My favourite revelation is the one we call Animal's Great Sexual Revelation and I'm transcribing it almost verbatim, the way he expressed it to Martán and me after a soundcheck as we shared a few beers during the febrile half an hour before going onstage at the University of Granada, where we were playing as part of the spring fiestas.

## Animal's great sexual revelation

Suddenly, lads, I understood everything. The male orgasm is an external celebration. Like the genitals themselves, which have been added on to the outside, our satisfaction is social, visible, public and not at all intimate: it's an expulsion of pleasure and liquids. This makes us entirely predictable: even our excitement is visible, externalised. And that dictates our relationships, because a man gets his satisfaction on the outside and not on the inside. Therefore, men are a sexual spectacle, like fireworks.

The best way we have of showing a woman our appreciation is by blowing our load, proving to her that we're in good working order. The male orgasm is a village fiesta, it's a carnival, it's an amusement park, a public square in summer, and if we men are promiscuous it's only because any given day is a perfect day for throwing a party. You must fuck, always. So here I am, with a truckload of fireworks, ready to start a party wherever people need me. So speaks Animal.

## ugly things about me

I find ugly things about me on the Web whenever I sit down to trawl through it. There are good things too, I know, but they don't have the same effect on me, because the bad things are so much more effective, so much more believable than the good things. And bile finds very cutting ways of expressing itself, whereas praise is by nature discreet, measured, intimate. Otherwise it's little more than hagiography.

Sometimes the Internet's infinite magma provokes the same feelings in me that I had as a child, when I lived in a cul-de-sac and felt physically trapped. Whenever I find an old clip of us playing an early song there's always one commenter asking what album the tune is from, and then there's another answering what does it matter if the song is a piece of shit and the guy has an arse for a face. That's how it works.

One day I was watching videos of Nina Simone concerts and noticed there were a gazillion likes and only four dislikes. And I thought about the kind of people who'd put a dislike on her immortal memory. Who are those guys? Where do they come from? Why are they so full of hate?

Once, a young girl stopped me on the street as I came out of the metro. She had a small rucksack hanging off her back. She told me she really liked my songs, really enjoyed them. We shared a moment, one of us going up the stairs, the other going down, and I loved the intimacy of one person who makes songs and another who listens to them. If this meeting had happened on the Internet, someone would have felt the need to share their opinion, to insult her, to pick her words apart. 'Well I don't like it,' they'd have told her. No, anything that's too big is ugly. You never have a good meal at a wedding or at a table for forty: if you want to eat well, you sit down at a small table.

## ain't no place like away from home

'Ain't no place like away from home,' is something this decrepit actor used to say who I knew from countless jazz concerts. The chap in question had a bushy moustache and a voice that could be heard anywhere in the room, even when he was whispering. Everybody called him by his surname, Gamero, and at the end of his life he walked with crutches because he'd had to have three of his toes removed. Apparently, the surgeon had come to say hello the day after the operation and to warn him that alcohol had been a big factor in his illness. The actor replied, 'Alcohol? Impossible! Why, I haven't had a drop in nearly a week.'

It was thanks to Martán that I began to attend jazz concerts and festivals. Martán and Nacho. Nacho joined us at our shows on tenor sax when he was free and when we recorded he organised the brass arrangements, which always made me feel like a real musician. He loved playing – any excuse – and he was just as happy accompanying people making jazz, rock or *canción melódica*, with scant concern for anything other than his appearance fee and staying busy, busy, busy. His tour was a never-ending one. 'Ain't no place like away from home,' I kept saying to myself.

Nacho had a wife and two kids but he only saw them between shows. It seemed to me that he was living in a permanent state of flight.

'How so?' he asked me.

'I don't know, no one likes travelling that much. I'm sure that deep down you must be running from something.'

'We're all running away from something, always. But to come up with a decent excuse, we musicians invented touring.'

I recognised myself in Nacho when I released my first solo album after Gus's death: I, too, began playing everywhere, heading off after each performance to some other place I'd then leave the following day. It wasn't so much a case of not being at home as not *having* a home.

But after visiting every city in the country three times, with their three-star hotels and their sad train stations and their venues with terrible sound, there was no longer any sense of mystery or freedom. It was all so predictable and disheartening, and it was summed up eloquently by the graffiti we saw on the brick wall opposite the train station in Albacete, which made reference to the popular saying about that city which we'd translated many times for Martán: Shit, and get out. On that station wall, in enormous letters, someone had written: Don't even shit.


## we're all about the pitcher in these parts

'We're all about the pitcher in these parts,' shouted one of the women who'd joined the group of experts surrounding

225

Jandrón. 'Here, take it, if you don't mind drinking straight from the pitcher.'

'Sure, sure,' I accepted.

Within a second I'd already stained the front of my shirt while raising the clay jug, forgetting that you were meant to fold your arm and fill your mouth in a single action. I could hear the unrelenting voice of Jairo, who'd struck up conversation with an elderly besuited man and was saying, 'Yep, I'm the hearse driver and, to tell the truth, Daniel and I have had lots of time during the journey to get to know each other well. He's told me all about the village and his father. Really, you've no idea how much clients open up when you let them just talk. That's the thing about my profession, you see. More than anything it's about knowing how to listen.'

'Now, let me tell you the order of service,' Jandrón informed me, 'because it's time for me to fulfil my mayoral duties. Don't worry, mayor here is a non-political role: they choose me because I'm the only one who ever stands.

'Right, the most urgent thing now is to bury your father and then there will be time for celebrating. The funeral stuff comes first. Was the journey OK?' he asked, turning to Jairo as if he were a tourist guide.

'The three of us got here without any incidents,' he confirmed.

'The three of you? Did someone else come along as well?'

'I was referring to the deceased,' Jairo clarified.

Jandrón began speaking again.

'I put the ceremony back by an hour in case of any imponderables, but that's fine. We can just have a bit of refection in here and wait inside so that people don't bother you. You see, they're all so excited, what with a celebrity arriving, despite the lachrymosity of the circumstances that have brought you here. As a matter of fact, I was just thinking how you haven't been to these parts for perhaps more than twenty years now . . .'

Jandrón's enthusiasm, his exhaustive bank of information, the magniloquent mayor's vocabulary choices − Imponderables? Refection? Lachrymosity? − his referring to me as a celebrity: they were all terrifying hints of what awaited me. I made up my mind many years ago not to try to resist total dullards. It's very common to arrive in a city or town and be received by local promoters, city councillors or the fan who arranged the gig. Many of them are friendly, discreet and sensitive people, but a good bunch of them can also be tactless, fawning and intrusive. It's pointless to fight them: the moment you decide that the person in question can do what they please with you and that you won't resist any of your host's whims or foibles is the moment you begin to discover surprising things about them. Everyone has a story, everyone has their own personal adventure.

Animal always asks me why I bother starting conversations with all the tedious people we meet on tours and my answer is that I don't start conversations, I simply direct them. I ask the person about their life, their background, their family history, what they're into. It's not a sign of generosity, it's a survival tool: in our business − as my father used to say when describing his profession − we have to listen to stories as well, because we want to tell them ourselves, reach those people with our songs. I'm not sure if you can inherit that willingness to listen to others, but I know for sure it has its uses.

The local ladies kept peering in through the grated window, along with a kid who asked, openly sceptical, if it was really true that I'd been on TV.

'I didn't realise so many people lived here,' I said, not attempting to dress it up as praise.

But Jandrón seemed delighted.

'They're here for the party, man. You already know that our biggest celebration coincides with the feast day of Spain's patron saint. There are only four oldies and two Romanian labourers who actually live here, but everyone comes back for the festival.

'People from the village are very attached to their roots; Garrafal makes you love it, it ensnares you. I live in Salamanca myself; I teach at the business school there. The mayor thing I only do out of love for the village.'

'So you're saying the fiesta's happening right now?' I asked.

'Of course! That's why we agreed this date for your father's thing, so that the two would coincide and you could be our guest star. It's so nice to have a famous person like you here, especially when you're also a son of this very soil. And even though I'm sure your head is always in a thousand places at once, you never forgot about your origins, did you, and you've chosen to do a wonderful thing by bringing your father's bones here so they can rest in the same clay that witnessed his birth. Maybe you'd even like to be buried here yourself. That would be a great honour for us.'

He turned to take a look around the tiny living room and for a moment I thought he was going to order those present to bury me alive right there and then.

Jandrón didn't take a single breath while he talked. He must have considered breathing a luxury one can't afford when there's so much to say. He offered Jairo a drink.

'He's spent the whole journey telling me about the village. Of course, you never forget the place you grew up.'

'No, no, this isn't where I grew up; it's my father's village, not mine. I only ever came to—'

'Sure, but remember the summers we spent here together,' Jandrón countered, slapping me on the back in a way that was meant to be affectionate but felt more like the first punch thrown in a fight.

He then introduced me to the councillor for festivities, the

228

suited man who'd struck up conversation with my driver and whose mournful face was contained within the quotation marks of his eyebrows. The councillor, in turn, introduced me to his wife, whose face and body language didn't suggest any kind of festivity whatsoever; when she spoke, her voice sounded exactly like a crane and for a moment it felt as if we were in the Doñana National Park.

I wanted to tell her that in Japan the crane is a symbol of good luck, but just at that moment Jandrón made me turn round again so that he could introduce his children, two boys whose faces were the spitting image of their father's during that summer I spent with him. Luci shoved the boys in my direction to kiss me on the cheeks, then took a step back to observe me closely.

'You're as thin as a rake. All that Japanese food, I suppose,' she said, to general laughter. 'You didn't bring your kids? Your father showed me a photo of them, but that was ages ago. They must be almost as big as these ones, no?' And she pointed to her two sons, who stood there in silence, showing those faces they'd been loaned by their father.

'Mine are a little bit smaller,' I said, 'in every sense.'

I remember the photo of my children that my father used to carry in his wallet. I'd given him a copy, but Kei had actually taken the picture of the two of them, lying on the ground, their hands on their cheeks.

'All of us in the village have been closely following your career,' Luci continued, 'and you haven't once mentioned this place since you became famous.'

Actually, I stopped mentioning it long before I became famous, I nearly corrected her. People often attribute certain character traits to fame. When they say fame has made someone more self-absorbed, more selfish, more miserable, they're forgetting that the guy in question was already self-absorbed, selfish and miserable, and that fame has merely given him permission to act that way without fear of reprisal.

'And what about your Japanese wife? You've never brought her here, either. What's the matter, are you ashamed of us?'

'Actually, I did bring her here once, when I played in Palencia several years back. It was winter and we passed through the village in the van. But I didn't want to bother anyone.'

'Ah! we almost never come in winter,' she explained.

'But if you're in Salamanca, let us know; we'd be delighted to put you up and show you around,' Jandrón suggested.

'Anyway, am I right in saying you've separated?' his wife added. 'I read about it in a magazine.'

'Well actually, we never got married.'

'You don't think having two kids counts as marriage?' Luci argued. 'Honestly, the things you hear these days.'

'So, is this where Granddad used to live?' Kei had asked as we passed through the village without stopping. That's how she used to refer to my father: Granddad.

'Yes, until the war broke out. He's been in Madrid ever since,' I explained.

Kei took a few photos through the window of the van – the church, the adobe houses, the former school, now in ruins – and later she showed them to the kids.

'Doesn't anyone live there?' Maya asked.

'There are very few people left now,' Kei answered. 'And I didn't meet any of them because your father didn't want to stop to say hello.'


*being alone*

It's hard work being alone. In Japan I remember the long walks, the unfamiliar faces, not knowing anyone, the feeling of being uprooted, how at the beginning entire days would pass without me uttering a word to anyone. Not knowing how to read signs or the small print in the papers, being an extraterrestrial on your own planet. I remember learning the numbers from a calendar and the overwhelming logic behind the figures they use to represent them. One is a horizontal line, *ichi*, and they expand from there. Learning how to read, how to speak, being nobody; erasing yourself and starting again from zero.

Japan. What took me to Japan? Perhaps it was another kind of escape. One I neither planned nor recognised as such. After Gus's death I struggled to decide how I was going to continue making music. Without him, the group lacked any meaning and it was impossible to imagine playing our repertoire without both of us.

'There is no group,' I told Martán and Animal. 'Without Gus, there is no group.'

Also, we didn't want to exploit our national tendency towards necrophilia. We're a country that's better at burying people than it is at allowing them to live: I felt an angry pain when I became aware of all the praise being showered on Gus for the simple virtue of being dead. Just as in the world of art dealing, this fact raised his worth significantly.

I cut myself off from everything, and Animal and Martán began playing with other bands. Occasionally we'd get together to perform, dust off our back catalogue; the songs took on an air of nostalgia, which is perhaps what made me reject them. I was repelled by our generation's fetishistic, kitschy, premature infatuation with the past, and I hated it when people came up to me and said things like, 'Remember the time . . .?' or 'I saw you at your first show.' I've seen venues packed full of people all there to witness the reunion of a group that broke up years ago, the very same venues the group had never been able to fill when they'd been active the first time round.

I began writing again and found myself alone, playing the guitar in order to enjoy once more the pleasure of lifting a song out of nothingness. I decided to become Daniel Mosca, a name that simultaneously recalled the group and also acted as a declaration of independence. I didn't want to sing with my own name: a family name is for gas bills, not for the stage.

One day I realised that I'd nearly completed an album. I'd never worked like that. Holed away in Ramón's studio, we'd begin with an idea then develop it. As I taught myself to operate the mixing desk, I did one song after another, with no particular connection, without showing them to anyone. Together, they all gained a strange sense of continuity, with interlinked characters, an air of operetta about them.

To everybody's surprise, when it came out people found that it was overflowing with humour – too much humour, according to some, for a person who was meant to be in mourning. A bold dose of the stuff, with uncomfortable results. Because humour is taken to be less direct, less profound, and just when people were likely expecting the melancholy and despair of someone who's lost their partner in crime, I gave them the opposite. Perhaps nobody realised that humour was an act of revenge against sadness.

I was in a such a bad way that everything I wrote was comical. That's how 'Four Days' was born. Animal and Martán joined us to record the backing tracks, which meant we did play together again, though not as the group. Their friendship, care and full participation all reflected well on the songs; the choruses became something revitalising, gaining a raw, energetic sound, like a funeral where everyone suffers from fits of giggles. Perhaps it was the funeral we were unable to give Gus.

## *the art of not doing what's expected*

The art of not doing what's expected demands the precision of a surgeon and the determination of a madman. It was obvious this wasn't the album the people at the label were expecting. The demo was quite advanced: we'd already recorded Animal and Martán's parts, as well as those of a few other musicians who'd come along to help with that first coat of paint. Among them was Nacho, who'd added in a brass section consisting of a group of Cuban boys, recent arrivals amid the waves of exiles. They sounded glorious.

The label didn't like the record. I knew it from the first words Bocanegra uttered.

'I like it, I really like it, but we're going to have to think long and hard about how we're going to sell it.'

That's the music world for you – everything they say means something different. And when Bocanegra said, 'I don't know if people will understand,' what he meant was that *he* didn't understand.

'What you gotta do,' he tried to convince me a few days after, 'is reactivate the group. Don't throw away everything you've achieved.'

From his perspective, it made no sense to start again with a whole new brand. But the discussion lasted barely a second.

'We can't be what we were with Gus without Gus.'

The top honchos at the label thought I was trying to be difficult, but Las Moscas had simply ceased to exist. When they listened to the album again they found another cause for concern: there was a potentially controversial song mocking the Catholic Church, which I wasn't prepared to sacrifice. Bocanegra tried to dissuade me with one of his usual diagnoses.

'Surely you don't want to become a singer-songwriter?'

He said it with the same disdain he'd have used if I'd decided to record an album of boleros or take part in Eurovision. I knew he wouldn't dare to kick me off the label at such a delicate moment, so I asked them to give me two albums, two experiments, assuring them that, with a good producer and the ideas and sounds I had in my head, they'd get something full of noise and atmosphere, something they could sell.

We took our time making it. I wasn't in a hurry, not with this repertoire of songs all based around different narratives and characters, brain-dead morons, street-dwelling losers and helpless souls straight out of some kind of roguish zarzuela. One song was called 'A Maths Teacher Forgets How to Add' and I think it's the first song in the history of music to be dedicated to a maths teacher, in love and completely defeated.

We made the band sound less rock guitar and more festival orchestra. The producer came from London, a luxury the label coughed up for because they preferred to have someone with an international name doing it rather than Ramón. It was the producer's idea to base the instrumentation on the music of the Balkans, which was fashionable at the time because of the films of Kusturica and Bregović. We had fun loading the backing tracks with trumpets, klezmer clarinets, a variety of percussion and some accordions, which gave all the joy a certain melancholy, a touch of the sadness that lingers once the party has come to an end.

Almost by accident, Animal discovered that his drums sounded amazing through the studio monitors and he set about exploring this effect. At the end of each day he'd stay behind in the studio for hours and the following morning, happy and exhausted, he'd show me what he'd managed to get out of the percussion. I loved seeing how dedicated he was. Martán acted as a special envoy for all things innovative, which included everything from toy instruments he'd stumbled across at the Rastro flea market to electronic programmes we used to create a strange atmosphere beneath the recording, sometimes rainy, other times volcanic.

The initial critical response highlighted something that had all but passed us by. The album was theatrical and each song narrated unexpected incidents in the lives of the characters: they were portraits, etchings, like Anders Petersen's bar photos. There was more pathos than romance, which is unusual for an album by a young, successful artist. People said the record sounded hurt, sarcastic, that its humour was born from despair, and maybe it was. It certainly was true that it had lost the playful frivolity Gus used to bring into the mix. My music sought to travel to a different place, but everyone else insisted I'd become a victim of McCartney syndrome, the musician who survives their bandmate and is then singled out for committing the only unforgivable act in the music world: still being alive.

And yet there was a party atmosphere at our concerts, with the whole audience singing along to the chorus to 'Four Days'. We'd extend the song when we played it live, turning it into a cathartic experience, and we soon noticed that it had become something of a hit: its catchy chorus could be heard at bars at closing time and it was even ripped off for a life insurance advert. We played in so many places – in any venue that offered us a good deal – and I've always believed that album ended up being a success through sheer persistence.

Then there was the scandal caused by the song about the paedophile priests, as people began to call it, and the accusations in newspapers and on radio shows; there was even the threat of a complaint to the Episcopal Conference, which never actually materialised. Some record shops stopped stocking our records and a few concerts were scrapped in the more conservative areas. All of this helped sales, especially when our concert in Miranda de Ebro was disrupted by a group of young ultra-Catholic conservatives. I became the 'Missionary Position' guy, the one who'd sung 'Let the little children come to me / and let me savour the bitter taste of sin.'

Very few people understood that the song was about guilt and the people who rushed to my defence were just as mistaken as those who attacked me. I was most encouraged by the obsessiveness shown by a highly popular radio presenter, who exhorted the mayors of Tomelloso and Calatayud not to book me.

'Tomorrow, this stuck-up city boy will be playing in your town square, next to the church, singing songs that are highly offensive to all believers.'

It was a wonderful thing to know someone hated you that much.

Of course, my father couldn't miss an opportunity to get involved in the debate and, naturally, he took the enemy's side.

'You've insulted the things people hold sacred.'

'Nothing's sacred for me, Dad,' I replied.

'One day, I hope, all the rage you carry around inside will be gone.'


## *the rage you carry around inside*

Years later, my son's teacher warned me he was experiencing difficulties with his studies and he was struggling to socialise, that he always sat at the back of the class, somewhat detached. She told me that Ryo was ceasing to be a child and that this fact was troubling. 'He needs help.' I understood her uneasiness, because I shared it, too. Perhaps you can inherit that . . . And I remembered a time when I, too, had to abandon my musical childhood, the weightless joy of play, to face up to the evolving, maturing nature of my profession.

For a while there was a certain excitement surrounding me at the label. They wanted to fabricate a rivalry between me and two or three other artists, to turn us into the Spanish equivalent of Oasis, Blur and Pulp, but our promotional artillery was completely blown out of the water by the bombing missions brought from overseas by the battleships of MTV.

All I did was try to chart a course across what Renán called 'the choppy waters of the music industry'. Perhaps I could have made the jump into higher sales – serious figures, numbers that would have put everyone in a good mood – but the people who came on board at that time, the new audience, never got fully acquainted with all the songs from the Gus era. Our older fans left and never came back: they associated me with a group from their youth and, while I myself was growing, they'd decided not to accompany me in the process.

I missed having Gus near me, I missed Oliva, and I missed Fran too, never mind the fact that Animal and Martán remained at my side. They were devoted to playing the same old pranks: filling my bed with cornflakes when they thought I might get lucky, calling radio stations where I was being interviewed pretending to be furious bishops, or replacing my shoes with slippers emblazoned with the Real Madrid crest, which meant I had to play several gigs barefoot. Death rather than sin.

I had to clarify that I hadn't robbed a bank when I handed my father a cheque covering my mother's care home fees for the entire year.

'Let me take care of this, Dad.'

'You really make that much from this music nonsense? The world is getting crazier every day.'

'As long as someone wants to give me money,' I told him, 'then I'll make a living from it.'

In this business, you don't retire and you don't make plans. You don't have a career, you just career along.

A kid was holding a scrap of paper for me to sign through the window of the school building. My limited experience tells me never to sign the first autograph or pose for the first photo when there's a big group of people, because it produces a domino effect and then everyone wants one for themselves, even if they aren't quite sure exactly who you are. It gets to be a real nuisance, with you becoming the collector's item, the butterfly to be skewered with a pin on a board.

Where do autographs end up? You might as well ask where all the pairs of odd socks disappear to: I'm sure that somewhere there are whole armies of odd socks ready to rise up one day against their twins. Likewise, there must be illegible autographs on yellowed scraps of paper all over the world, blurry photos of unrecognisable celebrities standing next to complete strangers, records with dedications written on them lying in the corners of church fetes and flea markets.

But Luci was more decisive. She moved her hips, walked up to the window and gave the boy a slap through the window railings.

'Nothing until after the burial,' she reprimanded him. 'Don't you realise this is an official function?'

I was about to stress the importance of getting on with the burial, which was what had brought me here, after all, when everyone began to make way for the village priest, to shouts of 'Look, here comes the priest.' I was surprised by how young he was; with his glistening, vivid black eyes he looked more like Jarvis Cocker from his 'Cocaine Socialism' era than a small-town cleric. There was something effeminate about him; he was wearing jeans and a cross carved from a piece of wood, quite possibly carved by the priest himself during an otherwise dull walk over the fields.

Jandrón introduced me.

'He's the parish priest for this village and for the other villages in the area.'

'Pleased to meet you. My name's Javier,' the priest said.

I saw several different bracelets on his wrists, one displaying the faded colours of the Spanish flag. Did he sometimes forget where he was, too?

'I'm not sure if you wanted anything special for the burial,' he asked me after we'd greeted one another. 'Music, a reading? I like a burial to be guided by the family, the way they want it. Perhaps you might like to sing something?'

'No, no.' I shook my head. 'I'm just doing it for my father; it's not for me.'

The idea of being subjected to yet another funeral Mass hadn't even entered my mind, but I didn't tell him that.

'I bet you were expecting someone like old Father Teófilo, am I right? Nothing of the sort!' Jandrón slapped the father on the back as he mentioned the old parish priest we'd had to endure in our childhood.

The councillor for festivities explained that the priest had died in a home, at almost one hundred years of age.

'He died all alone. He wasn't all that well-loved, truth be told.'

'Yes, well,' his young replacement said, 'he belonged to another era. Times change and so do people.'

I suddenly became aware that one of Javier's eyes was made of glass.

'I'm from Alicante,' he told me. 'This isn't my region, but I've grown fond of it. Deep down, this landscape also has something of the sea about it.'

'You'll have plenty of time to chat later on,' Jandrón

interrupted. 'The church was a complete wreck, God forgive us, but thanks to Javier it's looking great. He takes care of things; he doesn't just say the rosary for the old dears and call it a day.'

'Well, the Church has to evolve,' the priest said timidly, uncomfortable with such praise.

I said nothing. I was still unsettled by what Jandrón had said, about how the priest and I would have plenty of time for chatting. For the first time that morning I tried to take control of the situation.

'All right, I think the sooner we head to the cemetery the better. You see, I have to get back to Madrid—'

'Oh, no, no, no, you're not going anywhere. Today's for organising. Of course, I haven't gone through the order of service with you yet. It's just that everything is so full on.'

I stopped listening to Jandrón and looked towards the window; in order to escape, I'd need to get through the iron bars first. Too complicated. But on the other side of the window I saw a face that stuck out among all the others. The girl looked like someone who'd been brought in from another planet, with an intelligent, somewhat defiant look on her face. It was out of sync with the simple-minded spontaneity of all the young lads piling up around her, their hair cut short like football players, the bovine look in their eyes reinforced by their flabby cheeks. And then the vision was obscured again by the gaggle of curious youths, grabbing onto the bars like they were watching a football match from the front row – or perhaps a cruel form of execution, with me as the victim.


*with me as the victim*


One afternoon I was singing to my mother at the home. She always liked watching me play the guitar. If it was cold outside, she'd still warm my hands in hers and say, 'But your hands are so cold,' and then ask me the same question seven or eight times: 'Is it very cold out there?'

The doctors explained that musical memory was the most resistant kind and that many patients clung onto songs even after losing everything else. The shipwrecked gaze with which my mother pretended to look at me had long ceased to plunge me into a depression, but, I asked myself, if everything in life ultimately comes up against the absurdity of decay and oblivion, then why all the effort? Several times, while fucking, I'd been surprised to find myself seeing it as a vengeful act of defiance against death: sometimes I'd fuck against the world, sometimes I'd fuck against love and against couples and against commitment – and sometimes I'd fuck against so many things that I wasn't fucking *for* anything at all.

Marta was the physiotherapist who worked with my mother two days a week; she liked my songs and would pop her head around the door of the room while I played for my mother. We were seeing each other for a while and one night she told me I was very serious during sex.

'You look so serious when you're fucking, it's almost scary.'

It made me feel ridiculous, but it was an accurate description. Sometimes she'd straddle me naked, showing me her beautiful back; she said she preferred looking at my feet while we made love. 'Your feet are the nicest thing about you.' And she'd done a course in reflexology, which meant that she could use them to touch every part of my body. But no matter how hard she tried, she could never find the root of my sadness, and that disheartened her.

One day, as she was leaving, she said, 'You write such funny songs; so why are you so serious?'

Marta went to live in Pamplona, her home city, when she found work there.

'I was only ever a rebound for you,' she told me when we saw each other again, 'just the kind of girl you need to get yourself out of one important story and into another. Because you're married now, right? And you have two kids.'

She occasionally comes to see me at concerts and with those girlish eyes of hers she's as open as ever, though she's the mother of three children and her husband is a firefighter in Estella, with a threatening physique hidden beneath his good-natured exterior. One day I asked Marta if her husband knew we'd been together and she'd cut me off: 'He's a fireman, not an idiot.' She also told me that I didn't seem as serious as before, which made me happy. And she said again the thing she'd always told me, that I had the perfect job: no boss, no timetable, no ties.

Back when we were seeing each other in secret I wrote a song called 'A Taxi Driver Whistles' and I wanted it to have the jaunty feel of the songs I used to write with Gus. It came to me in a taxi, at a time when I felt everything that once held me up had collapsed – my parents' home, my love life, the company of my friends. Suddenly, I heard the driver break out into a whistle, completely oblivious to the outside world; I wrote the song there and then, and in the final part I whistled part of the melody. Gus always used to say that the thing I really did well, my main talent, was whistling.

'You can hold your own with everything else, but when it comes to whistling you're a true maestro.'

When I feel like whistling onstage I play that song and whistle for a while with my lips glued to the microphone while Animal plays the drums with his brushes. Gus was right: whistling is what I do best. Marta was also right: my feet are the best part of my body. There's no use claiming otherwise.

## it's Serrat

'It's Serrat,' said the voice on the other side of the phone.

And, indeed, the voice speaking did belong to Serrat, that giant of Spanish music, a voice I'd occasionally parodied, exaggerating his tremolo. Serrat calling me was a knowing wink from destiny, one that ended up changing everything.

'I'm going to say this without any circumlocutions.' *I mean, who uses that word?* 'I'm doing a tour of Spanish cultural institutes over half the globe and I need a support act. It must be someone I like, but most of all – and this part is crucial – they can't be better than me.' And he burst out laughing.

'I don't think it'll be too difficult to find someone who's worse than you,' I replied.

'Sure, right, but someone I like . . .'

And I believe I told him I wasn't a singer-songwriter and that cultural institutions sounded a bit folksy to me.

'Look, son, any singer who sings their own songs is a singer-songwriter and any building dedicated to culture is a cultural institute.'

I was suddenly overcome with embarrassment.

The conversation didn't last much longer. I ran out of excuses, reasons to say no. I'd be playing alone, I'd always be travelling with his musicians and I'd never play for longer than half an hour. There wasn't much money in it, but it meant I had fifteen performances scheduled within two months.

'Travelling with Serrat,' Bocanegra said after we'd agreed and coordinated our calendars, 'also means eating like a fucking king, swanky hotels and being treated like the dog's bollocks wherever you go.'

In my stupid head, agreeing to be a support act meant taking a step down the ladder and the label felt that it was crazy for me

243

to work a circuit that wouldn't bring me any sales or new fans. But it was the perfect excuse to escape my musical routine. It was an opportunity to test out six songs with only a guitar and to do some stripped-down performances to audiences who'd never heard of me, in countries far out of my reach. I'd reinvent the most relevant songs from the previous era and keep the ones from the last album that best held up in this format.

When I told Animal and Martán, they understood I was going to accept the job and that this would be the end. To persuade them otherwise I agreed to do three performances with them when I got back, in December 1999 – it would be a nice way to bid farewell to the millennium. But I couldn't get the idea I was boycotting my own career out of their heads or mine: faced with the motorway of ambition, I was choosing a private side track – quieter, more discreet, more comfortable.

## the past is everywhere

The past is everywhere. The past rests on us like dust on furniture. There's past in the present and past in the future. Coating everything, cheek to cheek, diluted, blended, mixed, stuck together, blurred. There's past in memory, in facial expressions and features, in words yet to be spoken, in solutions. There's past in the steps not yet taken, in the road ahead, in a look, in stories, in fabrications, in taste. Songs are made of past. There are no songs of the future; songwriting is an art form that has no science fiction. There's past in passion, in displeasure, in dreams. There's past in things to come, in future plans, even in mortgages. There's past in your kids, your grandkids, in their faces, their names. There's past on the streets of your city, in its outskirts. There's past in every single person, including those not yet born.

We flee from the past, but we return to it to seek shelter, in an endless cycle. The past is our future: emigrants long for the past and they also fear losing it, no matter how many miles they travel in search of a better life. I saw this up close when I met a few of them on the tour with Serrat; the different generations struggle to get along because they don't share the same history and some consider the newer arrivals to be trampling on their past, like unruly youths walking over manicured lawns.

The remains – sad, filthy and spent – can be found in the flea markets of every city, the devaluation of what was once important. Someone is screwing around with your childhood, while others play football on your parents' graves. And petrol stations or bank branches are being built in the field where you had your first kiss, or the bakery you used to go every Sunday after church.

The struggle is to leave something lasting, permanent, indelible, and the tragedy is that little more remains than the statue half buried in sand on the beach, like that film we loved as children. Like when you record onto tape and the previous take gets submerged beneath the new one. And the arrival of the CD finished off the cassette tape, and then vinyl became the domain of the fetishist. And when songs ceased to have physical formats and were instead hosted on digital platforms, we still kept producing thousands of vinyl records in order to leave something physical, something palpable behind us, like those who insist on still printing photographs on paper, because deep down we suspect that whatever isn't solid ultimately won't survive. We're taking part in an exercise in regression in order to reaffirm ourselves; we're going back into the past because we're afraid of not existing for the future, of belonging to a species that will go extinct without leaving any traces, and thus without ever having existed.

## *yira, yira*

*Yira, yira, cuando estén secas las pilas de todos los timbres que vos apretás* . . . and on and on went that desperate tango we learnt from Serrat's pianist during those months on tour, trips that were spaced out enough to allow occasional visits back home to Madrid. We started in Geneva, playing before an auditorium in which every last soul was Spanish.

'This looks like Badajoz,' the guitarist said to me when we peeped out through the curtains.

But Serrat knew how to make this audience eat out of his hands, these ex-pats who took such great pleasure in hearing words they felt belonged to them, the melodies of their yester-years. It was different with me; people would just sit there chatting to each other as I fiddled with my guitar. I was just the support act, filler; that crowd knew none of my songs. The rhythm-driven melodies of 'Play for Me' and 'The Dumbest Song in the World' still worked, but I couldn't get 'Four Days' to soar at all; without the backing of the drums, I felt like a magazine cover star doing a tour of geriatric homes.

Every time Serrat came out and played his greatest hits, I was swept off the stage like starters from a table as the main course is served. Serrat spoke about me at the beginning of his set: 'I hope one day the kid who just played for you will be asking me to be his support act. I'm certain he'll do great things for Spanish music.' I took this simply as him being professional, but even so, I almost burst into tears, tears of anguish rather than of joy. Spanish music? What the hell was I to Spanish music? He repeated those comments in every city we visited, without altering a single world. And each time I was overcome by the same feeling of despair.

In Munich it snowed and I caught a cold. During the concert

my voice failed and I ended up having to croak out the words to 'The Mumbliest Song in the World', as Serrat's guitarist jokingly renamed it. That night Serrat took me out to eat in a good restaurant, where I confessed my fears to him.

'Look,' he told me, 'in this profession the best thing is not to move around too much and just do what you want to do, because every now and again the world turns and you become fashionable again. But if you're always looking for praise, if all you seek to do is please, then you'll always be lagging behind, five minutes late for everything.'

Then we spoke about his songs, how he'd decided to become a singer, the extent to which he poured his own intimate feelings into them and how the key to this profession, like life, lies in finding the right mix of ingredients.

'You have to be you in your songs – of course you do – but without going too far. I put my real phone number into one of my early songs and you know what happened? I had to get a new one within days. Your audience is a monster and it's quite capable of devouring you.'

I confessed that I felt lost onstage without Animal – I needed his drums behind me and I felt that everything would be better if he was with me.

His response was, 'I'd be fine with a pianist, but a drummer . . .'

He accepted my proposal following a terse negotiation and we returned to Madrid after the performance in Brussels. I called Animal and we locked ourselves away to prepare the songs as a strange new duo. He was motivated by a desire to overcome his fear that we'd never play together again and brought along a whole load of percussion instruments, including tap shoes and even castanets, which drew resounding applause from the audience in Toulouse when he used them in a solo during 'Four Days'. Animal standing onstage and tap dancing while playing the castanets was our personal highlight of the tour.

Transforming our set to be played live with Animal's help encouraged me to write a new song for voice and noises called 'My Place in Spanish Music', which parodied the young singer I'd once been:

*No one queues when I play*
*No one cares what I say*
*My applause is mostly muted.*

Really, though, it was about feeling out of place wherever I went and how I'd made a gamble to get away from it all.

*I've checked the reviews*
*Looked all over for news*
*Of my place in Spanish music.*

It wasn't long before we began joining Serrat for the final encore of each concert, when he'd play 'Hoy Puede Ser un Gran Día', a song we used to hear playing from neighbourhood radios when we were twelve years old. Animal immersed himself in the lives of Serrat's band. He did everything with that bunch of veterans and it really toughened him up. Like every young singer, I'd come to knock Serrat off the road as I overtook him, but on those stages I discovered that the only possible road to go down is that of resistance.

We opened first in Moscow and then at a disastrous concert in Prague, where Animal came to blows with the hotel receptionist after our rooms appeared to have been burgled. We'd wander the streets until we found an all-night place that let us drink until dawn. We were touring musicians, taking restorative siestas in chaotic hotel rooms, attempting to resolve the historical controversy about whether it was bad for the voice to ejaculate before a concert, as Raphael Martos Sánchez maintained, or if the best thing to do was just climax in twenty strokes or less. This, apparently, is what Sinatra used to insist on during the rushed blow jobs he received moments before going onstage.

It was in this festive, almost familial atmosphere that we found out about three further performances in Japan. We'd begin in Tokyo and then go on to Kyoto before finishing up in Osaka. These destinations promised an exotic end to the tour and I was still unaware that the exotic would soon become my daily reality.

## and the village will be made anew each year

'And the village will be made anew each year,' Javier, the priest, recited.

Juan Ramón Jiménez's verses took me back to all the time I spent reading Spanish poets in my quest for the perfect rhyme, something that came so easily in English with all its monosyllables – up, down, shot, rush, love, find – and was so much tougher in Spanish, which was full of wild, untameable words that creaked and crunched: *arriba, abajo, disparo, deprisa, amor, descubrimiento*.

The village cemetery was smaller and more intimate compared with the vastness of Madrid, a setting my father would have appreciated. Every stone bore the same name: Campos, always Campos – a Campos over here, a whole family of Camposes over there. The cemetery had whitewashed walls and was situated on a slope on the outskirts of the village; I remembered having been there as a child, gathering snails, larvae and sometimes poppies. It was one of the village's four cardinal points that out-of-towners like me used to orientate ourselves when we got lost among all those identical houses.

The gravedigger showed us the hole he'd dug by the vault, waiting to be occupied. As a gift from the council – as he and his wife hammered home to me – Jandrón had taken care of the marble stone that bore my father's name along with the dates of his birth and death, all of his eighty-seven years summed up in just two lines. They hadn't held back from finishing off the inscription with a line from one of my songs, lapidary in both senses of the word, placed between inverted commas: 'It would be nice to go home.'

They'd interpreted it completely differently from what I'd intended it to mean; what I lacked when I wrote those words was a house to return to, and that's what I was trying to get across. Not some nostalgic desire for a return to the past, that subterranean homesickness I lack, but simply a corner for me to carve out for myself. It would be nice to go home.

The priest gave a short funeral oration in which he spoke about the kingdom of heaven and the resurrection of the dead while gusts of wind raised a carpet of dust into the air. We'd arrived at the cemetery in a procession, led by the hearse, and I knew my father would have loved this sight: the arid path, the coffin being carried like that and the air coarse with the dust of a July day blown into the air by the breeze.

'For believers, death is a joyful affirmation of life. This is what makes us different from those who don't believe in God and the Resurrection. But we shouldn't use our good fortune to attack others, the sceptics and the unbelievers. Quite the opposite: if they love us, then let us ask them not to suffer for us but to watch us go; when they think they are losing us, let us tell them tenderly that we are not going very far; let them sense our hope and our joy at coming at last to God's call.'

Javier, the young priest, spoke naturally, calling my father by his name and expressing certainty that he'd 'Enjoyed a full life, wouldn't you say: rich in years, in ups and downs, and with the undying affection of a son, and of all of the people who knew him and who did business with him. If he has left us, it's so he can prepare for the day we reach the kingdom of the Lord, to ensure that we are welcomed with great care and attention.'

I couldn't imagine my father going to much effort to make sure my arrival in heaven was a comfortable one, but maybe at least he'd finally let me take a damn shower without shouting at me to turn off the tap. I struggled to imagine the reunion the priest was talking about. At most, my father would greet me with his customary 'I told you so.'

'For those who do not believe,' Javier continued, 'death leaves them inconsolable. At times they judge our beliefs to be mere sedatives, but they are wrong. Our project is one of life, not one of death. Let us all share this idea of hope that was so strongly held by the person we are saying goodbye to today, in the village of his birth, to which he has now returned for his second birth. And let us remember the words of Luke, when he said that if there is light inside us then everything around us will shine. And now let us say the Lord's Prayer.'

He didn't make this request with the sinister authority of my childhood priests and so I felt obliged to accompany the others in their melodious chanting, proving what Gus used to say about me, that I carried Catholicism around inside me and would never be entirely free from it. In the middle of the prayer I realised I didn't know the modern version, so I decided to keep quiet.

Just when I thought the service was over, the young priest spoke again.

'Ecclesiastes tells us that the good man leaves an inheritance to his children's children. Let us hope it turns out to be just so and that when Daniel's time comes he, too, can bear testament to this truth and recognise, in those who follow him, those who came before him.'

I looked at him without fully understanding, or perhaps understanding all too well. He smiled and invited me to say a few words. I declined with a hand gesture. I managed to stammer out a 'No, no, just thank you to everyone for coming.'

Suddenly there was spontaneous applause, the kind learnt from TV. Jandrón stepped back and, after announcing in his foghorn of a voice that he would say a few words in the name of the village, he took a piece of paper from his jacket pocket.

'From councillor to councillor, with total loss of enthusiasm,' Gus used to joke whenever we showed up in a city or town during a tour only to be confronted with mayors and councillors, CEOs and festival organisers, all of them clearly hungry to hold a microphone. Second-rate players in the game of life, keen to get their five minutes in the spotlight.

Jandrón placed his mace under his armpit and unfurled his piece of paper that had been folded into sixteen segments. It took him what felt like hours to do this until eventually he began to speak, as if reciting.

'Today, we are witnessing the fulfilment of a promise made by a son who wished to carry out his father's last wish, which was to be buried in the village in which he was born.'

Then he went rambling on, moving from one topic to the next. I think he even included from dust we came and to dust he shall return, as well as the one about death being the final abode.

It wasn't until I was living a stable life in Japan that I was able to recognise myself in the Spain I'd left behind. Distance reaffirmed the connection. When you go out and play for the first time you don't consider yourself to be the continuation of anything. Your influences are accidental and the radio station you used to listen to is more important than the city in which you were born.

In Spain we lacked a tradition, so we had to try to have the

Anglo-Saxon ones implanted in us instead. You followed those groups because they brought you to rock, blues or country, just as kids today flock to hip-hop and gangsta rap. But we were imposters, in a way. We could never be that thing. We can't fully be it. Where was our authentic past? It was like growing with no soil.

I'm from Estrecho. Going beyond Cuatro Caminos was already like an adventure into outer space: I think I was fifteen the first time I went to Plaza de España. In Estrecho, we lived in Estrecho, not Madrid. I remember that my father once took me on an excursion to see the river Manzanares, via Paseo de la Florida. We spent the whole day there, with sandwiches and everything. Like we were abroad. So for me, being in Japan meant learning everything again from scratch. And it wasn't even Japan but Tokyo, which is several cities in one.

I'm not sure if being over there changed me much, musically speaking, but it did make me more aware of the war between tradition and modernity in Spain. In Japan too, the old folks have lost grandchildren, who now spend all day glued to screens, shut away in *manga kissa* or in the cubicles of cybercafes. It's a perversion born out of contempt for the real world.

Jandrón's diatribe continued. 'Garrafal de Campos is honoured by our friend Daniel's visit. I remember him from many years ago, a whippersnapper scuttling about the square and the backyards, hunting flies all day long. You remember the flies, right, Dani? That must be where your group got its name.'

For a moment I feared he was going to recount the scene with the hen, or describe the two of us with our dicks in our hands, trying to be men without a great deal of reference points. But no, he chose instead to invent a memory of his own, one perfectly suited to the occasion. He said that one afternoon he'd asked me what I'd like to be when I grew up.

'And do you know what he replied?'

There was a theatrical pause. My eyebrows were raised so high they'd pushed my sunglasses up above my eyes.

'A singer, he replied, I want to be a singer. Well, it looks like his childhood dream came true. And when it came to choosing something to go on his father's gravestone, we were inspired by some words from one of his songs, words that clearly express the desire we all share to go back to our origins.'

> It would be nice to go home
> But it's just got so late.

That's not it, Jandrón, that's not it at all; it's the exact opposite. Sometimes songs are works of fantasy, of wish fulfilment. Why are you also obsessed with taking things literally?

Jandrón finished off his speech with a cry consisting of two *vivas*, one to the village itself and the other to the patron saint, which everyone chanted back in unison. It felt strange to be shouting 'long live' in a cemetery, but then such was the euphoria of the moment.

Jairo, who had become my closest relative, proceeded to round up the village strongmen to get them to place the coffin in the ground. An instant later the gravedigger began inserting the gravestone into the vault and we all watched him using a silicon injector to carry out this procedure which, somehow, suddenly turned the burial into a building site.

## the first one to see her

Animal was the first one to see her: he just whispered to me, all agitated, 'Have you seen the cellist?'

We'd gone into the National Museum, motivated more by

the rain than by cultural curiosity; exhausted from traipsing all over Tokyo, we'd gone to rest in the gardens, only to be surprised when the skies opened. There was an enormous hall dedicated to paintings of almond trees in bloom and women with parasols standing by bridges in fancy gardens. I turned to look in the direction Animal was pointing.

There was a classical quartet at the back of one of the rooms, performing so delicately it was as if they were playing on tip-toes; the girl on the cello was dark and pale, concentrating on the oscillating sounds she was making. When she looked up I saw her beautifully proportioned face beneath her fringe. It took a second for me to take in the stunning beauty that had caught Animal's eye. Maybe the music helped to stimulate all of my senses, but I found myself paralysed, completely absorbed by the scene.

We devoted a few moments to admiring her sitting there with her three fellow musicians, among them a much older woman with a jolly, insubstantial look about her. We couldn't quite determine the exact age of the cellist, but her features were the fruit of individual merits that had accumulated over many generations, culminating by pure chance in her total perfection.

Her hair was extremely straight, tied up in a ponytail that swayed when she moved, and her upper lip formed an arch that harmonised perfectly with her jaw, which was the colour of rice paper. The crowning touch to her beauty showed itself when she closed her eyelids to reveal an impossible tiny mole painted right there, which appeared and disappeared with her eye movements – now you see it, now you don't. It was a real struggle to tear ourselves away from that spot; the cement on the floor had set with us in it and the music lingered in the air, ringing out to eternity.

I suddenly noticed the echo of the music fall silent. I shouted at Animal and began to run. 'Come with me.' I had to go back and look at that hidden mole on her eyelid.

The four musicians were gathering their scores and music stands together. I walked up to the oldest, who appeared to be both the leader and the most approachable of them. I spoke to her in English, but she barely understood me, and she scrunched up her face affably behind the enormous lenses of her spectacles. Convinced that an ill-timed look would break the spell, I didn't dare turn towards the cellist, but then she came over to join the conversation; she spoke better English than her colleague and offered to translate for me.

I looked up and there, a hair's breadth away from me, everything Animal and I had seen from afar was confirmed. I explained that we were two Spanish musicians touring the country, that we had three performances ahead of us and that we were looking for a cellist. Animal, whose English consisted of little more than different ways to order alcohol, just looked at me with curiosity.

'We need a cellist to accompany us on four songs. It's a simple job, but we don't know anyone here.' I mentioned the cultural institute to clarify that the performance wouldn't take place in some filthy hovel. 'Could you do it?'

She smiled and didn't let me continue.

'I don't think I can,' she said politely.

'Sure you can; it's really simple. It will only take one rehearsal. We can explain it in more detail.'

Animal came towards me as I pointed him out to her.

'What is it? What are you telling her?'

She put out her hand to stop me in my tracks and gracefully wrote something down on a page from her notebook. She tore it out and handed it to me. She'd written down a name and a telephone number. I read it out loud: Kei.

'You're Kei?' I asked, intrigued.

She nodded and repeated the name, far more elegantly than the crude way in which I'd pronounced it.

'Keiko,' she said.

I kept that piece of paper for years, folded away in my wallet next to my ID card. When it began to come apart at the edges I put it in a drawer, where it must still be, the last fetish of that first encounter.

'We're going to put a cello in the songs,' I announced to Animal as we watched her walk away with the rest of the quartet; Kei gave the impression that with each step she took she left pearls in her wake.

Then Animal destroyed the moment.

'You're gonna fuck her. You're the dog's bollocks, bro, the big man. You pretended we needed a double bass just so you can fuck her.'

'A cello,' I corrected.

'And how the hell are we going to put a cello in our songs?' Animal asked.

## good memory factory

A good memory factory, that's what we are during our best performances, a good memory factory, our only concern being to create unforgettable moments. Over the next few hours Animal and I laughed and joked so much – falling about laughing on the floor as I talked about the Japanese cellist who was going to be the mother of my children, the wife they'd bury me with, my life partner – that we became almost feverish.

'But look, however fine she is, we're playing in two bloody days and we've got no idea how the hell we're going to put a fucking cello into our miserable songs.'

But a while later I called Kei and made a date for the

following day at the concert hall, at a time when she was free, and hummed the initial melody to her. During 'Four Days', the cello could come in during one of the verses and though my ideas regarding string arrangements weren't all that precise, all Kei needed was to hear the phrasing before she moved her bow over the cello and gave the song a completely different feel.

She was sitting in front of me, the body of the instrument between her legs, which were covered by a long, drawn-in skirt that showed her almost-schoolgirl socks. She smiled with her eyes, seemingly keen to test, at her own pace, just how serious our proposal and our determination were.

Animal modified his usual hammering to fit the rhythm of this new sound, giving her notes that were about as precise as those a miller might give if he was put in charge of a philharmonic orchestra.

'A bit more *jaaa* there, then some *voo*, *voo*, that's it, perfect, the one that sounds like someone puffing.'

Perhaps, at that moment, the course of my music changed just as much as the course of my life. Perhaps they're the same story, the same infinite quest. Animal hit the cymbals to make way for my voice, and I tried to sound more powerful and assured over the strings. When the song was over, Kei broke into a beaming smile, said 'It works,' and then told us something we didn't understand about how the instrument was tuned in parallel fifths. Well of course it worked. I looked at her face again, at the mole on her eyelid – yes, there it was – and I felt happy at having added so much beauty to our efforts.

She then asked me to translate the lyrics to another song, 'Extreme Sport'. She wasn't exactly sure what kind of tone to adopt without knowing what I was saying. And so, in English stiffer than a sheet left to dry in the sun, I whispered slowly:

*If we see each other again*
*I hope it's like it was back then.*

It was a song written for an imaginary Oliva who, though distant, lost, still emerged through my songs, like reflections of the sun:

*When loving each other*
*Was our extreme sport.*

## I met you in a museum

'I met you in a museum,' I used to tell Kei when we looked back on those days. 'Maybe that's why I've always thought of you as an artwork I stole from the exhibition.'

But Serrat was more to the point when I introduced her to him half an hour before the concert, saying that she'd be playing with us.

'There's an old and very wise Spanish saying,' he warned me, exactly as my father would have done. 'Keep your cock out of the stock.'

Animal agreed to split the money between the three of us.

'It's not much. I hope you're OK with it,' I told Kei.

'I often play for free, like with Mrs Tanaka's quartet, in the museum where we met,' she explained.

What would Gus have thought of all this? He always appreciated beauty; sometimes he'd stop when he saw a lettuce leaf on his plate and say, 'Look at this, it's like a fully spread-out fan,' and he'd put it aside, unwilling to bite until he'd had the chance to admire it. He would have liked Kei.

The first concert went remarkably smoothly and when it was over, I glanced in amusement at Animal and took Kei's hand, so that the three of us could face the audience before we left the stage. That was the first time I touched her. Up until then I hadn't dared place a hand upon her, not even as I greeted her with two kisses when we met for the second time.

I experienced a small electric shock as I felt her fingers slip between mine. A minute later she introduced me to a guy holding up the base of the cello as she moved it into the wings of the stage.

'This is my boyfriend,' she said.

Serrat had just begun his section of the Tokyo concert. I greeted this fellow, grinning idiotically, his black plastic glasses sliding off tip of his nose like a toboggan. I think I heard him say his name was Mitsuo, but to me he was little more than a traffic light in open country, an obstacle blocking a beautiful view.

## growing without soil

Growing without soil. You can't grow without soil and yet sometimes I've felt as if I was doing just that. That's why I was so thrown when Jandrón had said I'd come back to the village because I was proud of my origins as he introduced me to his mother. She gave an almost poetic response: 'Naturally. After all, you can't grow without soil.'

Jandrón's family's house in the village was one of the biggest to have been preserved. Constructed from adobe, reinforced with a mixture of clay and straw, they'd added a concrete frame to strengthen the door. It had doors that led out onto two different streets, but we'd been taken to the dining room to taste the lamb, among selected guests. It was reminiscent of those locked rooms you sometimes see, with the expensive furniture covered by plastic sheets; a kind of sealed-off paradise, a museum within a house.

There was a completely random range of different kinds of seating laid out for us to use. The grandmother sat in a maroon fake leather armchair while the youngest diners perched upon a chest they'd manage to find in the house. The rest of us divided up the chairs, one made of wood, and four or five of them finished off with a green Formica that hurt my eyes. By now, the mayor and host had brought me up to speed with the agenda for the day, with occasional underscoring from the councillor, corroborated in turn by his wife in the form of a sinister head movement.

First, we'd attend the inauguration of the new cultural centre.

'We finished the building works two and a half years ago, but today seemed like a perfect occasion to inaugurate it officially and unveil the plaque,' Jandrón told me. 'Didn't I tell you we've got a plaque with your name on it?'

I said nothing.

'The idea is to have a museum full of agricultural tools, together with some historical photos. I'll show you my treasured collection later on; I keep it in my father's yard. It's an excellent collection, if I'm honest, and crucial for these kids nowadays. They've absolutely no idea how we used to work the land.

'We really care about preserving our roots here, so that visitors can discover our origins, our ancient past, and that's my main role as mayor. But of course, it's also an honour for us to have your name on the centre and, I can assure you, it will seriously piss people off in the surrounding villages because not many famous people originate from here, as I'm sure you're aware. The library in Cejuños de Campos had to be dedicated to Paloma San Basilio, and only because her great-grandfather came from there, need I say more.'

'So they claim,' his aggressively sceptical wife corrected him.

Javier, the young priest, had barely touched his lamb, and

was nibbling away at the lettuce and tomato in the salad bowl. He smiled as he observed me becoming overwhelmed by my agenda and all the duties hovering over me. When I tried to make Jandrón understand that I didn't want to be honoured and that it felt ridiculous to give my name to a place I'd only been to seven times in my entire life, the priest shook his head as if to say, you're not going to change his mind.

'Come on,' Jandrón reasoned, 'the plaque's already been made and everything, you can't get out of it now. We'd already guessed that you'd either use your father as an excuse or slope off like you've always done, isn't that right?'

'You're not going to interfere with our modest plan now, are you?' Luci asked as she used the nail of her little finger to remove a tiny string of lamb from between her teeth.

'But the thing is, I'm not a local and I've only ever been here for a few days at a time while on holiday. I'm sure there are some old folks about the place who merit the distinction far more than I do,' I said.

'You and your old folks. You're famous, for fuck's sake,' Jandrón countered.

'Not that famous,' I said with conviction.

'Believe me, man, we'd love nothing more than for Madonna to be a daughter of the village, but this is what we've got,' Luci concluded. 'Some stupendous people have come from this village – one even became a millionaire from selling PVC pipes – but no one knows any of them from Adam. B-lister or not, at least people have heard of you.'


## the wishing tree

Maruyama Koen, a Zen garden in Kyoto, is home to the wishing tree, which sits at the base of a bridge crossing over a little stream. We went there with Animal and two or three other musicians from Serrat's band. Kei explained to us that people make wishes underneath the cherry tree, that the wishes melt into the flowers and that when the petals drop, the wishes come true.

'Don't tell me what your wish was,' Animal joked, his eyes on me, amused by the way that mine were fixed on Kei.

I waited for the others to move on before talking to her.

'I wish you could always play with me,' I told her, taking her fingers between mine again.

'You're so nice,' she said.

'That was my wish,' I explained.

'You can't tell anyone your wishes,' she reprimanded me.

Love has its own amusing way of putting your hopes and dreams to work. I wanted to kiss her, but I didn't attempt it. Kei raised her hand in a gesture intended to make me, and perhaps also the moment itself, come to a halt, protect her from my words. She stepped away and was serious for the rest of the walk.

When we met later to go to the venue together she barely spoke, keeping up a polite, distant reserve that didn't in any way affect her perfect playing during the performance. We gathered our instruments and watched the rest of the concert from backstage.

Though I'd feared he would, Kei's boyfriend Mitsuo hadn't travelled to Kyoto. The first day I'd gathered, through his incomprehensible English, that he worked in car insurance and though he was trying to be friendly, I refused to accept his overtures. The following day, travelling on the bullet train without him, I had the opportunity to talk to Kei under Animal's curious, watchful eye.

'Are you seriously gonna go for it?' he asked me during a quiet moment together.

I shrugged. 'I can't stop looking at the mole on her eyelid. Can you?'

'Oh, man,' Animal puffed.

## japanese sadness

I didn't know it then, but Japanese sadness is silent and contained. Both of my children have inherited it and I'm always unsettled when they get like that, sometimes over the tiniest things. You feel as if the ground is splitting beneath them and they're being swallowed up into a deep, dark breach: they're little and you want to hug them and rescue them, but they let themselves fall and won't allow you into their hole. And you breathe a sigh of relief when they re-emerge with a childish smile and renewed spirits, but you can never rid yourself of the fear that this melancholy will become their Achilles heel.

Over the course of those three concerts I came to realise just how much distress I was causing Kei, because whenever I looked at her I'd notice just how absorbed she was in herself, trying so hard to avoid making eye contact.

There was a bus booked for the journey to our last concert in Osaka and Kei sat at the front, next to the driver and our interpreter, obviously seeking peace and quiet. I moved from the back, where I was travelling next to Animal, and went over and sat in a free seat by Kei, ignoring the crude comments of my fellow musicians as they mocked my infatuation.

I asked her about the journey, the area we were travelling through, and gradually I noticed the tension easing. We talked about her career. She'd been studying the cello since she was a girl and at fourteen had left her parents to enrol in the Tokyo conservatoire, where she'd lived in a residence for musicians; she'd also had two long stays in London and Vienna, where she'd greatly improved her English. She hadn't wanted to enrol in a big orchestra, so once back in Japan she made a living from teaching and from playing with two quartets, who received state support to tour around the country and gave her the experience she needed.

Using a somewhat elaborate formula to try to appear as polite as possible, I asked her age. She said thirty and smiled when I said, 'Same here.' She thanked me for the work, assured me she really enjoyed playing such different music and then said she'd always wanted to go on holiday to Spain.

There was a naive purity about her, which I associated with her country's behavioural norms. There was also a cold distance, which meant I had to perform a tricky juggling act: conversation and seduction, courtesy and humour. I could hardly breathe; I wanted to kiss her even if it was the last thing I did. I wanted to uncover her body – always hidden beneath her elegant, rather shapeless clothing – that body I'd imagined possessing a weightless fragility, from her fingers and her wrists to the eyebrows that broke up her broad forehead.

She asked about my life and I rushed to make it totally clear that there was no wife or any children on the scene. Then I told her about my mother, the relentless march of her dementia and the cruel distance separating her from my father and me. She asked if I was going to get married, so directly that it seemed like a proposal.

'No,' I said, 'I don't believe in marriage.'

She burst out laughing. 'I like weddings, but not the way couples have to sign a contract, like someone starting a new job or signing for a delivery.' She laughed again. 'You don't know what it's like in Japan. Here, all the women dream of marriage.'

'Are you going to get married? To your boyfriend?' My second question had a funereal ring to it.

'I don't know; he doesn't like my job. He wants me to quit music.'

Then she looked out of the window, uncomfortable about discussing personal details, and before long we were floating through a light snowstorm. Someone attempted to get live information about a Barcelona match and I explained to Kei why everyone was so agitated.

'Is it your team?'

'No, I support Atlético Madrid,' I told her, 'a team that nearly always loses.'

I felt ridiculous talking to her about such things as I watched her lips, two pink dunes rising from her smooth face. The interpreter smiled and said something like '*kappuru narimasu*', which I asked Kei to translate for me.

'She's talking about the concert yesterday. She says we make a good pair. *A good couple*. Musical couple,' she hastened to clarify.

I smiled. 'I couldn't agree more.'


## a huge honour

'It's a huge honour. Yes, sir, a huge honour,' said Jairo, who was also seated among the guests at the banquet.

As he left the cemetery he announced that he'd have to take the hearse back to Madrid, but Jandrón wasn't having any of it.

'No, no, no, man, you're staying here to eat with us. We can't insult my mother like that. She's cooked a whole lamb! The woman's been preparing it for two days and you must taste one of our region's culinary glories. I'm sure you don't get lamb like this in Ecuador.'

'Well then, with great pleasure, but I'll have to leave the moment I'm done, because in my line of work it's not so much eternal rest as eternal rush,' Jairo joked.

266

'I hate speeches, I hate authority. Really, Jandrón, don't do this to me.'

According to the mayor, everything was in place for me to open the festivities.

'You only need to say four lines,' Jandrón reassured me, 'and there's plenty of time. You don't have to make the announcement until tomorrow, after the midday Mass.'

'That means spending the night in the village and I can't, I just can't.'

'Plenty of spare beds,' someone said.

'No, no,' I continued to protest without anyone listening to me, 'I'm just not a public speaking kind of guy. It was a big deal just for me to accept the plaque.'

'And tonight,' Jandrón announced, 'though this is up to you, we'd like you to open the dance, play a few of your numbers before the disc jockey' – *how many years had it been since I'd heard that term?* – 'but this has to come from you. Though needless to say, for us it would be like manna from heaven. In a modest village like this we don't have the funds to pay artists' fees and we've made such an effort to honour you.'

'One heifer,' the councillor for festivities said. 'We've only got one heifer to let loose tomorrow instead of two and it's not going to be much of a show. With two you always get a couple of blows in all the confusion, but with only one the poor thing will just be overwhelmed by all those youngsters piling onto it.'

'Oh no, I'm sorry to hear that,' I said, identifying strongly with the calf.

'No, no,' Jandrón replied, underplaying the importance of the situation. 'It's true that we've only brought one calf, but it comes from Cebada Gago, one of the best ranches in the business. Their bulls never fail; they're always the favourites at San Fermín. I think they have the record number of gores.'

'Do you like bull runs, or are you one of those animal rights people?' Luci asked, frowning suspiciously.

I shrugged. 'Do you kill the calf?'

'No, man, of course not,' was the unanimous, outraged response. 'We're not like those savages in Tordesillas. In our festival the calf has a great time. The lads spar with it a bit and then it's all over. It's more expensive if you kill it.'

Jandrón continued to rally to the town's defence by informing me that the village even had its own ecologist, José Ángel, Venancio the butcher's son.

'We let him read out a protest before we let the calf out of the whatsit, and then the kids throw tomatoes and lettuce at him. It's almost become a part of the show and it means everyone's voice gets heard. No one gets censored here.'

'Right, right, seems fine to me,' I said, attempting to excuse myself in my own stupid way while someone had already begun recalling the incredible goring of a fellow villager at a past festival.

'Listen good: three broken ribs and a ruptured spleen. That's quite something.'

'I won't ask you to wave a cape around in front of the heifer; that's up to you,' Jandrón said, 'but if you sing four or five songs tonight and give us a little speech about your relationship with Garrafal de Campos tomorrow then we'll be more than satisfied.'

I wanted to say something, but Jairo got in first.

'How can you turn down an offer like that? Why, it makes me want to stay till tomorrow; it's such shame I have to go back.'

I believe that after all this, Luci pointed to the table, covered in food and scattered breadcrumbs along with glasses filled with a red wine that no one could quite manage to finish, and said, 'You must try everything.'

I took a long drink of that plonk, which was almost black and had the consistency of a sirloin steak. Luci stopped me in my tracks.

'Look, before you come up with a new excuse, some things are non-negotiable.'

The thought of spending two days in the village terrified me. The guest room in the house of some relative, the snacks, the dinners, the warm welcomes, endless selfies: 'Hold on, can we take it again; it didn't come out so good the first time.' Friend-liness wrapped up in blackmail.

I was reminded of a story a friend from another band had told me once. He went out onstage to play, took a look at everyone, thought about his set list, looked back over his career and his life and then pretended to faint, just to get out of there. I began to speak.

'I'm feeling a little . . .'

'What you need is another little kip,' said Jairo. 'I think you could really do with a nice restorative siesta. He had a rather heavy night last night, you see, and it was all I could do to get him out of bed this morning. Barely got his head down at all. You singers must really live it up, am I right?'

'That's it, rest a while and before long you'll see everything in a different light,' repeated all the guests in ripples.

'Down into the basement you go; it's the coolest place in the house, perfect for getting forty winks,' Jandrón ordered. 'I'll wake you up in time for the ceremony.'

*no one loses their dignity just from losing a little bit of their dignity*

'No one loses their dignity just from losing a little bit of their dignity,' Animal said in that philosophical tone of his.

He wanted to convince me to go over to the other side of the hotel corridor and knock on Kei's door. We'd done our last show in Osaka and we were sleeping in a hotel that looked like a fortress from the outside. We took a semi-naked thermal bath in the hot tub on the roof terrace with two other musicians from the band; the cold caressed our heads gently as we watched the city's lights spreading out in the distance.

'All you have to do is drum your fingers on the door and she'll invite you in for a shag,' Animal insisted.

We'd been in the restaurant with the musicians until the bar had closed and Kei had gone up to sleep the moment we arrived back at the hotel.

'She wants you more than you want her,' said Animal, the two of us both emboldened by the alcohol.

I waited for everyone to go back to their rooms before crossing the carpeted corridor, dressed in one of the kimonos that the hotel had left folded up for us on our beds. You don't lose your dignity by losing it; I guess what Animal meant was that if you never risk your dignity then you'll end up losing it for sure.

I knocked on Kei's door with more insistence than I'd intended. Her finely tuned ear appeared to have signed off for the night. Then I heard Kei's voice on the other side of the door. She answered in English straight away; she had been expecting me.

'It's me.'

She opened the door dressed in a kimono, although hers had cheerful drawings on a black background. I held up bottle of white wine by the neck; it was the one she always drank at dinner.

'Last night of the tour,' I announced.

She let me in.

That was the night I began composing the only truly erotic song I've ever written. I found inspiration in the sweet contact with Kei's skin, in the discovery of each delicate fold, in my fingers caressing her pubis. In her moist surrender which followed our brief conversation and toast. When Kei moaned she was smothering the girl shut up behind those eyelids, transparent like a glaze. The timid stiffness she adopted as she lay naked for me on that unmade bed had nothing to do with the passivity of a dead cow, which was how Animal described the kind of women who give themselves to you without putting in any effort. Kei's skills accumulated until they formed a song, one I still sing if the venue I'm playing is intimate enough for my whispered voice, delivered straight into the microphone.

I discovered that passion grows with moderation and restraint, because sating your desire doesn't kill the hunger. Exhausted as if I'd completed the project of a lifetime, I lay there in silence for a long time stroking her back while she, somewhat shaken up, also said nothing. Her fine hairs had gone static against the sheets and were pointing towards the sky.

When I escaped from her room three hours later, she didn't even turn to look at me. She simply let her back say it all. Though I'd predicted the encounter would end, as so often before, in a sated disenchantment, something was still burning inside me when I got back into my own bed. The touch of her skin lingered on my fingertips and I couldn't find an excuse to say goodbye, no matter how hard I looked for one.

The tour had come to an end. Playing in front of audiences who'd never heard of us and who watched us with total indifference had fortified Animal as much as it had me: we knew the musical journey we'd gone on had been worth the pain.

On the last morning, we had breakfast together in the hotel restaurant, seated around the counter from which the cook tossed us prawns that we caught in our mouths like dolphins. All the musicians were happy to be going home and their bags were loaded with evidence of their recent shopping sprees, all weighed down with reasonably priced cameras and computers. A heavy silence surrounded me, but if anyone noticed they didn't say a thing. Whenever my eyes accidentally met Kei's, she'd lower her gaze and I'd find myself once more staring at the tiny mole on her eyelid.

Spain felt hostile and arid to me as we headed to the airport. I wanted to go home, to recover after the tour and rest in my bed, but all of I sudden I felt that Madrid was a city of apathy, of contempt for my profession, of constant opposition. But above all, it was the city of heartbreak. Despite all the time that had passed, there were still countless street corners that reminded me of Oliva: a hug we'd shared here, over there where we'd held hands, the other place we'd walked together, and in the corner my cul-de-sac of loneliness and absence – of Gus, of my mother, of my lack of a real place to call home.

None of it endured and I asked myself what exactly was waiting for me in Madrid. Going home stopped being something I longed for and became a mere obligation. I remember getting emotional at the Osaka concert, standing before a hundred pairs of silent Japanese eyes as I sang:

*It's the opposite of what they say*
*It just gets harder every day.*

I wrote those lines with Gus and Oliva in mind, certain that I'd lost them forever, and I now also believed that to be the case with Kei: we'd said goodbye at the reception of the hotel in Osaka, with all the musicians warmly embracing her except for me, more timid than ever. I'd never see Kei again, we wouldn't even share the bus back to Tokyo because she took the train, and her boyfriend would probably be waiting for her at the station so that they could run off back to their life together before we'd invaded.

The night before she'd played a pizzicato section during our final song, while Animal shook with each strike of the bass drum, and I thought about how, thanks to Kei, our music had been elevated to heights we'd never have imagined. When the performance was over, I said goodbye to the crowd in Japanese and I remembered the saying Kei had taught me one day while spurning my advances.

'The eyes invent what they see,' is what she'd said.

And I winked in her direction as I repeated it onstage.

'The eyes invent what they see.'


## the eyes invent what they see

If my eyes invented Kei, which I don't doubt, then she'd also reinvented my eyes. As they looked out through the window of the bus home, they saw everything differently now. I'd be getting drunk, that's for sure, the moment I got back, taking some time to remember the highlights of the tour with Animal. And I'd make some songs. Love songs, the kind you only write when the object of your affection eludes you, beautiful lies cooked up to keep up the smokescreen.

By this stage we knew that our profession, as composers of love songs, was one practised by impostors. But none of that mattered to me, that morning on the bus, as I put my headphones on to listen to The Smiths singing about the light that never goes out. Saying all that stuff about how dying by your side, even if it means being flattened by a ten-ton truck, is a heavenly pleasure.

Before saying goodbye I'd handed Kei the envelope with the money she was owed and she'd put it in her bag, grateful.

'I'd have played for free,' she assured me.

'Me too.'

I hadn't been able to hug her as we left the hotel, or even brush her hand, and she said goodbye to me by leaning her body towards me with her customary reverence.

Seeing me get on the bus, one of the musicians shouted, 'What the fuck, Dani, you didn't even have it off with her!'

But I was thinking only about what the classics say, which is that a secret love is more profound than a public one. No one, not even Animal, suspected that I'd been with her the night before, or knew that for me this separation was more akin to an amputation. I put up with the filthy jokes that continued even once she was out of sight as we drove away from that fortress-like hotel.

After pushing me into Kei's bedroom the previous night, Animal had gone out whoring. He'd walked past all the shop-fronts in the Tobita Shinchi, the red-light district that offered women for sale, and was insisting enigmatically that 'If you've never slept with a Japanese woman then you don't know what sex is,' to the laughter of the others, who kept asking for every sordid detail.

I'd cut my lip shaving in a hurry at the hotel and when I began to bleed again on the bus, someone handed me a towel. Everyone dozed as we drove along those roads in the hills of Tokyo, which seemed to have no end nor beginning. Animal was talking to the other musicians, and at that exact moment he was telling the story of how we'd begun to play and started the group.

'You should have seen the look on that priest's face when everyone starting shouting at him to let us play.'

There was a barely concealed pride in the way he told it and I liked being a part of what he considered an epic tale. Animal was convinced that our career had continuity, that what we'd started in that school courtyard with Gus would never end, but this only rekindled my fear and made me think about what awaited me in Madrid. Starting all over again, again.

We got off the bus at the entrance to the airport; the towel was covered in red blotches from the stupid cut to my lip. My leather bag containing my passport, my money, a few bits and bobs for the journey and my notebook hung from my shoulder. I took the guitar from the cart where all the musical instruments were piled up and I walked over to Animal.

'Take my things. I'm staying.'

There was a smile on his face until he noticed my inebriation, the state of rapture I was in. He didn't say anything and I silently asked him not to tell the others.

'Ah, come on, man, you'll regret it later. It's just a crush.'

I shook my head a few times and began walking away from the check-in desks.

'There's thousands of chicks in Spain.'

But his words lacked conviction.

'We were together last night,' I let slip as my sole explanation.

A long time after, he told me that Serrat had made a disparaging comment on how love songs were still doing serious damage. He liked telling people about an old friend who'd attempted to sue Frank Sinatra: he'd proposed to his wife while listening to 'Strangers in the Night' and he wanted to claim damages and losses. Someone, I no longer remember who, told me later that if literature and songs were dedicated to praising the timeless grandeur of a good plate of lentils, we'd all be travelling to the ends of the earth in search of the finest specimens. Maybe they were right.


*eat, eat, don't leave a scrap*

'Eat, eat, don't leave a scrap.'

Jandrón's mother continued to eat with an abnormally large

appetite, though the rest of us had all accepted defeat. Despite her slim, fragile build, she devoured the lamb ribs with her sharpened fangs and then licked every last drop of fat from her fingertips.

She pointed to the platter where a few pieces still remained, reminding me of my father, with that obsession of his about never wasting anything, eating everything up. 'Ah, if you only knew the hunger we had to endure after the war.'

One of Jandrón's sons was still eating leftover bits of pork rind and a baby in a high chair was teasing its emerging teeth with a rib, held aloft in its drool-soaked hand. This scene, this collective of carnivores at work, which I observed as if it was a nature documentary on TV, was suddenly interrupted by the sound of the double doors opening. The adolescent girl I'd previously seen poking her head through the window of the village hall came through them. Luci introduced her as a one of Jandrón's nieces, Paula.

There were several photos of Jandrón's father, who'd died some years earlier, on display around the living room; it didn't seem plausible that this beautiful girl could come from the same gene pool as the monobrowed man staring into the camera. By then I'd spent a good amount of time in the company of the less fortunate branch of her family's genes and her entrance on the scene perked me up.

Luci said I needed a nap and asked Paula if I could use her room.

'You don't mind, do you, Paula?'

'Of course not.'

I accepted the offer in the hope that, at the very least, the solitude and the rest would do me good. I didn't have a toothbrush or a change of clothes, and I couldn't remember whether or not I had an appointment in Madrid that afternoon. But it was better not to resist: some hostages die after attempting a show of force against their captors.

Luci, followed by Paula, led me to the basement bedroom and cleared the abandoned clothes off the bed, explaining that 'This one leaves everything all strewn about. You know what teenagers are like.'

She threw the clothes into a nearby sports bag while Paula flashed me an amused look and between the two of them they created enough of a space on the mattress for me to be able to sink down into it.

'I'm sorry to be a pain,' I said.

'No, no, it's fine,' said Paula. 'I'll get out of your way now.'

When the girl had left, I slumped onto the mattress without taking off my trainers, but Luci had other plans. I watched her pull my trainers off.

'You'll be comfier that way, for God's sake.'

I felt her hands pressing down on my ankles. For a moment I thought she was going to take them off with my feet still inside. She was still grumbling as she left the room.

'Now sleep, sleep. God knows what time you get your head down most nights.'

The bedroom, submerged beneath the house, smelt of damp and plaster. There was a sacred heart of Jesus above my head, tenderly gazing across the room. I took my mobile phone from my pocket and prayed that some signal could get through those thick walls. I called home to see how my children were getting on.

My daughter Maya told me that Animal was with them. Sometimes he'd show up unannounced, to keep his wild anxiety at bay; he'd come over to my house to pass the time and if I'd gone out he'd stay and play with the kids or take them out for a walk. He was my only possible salvation. I asked Maya to put him on.

'Hey, Dani, where the hell are you?'

I told Animal about my journey to the village, my father's

burial, and then asked him to get in the van and come and find me.

'You have to come to my father's village. You'll find it on a map, but you have to come now. Can you?'

'Sure,' he replied, clearly understanding the desperate urgency of the situation.

'Garrafal de Campos,' I repeated. 'It'll take you around three hours, so you'll be here around eight. Park at the entrance to the village and come and look for me. I'll be the one surrounded by people. I'll think of a way to give them the slip.'

'Dude, I've got no idea what's going on, but count on me. You know I can handle these things better than you.'

Paula's MP3 player lay on the dresser, the headphones tossed to one side. I scrolled through the songs and couldn't find my name among the predictable list of international hits. She had a field of sunflowers as her screensaver. I found the list of most-played tunes, put the headphones in, hit shuffle and let sleep close in on me.

*invading your life*

Invading your life, when you put it that way, sounded like a military operation. And indeed, there was something bellicose in my lightning-quick return to Tokyo. I'd booked myself into a hotel opposite the metro station from which I'd emerged after coming back from the airport to the city centre; it was called Hotel Terminal, and it was narrow and tall, like a phone box crammed between the other buildings.

The room was tiny. I tumbled onto the bed after tearing off the quilt: hotel bed quilts are living organisms, containing the ominous residues of previous guests, filthy maps of a past you'd rather not know about.

I needed to think and yet at the same time I didn't want to think at all. I tried twice to call the number Kei had written down for me the day we met, but each time a different voice answered and I chose to stay silent. I went out onto the streets to eat something as the day begun to draw to a close, but didn't find the walk remotely relaxing.

I went back to the hotel and had a wank, which had a crushing effect on me, like having the act itself broadcast on national TV. I felt dirty, stupid, washed-up. And I felt guilty. I didn't dare to call her that night and I imagined my travel companions flying above me, on their way home, cracking jokes at my expense, picturing me sniffing and panting my way around Tokyo like a dog on heat. They'd never have believed that I was in fact alone, sprawled out on a bed inside a dingy hotel.

The following morning, I wrote a few lines in my notebook, attempting to write a song that would liberate me, but in the end the pages were condemned to the bin. The phone was screaming out at me from the bedside table, so I dialled her number again. Kei answered and when she heard my voice, a dark silence descended, a silence that soon turned to horror when I told her that I hadn't caught the plane. It was tough to hear her breathing like that, maybe crying.

'No, no, no, I don't want anything from you. I just wanted to say that I'm going to be around for a while. I want to stay here, get to know the country better, have some time to think. But I don't want to bother you.'

'Where are you?'

'In a hotel, near the station.'

I said its name; I think she told me she knew it. In my schoolboy English I made sure she understood that I wasn't trying to bother her, I wasn't planning on invading her life. I said it like that, in English, '*invading your life.*'

Inert, like a passenger no one shows up to collect from the

airport, I went down onto the street and spent a few hours in the *shotengai*, a nearby passageway full of shops. For a thousand yen I got my hair cut in a seventh-floor barbershop.

'You won't believe it,' I said to my father that day after calling to put him at ease. 'I've had a haircut.'

I told him I was staying in Japan for a few more weeks, that I wanted to explore the country, get to know it better. His desire for a more in-depth interrogation clashed with his certainty that the call I was making was bound to be very expensive and in the end the thrifty side of him prevailed.

'OK, you should hang up now. You can tell me when you get back.'

Then I wrote a long letter to Animal and Martán, to put them at ease, too, and to tell them not to be impatient, that we'd talk about work before long.

I took my time going back to the hotel, walking for a long time in no particular direction: I was desperate to avoid having to ask again if there were any messages for me and seeing the receptionist look at me with a mixture of suspicion and pity. I went up to the room and switched on the TV. I repeated the Japanese sentences phonetically, to the best of my ability. I tore the seal off the *yukata*, the cotton kimono, always placed at the foot of the bed inside plastic wrapping. I continued to repeat the catchphrases from the cooking programme, presented by an effusive young guy with hair that was frizzed up in every direction.

I tried playing the guitar for a while, but nothing came to me. I played aimlessly, the way I'd been walking around the city earlier. After a few minutes someone knocked on the door and a guy who looked like the lift mechanic asked if it was me playing.

'Sorry,' I said, apologising in case the noise had annoyed people in another room.

'No, no,' he said, shaking his head, and he added something I didn't understand, crossed his arms like the blades of a windmill and leant over towards me, distraught at having interrupted.

We smiled at each other around a thousand times before I closed the door and went back to the guitar. I tried to play something that made sense, now I knew that I was being listened to, including some of the compositions I'd learnt with Don Aniceto. Why were they coming into my head now?

Several hours passed before the telephone rang – with the intensity of an air raid siren – and the shock made me jump up on my bed. I answered, but it wasn't Kei or her gentle trickling stream of a voice. In his hesitant English, the receptionist told me that someone was waiting for me downstairs. I took a deep breath and tidied myself up using the tiny bathroom mirror. I wet my hair like I was going into a job interview and I fooled around in front of the mirror, trying out a samurai's ritual cry to loosen myself up.

I saw him the moment the lift opened, had no trouble recognising him. It was Kei's boyfriend. He smiled and greeted me with a stammer that sounded like boiling water. Mitsuo talked about Kei.

'She send me,' he said.

His English was rudimentary, which made me worry that even slight nuances wouldn't be understood by him. Every sentence was primary-school level.

'She worry about you.'

'Tell her I'm fine,' I told him.

There was no emotion in his words, just a sparkling grin, as if he were actually talking to me about the city's must-see sights, but he mentioned their plans to marry and then explained that Kei was asking me to return to Spain.

'You will no pain to her, true?'

I had to make him repeat it maybe three times before I could understand the question. He embraced me warmly and I stood there, dismayed, feeling ridiculous, with the sinking feeling that I was a bad person.

What did that honest, affable chap expect me to do? Get out of their lives? You can't intentionally hurt a man with such a boyish smile, a man who smells like wet dog.

'You must go, you must go to your country.'

But what he didn't know was that I was here to stay, that I was descended from Spaniards and that I didn't care if it wasn't so much a conquest as a banishment, because we'd accumulated a great deal of experience in both. And what he didn't understand was that, with my hug and my smile, I sought to annihilate him completely. Such are the rules of love.

## you used to hate sleeping as a child

'You used to hate sleeping as a child. Look at you now.'

What? Yes, I did hate sleeping as a child; it always felt like a waste of time. My mother was alarmed at how early I'd get up on weekends, and once I'd started studying with Don Aniceto, I'd be sitting on the bed with my guitar the moment I got up. I later learnt to tolerate it, but for me sleeping always meant missing out on life, not enjoying it.

It was only when I was with Oliva, with whom I never got to spend long nights, that I learnt to appreciate the prolonged pleasure of falling back to sleep after waking up and then waking three more times, lengthening the slow procession of love in the morning. An indefatigable early riser, she only occasionally heeded my requests to stay in bed, not to be in such a hurry.

After her, I never slept the same way again. I wake at all hours and only exhaustion helps me to reconcile myself to sleep. My children brought another form of sleep with them, with a built-in alarm that made me jolt in response to any strange noise and a vague fear of sleeping deeply, as if their breathing depended on my alertness. I've written songs during the night, verses written almost word for word in a semi-waking state; the songs always feel fully fleshed out as I doze until the effect is ruined by waking: by the time they're put on paper they're a shadow of what I'd thought they were.

'You hated sleeping as a boy. When you came to the village you wouldn't even let us sleep during the siesta,' Jandrón complained. 'You said taking siestas was for old people. Looks like that's what you've ended up becoming. Come on now, wake up. It's time, Dani.'

I opened my eyes with difficulty. It wasn't possible that I'd already used up my siesta hours – I felt just as defeated as I'd felt when I'd fallen asleep. Paula's songs were still playing.

'You like that music?' Jandrón asked as I took off his niece's earphones.

'Yeah, no, I don't know,' I replied.

My ears hurt and I put my glasses back on to focus on Jandrón. At some point we'd have to bring up the time we showed each other our dicks and he initiated me into the world of sex with poultry.

'I'm sorry to interrupt your siesta, but you need to speak to the boys from the paper.'

'What?'

The boys from the paper were a noble-looking gentleman with a patrician face who covered village festivals for *El Norte de Castilla* and a pair of acne-ridden students, who made a video recording of my answers for a local news page no one would ever be desperate enough to look up. With the inertia typical of journalism, which formulates the same questions in every place and in all circumstances and never breaks with this rather pointless protocol, I responded to their friendly interrogation.

'What's your best childhood memory of the village?'

'The time I watched the mayor sodomising a hen,' I felt like saying. 'Do you think these villages have a future?' I was asked. I should have said, 'The past is the only thing that has a future.'

'Are the roots that tie you to this region present in your songs at all?'

All of my answers were disappointingly predictable and lazy. 'What do you think of people who illegally download your music?'

It still hadn't got any cooler, yet the neighbours were beginning to come out of their homes and surround the place where all the action was happening. And that's when the ritual of the selfie began. It was very common, even when walking around abroad, for a Spaniard to recognise you and ask to have a photo taken so that they could post it on social media. 'Are you someone famous?' people sometimes asked me. Often they confused me with someone else: 'You're Coque Malla, right?' 'Quique González?' Or they'd congratulate me for songs I hadn't written.

On one occasion, after signing an autograph, the girl who'd requested it reappeared to tell me she couldn't make out my name.

'Aren't you the skinny one from Pereza?'

The hearse driver also came over to me with his phone: 'You don't mind if we take a photo together, do you? We're like family now.'

'Sure,' I agreed.

'Do you know Enrique Iglesias?' Jairo asked. 'He must be a friend of yours.'

'No, I don't know him.'

'But you admire him, right?'

'Yes, of course I do.' What else could I say . . .?

'You could have brought Shakira,' some kid commented, almost drooling with lust.

'I barely know her,' I said by way of apology.

'Or Beyoncé and Rihanna' – which he pronounced 'Rijana' – 'they're so hot.'

'I'll tell you what, there'd be no more bull run if one of them came to play here,' chimed in another, slightly older brat.

There were even more people in the square and surrounding streets, arriving for the fiesta from neighbouring villages. Jandrón explained that many of the teenagers from the youth clubs were still having their siestas because they'd been up until the wee hours.

'There's going to be some serious hangovers! But then, that's also a fiesta tradition, am I right?'

'Sure is,' I confirmed.

The councillor was fighting with a mic cable in an attempt to extend it from the small collapsible stage in the middle of the square to the school gates. The square glimmered with decorations and multicoloured light bulbs and I remembered how during past fiestas Jandrón and his friends would try to smash the bulbs with rocks, double points for red. The councillor achieved his goal by violently yanking the cable and then moved on to the soundcheck, tapping the mic and softly growling into it, making a noise that sounded like the amplified cries of an approaching ogre: 'Aaah, uuuh.'

One day I'd have to ask Raquel calmly if they'd mentioned the extent of the programme to which I was to be subjected. It's possible she'd accepted it as a cold form of revenge, as she strolled down Copacabana with her new friend, payback for all the problems she'd resolved without so much as a word. Now, it was my turn to pay for it, all in one go. It's possible she even enjoyed the crazy idea of me, knee-deep in my father's native village, besieged by the great and the good. Sometimes she'd book me in for fundraising concerts, saying I had to do them, then take me to a radio performance to raise money for immigrants or a dinner in aid of the treatment of rare illnesses, or to play at an event in defence of traditional wine corks, organised by people involved in the preservation of cork oaks. It was her way of getting back at me for my manias, my demands and my whims – like the time I insisted on taking a walk around my childhood neighbourhood for one of my videos and ordered an enormous sunset to be painted on the wall of our cul-de-sac in Calle Paravicinos, hoping it might brighten up the lives of the residents for a few months.

My other artistic extravagances were limited to insisting on having clean towels, toilet paper and running water in the dressing room; that is, if there even was a dressing room in the venue we were playing at. Once when we played in a village in Huesca, I inquired about the nearest toilet and the mayor, a very affable chap, handed me a mop bucket and told me, 'Do it here. I'll get rid of it after the concert.'

'Did you sleep well in my bed?'

Paula touched my shoulder after I'd finished posing for another photo with Aunt Dorina's fourth cousin twice removed. She was the kind of young girl who sparkled wherever she went and I was delighted to see her.

'At least the room's nice and cool, right?'

'Yes,' I conceded, a little stunned by her beauty. 'What are you up to? Partying with your friends?'

'I'm seriously hung-over,' she confessed. 'We had a big one last night.'

Her fellow villagers continued to take snaps of me with their phones and the bright flashes left blinding white blotches in my eyes.

'What a bunch of losers, right?' she said. 'They won't leave you alone.'

'It's OK; it's only one day.'

'But they've really pulled a fast one on you! Jandrón wants you to sing tonight,' she told me.

'Yeah, he told me already. Well, at the end of the day, how can I refuse? It's my father's village and it's the least I can do.' I'd started playing my role.

'Did you come here a lot when you were little?' she asked me.

'No, like you, I guess – the odd fiesta here, a summer there.'

'You must have known my mother, then. I'm not sure if you remember her. Her name was Ignacia.'

'Ah,' I responded, my mouth wide open as I suddenly understood the origin of those brilliant green eyes, that childhood infatuation suspended in time.

Into that poignant moment burst Luci, seemingly from nowhere, with that special knack for pouring cold water on the party.

'What, trying to get the youth on your side, are we?' she asked.

'No, not at all. Paula doesn't even like my songs.'

Paula smiled and I confessed I'd taken a look at the songs in her collection.

'I've heard one or two. My friend likes the one that goes 'play for me'. Is that what it's called?'

'These ones now wouldn't dream of buying a record; nobody does any more. With everything that's happening I've no idea how you make a living off it. And on top of that, all the councils are broke and we have to balance the books when we organise these celebrations, you know. They won't tell you that, of course, but that's how it is,' Luci interjected.

'Yes, yes. Someone already told me that you've only been able to sacrifice one bull this year.'

'If only that was all it was,' she replied.

I shrugged my shoulders ironically, directing the gesture at Paula.

'Don't worry. I'll download one of your albums off the Internet,' she said, flattering me.

A moment later she said goodbye.

'She's a ray of sunshine, that girl. My niece, you know. Now, you, you'd better keep quiet and no moaning. We're treating you like a king here.'

## waiting nourishes

Waiting nourishes the heart. If there was anything that really got on Vicente's nerves, it was anxious people. That's what he told me in his house one afternoon as we went through his neatly ordered shelves of vinyl records and tapes. He was looking unhurriedly for a particular song for us to listen to together; although it was entirely possible he'd find something else to show me along the way. Maybe the thing he found annoying about Gus was his lack of patience, the way he wanted everything now, right away, like a child. And so Vicente always said that waiting nourishes the soul.

His verdict on the arrival of mobile phones was withering, not because of the obvious service they'd provide, but because of the immediacy.

'It'll be awful, you'll see. If we do away with waiting, pauses, periods with no communication, then nothing will ever happen by accident, by chance, on impulse. With mobile phones it'll be impossible to fall in love, because everything will get instantly resolved. Love is all about waiting.'

I've often thought about this and it's possible that Vicente's words did indeed turn out to be prophetic, even though he always ended his laments by saying, 'Oh, don't listen to me,

I'm just a presenter with no programme. The typical old guy who thinks that just because he's finished, the whole world has to end with him.'

I kept my mobile in my suitcase. It was too expensive to make calls with it while I was in Tokyo and it took me back to an earlier time, before such easy communication existed. Besides, Kei kept silent for several days. The wait didn't so much feed my heart as my imagination. My dreams at night consisted of weird disconnected scenes: I'd be walking a dog through the woods, at times trying to spur him on, play with him, other times losing sight of him. Then I'd call after him. But it wasn't my dog, it wasn't my Lindo Clon who my father was looking after in Madrid. My voice would resonate among the trees just as it had resonated earlier that afternoon, beneath the enchanted bell in a temple I'd visited, and the echo was a musical one.

For breakfast I'd have raw fish and green tea in the hotel restaurant. The guitar always resting in its case by my side, like a friend, a travel companion. I liked to play sitting down on one of the benches near the emperor's gardens, busking and smiling back at each smile I received from passing joggers, who always ran in the direction and within the space clearly indicated for them by the city council. I'd invent melodies but make no effort to memorise them, convinced that any song that came out of those circumstances would be no less embarrassing than my current frame of mind: the circumstances were perfect for self-help songs, self-indulgent songs – that is, the worst kind imaginable.

I'd found the perfect place to eat near the centre, in a bar where people smoked and drank, with an unmarked wooden door that gave onto the street. I spotted a man stumbling out of it the first time I walked past: old drunks are the best guarantee of the quality of a place, like the lorries parked outside roadside cafes in Spain.

That bar turned out to be absolutely irresistible, with adjoining tables enveloped in cigarette smoke and glasses of beer and saké everywhere. With time it would become one of my favourite spots; the clientele was older and worn-out, all uninhibited senior gents who'd occasionally collapse, drunk and defeated, onto the tables in front of them. That was where I got into drinking *nihonshu*, and the soup, the fried food, the smoke and the noise all formed a secret connection with so many dives I'd known in Madrid.

Back at the hotel, I met the older man who'd rung at my door a few days earlier and who I discovered did maintenance at the hotel. He pointed at the guitar. I could barely understand him, but the receptionist told me he wanted to know if I gave guitar lessons.

'Lessons?' I asked.

They briefly exchanged information between themselves and then the young man told me that the older man had a grandson who wanted to learn Spanish guitar. He was asking if I'd teach him.

Of course I would.

The man handed me a card with his address and telephone number so that I could come over to see him the following day. We shook hands as we agreed on the time: four o'clock. I was overcome by a joyful mood that lasted until well into the afternoon, by which time I'd already taken the decision to move to a cheaper place, further away from the commercial district.

It turned out that the guitar lessons were actually for two of the man's grandsons. They were thick, grinning boys, their fingers slow and weak, almost comically unsuited to the instrument. The man paid me an indefinite amount of yen every time I went to the house. The lessons took place twice a week, on the afternoons when he looked after his grandchildren, and his wife would prepare a snack for us, which I'd devour while communicating solely through smiling and pointing.

Not long after, I convinced him that while his grandsons might make fine soloists on the *zambomba*, they'd never play the Spanish guitar. It was a shame, because by then both the man and his wife, Mr and Mrs Utamaro, had become friends, and I'd visit them even when I wasn't teaching the boys so that I could let them get me drunk, something that gave them enormous pleasure as hosts.

One day, as I arrived back from one of these guitar lessons, Kei was sitting on the sofa in the lobby and stood up when she saw me. It was like a vision, an illusion. Before she could say anything, I explained to her that I already had a job.

'Yes, the receptionist told me. You're a guitar teacher.'

I burst out laughing and then opened my arms. She almost ran to take refuge in them. It was a chaste hug; we were more like siblings than lovers. We remained like that for a long while, witnessed by the shocked eyes of the receptionist, who'd already marked me out as a dangerous, solitary criminal. Then, in order to demonstrate my knowledge of Japanese to Kei, I tried to say one of the phrases I'd learnt.

'*Ashita no asa hachi ji ni okoshite kudasai.*' I pronounced it delicately into her ear, like a profound declaration of love, though what I'd actually said was: 'Please could you wake me at eight in the morning?'

We went out to have dinner in a nearby restaurant and spoke quickly, without exchanging any meaningful information. I told her about my solitary days in the city and she asked me how the hell I'd managed to end up being a guitar teacher. I described how the man had appeared at the hotel and the bar, full of drunks and smokers, where I ate. She told me she thought I'd left after her boyfriend's visit and that she'd only called the hotel that morning to find out if I was still there.

'Is there still a foreigner staying?' she'd asked.

The reception boy had answered with another question.
'The Spaniard with the guitar?'
Then she'd decided to come and see me.

I told her about my method for learning Japanese, which consisted of memorising ten words a day and finding any excuse to use them in conversation. One day it was tuna, teaspoon, glass. Then next day it was book, house, brush, then sun, cloud and street, or *taiyo*, *kumo* and *tori*. Maybe this was another explanation for the receptionist's obvious discomfort around me: every morning I greeted him and then pointed first to his pen, saying '*boorupen*' and then at the telephone, adding, '*denwa*'. So as not to boast too much in front of Kei, I confessed that for every ten words I studied, the next day I could only remember four. At that rate, I'd have a vocabulary of 8,000 words in six years. I was a man with a great future ahead of him.

I ordered white wine, not wanting her to know about my addiction to *nihonshu*, but Kei only had a few sips, whereas I got drunk. Then we went back to the hotel. I didn't ask about Mitsuo the whole afternoon and she didn't mention his name; she just told me she couldn't stay when I invited her up to the room.

From that point on, we established a kind of pact of practical friendship: Kei helped me to find an apartment to rent, one that satisfied all of my needs within a space no bigger than three lunges. We bought the bare minimum I needed to get by: clothes, towels and kitchen essentials from Tokyu Hands. I let her be the one to suggest going out somewhere or visiting a museum or some other public space. She let me take her by the arm on the street and even briefly kiss her on the cheek when we parted ways.

Sometimes Kei cried and sometimes I ran my mouth off. I was in the habit of carrying around a notebook, which I used as a convenient personal dictionary to jot down new words or phrases. I took it out whenever there was an opportunity, practising with Kei or asking her to write things down for me.

After a performance by her quartet she'd invited me to, I tried out a well-rehearsed sentence on her – 'Would you care to dine with me?' – enunciated in what I imagined to be perfect, neat, formal Japanese. But it made her companions burst out into childish fits of laughter until they explained that I'd actually said something like 'Are you wanting me to dine on you?' It wasn't a completely ridiculous idea.

## sometimes darkness scares me, other times it's heaven

One night I wrote the lyrics, 'Sometimes darkness scares me / other times it's heaven', before hurrying to lay down the simple melody on a portable recorder I'd bought from one of those seven-floor tech supermarkets. It was a special song, not about anything going on at the time, or maybe it was: songs, like people, belong to their birthplaces and this was my first Japanese song.

It described Madrid the way you can only describe a place you're longing for. Often, songs are ways of getting back things that are absent, because when you write you're always writing about what you've lost. My first Japanese song went through several versions and variations until one afternoon I asked Kei to let me play it to her. She didn't want to come up to the room, because the last time she did I'd tried to kiss her; she'd been furious and had refused to call me for two days. So I played it to her out on the street and I stopped at the points in the song where I thought a cello would sound great.

'Here, and here, when I say the bit about lifting the veil of my dolour.' A word I'd picked up a long time ago, from the poetry of Garcilaso de la Vega.

Not long after, she told me that a friend of hers had a place to record in Yokohama, less than an hour's train journey away; we could record there when there was nothing else going on in the studio. Haruomi was a kindly forty-something who helped us to bring in some strange keyboards, with an old Farfisa organ I remember using once with Gus, on our earliest recordings. His involvement helped to give the song a Japanese flavour I'd never dreamt of.

Kei seemed content to watch me compose and sing my Japanese song, and the three of us sat down to listen after her friend had ordered some dinner from the Chinese takeaway next door. We ate it straight out of the box as we corrected the levels, although the recording was very basic. Kei insisted on double-tracking the cello several times and giving the accompaniment more texture, and for an instant it seemed like I was in a group again, a strange mixture of people brought together by the mysterious process of making music.

It got late and Haruomi offered us the guest bedroom, which was there for when a recording session went on too long and someone needed to get their head down. There were no more trains back and Kei accepted; though I noticed the look of fear on her face when her friend said that he'd go up to his house to sleep because his family was waiting for him.

We stayed there playing for a while as he gathered his things to leave. I think Kei really wanted to give her friend the impression that our relationship was purely professional, but I knew tonight was the night, almost a month since I'd decided to stay in Tokyo, and I embraced Kei with a renewed forcefulness, caressing her body over her clothes. She played her erotic game of resistance until finally we joined together the twin beds in the room.

All those days of self-control, the distance she'd imposed every time we saw each other – it was all gone in an instant. It was total surrender. We slept in each other's arms, in that un-comfortable bed that opened up in the middle like a geological fault. Once our naked bodies had regained their sense of shame, we threw a worn-out cover on top of ourselves. Kei fled at the crack of dawn, without taking a shower, bathed in my odour, something that didn't seem to bother her.

I waited for her friend to return and open up the studio. We ate breakfast together. Haruomi must have sensed something, because he laughed like a schoolboy every time he looked at me. We listened to the song again before the studio filled up with clients. I remember that song being a revelation: I felt it was the artistic equivalent of a bespoke suit in a world that was getting faster every day, where paying attention to something that lasted longer than three minutes had become impossible. It was a reminder that a song could still have a heart, you only had to create an atmosphere, a sonic background, and let the melody and the lyrics pull the light out from the inside – like the best paintings, which create a focal point that draws in the viewer's eyes.

Through Haruomi I managed to find a venue that let me play my songs twice a month to a chatty crowd who were completely indifferent to my Spanish songs, accompanied by my electric guitar and Kei's cello.

*Sometimes darkness scares me*
*Other times it's heaven.*

That was how the song I called 'Calendar' began. It's the one song I always have to play at concerts, even though it reminds me of wearing nothing but a *fundoshi*, sitting on my bed in that tiny Tokyo apartment, and being between the sheets with Kei in Haruomi's miniature studio, happy at having discovered I could make songs there, with her:

*Sometimes darkness scares me*
*Other times it's heaven*
*I want to show you my city*
*Let's experience it together.*


## I want to show you my city, let's experience it together

'I want to show you my city, let's experience it together,' I proposed to Kei. 'Come with me to Madrid, just for two weeks. It can be your holiday.'

It was crucial that I went back to Madrid for a while. My tourist visa was about to run out and I needed to clear up a few things, talk to Animal and Martán about our future, and sit down with the people at the label.

My father seemed unsettled when I called, insisting that I was hiding the truth and that there were other reasons behind what he called my *espantá*.

'The *espantá*,' he explained, as ever taking a backwards glance towards the mythology of bullfighters and zarzuela, 'isn't, as you know, just about being afraid of the bull, as Rafael, *El Gallo*, used to say. No, it's the art of putting ground between yourself and the bull when your legs and your heart falter.'

For him, my *espantá* was all about my inability to get my life with Oliva back.

'Let's see, Dani. Is there a girl involved?'

'Of course there's a girl involved,' I answered when he asked me directly, 'but it's not just that. I want to be here, I want to get to know another country.'

At this he sounded relieved and confessed he'd assumed I'd been arrested for some drug-related issue and that my highly punctual phone calls, always on the same day and at the same time, could only have been the result of prison–imposed discipline.

'If I call you at regular intervals it's because you yourself love prison discipline,' I told him.

I really did want to get to know the country better. Kei had some work that meant we wouldn't be able to see each other for several days and I'd planned a trip somewhere, away from the big city, hoping to discover Japan from a train window. It was ridiculous for me to be spending my time like that, tramping around old temples, mountains, hotels and *ryokan*, however exciting it was to be submerged in the completely incomprehensible conversations of the people around me. Or for me to accept invitations to get drunk on shots of saké – which was the main way for Japanese people to show friendliness to tourists, or *gaijin*, as they called us.

'What will you live on? What about your mother, aren't you going to see her any more?' my father asked.

I said of course I was, then I told him about the guitar lessons and explained that musicians could live anywhere. But it wasn't true. I was frittering away all of my savings in that costly, perplexing city.

'They'll forget about you. Everyone will forget about you,' my father warned.

This wasn't all that different from what the people at the label company kept telling me, Bocanegra in particular.

'You need to make yourself visible, or the public will wipe you off their radar.'

As my career stagnated, Kei's flourished and one of her quartets was beginning to get some highly tempting offers, including dates abroad. The three other members were all easy-going Tokyoites who approached classical music without any elitist pretensions. They'd decided to focus on Scriabin and were getting an album of his music together, which included some jazzy interpretations.

I visited them in the studio and was overwhelmed by their

incredible precision, the way they played bits over and over again, constantly editing and improving certain moments they wanted to perfect. Their approach to music couldn't have been further removed from ours. I admired Kei and her musical expertise, the skill she'd acquired by sacrificing her childhood.

Sitting next to their technician I learnt how to operate the new mixing desks, the digital equalisers, alter the frequencies, mic up each instrument, and filter or revert the atmosphere. I became the sound engineer's helper, something Kei observed with a mixture of surprise and amusement.

'I never knew you liked playing around with these toys so much,' she said to me.

Sometimes we'd stay after hours to record a demo and her musician friends would add a little twist or a variation, despite not understanding a word of my Spanish lyrics.

One afternoon in the apartment, I listened to a conversation my neighbours were having. They were a polite, discreet couple, who always lowered their eyes in greeting when we met each other on the stairs. But that afternoon they were having an argument that was sounding more and more violent in tone, and I thought I heard something being shoved against the furniture, someone being hit perhaps. This was followed by silence and then by a conversation that played out in sobs.

It became a ritual, the daily brawl between this couple, so friendly on the outside and so hostile on the inside. I suspected there was something hiding behind all this repression. The grandparents of my guitar students were similarly restrained and friendly, but when the woman got drunk a cruel look would appear on her face and she'd come out with cutting retorts which, though I couldn't understand them, clearly silenced those around her. The widespread alcoholism and blatant machismo shocked me every day and made me feel worried for Kei. I had no idea what was going on with her other relationship, in her other life.

'You don't understand, OK?' Kei was clearly irritated when I tried to talk about her relationship with her boyfriend. 'When you go back to Spain, this is all over,' she told me.

'Why don't we go to Spain together?' I suggested.

She told me I was selfish, which was true.

'But sometimes you have to be selfish, you have to do what you really want, what you feel,' I insisted.

Kei found it difficult to explain, but she kept her eyes fixed on me. It was the best reply she could give: a cold, petrified stare.

'You'll be gone soon, right? Well that's it, then, it's all over,' she said.

I realised that for Kei my journey to Spain confirmed my escape, the end of our relationship: for her, I'd never stopped being a strange parenthesis. That afternoon, I put my arms around her shoulders as she began to walk down the street. I'd come from a lesson with my guitar on my back, and she'd just been rehearsing and so was carrying her cello. We were four lovers walking in opposite directions, broken, desolate, futureless.

Kei was on the brink of tears and we came to a halt on a bridge. Down below us the canal water was flowing and the cars were going by. I rested my guitar on the railings before freeing her from the weight of her cello case, which I rested to one side. All of a sudden I noticed the instruments standing there, propped up against each other. I pointed to them and smiled.

'They make a nice couple, don't they?' And then I falteringly repeated the expression, '*kappuru nimasu*'.

There was a worn-out rock, surrounded by chains, indicating the milestone's historical significance. Next to it was a small plaque bearing the logo of the bank that had met the costs of its restoration.

'They stopped here while they were preaching the gospel,' Jandrón pointed out for me. 'In Garrafal itself.'

This was another of his initiatives as mayor, to reclaim the route taken by the Apostle James on his way back to Jerusalem after disembarking in Galicia and his unlikely stop along the way, exhausted from so much preaching.

'No one has given us much credit for it so far,' Jandrón elaborated. 'But in 2033 we plan to celebrate 2,000 years since the events took place. The old folks around here have always told us the Apostle stopped to rest on this rock, and who are we to detract from that?'

I consoled him by mentioning that several different places all claim to hold his remains, that his horse's shoe is kept in a monastery in the north and that at the end of the day that's what legends are for. If it was simply a question of veracity then we'd have to close all the cathedrals, along with a great number of museums.

'The truth is a pain in the arse,' Jandrón agreed. 'But you can never kill people's hopes and dreams.'

We walked back towards the square, where someone placed a small bottle of beer into my hand, followed by another.

'Drink up, it's hot,' Jandrón ordered.

While I'd been surprised by how willing Japanese people were to get drunk after a certain point in the afternoon, what struck me about Spain was the booze-tinted hue of every village fiesta and how cruel so many of its traditions were. After playing a great number of outdoor dances and feast day celebrations, I've concluded that the cruelty practised at such events is a kind of rehearsal for the real world – a re-enactment in which the weak are always punished by the strong and powerful – and running away in terror from a beast in pursuit is just another form of training for our everyday lives.

The brass band appeared at one corner of the little square, playing as they walked, and with that the celebrations began in earnest. There were only six of them: two trumpets, one sax, one clarinet, one horn and a guy with a drum, who couldn't really keep up with the rhythm because he'd lost one of his shoes. I've always liked the sound of brass bands. The musicians, clad in sweaty Terylene shirts, were escorting the godmother of the fiesta.

'We're real feminists in this village,' Jandrón asserted. 'During the fiesta the godmother becomes the highest authority, higher even than the mayor. She presides over the events, carries out the offering to the Apostle and leads the dancers.'

'And who is she?' I couldn't quite make out the godmother, who was dressed in the typical uniform of embroidered apron and headdress.

'You don't know her? Come on, man, she's related to you! That's Juliana. You must have heard of her daughter, she was a missionary in Africa and got killed out there when we were kids.'

'Right, right.'

I raised my eyes to try to see her as she came closer, none other than my biological grandmother. One of my father's regrets after my mother got sick, I remembered then, was that she'd never get to be godmother when her turn came.

When she got to me, the godmother planted two kisses on my cheek and Jandrón led the two of us to the school gates. Juliana, that was her name. I scanned her face beneath the black veil for any family resemblance; I felt ridiculous for taking this sideways glance at my past, for seeking that which cannot be found.

The musicians stopped playing and Jandrón asked me if I'd like to say a few words.

'No, no,' I said apologetically, 'I said no speeches.'

He grasped hold of me. I felt tiny under his armpits.

'You're really shy, you are, much shyer than you look when you're singing.'

He put me down, like an exhausted child dropping a teddy bear, and then the godmother kissed me again and asked if I remembered her.

'Sure, of course I remember,' I admitted. 'You always used to come into my house for a drink of water.'

The festivities councillor helped us to open up a little corridor between the crowd so that we could make our way to the facade where the commemorative plaque we were about to unveil awaited us. The hearse driver hugged me with excitement as I passed him.

'Oh, Jairo, you're still here!'

'Sure am. I wasn't going to miss such a lovely occasion, now was I?'

We came to a halt next to the curtain that covered the plaque and the band played something that sounded like the *paso doble* of Manolete. A man gave me a powerful hug.

'It's Ciriaco, Antonia from the phone switchboard's son, remember?'

But Luci authoritatively pushed him to one side: 'Not now, they've got to unveil the plaque.'

Yes, I remembered the only phone in the village when I used to come as a boy, from which I called my mother a couple of times without daring to ask about her hospital visits – 'Everything's fine, Dani, don't worry' – and though I didn't tell her because I didn't want to make her sad, I missed her.

Once the music had finished, Jandrón grabbed the cord on the curtain that covered the plaque and invited me to pull it. I did so several times, but it wouldn't budge.

'Shit, man, pull it harder,' a local shouted out.

The councillor's wife accused me of ruining the ceremony.

'Come on, it worked fine before. I tested it myself just after lunch.'

I pulled it again, one, two, three times, but still nothing. Then Jandrón placed his hand on mine to give the cord a real good tug and the whole curtain came down on his face. In a single swipe, he unveiled himself.

'The Daniel Campos, alias Mosca Cultural Centre, is now officially open, in tribute to this son of Garrafal, on the feast day of the Apostle James.'

And then he added the year and let out three *vivas*, one for the village – *viva!* – one for the Apostle – *viva!* – and one for Dani Mosca – *viva!*


## every goodbye is a rehearsal

Every goodbye is a rehearsal for the final one. Kei insisted on coming to say goodbye at the airport, despite me asking her not to, to spare herself the pain of trying to train a muscle that's incapable of learning. But still she came. I wanted to look calm and collected, convinced as I was that I'd only be gone for a month, that I was only going to get my affairs in order. But she suspected it wouldn't be so simple.

'You won't come back,' she'd assured me three evenings earlier.

When I attempted to explain my relationship with Kei to Animal or Martán I felt selfish again, like I was putting my emotions before our collective endeavour. Martán was busy with his job at a computer games company and sounded enthusiastic, downplaying the fact I was so far away. Whenever I needed him, he'd be there – he didn't rely on our musical activity to survive. That wasn't the case with Animal. I noticed that he seemed resentful.

'What are your plans now? Anything new to tell me?' he asked.

But I didn't even have a plan for myself and I tried to clear the air with Animal. By the sixth or seventh beer, his joy at our reunion had blunted the edges of his grievances. Not so with his worries about the future. On his return from Japan, Animal had tried to live out his own love story.

'I was jealous of you, seeing you all loved up like that, your passion so inflamed,' he told me.

He'd met a girl and they'd begun something resembling a romantic relationship; she was called Mamen and I knew her because she'd worked for the label for many years until founding her own promotion agency. Her life story, like Animal's, bore all the hallmarks of an indomitable personality. According to him, she had an album cover attached to her bedroom wall signed by a certain AY, who had written something like 'For the best blow job in my life'.

'But it took her years,' Animal told me, 'to figure out that the word blow job had nothing to do with the promotional work she'd done for the group in Spain.'

My flat by the Bilbao roundabout felt enormous compared to my tiny Tokyo apartment. All of our shows were sold out and very quickly the idea of going away again felt like madness: something was trying to pull me away from Kei, now that I was back in such familiar surroundings. Nevertheless, when Martán suggested he move into my flat I said yes and that I wasn't thinking of sticking around in Madrid. He told me it was Animal who needed me most.

'Sure, he's living with this girl, but it's no love nest. It's more like a hornet's nest.'

And it was true, Mamen soon grew tired of Animal and threw him out.

'I wasn't designed for this love scam,' Animal said, retracting his previously stated intentions.

He'd got a small tour playing drums with a band from Zaragoza and those shows had helped him to overcome the suffocation of cohabiting.

'And anyway,' he explained, 'Zaragoza's the funnest city in Spain, so I spend half the week there.'

A few days later he introduced me to the lads he was playing with, one of whom was clearly very excited to meet me.

'Man, we've grown up listening to your songs.'

I felt time crashing down upon me.

I spoke to Animal about the possibility of coming to Japan and helping me to record, playing with me. His only reaction, I recall, was to make the sign for cash by rubbing the tips of his thumb and index finger together: 'And where will we get the bread from?' He'd been playing with a star of the moment, standing in for a drummer friend, and they paid cash in hand and off the books.

The year 2000 had arrived and I was thirty years old, just as we'd calculated so many times as kids back when that date felt iconic and our predictions of what it would be like were pure science fiction. It was depressing to hear Animal speak so admiringly of this guy he'd played with, who dragged around a sports bag full of banknotes after each performance.

'Seriously, that's your dream?' I asked him.

Bocanegra painted a seductive scene for me. He'd risen to the top of the record company and become one of its head honchos.

'What you gotta do is to come back here, where there's money.'

Renán now represented so many artists that we no longer meant much to him; all the big money was destined for other performers currently making a name for themselves on TV. Bocanegra assured me that with him as our manager we'd get enough performances to do a summer tour. Then I'd put all my efforts into a new album.

'What you gotta do is make a new album, right away. No more waiting.'

My relationship with him was one of cordial distrust. When Gus was alive he'd helped us to get established, supporting groups that packed out venues. He'd been affectionate and respectful – *whatyougottado* is this, or that, a tour of city venues, summer fiestas, another album. He was corrupt and profligate, and though everyone felt he was stealing from us, he did it in the exact same proportions as with larger groups.

Every year he'd move into a bigger and more spectacular house, spurred on by what he said were the whims of his wife with whom he'd had two kids he'd been dressing up as rockers since before they could walk. He loved pushing around a pram containing a baby shoved into a Ramones or Stones T-shirt, despite the fact he made a living from producing romantic balladeers.

Spain nurtured guys like Bocanegra: shameless, enterprising, entirely without scruples. There was a copious flow of money for expensive wines, fashionable restaurants, sports cars. It was easy to get used to such an environment, provided you weren't footing the bill. Of course, as is always the case, all that hospitality was paid for with money generated by us. But at least Bocanegra was nice. He insisted on going bankrupt every five years as a matter of hygiene, like a gut cleanse, and yet he always knew to step out of the vehicle just when the brakes started failing.

But my destiny, I felt, was to forever be turning into dead-end streets. At the end of the day, I was born in a cul-de-sac and perhaps I'd never leave one.

'I need to sort out my private life first,' I told Bocanegra.

'Being a musician means singing to other people about your private life,' he told me, without even listening to what I'd said. 'Let people come along with you. Sing to them about it. Got doubts? Sing about them. Wanna fuck an oriental girl because you're tired of fucking the Spanish ones who go to your concerts? Put it in a song; they'll lead the way for you. The audience dictates.'

He always claimed that the truth lay with the audience. For him, our profession couldn't be kept apart from our personal lives: 'When you go under you lose everything: friends, partner, social status, power. There's no such thing as public or private lives, man. In this game, you slit yourself open and let other people gobble up your insides, because that's what makes you rich.'

He asked me for a taste of what I'd been working on and I gave him just one of the songs I'd recorded in Japan, which had been inspired by my fears that my return was actually an escape. I hadn't been anywhere near a studio; it was just guitar and voice in my bedroom.

'What you gotta do is bring me ten songs like that and we've got ourselves the album of the millennium.'

The song was called 'If I Were Me' and the title had come from a conversation with Vicente in which I'd shared the same anxieties I'd discussed elsewhere.

He'd just replied, 'Be you, Dani, you have to be you.'

But what do I have to be to be me? What would I have to do if I were me?

## if I were me

Being back on the scene in Madrid, having nights that ended at five or six in the morning, did nothing to stop me from thinking about Kei all the time; I didn't call her, because surely my silence was better than any words. I'd later understand what was happening to me more clearly: if someone had inspected me with an X-ray machine back then, they'd have found a hole going all the way through me, a void that I haphazardly tried to fill.

The idea, the thing that Oliva — now so distant and irretrievable — had taken with her, was the idea of love. And I was determined to fix it. Whatever it took and no matter the cost. And I began to think I couldn't live without Kei, without being near her, when really the person I was missing most of all was me.

'I've seen a ton of people completely fuck their lives up because they believe love is more important than eating or doing the laundry. Are you going to make the same mistake? Loving is all well and good, but it's no better than having a dog or playing tennis,' Bocanegra told me as he drove me to the airport.

Animal couldn't be relied on so early in the morning; he'd have got drunk the night before and there'd be no way of waking him. In the mornings he was a complete dead weight, lying there on the mattress or the floor wherever he'd happened to end up, even in the flea- and cockroach-ridden guest houses we'd stayed in on our first couple of tours. He wasn't bothered about crashing out in the bathroom, on a fluff-covered mat. He slept how he always did, extremely heavily.

Bocanegra came to collect me in a grey Porsche.

'It's not penis envy, I swear. It's Porsche envy,' he said when he noticed the weary look on my face.

On the way to the airport he told me he'd let Luz Casal hear the demo of my song.

'I told her you're going to record it and that you've got a new album coming soon. But she loves it and wants to include it on her new record. Before you say anything, have a think about how it would sound with her voice. Let her have a go.'

'Tell her she can have it,' I replied.

To say I gave it away would be lying, though, because a few months later it became the steadiest source of income I've ever had, one of the biggest-selling, most-played songs for a whole decade. 'If I Were Me' would always be associated with that other beautiful and nasal voice:

*If I were me*
*I'd take what I get*
*And stop looking.*

Those royalty cheques made getting set up in Japan a breeze and the song won me a reputation as a composer of romantic ballads for female voices, a skill I turned to my own advantage when my own career was stuck in limbo.

Ana Belén would later record another tune of mine, also seeped in my effusive idea of love, and in a far more brazen display than in my own songs. Writing for other singers, some of the best female voices in the country – Sole Giménez, Concha Buika – taught me that you're never more honest than when speaking through the mouth of another.

Bocanegra then asked me for two more compositions for a San Sebastián group who, despite being on the cusp of hitting the big time, had lyrics that were barely preschool. They soon became one of the bestselling groups in the country and I earnt so much from those records that I came to believe that my future lay in writing on demand. That was until two years

309

later, when Bocanegra destroyed a song I'd put a great deal of effort into by giving it to a truly appalling artist. The ensuing argument was so heated that I decided to stop composing for other singers. The easy life, away from the limelight, came to an end.

Bocanegra left me on that muggy morning at the terminal in Barajas. I wasn't in the best of moods after having another argument with my father, who was annoyed about both my trip and my absence.

'You think your mother doesn't notice, but she does. It's convenient for you to imagine that she's ill and oblivious to everything, but she knows you're shirking your obligations.'

Only a father can wound you where it hurts the most. And he did it standing there, holding on to my dog's collar so that I wouldn't be tempted to take him with me.

A melody came to me on the plane back to Japan and I began scribbling lyrics that would become the song 'Live It the Way It Sounds', the centrepiece of our next album. I wrote almost the whole song, ready to be recorded, as the flight took off after a stopover in Helsinki. I was hit by a wave of euphoria, because it was a happy song, full of new life:

*I'll dry my eyes, won't let it bring me down*
*I've decided to live it the way it sounds.*

## live it the way it sounds

I remember that Gus was always incredibly keen to get what he wanted. Thirst, thirst, thirst, thirst. And I also remember how excited he was when the money first started to come in. How it quenched his desire for fame and success, which was undoubtedly far more urgent than mine, so much so that he took me to a seafood place that was very highly regarded back then and ordered gleaming trays full of goose barnacles, lobster, crab and oysters.

'I'm happy today, the way it sounds.'

And the phrase came back to me, to help me be happy, to aspire towards it, insist on it. Live it the way it sounds. Gus loved goose barnacles. He called them dinosaur feet and when the liquid splashed out, he'd celebrate them as orgasms of the sea. For Gus, such moments of euphoria were always work-related: a good gig, a good song, finishing the recording sessions for an album, meeting our loyal friends in the provinces, that Paris gala where we played with a bunch of European groups.

I talked to him about it once.

'How is it possible for you to only feel joy about things related to work? You never celebrate personal stuff.'

With a half-smile on his face, he responded, 'You'll understand when you come to realise, as I have, that your work *is* the most personal thing in your life.'

I'm not sure if he really believed that or if it was just his way of getting back at me, challenging me for spending too much time on my relationship with Oliva, or for suffering for it afterwards.

Living it like it sounds was a perfect description of my frame of mind when I got back to Japan, with so many unknowns to resolve. Martán had decided to stay in my apartment and would continue to pay rent to me erratically over several years to come. I'd never return to the flat by the Bilbao roundabout, which we'd sell to buy our next house. Nor would I ever again see my dog, Lindo Clon, who died during a gruelling walk with my father and was buried right there, among the pine trees in the mountains outside Madrid. He told me over the phone, with that astonishing ease he always had: 'Oh, that's right, Lindo died.' My father belonged to a generation who observed animals without the levels of sentimentality that would come later, once people had begun to feel helpless and alone.

I returned to Japan carrying a suitcase packed with clothes and little else. The rest I left on the shelves in the flat. Kei came to the airport to pick me up. I saw her when I came through the arrivals gate, but she took some time to spot me. She'd cut her hair and dyed the tips, raised like a weightless dandelion and held in place by a black velvet headband tied behind her ears. She was wearing purple lipstick and showing off the full exuberance of her personality, previously so withheld, as if celebrating my return.

I dedicated the time she took finding me to contemplating her beauty once more. It wasn't just a fantasy; the glimmer was still there. I hugged her from behind, without letting her turn around.

Kei and I rented an apartment in Tokyo, near the Koto neighbourhood; it belonged to a music colleague of hers. That was when she finally came clean and told me that Mitsuo had never been her boyfriend: he was just an old friend she'd asked to play the role of her partner so that I'd go back to Spain guilt-free and give up on the idea of staying in Japan.

In my eyes, the risk she'd taken with this well-thought-through strategy transformed her into a kind of hero. In a similar way, she'd later demonstrate her ability to be strong-willed and resolved even when I was in a slump.

'I won't let you get depressed, you Spanish fool. I won't hear any more of it.'

The flat we found had a guest room, for potential visitors from Spain, and a room with soundproofing for us to practise in. And though the neighbourhood was pricey and the rent excessive, Kei had been accepted into the orchestra she'd been trying out for and her new salary made us decide to get a bit further away from the hustle and bustle of the touristy area of central Tokyo.

Within two months I was playing every Thursday in a European-style bar called Continental, situated inside a shopping centre. I did two half-hour solo sets with my electric guitar – though I quickly recruited two musicians who also performed there – and sometimes Kei would join us onstage as well. I tended to play other people's songs, chosen from a repertoire that was familiar to everyone and sung in my blunt, coarse English, but I later began to include one or two Spanish numbers, which I introduced with a more or less accurate explanation of the lyrics.

When Kei got pregnant, I tried to convince my father to come and visit me, but I knew there was no chance he'd do it: the idea of getting on a plane terrified him. He'd die without ever trying, the last remnant of another era. That was around the time I wrote 'Rising Sun', the last song on the album and my final step towards announcing that I was recording again. The project was closely linked to the pregnancy, which meant having to lay down roots in another place and see another sun, another landscape, every day.

'It's lucky your mother doesn't know how exactly far away you are,' my father told me.

He, too, would have preferred not to know, not to have his son so far away. 'So far away, so far away,' he'd always say when we spoke on the phone on Fridays.

Kei had started travelling more with her orchestra job, earning good money, grasping at the professional dream. The orchestra was like a clock that kept perfect time. Less fun than the quartet, in my opinion, but they toured prestigious venues throughout the world, theatres and auditoria, something I, having spent my career in fleapits and noisy bars, greatly envied.

Kei radiated beauty as she grew bigger and bigger, and we'd sit down together to listen to classical music. She said it would shape her yet-to-be-born daughter's taste while also opening my ears to composition, to polyphony, to harmonies that were out of my reach as a guitarist. I'd carefully watch Maya during the scans, as detailed as a portrait. I'd walk over to the belly that housed her and sing her Joaquin Sabina's 'Caballo de Cartón', so that she could learn my city's metro stations off by heart, along with 'La Nana de una Madre Muy Madre' by Vainica Doble, which would end up being the song that sent my children off to sleep at night.

Entering the practice room after Kei had been pulling apart the impossible notes of Schoenberg or Hindemith for me, I couldn't help feeling like a pauper, a professionally bankrupt boy just pretending to be a musician. But this stark contrast helped me to remember the playful joy of pop music, the need for simple lyrics and danceable rhythms.

As one critic later put it, my next album was the happiest of my career, perhaps because it contained a note of reconciliation with my musical beginnings. My uninhibited compositions allowed me to leave behind that stupid desire for meaning that's so tempting to musicians – that need to be important, to *sound* important, to sell yourself according to phoney rules dictated by whatever the trend is at the time.

The pregnancy wasn't planned, but we did nothing to stop it. Our sexual attacks on each other were so frequent that sometimes we forgot to eat. The fact that our daughter came into the world not from a premeditated decision, but from a state of transition between lives, between continents, helped me to realise that people are born the same way songs are, from nowhere. You're not born from an equation, but from a rippling of accidents and chance occurrences, something that should help us to tread through life more lightly.

I met Kei's parents in the province where they lived. She'd lived away from them since she was very young, when she'd chosen to train as a musician. They were friendly with me. They took me to the tomb of their ancestors and her mother smiled and took me by the hand, incapable of understanding a word of my stuttering Japanese.

Animal congratulated me, so to speak, when I told him over the phone that I was becoming a father.

'You're really in the shit now. They've got you pinned down forever.'

We found the perfect dates for Martán and him to come over and record. Everything had to be assessed and synchronised. I wanted the record's release date to coincide with Maya's birth and I wanted it to be recorded live, in the venue where I played from time to time. I wanted the album to be called *Live in Japan*.

We'd record it over the course of three live performances at the venue, with barely any audience, accompanied by a keyboard player who also programmed synths, a percussionist who played with Kei in the chamber orchestra and Kei herself, who was just as involved with the project as the rest of us. 'Spanish Fool' was another song from the record, probably the one that got the most airtime. It was a short tune, very simple, inspired by the insult Kei often used against me, when we were arguing or fighting about something.

It was a story taken straight from real life. One evening, Kei and I went out for dinner after I collected her from one of her orchestra performances. She looked so happy with her huge belly that I asked what she'd have done if I'd never returned from Madrid, if I'd believed all the lies about Mitsuo being her sweetheart and not come back.

She raised her neck powerfully, laughed and said, 'I'd just say that once upon a time, I met a Spanish fool.'

*spanish fool*

I'd managed to spot Gus's sisters among all of the people swarm-
ing the village square as we unveiled the plaque with my name
on it. Surrounded as I was by Jandrón and his councillors, it
wasn't easy to get to where they were standing, set back from
the crowd because they didn't know anyone else. Dressed in
their Sunday best, time had clearly done its work and they'd
become two old ladies since I'd last seen them, years back, at
Gus's funeral. They were surprised that I recognised them and I
asked Jandrón to let us take refuge inside the building so I could
talk to them alone for a second.

'They're Gus's sisters – the guy who used to play with me,
remember?'

'Ah yes, the one who killed himself,' said Jandrón.

'We read about you opening the fiesta in the paper and as
we don't live far from here we thought we'd come and see. It's
been so long,' they said.

I'd held on to the affection Gus used to transmit every time
he said their names. He had a favourite anecdote about the
record that had changed his life. I don't know if Gus invented
it – it sounded like he did – but it dated back to one of his
childhood birthdays. He'd turned nine or ten, and his sisters
gave him a record by María Jesús and Her Accordion, who had
a huge hit at the time with the ubiquitous 'Los Pajaritos'.

Gus said he was really excited to have been given that record,
which he used to dance to at every family gathering, but when
he went to listen to it, it turned out that someone had switched
the contents and the record inside was actually Bowie's 'Ashes
to Ashes'. Gus's version of the story never made it clear whether
his sisters had switched the two records on purpose, or if it
was an accident involving some record shop employee who'd

316

looked at the cover, which showed Bowie's face painted like a Pierrot, and assumed that it was aimed at kids. Regardless, the point is he listened to the song on repeat and that was it: a record he'd come across by chance changed his outlook forever.

I smiled at his sisters. They'd aged, and one of them had got a little chubby and looked like Elton John. Perhaps Gus, who always used to sing 'Tiny Dancer' in his falsetto voice, would also have ended up looking like that. I imagined them during the time they witnessed their younger brother transforming into that gleaming, extrovert character who'd broken the seams of their ultra-conventional family.

'We shouldn't disturb you,' the older one said, 'but we thought you'd like to have this.' She turned towards her sister, who searched around in her bag and took out a small notebook with a card cover. 'It's Gus's,' she announced. 'It's some kind of diary.'

I took the little notebook in my hand and hesitated to open it. I wasn't sure if I should. On the first page he'd just written the word diary, but it was underlined three times with an insistence he clearly hadn't kept up, as only the first four pages had any writing on them. The rest were blank.

'You know how he was never very consistent with anything,' smiled one of the sisters. 'He began it when he arrived in Madrid,' she pointed out, and it was true. 'We found it when Aunt Milagros died, among all of her things in the guest house.'

The first notes, in Gus's untamed handwriting, simply registered his arrival:

I'm in Madrid. I've decided to keep a diary. I'll write down my life here. I live in a neighbourhood called Cuatro Caminos, in Aunt Milagros's guest house. Nobody recognises me when I go out on the street. *It's a wonderful town.* The street's called Calle de los Artistas. Artists' Street!

I smiled. It was unmistakably how Gus used to express himself. Further on he wrote about his first day at school and the first afternoon when he'd gone to see *Rocky Horror* at the Regio cinema. Alone. The notes were hurried, almost telegraphic.

> I have a friend. He's called Dani. He lives near school,
> but in the ugliest part of the neighbourhood, in a dead-
> end street. When school's finished I walk back towards
> his house with him. He's an only child, but he's one of
> the more popular kids in class. We went to see *The Blues
> Brothers* at the Griffith and stayed to watch it again at the
> next showing.

I looked up and both of Gus's sisters had their eyes fixed on me, looking somewhat embarrassed. At that moment I feared the diary might contain some intimate information, reveal some detail that I didn't remember. Me, popular in class? I'd never have said that. Another note read:

> Music, music. We're going to start a band. Dani's amazing
> at the guitar. We bought some records he says we need to
> hear.

He was referring to our afternoons in a record shop on Calle Goiri, where we spent our time not so much buying records as stroking the sleeves of the ones we hoped we could afford one day. I turned the page to find a whole sheet on which Gus had written down every possibility as he searched for a name for the band.

> The Hoagies, The Bogies, The Stoners, The Loners, The
> Ones, The Twos, The Slackers, The Pennies, The Pesetas,

Dollar, Dollars, The Fucks, The Flies, Las Moscas, The Artists, Los Quién, The Gentlemen.

I imagined him in his bedroom, hostage to his own enthusiasm, before he came and told Animal and me that we were going to be called Las Moscas. It was decided.

There was one more page, but it was odd. He'd only written one sentence: 'Today we made our first song. Yes.' But he'd scribbled something else along the edge of the page, like a decorative border. The letters were jumbled together, but you could clearly make out the same word repeated again and again: 'danidanidanidanidanidanidanidanidani'.

I didn't dare look up, paralysed, my eyes locked on this chain of letters. After a strange moment when I felt like I was falling into that pattern he'd drawn on the edge of the page into a deep, distant place, I snapped back to life. I leafed through each one of the pages that followed, all of them blank, all the way to the end of the notebook. I stroked the book with my fingers. Gus's sisters, sitting either side of me, were holding back their tears when our eyes met again.

'He loved you so much,' one of them said.

I nodded.

'He was always in love with you,' the other one ventured to say.

I rested my tense back against the chair. In love? I don't know. I think it was something else. Something even better.


## always Gus

Always Gus, always a memory involving him, something that would happen and make me think about what he'd have done or how much I'd have liked to be able to tell him all about it.

Gus finishing off a song or negotiating a contract. What would he have said?

The circumstances of Gus's death had come back to me on one occasion, after the births of both of my children, during a journey from Tokyo to Madrid. I was flying, I recall, in order to promote the last record I ever recorded in Japan. As I waited for my suitcase at the terminal, an unremarkable man approached, greeting me timidly. At first sight he didn't look like a typical fan, so when he spoke to me I looked up, eager to inspect him.

'You don't remember me, do you?'

I shook my head. I hate these riddles – at my age I barely recognise anyone.

'I was the police inspector looking after your friend's death.'

Gus, of course, there he was. The man held out his hand and explained that he'd already taken retirement.

'Such a sad story.'

'Yes,' I said, shaking my head.

'You were right,' he confessed after lowering his voice a little. 'It wasn't as simple as it looked.'

I looked at him.

'Do you remember the details? The lost shoe, the hunting jacket he used as a pillow when he was abandoned, still alive, in the entrance hall.'

'Yes, of course. How could I forget?'

'They never let me look at the case for what it really was. There's a crime called failure to act. And there was an element of that.'

I gulped. I didn't know if I wanted to hear more.

'No, look, don't expect me to tell you anything important. I don't know anything, except that your friend was at some party and the people upstairs weren't interested in knowing who else was there.'

'People upstairs?'

'The people in charge. Catch my drift?'

'What do you mean?' I asked. 'Did they know something?'

'Nothing. No one was keen to implicate the child of someone important, some youngster who was fooling around with all that stuff, like your friend.'

Right. I remembered how frustrated I'd got back then from talking to the police, by everyone's assumption that it had just been an overdose and by their refusal to investigate.

'The only thing that's certain is that the girl was with him.'

'Who? Which girl?'

'The model, she was with him that night. That's as far as I got.'

'You mean Eva?'

'Yes.'

I was unsettled for weeks on end. I considered talking to a journalist friend of mine, but stirring up what had taken place so many years earlier wouldn't bring Gus back to me.

Years later, when we were back in Spain and Raquel was in charge of my career and my diary, she booked me in to play a private show for the guests at the wedding anniversary party of a textiles impresario. We'd sometimes accept this kind of request when they were willing to pay our fee. Apparently, he and his wife had a favourite song of ours from when they'd got together years ago. It was 'Lol-li-pops' and they'd heard us playing it at El Escalón, near Chamartín. I sang it to them one more time that night, albeit sounding rather different from the way they'd have heard it as young sweethearts.

The party was attended by a select group of elegant-looking people and it was there I bumped into Marina again. She greeted me cordially, as if we'd seen each other only yesterday. The years had treated her well and though as a young woman she was never quite as beautiful as all the girls surrounding her at the atelier, she was more attractive than ever as a forty-something.

A long time had passed since we'd last seen each other, probably at a concert in Valencia. Something she said, as she lifted her champagne glass to her mouth, really stuck in my mind.

'Well, well. I fear we've reached an age where we attend more funerals than we do parties.'

That was her way of saying 'hello again', her seductive invitation to make the most of the remaining time. We swapped numbers and the next time I played in Valencia I rang her and she invited me over to her house, the same one with the amazing terrace looking out over the city, where she'd once organised that kind-of orgy.

My cohabitation with Kei was beginning to fall apart – happiness for me was always a perishable good. I slept with Marina again, and did the same every time we saw each other. Sometimes I even made up excuses to go to Valencia, or if she was passing through Madrid for a fashion show or business meeting we'd meet up in her hotel and spend some time together. It was an infrequent, casual relationship, neither of us looking for anything more profound than simply to have a good time together. Marina enjoyed saying we were lovers.

'Lover sounds better than wife, right?'

She was the one who told me where Eva was working and one day I went along to the clothes shop, near Calle Serrano, where she did PR. I entered, inquired about her and was led to a small office connected to the storeroom, which was surrounded by scattered items of clothing. Her perfect teeth were now grey, with rotten molars and black circles on her gums. She still looked thin and stylish, but her thinness now gave off an aura of decay and her style had more to do with her expensive clothes than with the way she carried herself, though she hadn't completely lost the sophistication that Gus had adored.

I don't really remember which one of us started talking about Gus, but Eva looked at me from a place that was right at the back of her blue eyes.

'Do you remember him?' I asked.

'Every day,' she confessed.

'I miss him, too,' I said and promptly added, 'Eva, I know everything. I know he was with you that night.'

There was a long-drawn-out silence.

'We were very young back then.'

I told her about my encounter with the policeman at the airport, about the chap who'd looked as grey as that sad morning. Eva looked away from me for a moment and spoke into the empty space for a while.

'I couldn't say anything. I was with a group of people, I wasn't sure who, all hangers-on, and someone invited us up to their flat near Colón, a really plush flat. We'd been drinking and we took some pills and I came up really quick. I was with someone and we left early. I didn't know about what happened until after, that Gus had fainted and that he wasn't breathing.'

She swallowed and slowly told me the rest of the story, how the following day he'd been found sprawled out in a nearby building. How she was afraid of saying anything and getting her friends into more trouble.

'It was an accident,' she said finally and stayed quiet.

'It's always an accident,' I said, furious. 'I suppose you thought you were all too important to deal with something like that, right?'

'Dani, please, it was a long time ago. What do you want from me?'

I looked towards Eva and realised what she was trying to say. The woman resembled a beautiful corpse. What was the use? No one could bring Gus back. She'd probably constructed a purpose-built lie to get her off the hook.

I couldn't say goodbye to Eva. I just got up and left the clothes shop and didn't look back again, overcome as I was with disgust – disgust for her and for all the people who surrounded her back then. People Gus had been all too happy to entertain because they offered him something he craved, and helped him to bury his provincial self once and for all.

Furious, I walked for a good while beneath the Christmas lights that lined the spruced-up streets of the centre, unlit because it was still daytime. And I'd have kicked something to pieces if I hadn't known that doing so wouldn't bring Gus back to where I wanted him to be. Right by my side, always Gus.

I walked up to the school gates with Gus's sisters, where the crowd was still huddled together, watching the kids' entertainment. Onstage, medals were being given out for some game or other and the kids were making their way up to collect their trophies. Perhaps it was that, as well as my own recently inaugurated plaque, that made me think about Gus. A hero without a medal.

As I watched his sisters depart, with their mannered way of walking and their well-kept clothes – their bags over their shoulders and holding jackets just on the off-chance that that blisteringly hot afternoon might turn into a cool evening – I couldn't help but think about Gus's achievements. His bravery in getting away from the predictable and sinister environment of his childhood and becoming someone who was truly free.

He had jumped straight onto the stage from that bedroom where he used to dance alone, dressed up in front of the mirror, singing songs in that made-up English he always used when composing. Just like what happened when he erupted onto the scene at school, opening up a window for a gang of morons schooled in repression and intolerance, a window through which we could aspire to be what we wanted to be. And I knew his sisters were as proud of him as I was, because we knew where he came from, that none of it had been easy. I would put that notebook away in my pocket and keep it as another memento, one more relic telling the story of our lives.

'So, are you going to sing then, or what?' Paula came up to me, followed by a couple of friends her age.

'I don't know,' I replied and we came closer to each other so as not to have to shout above the noise.

'You'll have a good time if you stay the night. We're throwing a party at our club,' she proposed.

She bit her lip. I remember how obsessed I was with her mother during those childhood summer days.

I just smiled and said, 'I fear I'm too old for that kind of party.'

'I've got a lot of love for these people, believe it or not,' she suddenly confessed, perhaps sensing my scepticism. 'My parents died in a car crash six years ago.'

'God, I didn't know. I'm so sorry,' I said moronically.

All of a sudden, I was filled with sadness by the idea of Ignacia, who'd been so beautiful as a girl, also being dead. All dead.

'Your mother was incredible, she really was,' I told her. 'I remember her from my summers here, she was really special.'

'Yeah, well,' she intervened, 'I've grown up with my uncle and aunt, that's why I keep coming to the village.'

'Of course. Well, I guess Jandrón's been like a hen for you.'

I didn't realise what I'd just said. Paula laughed freely.

'What did you say?'

I was surprised myself and a jet of beer escaped from my nose.

'I'm sorry, I don't know what I'm saying.' I coughed several times.

'Something about a hen,' she clarified for me.

'No, no, I meant he must have been like a father to you. Excuse me.'

325

'What were you thinking about?'

'What fun, everything's going so well,' said Jandrón, coming down on us like a monster's claw nabbing a child in a horror story. 'Go and check out the chorizo, it'll bring tears to your eyes; there'll be none left soon.'

'I'm not hungry,' I replied.

Now I understood where the strong smell filling the air was coming from: the chorizo stand outside the club.

'Eat up, get it down you. You're going to need a full stomach, because we've got a long night ahead. Come with us, Paulita, I want to show Dani the farming museum at home.'

Jandrón put his arm around my shoulder and began leading me out of the square, pushing away well-wishers the way a bodyguard might do for a celebrity leaving a courtroom. The band had finished playing and were leaning up against the wall. They greeted me one by one after putting down their sandwiches and drinks cans and wiping off their sweat- and fat-drenched hands on their trouser legs.

'Pleased to meet you.'

'Likewise. Are you from the village?'

'No, no, we come from Zamora.'

I checked that Paula was still right behind us and that her friends were still by her side.

'Come on, don't get distracted now.'

Jandrón kept on pushing me and talking at me, putting equal amounts of effort into both things.

'Aren't you happy? Surely there are scores of singers who'd love to be honoured in the way we've just honoured you?'

Before I could answer, I was embraced by a man with a moustache.

'I'm Luciano, Honorio's grandson, do you remember? The thresher?'

'Sure, of course. How are things?'

'Please, try the cheese, it's from Villalón,' Luciano said, putting a piece into my hand.

'These are all different flavours of the region. We organise a travelling market selling local produce,' Jandrón explained after making me eat the piece of cheese, followed by six other different varieties. 'For me, it's a matter of great pride to work with the council to ensure that these traditions don't get lost. Modernity and progress are all well and good, but we have to stick up for the places we come from.'

Some senior villager appeared and said, 'Here, Mayor, how's about you do something about the street by the river, it's in an awful state. It's not all about the fiesta, you know,' he complained. 'It'll all get sorted. We just need to get out of this damned crisis.'

We entered his house through the back door. Paula and her friends followed.

'What bollocks,' said Jandrón. 'Why, you know as well as I do that the so-called crisis isn't really a crisis. We're simply going to have to live like this now, with half of what we used to have. It's the same all over Europe, you know, because we've got competition from the Chinese and the South Americans. They all want to live like kings now.

'They can see from the TV that things aren't the way they used to be and they certainly won't be saving any seats for us,' Jandrón confessed, and for the first time I caught a glimpse of the lecturer in business economics who taught at the university when he wasn't being a mayor with a ceremonial mace in his hand. 'Europe must reinvent itself.'

'Yes,' I said, 'I've heard that somewhere.'

We went through the backyard and into the area that once housed the chicken coops and rabbit hutches. Jandrón had constructed a museum with the old tools once used for sowing and tilling, each recovered item hanging from a wall hook.

'This is a hoe, this here they used to call a harrow,' he explained. 'Anyone know what this is?'

He lifted up the tool by its handle and one of Paula's friends said it was a trident, like what the Devil has.

'It's called a pitchfork and pitchforking used to refer to throwing the thresh up in the air so that the wind could separate the wheat from the straw.'

I noticed the joyful look on Jandrón's face, miming each action as if he were actually standing at the foot of a stack of threshed grain. There were also implements used for slaughtering and he began showing me photos from a big album depicting life back then. He explained all of it to me and to Paula and her friends, who listened attentively to his descriptions.

The tractor was abandoned and covered by a film of dust and grease. But Jandrón seemed determined to remove this veil of neglect so that you could experience each item as it was once used. It got all over his hands and his beige suit, and yet he seemed happy and proud. I suddenly began to take to the guy. I began to make out the boy I'd had so much fun with that summer and I was genuinely moved by the effort he took to recreate every element of a story that he considered his and, by extension, mine.

'When I found this it was a total wreck, rusty and completely covered in muck. A local blacksmith helped me to get it back in shape.' Jandrón gripped the reconstructed plough and explained each part to us, taking care to mention all the names. 'Beam, stay, mouldboard, share,' and he hooked his foot in to demonstrate.

Paula laughed and her friends, who seemed to be interested solely in breathing in her aura, mimicked her reaction. I looked at the huge figure of Jandrón playing at being one of his grandfathers, finding the image very touching.

'Someday perhaps you lot will also feel the need to collect

objects from today to show to your grandkids,' he told them, 'like, I don't know, mobiles, tablets, laptops, all those things that will be ancient and obsolete by then.'

'Right,' said Paula.

'I don't think so,' said the friend who wanted to appear the most interesting, 'a mobile isn't the same as a plough.'

'That's what you think,' replied Jandrón, and at that moment I felt enormous admiration for the man.

Among the photos in the album that Jandrón showed me were ones of the school, 'Where your cultural centre is now,' he pointed out. 'Look, this is when I was little and this other one was taken in class, see, because Don Nicéforo was still the teacher and I knew him. Yep, look, I've written it here on the back, 1965. Half a century ago, see.'

'Look, this one here is Lurditas, who was killed in Africa. She'd be Paula's age here, more or less.'

I peered at that face in the school photo. The same honest and open smile I'd seen in the other ones. Why couldn't I have that smile? How do you explain a smile like that on the face of someone who was never free, who trusted her fate and let it carry her along, especially given how cruel the destiny awaiting her turned out to be? She looked like a beautiful young girl, surrounded by kids who looked as dumb as oxen, with haircuts like brooms and menacing eyebrows in need of a good trim. I've inherited those eyebrows from my father and I like to leave them untamed because they remind me of him: every time I'm getting my make-up done for a TV interview I have to stop people going at them with scissors.

Lurditas was wearing a home-made dress and had her hand, with its long, thin fingers, resting on the desk. I felt a strange stabbing pain inside me, surrounded as I was by all those items on display and that image of my biological mother at the end of her adolescence, not long before she'd become a nun and travelled to Madrid to seek refuge in my parents' house. And I tried to understand that perhaps she, too, had wanted to escape from there. That studying to be a nun was the only opportunity she had to get out and that destiny had then tied everything up into a knot that I'd never be able to untangle, because within that tangle lay my origin.

## it's all in the songs

It's all in the songs, all poured into them. Songs were a form of biography. You place your feelings there, where they stop being your own private, intimate thoughts and become part of a larger communion of feeling – and then, maybe, you move beyond them. I wrote more songs, adding a dozen more with each album, and I asked myself where they all went and what would become of them when they stopped getting played, when I stopped taking them out for a walk at concerts. They'd become like orphans, like dead soldiers in a lost battle, like letters that never reached their destination.

The fact that a Spanish musician was living in Japan inspired numerous takes in the press, many of them hackneyed and an equal number gratefully received. Dani Mosca became someone who was too far away to disturb the local heroes or cause too much fuss. I'd asked Vicente to write something for the liner notes and he gave me a wonderful text. I never got to Madrid in time to see him before he died, but I knew he wasn't well and asking for some words was a way of bonding with him for the last time.

The final sentence he wrote for the record felt to me like a friend's goodbye, honest, gentle, true. 'Where will this road Dani Mosca has taken lead him? He will travel through a thousand places before going back to where he came from.' Doesn't that always happen? Thinking about Vicente I understand that some people help you to forge your own way because you know you've always got them watching over you.

My daughter was only four months old when we travelled to Madrid to do a promotion for the 'Japanese record', as we all called it. We took her to my mother and placed the baby in her hands; she held up tiny Maya with a big, almost childlike smile, seeming to take it all in, way beyond our own understanding.

'Clearly your genes are far stronger than ours.'

My father spoke to Kei the way he'd speak to a deaf person and he did his usual thing of showing affection through imparting aphorisms, which Kei, being Japanese, interpreted as a sign of wisdom. You could see how fond my father was of Kei by watching his body language around her; he found her so beautiful that he'd do little more than grasp hold of her hands, with great feeling, or follow her around, all the time clinging onto her slender elbow like a guide dog.

I showed Kei around bits of Madrid. I rediscovered the city through her eyes: the filth, the noise, the smoke-filled bars, the delirious, packed streets at night or at the weekend. We also visited places I didn't know at all, like the botanical gardens, the Retiro park, the Prado, the Opera, peaceful spots I'd never visited in my youth and which I thought she'd love.

Kei didn't spend the whole time fretting about the baby; instead, she'd let me be the one who had to keep up with Maya; carry her, kiss her, toss her into the air, the one to get down on my hands and knees to play with her. Kei massaged her before bed and kept her engaged with psychomotor exercises, as if she'd been on a course that I'd totally missed out on. She was very gentle when playing and singing to her, leaving all the noise and frenzy to me. We were the perfect parents, combining the expertise and harmonic sophistication of one with the brutish affection of the other.

The convenient thing for us to do to get our papers in order was to get married, but I knew how big a deal this was for Kei, so immersed in tradition.

'Why don't you get married, son?' my father would repeat, with her support.

But I resisted. I didn't want to betray my principles so easily. I didn't want to turn love into a bureaucratic process, ask a notary to make a written record of our passion, or a registrar to measure the imponderable dimensions of my bedroom. Kei laughed, accepting such eccentricities as simply the quirks of my trade.

'Daddy's a Spanish fool,' she'd say to our daughter, and it ended up being Maya's first word: not water, not ama, not dada, not oto, but fool.

Whenever we met up with friends during that stay in Madrid, Kei would go completely silent, not venturing to say a single thing. She ended up sending me out alone and would watch me come back at dawn, my mouth all pasty from too much beer and the stink of other people's cigarettes on my clothes and hair.

I'd have recurring nightmares about the lack of trust between couples who don't share the same culture, the impossibility of understanding the hidden corners of the language, its tones and inflexions. Back then it felt like a source of mystery, an unknown region that I filled with my imagination; later, I understood that the distance was unbridgeable. At one of the first concerts we played during those three months in Spain Kei suddenly seemed to realise that I was well known, that my music had a place – albeit small – in my country's pop culture.

I was unfaithful to Kei for the first time on that tour, at the concert in León, when a girl shoved me into a friend's bathroom, attracted by my apparent coldness. Then there was this

332

incredibly beautiful fan who came to both the Bilbao and San Sebastián concerts and stayed in my hotel bed until dawn, her incredible body entwined in the sheets. I escaped at sunrise and wandered the streets aimlessly, praying she'd have left the hotel by the time I got back: you can be unfaithful in bed, but never at breakfast.

Although Kei and the baby had already gone back to Tokyo, such chance encounters – and chance could be so predictable – made me realise that I had to stop playing concerts in Spain, with that empty, nocturnal routine that takes you away from home and into the heart of nothing. I had to return to my private quarters, to the hideout from which that album had emerged. I knew that the only musicians in the business who led structured and orderly lives were those who'd shut them- selves off, almost like monks.

However tempting the world of live music was – with all its promises of fun and freedom, that nocturnal trail from one beautiful body and undiscovered bed to the next – I under- stood that my place was in front of my daughter's eyes as they opened in the morning, not in urine-covered toilets where you had to piss on tiptoes. I knew I'd rather teach Maya to ride a bike than steal a kiss from some hot girl who'd turned up to a gig.

Animal told me that without night there was no music. And therein lay the conflict: I began to feel like a sailor who was scared of going to sea, a lorry driver who was reluctant to get on the motorway, a bullfighter who was terrified of the ring.

A young singer in a Catalan group that was big at the time shouted at me, 'Look, dude, what do you want to be? A family man or a musician?'

I didn't respond, but I thought about how fun stops being fun when it becomes an obligation.

## being twenty without being twenty

I wasn't tempted by the effort involved in being twenty without being twenty. Madrid presented the prospect of an almost infinite night – each dive leads to another dive, each one staying open later than the previous one, and there's always one more friendly face wanting to tag along with you. You gather more and more people in each bar until you've amassed an army, which you use to conquer another hill, another bar someone knows. The moment night falls it becomes a happy city: at night Madrid shakes off its airs and graces and enters a state of anarchy.

The verb 'to age' is the one that musicians are forbidden to conjugate. My father had a proverb he always quoted to warn me of my fate: 'Old age brings great evil to the harlot and the minstrel.' I knew and adored some seriously talented singers, true maestros, who had got old and felt the need to take shelter behind a young, devoted woman to dilute their whisky for them or hide their cigarettes. Prisoners in their own houses either because they'd imposed this hospital-like discipline on themselves, or because they simply wanted to give themselves over to an accelerated process of decay.

One night while staying in Spain for a few weeks doing summer shows, I hailed a cab in Barcelona and was surprised when the taxi door didn't open automatically or slide round to the left to let me in. In my drunken state, I guided the taxi driver. 'Go straight until you get to Koto district, then turn down Ariake Avenue,' continuing until the guy turned to face me in irritation and said, 'Hey, man, this is Barcelona.'

I decided I no longer wanted to go to a new hotel every night, or have to take the shampoo sample with me in case the next place didn't bother providing them in the showers. If there was something truly interesting and someone was willing to pay for my return flight, they only had to call

I lived in Tokyo for a total of five years and my trips back to Madrid were so short I didn't even change the time on my watch, so that I wouldn't have to deal with jet lag on my return. I'd strike and retreat, like a game of hide-and-seek. Poke my ears out into the world of music and then go home, safe and sound. I was a cockroach, because I knew that when the lights go on and people start treading on you, only the fastest and most cowardly are saved. And I wanted to be saved.

Kei got pregnant again and Ryo was born one summer while her orchestra was on a break. I enjoyed the days when I was left alone with Maya and her new brother. We'd do kids' things and then each day I'd spend a few hours just doing music. I was listening to everything coming out around the world and writing a monthly column for a Spanish magazine that paid me a pittance just to keep the lines of communication with my country open. I was studying composition with one of Kei's friends, a piano teacher, and I had the extravagant idea of composing a whole album of adaptations of poems by Bai Juyi, a Chinese poet widely read in Japan.

I wanted to experiment, to test out the thing Brian Eno said about how art is the only profession where you can crash your plane and walk away from it. From Madrid, Bocanegra implored me to record another album every time I started thinking about all this stuff.

'This is your pretentious opera,' he told me, 'a virus every musician contracts at some point.'

I'd fly over to Spain for the juiciest shows and travel to Latin America in several vain attempts to make a name for myself over there. Animal was drinking non-stop and no longer spending so much time with Martán, who'd also become a father, so when I brought them together to play a few shows they also seemed happy to be abandoning their routines.

One week, during a trip to Madrid, I felt as if I had the whole city at my feet. I visited my parents and slept with the girls who cared least about being abandoned at dawn. Both my strength of will and my vows to change my ways lasted as long as it took for the blood to come back to the tip of my dick.

In order not to disrupt Kei's career it was crucial for me to plan ahead and look after the kids when she was away. Kei played a Venetian cello that was more than a hundred years old and that she handled with the utmost affection and care, treating it with a natural oil she got from somewhere or other. It was her baby and when our children were born I made sure it wouldn't mean her having to give anything up or make impossible choices: she shouldn't have to let her career go off the rails or put the cello away in a corner somewhere just to look after the kids.

Captive mothers always terrified me, especially when their captivity was for a noble cause. I couldn't let family life become a form of slavery, robbing her of her autonomy. I knew she was happy when she was playing, just as I was. Surrounded by her scores, wearing her round-rimmed glasses that would slide off as she played and which she'd have to use her thumb to put back in place. And she always did it in time with the music and without letting go of her bow.

I loved bottle-feeding Ryo, a bright, wide-awake child, when his mother was off playing somewhere. I loved learning the language with Maya, sprawled out on the floor and poring over enormous books filled with drawings and signs. And I loved handing her over to her mother before shutting myself away with the guitar for hours to extract something that had been bouncing around in my head while they painted their nails bright colours.

Sometimes there were logjams, conflicting interests, the

sorry anguish of wanting to sit down and play, to nail down a melody, feeling that urgent and pressing need but always being tied down to the kids and to family duties. At those times I felt like a fraud of a musician, a coward, but I always tried to avoid those fleeting moments of unhappiness becoming a burden on Kei and her independence. Besides, that independence brought us in a nice sum of money, even paying for the lady who helped out around the house, and sometimes took Maya and Ryo out for a walk in the nearby gardens.

By the time Ryo was born the Japanese economic crisis had become a chronic illness and the country's self-esteem no longer gleamed brightly, instead showing signs of a depression that dated back years while the government, cloaked by light online censorship, injected money into the market. There was obvious overemployment: you'd find three people doing a job that could easily have been done by one. The sponsor of Kei's chamber orchestra pulled out and the star violinist left the group to go and live in the USA. Just two months later, the orchestra was dissolved.

I found out about the explosions on the trains at Atocha and El Pozo from Martán after he called me.

'It's a fucking inferno.'

I ran over to the computer and logged on to the Internet, not even sitting down to eat with Kei and the kids. I did feel a certain sense of pride at seeing the huge demonstrations in Madrid that were all over the news, but that strike in the heart of the city, against people going in early into their class or offices or workshops, was too cruel. Messages came in and I spoke to a few people on Skype. Animal lived close to the station and I felt restless until I got through to him. He'd been in a drunken sleep all morning, not even realising what had happened. Everyone knew one of the victims. We'd played in Almería the

337

same night the Twin Towers in New York had been attacked three years earlier, without much awareness of where we were headed. We felt something distant and muddled. Shock blurred by tears.

I remember the attempts by the government, who were approaching an election, to twist what had happened in its favour, and the fury of my friends who kept me up to date at all hours from Madrid. During that period I'd take the kids to school as usual and then burst into tears on the street after I'd left them. I cried because I was far away, because I'd repeatedly denied the blood ties I still had with that thing called *your city*, *your people*, and now I felt I'd abandoned them to their fate.

One night I got into bed with Kei, slipping into the sheets that had been warmed by her sleeping body. I kissed the porcelain skin around her shoulders and her swanlike neck, pushed aside her black hair until it was gathered around the nape, and stared at the mole on her eyelid for a while. When she woke up I brought up the idea of us all moving to Madrid together.

'I was hoping you'd suggest something like that,' she said. 'I thought you'd be ashamed of living with me in your world.'

The decision, which we took within a few hours, came as a surprise to me as well. Her parents' farewell lacked the melodramatic eloquence it would have had in Spain, but we still went to visit them, spending five peaceful days explaining the reasons behind the move. Before we packed up the flat, Kei received an offer from a German musician friend to join his group, which was something like a progressive jazz quintet. Madrid was a perfect city to be based in, as long as she was prepared to fly out to international concerts and festivals. At the time all I wanted was to see Kei smile. I wasn't even thinking about myself, or what it would mean for me to live in Madrid again, with my two children and my Japanese partner.

Hans' offer materialised. He was a German musician, ten years older than us, whom Kei had played with on several occasions during his Japanese tours. He had an unshowy intelligence and a musical knowledge that left me open-mouthed every time we had dinner together, as I finished off the bottle of wine to myself while he drank Coca-Cola with ice. He lived in Munich and wanted to get the quintet up and running, and for Kei to join it.

The demands on Kei would depend on what work they were offered, but over the following two years it would be limited to a few months of intense activity followed by sporadic trips abroad. According to Kei and her minutely detailed diary, that would allow us to live together in Madrid and for the kids to spend at least a few years immersed in their father's culture.

I found it strange that she was the one worrying about that, but after all, her code placed a higher value on roots. She could travel from Madrid to Munich when she had to, a far more comfortable proposition than travelling there from Tokyo.

'Wouldn't you like the children to go to a school in Madrid, make Spanish friends?' she asked me.

I spoke to my children in Spanish and without too much effort I'd got them to be able to maintain a decent level of conversation. I loved hearing them speaking in Japanese and English, the house transformed into a tiny version of the UN General Assembly.

During my last days in Tokyo I'd go out for walks in the gardens of the Imperial Palace and remember my first desperate stay in that city. I liked sitting down to watch the tourists, all disoriented by the magnitude of the city. *That was me*, I thought, *just one more gaijin*. I'd never live in Japan again.

I was happy to be going home, closer to Animal. He'd come over to Japan for three long trips, though Kei had got angry with me during the last one.

'Don't you realise your friend, your best friend, is an alcoholic and that you'll never be able to do anything for him, never be able to help him? You just laugh at his jokes because you don't have to put up with him every day. You don't want to accept that he's slowly killing himself.'

Animal was living in Lavapiés, coming home drunk every night to his grubby flat. Low-level dealers would rob him on the street, removing the money from his wallet and then placing it back in his pocket, with the insulting familiarity that comes with impunity. He bought his socks and beers from the Chinese shop next door; he'd put on weight and lost his shape; he ate at kebab places almost every day. His last girlfriend, hooked on nearly everything going, took the pillows and the TV with her, which is pretty weird. Animal would repeat to anyone who wanted to hear, 'What can you expect from a chick who leaves you and takes the pillows with her? The TV I get, but the pillows? A pillow's the only substitute for a woman left to a man who has to sleep alone,' he lamented.

A slave to his own personality, at nearly forty years old Animal had lost the charm of my old school friend and now more closely resembled a swallow trapped in a pool of tar. His excesses had distanced him from Martán. The mother of his child couldn't stand Animal and besides, she was jealous and wanted Martán to give up music for good. Whenever he got back from one of our trips she'd make him ejaculate into the palm of her hand, to check if the consistency was as you'd expect it to be after a few days of abstinence, or if he'd been cheating on her. We'd laugh at Martán guzzling down bottles of soy milk in the van on the way back to Madrid, because he'd been told that doing so increased the flow and would help him to get round this harsh fidelity test.

It took several years after I returned to Madrid to get Animal to seriously consider the idea of giving up drinking. He thought of himself just as a sixteen-year-old boy who liked beer and refused to see that he was an alcoholic. I gave him a monthly wage so that he could have a fixed income and not feel obliged to go looking for other groups to tour with, because that meant danger.

After several attempts to quit drinking off his own back, he agreed to go to rehab. But then one night he showed up at my house after running away from a sanatorium in Guadarrama; he was barefoot because they'd taken his shoes away when he'd entered three days earlier. When I reproached him for escaping, he insulted me and then Kei before laying into us both with all his deeply held grievances. How we were such a conventional couple – all the bitterness of a close friend who's been replaced, a bitterness that had spent too much time festering inside him. I threw him out of the house and we stopped seeing each other for a while. I feared I'd lost another friend forever.

I wrote songs about couples breaking up when my friend Claudio got separated; he had got married after living with his boyfriend for ten years. This was during those euphoric days following the legalisation of gay marriage and Claudio asked us to play at his wedding.

'It's a gay wedding,' Animal explained, 'so Martán won't try to fuck the bride.'

When Claudio was abandoned by his husband, a much younger actor who owed his career to him, he fell into a deep depression. He'd spend hours locked up in his house listening to Maria Callas full blast on his stereo, which to me felt like a scene taken straight from a nineties queer film.

'I can see him there, Dani, perched on the edge of the coffee table the way he always did when he was changing the channel,' Claudio told me as he looked back over his life.

I tried to console him, but I learnt from sitting next to him on those afternoons, filled with a sadness that couldn't be shared, that the word love never echoes as resoundingly as it does in an empty house that was once shared.

Kei and I looked for a place in Madrid to settle down with the kids. Bocanegra gave us his advice.

'What you gotta do is buy; it works out cheaper.'

Choosing the right school kept me up at night, convinced as I was that it would determine the children's lives for good; choosing a school feels far more monumental than the name you give them, the city where you raise them, their gender and, it goes without saying, any form of baptism. The school we finally went for, recommended to us by the few friends we could trust on such matters, took us out of the city centre. It was in a working-class neighbourhood where some small dwellings remained. Hemmed in on all sides by apartment blocks and charmless duplexes that perverted the personality of an area that had been built in the twenties as a holiday colony for people from Madrid, it was now just a stone's throw from the airport – a fact that put Kei, thinking of tours to come, at ease.

We found a semi-decrepit maisonette with wooden floors and two levels for us to spread our things across. Suddenly that house, which belonged to an older lady whose eyes were painted the same intense blue they'd used for the facade, began to feel like it could be our home.

'You don't know how pleased I am that the house will be going to people like you. It's quite wonderful. It sounds silly, but it's nice to think of your house living on when you're gone, giving shelter to the happiness of others.'

The first time we visited the house with the children they ran off to divide up the rooms. On the other side of the garden there was an enormous woodshed, covered in mould, and a detached hut that used to be the servants' quarters. The residue of a whole lifetime had accummulated here: old kids' bikes, rotting wood, empty jugs, sacks of lime and cement wasting away, filthy and worn-out rubber rings, a parasol with no frame, several deflated leather footballs and broken baby prams. We transformed this space into our music studio for practising and storing our instruments; an architect friend, whose brother had mixed my last record, confirmed that the beams and pillars were in a good state and that it was possible to turn it into a liveable space.

Needless to say, Kei was interested in which way the rooms were facing, the sunlight and the positioning of the bedrooms. I simply looked at the ruined woodshed and imagined myself locked away in there, devoting myself completely to making songs. I never suspected I'd end up living in that corner of the house, on the other side of the garden, protected by the hundred-year-old vine in its iron trellis and a mighty chestnut tree that lost its solid green leaves in winter.

We kitted out the studio with the insulation materials Ramón had given me when he'd shut down his business. He'd retired from production to live in a village with his son, Bambi, and his wife. We also installed a small mixing desk and control panel we got from some bankrupt technicians, ruined by the fall in CD sales and the precarious nature of an industry in peril. Recording an album had ceased to be a musician's ultimate goal; it had become an indulgence, a way of getting your new songs out there, and because of that it had to be cheap and underdeveloped.

The business seemed completely different on my return to the city. Even Bocanegra was sacked after the company's pen-ultimate round of redundancies and now had to get by on the seven-figure severance pay.

'This business is stone dead. What you gotta do now are shows, because they can't be packaged. You can only make a living from playing live.'

Kei always found my idea of having a studio that was separate from the living space threatening. She suspected I was using that place as a refuge, that I'd spend all day there, too far away, cut off from life in the house. She felt that one day I'd end up dragging along a *tatami*, putting in a couple of cupboards and turning that place into my own separate apartment, which is exactly what happened a few years later.

From time to time my father would burst in to disrupt the refurbishment works with his own catastrophic vision.

'Too many stairs,' he gestured. 'When you're old and you can't get up or down, you'll remember me.'

He thought the bedroom was rather small, but then again he'd read that the Japanese sleep in capsules. He found the kids' rooms unnecessarily big.

'They'll just fill them with junk in no time.'

Nor was he convinced by the pine floor.

'It wears away with use.'

Even crazier to him was us keeping the old wooden windows.

'Wood is alive and has to be maintained; it's a mistake. There are far more durable materials available nowadays.'

I tried to explain to my father that I liked living materials. I wanted time to have its way with my house, like it did with us.

'That's just poetry, Dani. Write a song about it if you like, fine, but houses are made with cement, not pretty words. Pretty words don't keep out the cold.'


*pretty words don't keep out the cold*


'I hope we can keep in touch from now on and that it's not so long before we see each other again,' Jandrón said.

His wife's head appeared through the door connecting the house to the yard.

'Listen here, you stop pestering Dani with your nonsense. There's some fellow here looking for him.'

That's when Animal erupted into view; behind him, looking halfway between shy and astonished, came my children. Ryo started to cry when he saw me and threw himself into my arms. I gave Maya, who followed just behind him, two kisses on the cheek.

'Here I am, bro. Whose legs do you want me to break?' said Animal, sizing up Jandrón.

'No, let me introduce you. This is the mayor. These are my children and this is Animal, the drummer who plays with me.'

'Sure, I recognise you from TV.'

Jandrón and Animal shook hands, like elks clashing their horns against each other before battle.

We walked past the well. I remembered how my father used to like washing his hands with the water from the basin in the mornings. Even after bathrooms had been installed in the houses, he continued to wash his hands like that, with fresh water from the well, just like when he was a child, and I'd watch with amusement as he did it. During the last days in his hospital room I noticed his beard had grown, giving him an air of abandonment that he'd never had before. I took his electric shaver from his washbag and spent a few enjoyable moments restoring the well-kept look that was his trademark. Then I wet his skin with his cologne, as he used to do every morning.

'Look at the well,' I said to my kids.

But it was impossible to explain. How could I make these children understand that their grandfather grew up without a toilet? These children who, even in Madrid, missed the sophistication of the Japanese TOTO toilets, with their cleansing jets of water and thermostats on the seat. They'd made me install an *otohime*, or princess, a kind of sound system that emulates a waterfall to hide the noise when you're doing your business.

How to explain to them the other world their grandfather had inhabited, where you shat surrounded by hens and washed your hands with two dunks into a basin of freezing, freshly drawn well water?

'Have you buried Granddad already?' Maya asked.

'Yes.'

'Can we go to the cemetery? Ludivina prepared some flowers for us.'

'Give them to me; I'll put them on tomorrow. We've got a performance now,' said Jandrón after tearing the small bunch of daisies from my daughter's hands and resting them in the sink.

I noted that both of them had been dressed with a certain amount of care. Ludivina must have got excited by the idea of a funeral.

'You don't mind that I brought them along, do you?' Animal asked.

'No, no.'

'I asked to come,' Ryo explained, 'and Animal let me drive a bit of the way.'

'Only holding the wheel,' Animal clarified.

We went through the house and onto the street. Jandrón and his wife were setting a fast pace and I led my children along by the hand.

'Dad, I'm hungry,' Ryo said.

But Jandrón got there first.

'Do you like *longaniza*?'

'I don't know what that is.'

'It's like chorizo and *morcilla*.'

'Yes,' said the boy.

'Not me,' said Maya.

'There'll be chocolate, too,' Luci announced, 'and biscuits.'

'Just what have you got yourself into?' Animal asked in an aside. 'The local fiesta?'

346

'Something like that.'

My daughter stopped as we were about to enter the church. 'Are we going in there?'

She was panicking. When she was small I'd taken her to the Prado and as we stared at Velázquez's Christ I noticed her squeezing my hand and asking me to explain what it was. *Ah,* I thought at the time, *how incredibly lucky my daughter is, to be six or seven years old and still not know what that recurring image from my childhood, the crucified Christ, even was.*

Priest Javier swiftly won my kids over. He had some gummy sweets in his pocket, among other things. Inside the church he showed us the little unfinished mural dedicated to Lurditas.

'For us she's as important as a martyr,' Jandrón explained.

Using some photos laid out in chronological order, I explained to my children about her work in missions and her violent death. I was overcome with pride as I looked at the photo of that tiny woman surrounded by children, that hopeful look on her face going all the way through her.

'I'm trying to compile all the material about her I can find,' Javier said, 'to present a dossier to the Vatican asking for her beatification.'

I was amused by the idea that one day my Wikipedia page might say that Dani Mosca's mother was literally a saint.

'Why did they kill her?' Maya asked.

'They killed her while she was doing missionary work in Zaire,' I explained.

This detail attracted the attention of Ryo, ever on the lookout for all things violent and gory.

'How did they kill her?'

'I don't know; it was some kind of war.'

'Was she related to you?' he asked me.

'Yes. Closely. She was called Lourdes, but I barely knew her.'

'And is there still a war in that country?'

'Yes, sure, I imagine so.'

'Did they eat her alive?' he asked.

But before anyone could answer, Luci chuckled and said, 'My goodness, Dani. What kind of bedtime stories have you been reading to your son?'

Jandrón pointed to the scaffolding next to the church altar, with the small imitation baroque altarpiece.

'We're restoring it; we've got a sponsor.' He shared a knowing look with the parish priest.

'Some sponsor indeed,' the priest commented.

'Look, he's local, he's a believer and that's that.'

'Please, Jandrón,' Javier cut in.

It seemed like an ongoing dispute between the two of them.

'You didn't happen to notice a brothel called Borgia as you were coming down the main road, did you?' Jandrón asked.

'Borgia 2?' I said.

'Yes. There are six between Benavente and León. It sucks, but that's the way things are. The recession never affects that kind of business,' Jandrón explained.

It turned out that the guy who owned all those whorehouses was the one paying for the restoration of that part of the church.

'Seriously? What's the deal, guilty conscience?' I asked the young priest.

'I fear not,' he responded.

'Of course it is, for fuck's sake,' Jandrón interrupted. 'Cañamero's as pious as they come.'

'He's got money coming out of his ears and he wants to keep the locals on his side,' was Javier's response. 'And now I must keep my mouth shut, because this has come down from the diocese. I've already told them it's dirty money, that it comes from exploiting women, but at the end of the day, money's money,' he shrugged.

'OK, OK,' Luci interrupted. 'Dani hasn't come all this way

348

just to watch us air the village's dirty laundry in public.'

'Something tells me you're in on the secret,' I said to Javier with an ironic smile on my face as we moved away from the others.

'Which secret?'

'You know which secret, because you're in on it. You know that, deep down, God doesn't exist, yet you're still a priest.'

Javier let out a chuckle. 'No, absolutely not,' he countered. 'But I'll tell you one thing, even if God didn't exist it wouldn't matter all that much, would it?'

'What do you mean?' I asked, genuinely curious.

Javier took out the key to lock the church door as we left. Then he gave me an intense look.

'Didn't you say something like that in one of your songs? I can't remember properly. It was something like "even if love isn't real, we must love each other still".'

That was a line from a song on the record I made after returning to Madrid, a love song that I hardly ever sang live any more.

'Well, it's no different from that,' was Javier's verdict.

Then he turned out the lights that he'd switched on to show us the church.

'Mustn't waste electricity.'

## escaping from home

Escaping from home, that's what it was. Kei and I separated bit by bit. We immersed ourselves in the kids because they'd become newer and more exciting to us than we were to each other. I started playing live more often again and hanging out with friends. I met Raquel and she organised my diary so that I played a concert almost every weekend. We released a sixteen-song record called *Coming Back Home*, with a symbolic cover

349

showing a guitar plectrum that had been turned upside down to resemble the outline of a house. Wasn't that my real home, after all?

Kei went to Munich often, to work with the quintet. Her concerts across Europe guaranteed her a steady income and the level of harmony she'd attained with the other members was exquisite. She and I both plunged into our love for our careers. We made love like marital bureaucrats. Not a trace remained of her wild flights in the bedroom, as she called them, her sensual fantasies, her poems of the pillow, her expertise at practising the Japanese crab, an erotic discipline that had left even Animal open-mouthed when he made me sketch it out for him in detail. But that was before; now, we always fucked with one eye on getting the chocolate milk ready for breakfast.

That was when I got back in touch with Marina and when I began committing more or less habitual infidelities every time I was off playing somewhere. Marina made light of my guilt, my crazy outbursts in which I'd swear I was going to tell Kei everything.

'Ultimately, we're just as conventional as our parents,' I complained and she laughed at my genuine despair with that Valencian scorn of hers.

One night I made dinner and opened a bottle of champagne to celebrate Kei's return from a tour with her quintet. I liked it when Kei dared to drink a little; it made her eyes shine beautifully again. Alcohol had an instant effect on her, as if her body needed only a small dose to let itself go. But that night she began to cry after the first sip and asked me to tell her if she was wrong to say that we'd stopped loving each other.

We separated without fuss. I moved into the studio so that she could have me close at hand and the kids only had to cross the garden to be with their father. When Kei was away the children were in my care, but the autonomy suited us, seeming to open up new spaces, and when we occasionally had dinner together we even laughed again, liberated from the forced discipline of couples.

The children quietly noted our separation but didn't ask questions or seek to clarify anything; they knew they could always find their father in his studio or, as they called it, his shoebox. The few friends who knew about the situation, including Animal and Martán, still didn't quite get it when they saw me so relaxed, even affable.

'Look, dude, you're going to have to explain your separation to me using diagrams, because I don't understand it at all. You live together, you raise the kids together, you eat together, you wash your clothes together, but you're separated. Shit, if only I could do that when I break up with a chick,' was Animal's response.

But Kei and I knew exactly what the separation consisted of. When her parents came to visit us we both took part in a convincing simulation, which extended to my father. They went on trips with their daughter to Seville, Cordoba, Bilbao and Barcelona and came back enchanted with the country, a little annoyed with me for never having told them how beautiful it was, something they insisted on proving with an endless selection of photos. They were happy to be back with their grandchildren now that they saw them less often, just one week at Christmas and a fortnight in August, when Kei travelled back to Japan with them.

After a few months had passed, Kei gave me the task of explaining the separation to the children, because it seemed absurd to keep up this orderly routine without telling them why, so one day, after picking them up from school, I did just that.

'Did you do something bad to Mummy?' my son asked.

'No, of course not. How could I do something bad to a wonderful woman like your mummy?'

'So why did she throw you out the house, then?'

'She didn't throw me out, Ryo. I'll always be near you,' I reassured him, 'but when you're older you'll understand that these things happen with couples.'

*Forget it*, I thought to myself, *you won't understand a thing. We never understand anything.*

Their uncertainty transformed into new, soothing rituals. And, worst of all, Kei and I also got used to the new order: we'd often eat together in the house and the kids would cross over to my shoebox so that I could help them with their homework, surrounded by all the guitars. They began referring to my studio as Daddy's house and our house as Mummy's house, and in this way the separation became a reality.

You can never completely know someone if you don't share a language, even when you live together and have kids. Kei's secrets were always unfathomable to me and likewise, she never knew everything that was going on in my head. I invented a perfect love to suit my own needs, mighty and romantic, full of generosity and occasionally even risk. A love that was consolidated, tied up in a bow with two children. We were happy, occupied and enthusiastic, but we never fully knew each other. I invented Kei in my head and she invented me.

Kei became closer to Hans, who sometimes came to stay at the house. One day she confessed to me that they were in love: it wasn't unbridled passion, it was more like a mature agreement. I felt a pang of jealousy watching Kei's beauty bloom again, watered by her new relationship. I recognised her in her love for someone else. They organised their life together harmoniously, with him living in Munich most of the time and the two of them travelling to their concerts together. When Hans came to Madrid it was he I saw each morning doing his exercises as I went up to the window that looked out onto the garden and gazed at my old house.

It was he who put his arm around Kei's waist when they left the house.

Hans was sixty but was in incredibly good shape, something he demonstrated by using the slightest pretext to stand on his head, to the admiration of my kids, who were both well aware that I sometimes struggle to lift my leg up from a chair when someone's trying to sweep under my feet. In such a way, the guy who used to stay in the guest room when he came to see us graduated to the main bedroom whenever he was in Madrid for a few days and my kids got used to calling him Mummy's boyfriend. There was a certain logic to their relationship; Kei was the most German Japanese person I'd ever known and he was the most Japanese German. Just as had happened years before with Oliva, something burned itself out in our relationship because, without wanting it, my world turned out to be absorbing, and took over everything else.

## getting older

'Getting Older' came into the world during that period, played on the keyboard in the studio where Maya had her guitar lessons, while I tried very hard not to be the teacher my father had been with me. I wrote 'Getting Older' on the edge of the previous day's newspaper, in tiny, messy handwriting. I wanted to explain to a child that losing isn't so serious:

*No one hears you say I'm sorry*
*You hug the air instead*
*It's nothing serious, you're getting older.*

And when I sang it to my daughter, she made a comment.
'You know what, Dad, your songs are sadder now. Of course

they are, it's because you're not with Mum any more,' she replied to herself, shrugging her shoulders.

I resolutely denied it.

'My songs have always been sad. The only time I made a record full of funny songs was when I was so sad I couldn't even write sad songs.'

'Oh, really?' responded my daughter, her curiosity seemingly awakened. 'And what had happened to you back then?'

My daughter was right – the song was sad, devilishly sad, because it was my separation song. There would be others, but that was the first one. It was a distillation of the pain of letting something that was meant to be so beautiful, so valuable, come apart. Of ruining the material with which I'd made my children, who'd come from love and who were now the orphans of that idea.

Being alone is a spiritual condition. It doesn't need to be physical. You can be alone on Gran Vía at rush hour. I'd always felt the temptation to be alone. I knew the risks but got on with the separation because I wanted to become reacquainted with solitude. 'Here I am again,' I wanted to say as it enveloped me in that embrace that others find so terrifying. But not me.

I wasn't offended by Kei's happiness; her relationship pushed me one step further, deeper into that solitude I'd made for myself. I was afraid of not being able to steal a bit of whatever she'd cooked in the evening, of never again sitting down to watch her marinate the fish. Or of having her hand me a cold beer from the fridge as I unloaded all of my professional grievances onto her, when she told me not to insist that my voice was horrible and that it needed to be processed every time it was recorded to give it depth, distance, resonance.

'You've got a lovely voice, Dani, stop tormenting yourself.'

354

There came a day, at forty years of age, when I found myself on a stage, alone except for my guitar, singing songs about my sadness to the rapturous applause of the audience. Since that first concert we played at our school, twenty-five years had passed. Bocanegra was succeeded by a cascade of young, inexperienced managers whose only responsibility was to cut staff numbers until eventually they were forced to get rid of themselves. Bocanegra had used his severance pay to fund a TV production company and though it failed spectacularly, he still had enough money left to sail around the world.

It was the people at the company who cancelled my contract, when it was absorbed from London by a bigger fish, dominated by hazy investment funds. Then I met Raquel, who seemed efficient, attentive and serious; she'd started off working as a roadie and you could tell – she was the kind of manager who solved rather than created problems. I asked her to work for me and she got me back in the saddle.

I told her about Martán and Animal, with whom there'd been no reconciliation since the argument in my house. Raquel went in search of Animal and when she found the sorry specimen he'd become, she explained that I was worried about him, that I loved him and wouldn't just abandon him as another piece of collateral damage over the course of my career. She convinced him to go into a clinic on the outskirts of Valencia, where another musician she'd worked for a while back had managed to stop drinking, and one day she made me go and visit him.

Animal's hug brought that long year of stubborn distance from each other to an end. When he asked me if I was writing any new songs, I let him hear 'Getting Older'. He seemed more serene, as if he'd drunk his way into sobriety.

'Well, you sure are fucked,' Animal blurted after hearing the demo recorded onto my phone. 'It's great, though; it's just a shame that you had to bite the dust before you could write such a beautiful song.'

When I told Animal about Kei's relationship with Hans, his first reaction was 'Let's kill him, bro. The son of a bitch stayed in your guest bedroom a thousand times, tossing himself off while thinking about her,' Animal explained graphically. 'Maybe even fucking her when you weren't looking, God only knows. Have you checked the bedcovers? They're bound to be covered in the guy's cum stains, going all the way back to the first time he decided he'd replace you. To think of your guest bed, where I've slept so many times, all covered in German jizz!' he exclaimed, pretending to be scandalised.

That morning Animal told me something I've never forgotten.

'We get older, but we don't get better.'

We recorded together the moment he was discharged. We started hanging out again and, despite the new sense of vulnerability that emanated from him, he seduced us all with the same outlook he'd always had. Especially my kids, who celebrated every time they saw him.

My father managed to catch his breath for once when I brought him up to speed regarding Kei's relationship with Hans.

'Wise up, Dani. The only Spaniard who ever dared to put the Germans in their place was Franco in Hendaye.'

Along with the tragedy of my mother, there was now his own ageing to reckon with: 'I've nothing left'; 'I'm living on borrowed time'; 'I'm got one foot in the grave'; 'I'm already dead – my certificate just hasn't arrived in the post yet'.

He loved the way the children greeted him with a ritualistic bow, the polite *teineirei*.

'They do it for everyone,' I explained to him as he lavished effusive praise upon Japanese manners. 'It's not just you.'

'I like it. I like the fact that my grandchildren respect me in a way my son never has,' he yelled once his deafness had made it necessary for him to raise his voice all the time.

His deafness was a good excuse for him to stop listening to my records, which he still kept neatly stored on his shelf at home, never taking them out of their plastic covers. Surprised that anyone made a living from a job like that, he understood that becoming label-less was a natural process and that it had to happen, sooner rather than later.

'And you don't even have a degree. What will you live on now, I wonder?'

From time to time he'd ask me to sign one of my records for his clients' children and made me write out dedications for the nephew of Encarnita, the one who lives above the hardware shop. I could never fill my father in on my professional worries; he'd have toasted them with his characteristic 'I told you so'.

When he saw me living in the studio, with a tatami surrounded by guitars and cables, he couldn't resist blurting out, 'This looks like the den of an eternal student.'

He was horrified by the fact that my only possessions were my records, some paintings by friends, and photos and books that were scattered all over the studio because I hadn't decided to arrange them or find a permanent space for them. And like Martán and Animal, he insisted I should find a flat in the city centre, but I convinced them otherwise by saying that my place was a stone's throw away from my kids.

Kei was playing in the Reichstag in Berlin when my father died. I asked my daughter to dial her number and tell her. Sometimes Kei would get very upset when she thought about her parents getting old so far away from her. Her father had been treated for a tumour and Kei's old friend Mitsuo – who I always suspected had enjoyed his weeks as her pretend boyfriend since it was obvious he'd been in love with her his whole life – went to see them every month and would send her a full report.

For years Kei came to the home with me to see my mother, though she never got anything more than some ludicrous comment.

'Who is that Chinese lady? Is she the new nurse? Are you shooting a film?'

I guess that every time she took my mother's hand she was also taking the hand of her own mother, so far away.

She gave her a precious painting she'd bought in Japan, of a maple tree with yellow and purple decorations tied around its branches, and my mother's carer told me one day that she always looked at the painting with great concentration.

'She stares at it for hours and when I ask her why she's always looking at it so much she always says the same thing: "I'm waiting to see if the leaves fall."'

'Dad's dad died.' That was the way my daughter gave her mother the news on the phone. 'Yes, Dad's right here,' and she handed me the telephone.

'Dad's dad', that's how a child sees what we always explain in such a complex way, the natural continuity of life.

'Do you want me to come back? They can get a replacement for tonight,' Kei offered.

'There's no need,' I said, 'there's nothing to be done. I'm going to bury him,' I added. 'I'll bury him and then I'll think about him for a while.'

'I'll think about him, too,' Kei replied and then she repeated something she always used to say to dispel my anxiety. 'You can overcome it. You *will* overcome it.'

We walked down the backstreets to avoid the square but even so, whenever we came across someone from the village they'd stop us and ask if those were my kids. And then they'd say, 'They're lovely,' and 'Have you got a kiss for me?' and 'You don't know me but I'm your father's cousin,' or 'I'm your father's great-aunt,' or 'Your grandfather and I grew up together.'

This happened so many times that Maya squeezed my hand and asked me discreetly, 'Is everyone here part of our family?'

'More or less.'

Jandrón pointed to a house at the end of the alley.

'All we need to do now is the dance in the godmother's house and then we'll go to the square.'

My son heard the word godmother and ventured to ask, completely straight, 'So fairy godmothers do exist?'

'Of course they don't,' his sister quickly clarified, 'it'll just be some old lady.'

Effectively, the godmother was just some old lady, Juliana, but she'd got all the dancers into her small living room, a group of young people dressed in spectacular nuclear-white suits with blood-red corsets and brightly coloured sashes. Sweets, caramel-coated almonds and two bottles of spirits, which they were drinking in small shots, were laid out on the table.

Outside, the light was fading at a leisurely pace and the summer was rewarding us with an orange-coloured night.

'Come, drink up,' the godmother offered.

'No, no, I don't drink any more,' said Animal, firmly refusing. 'I drank it all in my other life.'

The godmother was complaining about the pain in her legs.

'I'm not up to all this toing and froing.'

'I hear you. It's really tiring, this whole being an authority thing. Plays havoc with my knees,' Jandrón added.

My kids shared the sweets and almonds with the young dancers and when half the town crowded around the entrance to the house, which was right on the main road, the councillor for festivities interrupted our chat to tell us it was time to go out. Outside, the dancers were received by the band and began their performance in two interweaving lines. They took their wooden clubs from their waists and hit them against each other as they criss-crossed through complicated routines.

'Dad, they look like nunchuks,' Ryo pointed out.

And so they did: those dancers – all sense of precision lost from ingesting sweet liqueur – jumped and clashed their sticks in an almost ninja-like ritual.

After the dance was over the band played a polonaise on the way to the square and we began walking behind them. I knew the melody; I remembered the dance from my early years in the village. The clarinet player had taken out a *dulzaina* and now everything was dominated by that harsh, ancestral sound, whose origins dated back 5,000 years to Mesopotamia, Jandrón explained, sounding like he'd been there when they invented it.

I waited for him to walk ahead to shake his mace at the front of the procession and held back a little.

'What's going on? Have these bastards got you involved in their bumpkin festival?' Animal asked.

'You don't know the half of it! I've had to open a cultural centre named after me.'

'I saw; we drove past it. I took a photo to send to Martán. For fuck's sake bro, you've really hit rock bottom.'

The godmother was holding my kids by the arm and taking sweets from a little bag.

'No, no, please no more sweets.'

'Get out of here,' she shouted at me, 'it's a day of celebration.'

'I know, but they'll get cavities.'

'Don't be such a bore, Dad,' my daughter cut me off.

We were still walking behind the band and at that precise moment I'd have liked to tell my kids that that woman was their third grandmother, but I kept that genealogical muddle to myself.

'I remember your father when he was just like you two,' she told them. 'He used to love coming to the village, because as you can see for yourselves, it's so much more fun here than in Madrid. He was always inseparable from Jandrón and his gang when he came down.'

'Actually, I only came here for one summer,' I tried to explain.

'You used to love whistling, that I do remember. People could hear you coming because you always whistled when you walked.'

Juliana stretched out her wrinkled hand and grabbed my son's arm.

'What's your name?'

'Ryo,' the little boy answered.

'Wow! what a lovely name. We've got a *río* here,' she said, indicating the river, 'but it's dried up.'

'Actually, it's a Japanese name,' my son explained. 'It doesn't mean river, though it sounds the same.'

'Don't you worry,' Juliana reassured him, 'we all got given strange names, too. Look at me: Juliana. My grandchildren call me Juli, though.'

'Her daughter was the girl who got killed in Africa while working as a missionary,' I explained so that they could situate Juliana within what little they knew of the village.

After that, my children looked at the woman with a mixture of pity and curiosity.

'Lurditas,' said Maya.

'That's the one. The one I sang to when she was little and who had to sit on my lap because that was the only way she'd eat. I had to shove in a few spoonfuls as I sang. She was like a little bird; she never raised her voice.'

There was an odd silence during which Juliana seemed to have gone so far back in time that it must have taken a real effort to remove herself from the memory of her dead daughter.

As we turned the street people surrounded us again and there were more requests for photos. The councillor made his way through them.

'Man alive, they're áll waiting for you.'

Behind him came his highly agitated wife, all councillor and no festivities.

'We have to start the dance.'

I turned towards Animal.

'They want us to play a couple of songs.'

'You're joking. Here?'

I shrugged. 'Where else? What have we got in the van? A guitar, anything?'

'Yeah, I think so.'

And I explained to the councillor that we needed to bring the van closer.

'We have to unload some equipment onto the stage.'

'Now?' he asked, surprised.

'Well it's not going to be tomorrow, is it?'

The violence implicit in Animal's menacing retort persuaded him to obey straight away.

The band was winding up and I was walking over to them when a woman grabbed me by the arm and stopped me.

'Could you do a photo with my daughter?'

'I can't, we don't have time,' I replied, but then Maya held me back with a tug of the hand.

'Papá . . .'

When I turned towards the woman I realised the girl whose hand she was holding had Down's syndrome.

'Can we get a photo?'

'Sure, sure.'

She can't have been more than fifteen, but the girl gave me a lovely appreciative smile.

'She's called Susana,' the mother told me when I asked as she fiddled with the mobile so she could take the photo. 'Hold on, let's see, I'm almost out of battery.'

While her daughter and I stood still, smiling and posing, she kept talking as she messed around with her phone.

'You know, Susana has a teacher at her home and one day we were talking about the village and how you were born here and so on . . .'

'Well, my father was born here,' I clarified.

'Sure, whatever,' Susana's mother continued. 'Anyway, the point is she told me she used to know you, like really well.'

I was intrigued by her choice of words.

'Oh yeah?'

'Yes, she works at the centre. She's like a ray of sunlight and my daughter adores her. She's called Oliva. Ring a bell?'

'Oliva?' I don't know if anyone in the procession noticed how unsettled I became. 'Sure, Oliva, of course.'

'Well she's the one who told me she knew you. She works at the residential home; it's like an art and vocational training school in Palencia. It's really brilliantly run and she's just wonderful, isn't she, Susana?'

But Susana said something about Oliva that I didn't understand while she pulled my daughter Maya's hand and asked permission to show her something.

'She gets her words mixed up,' her mother explained.

'Can I go with them?' Ryo asked me.

'They're only going over there,' my mother reassured me, 'to look at the animals.'

I wanted to coax more information about Oliva from her.

'So your daughter studies in Palencia?'

'Well, I say studying, it's more like a place to learn manual skills and they get to do a few odd jobs. It's not quite in Palencia, it's just on the outskirts, in a lovely spot that used to be an old seminary. She's been going since she was two; she's very happy there.'

I knew that Oliva had returned from Boston; I'd seen her one night in a restaurant in La Latina, maybe three years back. She was having dinner with a group of friends and I was at a table on the first floor of the same place, but we saw each other through the window and stopped to say hi.

'Yes, I saw that you were living in Japan, from the records and the interviews, and I also saw that you have two children with a Japanese woman.'

'Yes,' was all I managed to say.

She told me about her return from Boston. I didn't ask her about Fran, but she told me he was still living there and that they hadn't been together for some years. Her eyes still sparkled, even behind her thick glasses, though her muscular shoulders had lost some of their power.

All I was able to say was, 'Have you cut your hair?'

She no longer had her curls but wore it short, which brought out bags around her eyes and the purple in her lips, like she was cold.

'I got tired of it,' she said, scrunching her face as if she suddenly regretted doing it.

She definitely noticed the look of disappointment on my face.

'I hope you don't report me to environmental standards,' she joked.

We made a few vague commitments, wished each other luck and I think I told her she was very beautiful, even though she'd got rid of her wild mane. Then I went up to the top floor, hoping she'd come and say goodbye before she left, but she didn't.

'Please forgive us. He has to go onstage now and we're already way behind with our timetable,' Jandrón begged, hoping to take me far away from Susana's mother.

'I'll look after the children for you,' she told me when she saw me being dragged towards the square.

The band had stopped playing and were crowding around near the stage. The one who seemed to be the leader smiled at me. He was missing two teeth, lost from playing his saxophone while standing on the cobbled squares and streets of so many villages. I approached him.

'Any of you guys fancy playing with me?'

'Sure,' the youngest two said.

'I'm not sure if I know any of your songs,' the saxophonist said apologetically.

'Everyone knows 'Lol-li-pops'. It's really easy, A major, B, then G and sustained F in the chorus,' explained the boy with the clarinet, with an infectious enthusiasm.

I liked the way he'd rapidly distilled the song into a language they all understood.

## sitting in the cinema one evening

Sitting in the cinema one evening, watching a romantic film I'd heard lots of good things about but that looked like every other romantic film, with its series of encounters and setbacks leading up to the final encounter, I realised I was no longer interested in love as a subject matter. That hidden, immense power, which had fascinated me for years and to which I'd dedicated my songs – or perhaps it would be more accurate to say to which I'd dedicated my life – had ceased to interest me. In the distance I could make out the muffled sounds of an ambulance's siren. Suddenly it sounded the way love does, like someone else's emergency: a far-off ambulance you haven't called and don't need, and therefore aren't eagerly anticipating. Love had ceased to form a part of my landscape.

Thus began a spell without love songs. I looked after my mother a little more, protected my kids a little more closely, looked for inspiration in other things and tried without success to prove myself wrong by falling in love again. I knocked at the door every night, in the hope of finding something deeper, but all I found were temporary moments of intimacy, which satisfied my curiosity more than my hunger.

I enjoyed the nudity, and I didn't want to talk to anyone about anything unless we were naked and in a bed. I'd fuck almost every night in a kind of continual flight, which meant I had to tiptoe across bedrooms in tiny sterile apartments, with shelves holding little more than a small pile of books and a few DVDs given away free with newspapers. Or an open laptop on the coffee table by the TV, playing a presumably endless list of songs from the Internet. Tremendously lonely flats, places of transit that had become homes without anyone investing in them, with no sense of permanence, with showers where the water had no pressure and bathrooms watched over menacingly by a set of scales. It was in those anonymous flats that I witnessed the true emotional catastrophe of our generation, our incurable loneliness.

Bocanegra wrote me an email from some exotic location. He brought me up to speed, with his habitual grandiloquence, about how he envisioned the near future in our profession. Too many prophets and not enough honest, hard-working craftsmen proud to wear that badge; that's what I thought every time I listened to a new diagnosis from him. I wrote back and confessed:

> I never thought I'd miss the label advance as a way of making me get on with writing. Look at me now; I used to think this was a vocation rather than a job.

I must have sounded disheartened, because he replied a few days later with an epic explanation of the reasons why the record industry had sunk and how this paradigm shift would end up shaking the worldwide economy, including not only publishers, radio stations, TV channels and newspapers, but also banks, politics, hotels, taxis, hospitals. But he finished with an outburst of lyricism, inspired by his wealth and his unhurried jaunt around the world.

> Everything's sinking, at least in the old way we used to know it. But when you immerse yourself in nature you realise how little all the things you used to care about matter. Come to Mallorca, to my house, bring the children, one week, two weeks, swim in the sea, watch the sky at night. The city's fucking killing you – everyone's depressed in Madrid. They all think the world has ended and they're stuck inside, unable to escape.

My disillusionment had been going on for months. I didn't go near my guitar, I never got out my phone to write down any lines to use in future songs. I found that I was empty, because everything around me already seemed full, brimming over. We were playing very few shows, our last record was already beginning to feel distant and the public's memory had become shorter, more immediate. Maybe what Bocanegra said was true,

I needed to look at life from outside that brick wall we call the city and, yes, maybe nature had the answers. And after listening so many times to Joni Mitchell's 'A Case of You', I summoned the strength to write something in her style:

> Let me tell you it's raining again
> And the flowers are out in the garden
> And spring is as stubborn as a mule.

## spring is as stubborn as a mule

For me, watching my children grow up was enlightening. While teaching Maya to play the guitar in her spare time, watching her weak fingers brush up against mine on the strings, I'd bring out my old teacher's tricks, the finger exercises and the scales that she agreed to repeat through gritted teeth. Like everyone else, I believed that in my day I was more driven and focused, possessing a passion she lacked. And maybe my daughter was upset, like all kids are, that her father wasn't proud of her, but it was just the opposite: I hoped that one day she could feel proud of me.

I liked looking after the flowers in our shared garden – a tulip coming up in spring was a cause for joy. Until one day I wrote a song and, when the children were asleep, invited Kei to my studio, a place she'd barely set foot in until then, always sending in Ludivina when she figured it was time for someone to blitz my lion's den. Without sitting down, she leant on the table and I sang to her, softly:

> If I was happy by your side
> I owe it to you
> I only hope I was
> Your greatest failure.

With her you always had to wait for a reaction. She wouldn't get excited or applaud or say 'how lovely,' simply and plainly; nor would she ask if it was for her or Oliva or another woman. No, Kei wasn't like that. She almost always waited until she had something professional to say, even going so far as to add a correction or a counterpoint.

That night she said 'Wait,' disappeared from my studio and crossed over the garden.

She came back with her cello and bow, closed the studio door and sat down to play at my side, tying up her hair with a purple ribbon.

'Let's see, how does the second part go?' she asked.

I hummed the melody so that she could try out her accompaniment and after a few attempts I sang the song again without any interruptions while she played. I enjoyed that moment, which felt like a reconciliation, though perhaps no reconciliation was needed between us. She finished with a few rasps of the bow that I watched in silence, in awe of her incredible ability to enrich the harmony intuitively. When I told her it sounded very beautiful and that we'd have to record it like that, she smiled and shrugged her shoulders.

'What's the point? Animal will just come along and swamp it with his drums.'

It's true, that is what happened. Animal would put his stamp on the songs and I was grateful, because it stopped them from sounding bland and turned them into something solid. When his percussive assault was introduced into 'Your Greatest Failure', it stopped being a melancholy ballad and turned into a Holy Week procession march.

'We've got a record, bro, we've got a record, bro, something tells me we've got a record,' he began shouting the moment we'd finished.

He was also waiting for the heavy grey cloud that had been

hovering over me those last few months to dissipate a little, to let the sun rays filter in. Friends always believe that they have the power to take a chisel to your sadness and smash it into pieces.

I like finishing records that way, piece by piece, with the patience of a fisherman. Three or four songs give you a certain security, a tone. They're the web over which you'll continue weaving all the others.

When my father died I went to sort out the house, where I discovered all of my records on his shelf. Without opening them, I looked at the back covers that listed the song titles. My mother used to carefully compile our family photo albums until one day she stopped finishing them. These days, all she did was pass the time every now and then leafing through the pages, pointing to my photo and asking, 'Who was this boy, then? He looks so serious.'

My kids made fun of the photos whenever we sat together with my mother at the home, and resorted to picking up the albums when there was no longer anything meaningful to say. My father and I were incapable of sticking them in: if any photo destined for the album ever fell into our hands, we just shoved it into the back pages, perhaps hoping that someday someone would perform the delicate task of placing them in in chronological order.

For me, the songs on my records were a bit like looking at old photos: some of them make you laugh, because of the look on your face, your haircut or the glasses you're wearing; others look more like you, so you can appreciate some trace of beauty; in others you look terrifying; and yet you're you in every single one of them. I also found the press cuttings my father used to keep in a drawer in his bedroom. In headlines you always sound either petulant or full-on moronic, but then I found some yellowing files in there, which dated back to the late eighties. They bore testament to the blunt reasoning of someone forced to make pronouncements about music or life, the country or current affairs, merely because he was promoting a record or playing a concert. 'The Spanish music industry is so underdeveloped that even we can be successful in it.' 'We don't make songs to please our audience but to please ourselves.' And in the photo we're jumping, the way Gus liked it – him and me jumping in the air.

I imagined my father had been incapable of understanding Gus's references and humour, but he'd still gone to the effort of cutting the articles and putting them away. 'This is my most grown-up record.' That headline was repeated too many times to be taken seriously. 'My name is Dani Mosca and I write songs.' And on the cover of a lesser-known but respected music magazine, run by a friend for a few years, which I handed to my father with a certain pride: 'Is this the best songwriter in Spain?'

This hyperbole felt like a good thing to shove in my father's face, but he immediately drew my attention to one detail with his habitual genius for such things.

'The question mark isn't a good sign, to be honest.'

I had my five minutes of pride with that cover, though I was never included in the magazine's lists of the hundred best songs in Spanish music, or the hundred best records, or the hundred best singers.

'I'm number 101,' I'd tell myself, 'that's not so bad.'

I put my father's clothes in cardboard boxes, saving the odd item: a jacket, a sports visor. Clearing out the house was a little like clearing out my childhood. I was happy that moving so often had eliminated many of my footprints, so much unnecessary paperwork, so many disposable memories. I was moving on without leaving too much behind. Unlike my father, I won't leave behind these huge piles of tickets, bills, wedding notices, death notices, Christmas cards and bank receipts, like exhibits in a pointless museum.

'Don't do it by yourself,' Kei told me when I told her I had to clear out the house, 'let someone help you.'

But who else was there that could enter the flat in Estrecho and figure out which things had sentimental value and which were just rubbish?

I looked for any traces of my biological mother left behind among the documents. I located the papers that had been such a revelation to me as a child: the adoption certificate, the photo of her in the village at fifteen or sixteen, the only visual trace left. Among all of the funeral notices, which my father treasured as if they were football cards, was hers: Lourdes María, died 13 April 1974.

Among my father's papers, I found two opened letters sent from the Congo.

'Dear Aunt and Uncle,' they both started, though they were sent almost a year apart from each other. Both were identical: a long, descriptive paragraph in which she told them about what her work entailed, the people she served, the widespread poverty and the most common diseases. She added a curious detail to the second letter.

The children here call me *Ngudi*, which means mummy, and that makes me very happy. I call them *Fibana*, which is something like 'my little children'.

And they both end with a request:

Please, pray for us every day and pray for all the people here. They need it so badly.

In one of the letters she described how the people over there

372

were so determined to be happy that it had ended up making her happy, too.

In the second letter she thanks my parents directly for everything they were doing, but she doesn't go into details and it looks like it was written in a hurry, because the handwriting is less careful. She does make a point of thanking them for a photo of the boy. 'He's so lovely and very big. He's so lucky to have wonderful parents like you,' she wrote, adding a forceful coda to the sentence: 'I know it.' She finished the letter with a tiny, unassuming signature. From the postmark I worked out that she'd have been twenty-two at the time and that she died a few months later.

I no longer retained that inner hunger I'd had when I was eleven and wanted to know the truth. Maybe it's because now I understood better that there is no order, that the order that children believe will explain everything – moral discipline, an exact consequence for our every action – does not exist. Maybe becoming an adult means accepting the chaos or at least learning to coexist with it – the chaos that makes children unsettled and causes them to invent a world that's as solid as the ones they create with their building blocks and with robust words like mummy, daddy, family, future.

I'd also learnt to stop aspiring to a position, to a career, to be someone. I no longer harboured any ambitions to see my name gleaming out from some shop window: I knew it could only ever be written in the condensation on the glass outside.

During my last visit to my parents' house I filled up two big boxes of things I thought might be of interest to my kids – not today but when they were older and began to remember the past with renewed interest. Perhaps at that moment what I needed was to get a head start for the third act.

Sometimes I'd take my kids to see my mother.

'Your grandmother was a wonderful woman,' I'd tell them.

373

'One time she fixed my knee using only the warmth in her hand. I was very small and I'd fallen off my bike on the street. She transmitted the heat from her hand to me and then I was better. She's lost her mind now, but you can talk to her about whatever you like. It's really fun – you just have to treat it like a game.'

Little by little the children stopped being scared about her illness and would engage in delirious conversations with her, and my mother would use her recurring soundbites to give ridiculous answers: 'drink your juice up quick or it loses its vitamins'; 'it's cooler at night, you know'; 'don't let the dogs lick your hand'; 'look properly before you cross'.

My son asked her what her favourite song was.

'Dad can play it to you.'

'Any song is beautiful,' she said, 'if you like it.'

And we all laughed, she most of all.

When my daughter got older she began to space her visits out. Ryo and I would go to the home without Maya because she said it gave her nightmares.

'I always get nightmares after seeing her.'

I told her they're not nightmares but reality. Yes, reality. Wasn't her grandmother, my mother, just someone else who'd wanted to escape from reality? She'd had a tragic childhood – losing her parents and her siblings as a girl – and it was easy to imagine her insecurities, her torment after my birth. Maybe her escape was just the result of too much reality; it was an escape to somewhere far away from pain and misfortune, where her nuggets of advice, loaded with common sense, were applicable to everything. My daughter was also escaping, exercising a child's right to escape from the world of adults and to head to another place, where tragedy and sorrow don't look you so straight in the eye.

*why are we waiting*

'Why are we waiting, we are suffocating.'

A few noisy boys were shouting the old chant, 'why are we waiting, why oh why,' so I blasted out a few riffs on the guitar while I tried to spot my children, feeling slightly uneasy.

Susana's mother pointed to where they were, climbing onto the right side of the stage with her daughter. Maya was carrying a tiny kitten in her hands. She was stroking it while Ryo was trying to get closer and touch it, both of them watched over by Susana, who was smiling with the undisguisable satisfaction of someone who knows that they've made children happy. I guess they felt more protected onstage with their father than out there with the villagers.

I felt Martán's absence, wishing he was here to play bass with us, certain that he'd have known how to get some interesting sounds from the DJ booth, which was already set up to open the dance.

When the guitar first rang out, the people at the back of the square came back towards the stage with their drinks in their hands. I looked in vain for Paula, trying to find a face to inspire me, but I could only see Jandrón and the other bigwigs in the first row. The rest was all darkness and the blinding reflection of a light that shone in my eyes. It came from the facade that now bore a plaque with my name written on it. I tried not to die of embarrassment.

Animal and the other musicians from the band had finished getting into position and I played the introduction to 'Ohio' by Neil Young, as I always do to loosen up my fingers. Some people began howling, because though the sound left a lot to be desired, music is always a liberation, a great excuse to lose your inhibitions. I remembered the calf they'd sacrificed so that

I could be up there on that stage and I thought to myself that all of those people deserved to have a good time.

I watched Animal, who had a snare drum hanging from a filthy strap around his neck, take a set of drumsticks from his pocket; he must have them found in the van or been lent them by one of the musicians. I caught his eye and he smiled back at me.

'Let's do it,' I said.

And we began playing 'Lol-li-pops'.

Animal nodded his head towards to the huge man with the bass drum and the rest of the band started up. When I heard them erupting behind me, I turned round to acknowledge them before the crowd, hoping that the applause would help rid them of their fear. The saxophonist smiled back at me from the corners of his mouth and I realised that they were enjoying themselves. That meant I had to have fun, too.

We'd never done 'Lol-li-pops' with a band like that. With every chord we came into our own more and more. It had an open-air dance feel to it and nothing could have made me happier.

I went over to the sax guy and asked him to do a solo; he nodded and stepped forwards to the edge of the extremely short stage. Within seconds, he was so immersed in it that he let out a metallic bellow and I began following him on my electric guitar for the final chorus. We'd never played that tune so well. I'd have loved Gus to be there on backing vocals, coming in where he always came in on that song; I'd have liked to have him onstage, next to me – the only place, I think, where we were ever completely happy.

The people in the crowd were shouting 'One more song, one more song,' but we had nothing left to play. The band didn't know any more of our songs, so Animal and I played 'Getting Older' to lower the adrenaline a little. I dedicated it to the village priest and to Jandrón, the mayor, which generated mock applause.

During the final chorus the saxophonist was bold enough to accompany us again, succeeding in sketching out something like what Kei added with her cello. We had to stop and get off the stage, so I strummed my guitar strings a little and brought my mouth to the microphone.

'Goodnight, everyone, it's been a joy,' I said, raising the volume of the distorted guitar to silence the cries of 'one more song, one more song' that were coming from the younger members of the audience.

I looked at the surprised expressions on my kids' faces. People often insist that having kids forces you to get old, that they flip through the pages of the calendar before your very eyes, but there's something else too, something connected with the way they were watching everything at that moment. Right there, Ryo and Maya, glued to the stage: it was as if having them near me meant I could rediscover life through their eyes, enjoy it again with the passion I saw in their gaze. It's the closest thing possible to a second childhood.

Animal whispered something I didn't understand.

'"Play for Me",' he repeated.

And, as if in a trance, he began hitting the drum until I began to sing that song we'd composed so many years earlier, silencing the cries that kept on asking for one more. A few mobile phones shone out in the darkness, recording us from the square.

By the time I'd unplugged my guitar, the DJ was already in place behind his table, about to start playing the canned music that would soon cover the whole place, like an aural pablum.

I went over to my kids, but before I could say anything Maya pointed to the kitten in her hands and asked, anxiously, 'Can I keep it?'

'Pretty please, Oto, let us keep it,' Ryo begged.

Susana's mother explained that it was one of her cat's kittens.

'It's a month old and you'd be doing us a favour.'

The cat was ash-grey all over and looked like it had been painted with smoke. I nodded and Susana smiled at my kids.

Jandrón embraced me enthusiastically.

'That was fucking fantastic.'

Animal came over and shouted at me over the music.

'What now? I pack away and we go?'

When Jandrón heard this he got angry and began protesting: I couldn't go, I had to be there the next day for the offering to the Apostle and the heifers – well, the heifer. They'd also be playing a football match against Mormójon, the neighbouring village, and they wanted me to do to the kick-off of honour, and then there was the speech after the Mass. But I was already holding both of my kids by the hands, and I told him I really had to go and couldn't stay a moment longer.

After much protesting he seemed to understand and he helped us to carry all the things Animal had got out for the concert back to the van. The guys from the band hugged us goodbye and I felt their sweaty bodies touching mine.

'Maybe one day you'll invite us to record with you,' said the saxophonist.

Jandrón ran off to find some sandwiches for us eat on the road. Maya and Ryo got into the back of the van together, once Animal had loaded up the amplifier. Maya was holding the tiny kitten in her arms, protective like a twelve-year-old doting mother.

'I'm going to call him Gris.'

'Because he's grey?' I asked.

'No, idiot, because of the film.'

I hesitated for a moment.

Animal explained as I put the guitar in its case and shoved it all the way to the back of the van like a coffin.

'*Grease*, not Gris. You remember how much Gus liked that film? He used to bang on about it all the time.' Animal slammed the van door shut and went and sat behind the wheel.

Luci came up to me for a moment.

'You remember when we were kids, right?'

I stopped to look at her, trying to figure out what she was referring to.

'Now I regret not letting you look at my tits.' And as she said it she regained her face from so many years ago, the one belonging to the feisty teenager she once was, and let out a chuckle.

'There'll be other occasions, I hope,' I replied.

'Whenever you want,' she said with her usual air of defiance.

Jandrón came back with four sausage sandwiches poorly wrapped up in paper towels and the councillor passed a few cans of beer to Animal. Animal looked at me as I held them and asked if they had a small bottle of water.

'Thanks,' I said to everyone and we got into the van before we were forced to say goodbye to all of them one by one.

From the car window I glanced at Javier, the priest, and nodded a goodbye, which was also received by the councillor's wife, making her smile, activating facial muscles that had been forgotten through lack of use in doing so.

Animal swung the van round, unconcerned that a few kids had to jump out of the way of his manoeuvre.

The hearse driver ran up to my window and shouted, 'It's been a pleasure. Are you off home now?'

'Yeah, have a great time. Thanks for everything. I thought you'd already gone.'

Jairo raised the beer can he was holding and I guessed that his night was going to be a long one.

'I hope we don't see each other soon,' he said, then shrugged and smiled in acknowledgment of his undervalued profession.

Animal followed the main road but missed the turning,

leaving the old adobe mansions behind. A bonfire had been lit at the entrance to one of the crumbling granaries and some youngsters were roasting sausages over the flames. Animal slowed down because one of them, dressed in their dancer's outfit, was vomiting in the middle of the road.

'These youngsters are the shit,' Animal said. 'It's not even eleven and they're already chundering their guts out.'

'Stop, stop for a second.'

Paula, illuminated by the light of the fire, had just shot me a farewell glance. When the van came to a halt she walked over to the road like a gazelle.

'Going already?'

I said yes.

'Are those your kids?'

Ryo and Maya's faces were pressed up against the back window and the flames of the bonfire were reflected in the glass.

'Yeah. All three of them,' I said, also pointing to Animal, who'd lit a cigarette behind the wheel.

'Four, you mean,' she corrected me, pointing with her finger at the kitten in Maya's arms. 'From Susana's cat, right?'

'Yes,' I said.

'The concert was great; we heard it from here.'

'Thanks.'

'Well, maybe we'll see each other in Madrid someday.'

They'd hung a spray-painted banner on a torn bit of bed sheet from the door to the barn, which read 'The Prisoners Club'.

'Why do you call yourself The Prisoners?'

'It's a long story. Last year the club met up in an abandoned depot, outside the village, and what happened was the door got jammed and we were trapped inside. By morning we still hadn't managed to open it, so our parents came to find us and they had to use a tractor to pull open the door. We were completely shut away the whole night and the name The Prisoners stuck.'

I noted the distant look on the face of one of the boys by the bonfire, assuming it was her boyfriend and that they'd got together the year before, during their accidental incarceration. The boy was staring at me with daggers in his eyes, the way young guys always look at us when we play concerts in villages. We always have to run away from jealous lads whenever we get approached by girls; on one occasion the whole group had to take refuge in a church because they all wanted to lynch us: I seem to recall that Martán had been messing around with a girl and her boyfriend's crew wanted to clobber us. Animal had to go up to the bell tower and sound the alarm for the authorities to come and rescue us from our enclosure.

'It's been a pleasure meeting you. Look after yourself, 'I said to Paula, whose mother came out in her smile for a brief moment.

I stuck half of my body out the window to kiss her on both cheeks.

'Who was that?' my daughter asked.

'A cousin of mine,' I replied.

'She's really beautiful.'

'She sure is. There are beautiful people in my family too, believe it or not.'

Animal looked very serious. 'Have you seen the tits these young girls have today? They weren't like that in our day, were they?'

With my head I gestured towards my kids in the back seat. 'The walls have ears.'

'Whoops, sorry,' he said, lowering his voice. 'They say it's got something to do with the hormones they're putting into chickens. The thing with the tits.' He gave the wheel a big spin and managed to turn onto the road by the stream. 'The thing that bugs me most is not being around for the heifer. Somebody told me they're releasing one tomorrow,' Animal complained. 'Do they stab it to death here or set fire to its horns?'

'No, I don't think so.'

'Right. That's a shame. Did you tell your kids about the time we played in Tomelloso when we went into the enclosure and the calf got you and you had to sing with two half-cracked ribs?'

I looked at Animal. 'Me? I don't remember that,' I said.

'What the fuck, man? Gus took you to be looked at and they put on a bandage or something so that you could perform. Then you got it on with the nurse.'

I shook my head again.

Animal turned back to look at my kids.

'Some father you've got. He only remembers what he wants to remember.'

We sped away from the village. Outside in the moonless night, the fields of grain blended into the darkness. Ever since Jandrón's emotional goodbye I'd had a niggling feeling that I was a fraud: I couldn't pretend that I belonged here, because I didn't. I remembered Gus, the way he used to laugh whenever people talked about their roots, when he'd renounced his. His own ties were to daydreams, fictions, fantasies. He was a Martian by calling.

'We're extraterrestrials, Dani, and we're going to get ourselves a planet and move there. We're the first generation in history to float, free, over the waves, with no land of our own.' That's what Gus would say.

I'd have liked to prove him wrong. Tell him that I had my roots, that that was where I came from. But I wasn't so sure.

I looked at my kids in the back seat. They wouldn't be able to bury me in a place that meant something to me, as I'd done with my father. Gus was right. Saint Gus. We were what we did – the songs, entertaining others, people dancing or clapping or humming – not a plaque or a headstone in a graveyard. What survives of my father is the look on the face of that flight attendant when she returned a favour that he'd done for her mother to me. Ultimately, Gus and my father were right. You get out what you put in.

'Shit, I'm not sure we took the right turn back there,' Animal complained. 'There's no bloody signs.' Then he sighed. 'Fuck the MOPU.'

My daughter, Maya, took a while to get to sleep. She was quiet, but she couldn't close her eyes and nod off like her brother, whose head was resting against the door after it had fallen onto her lap and she'd pushed it away.

'He might squash the kitten,' she said to excuse her lack of sisterly charity.

'Can't you sleep?'

She shrugged and looked at me with an uncommon intensity.

'When are you going to record another album, Dad?'

I was surprised by her question.

'Soon,' Animal intervened, addressing her via the rear-view mirror. 'Very soon. We've already got loads of songs.'

I nodded in agreement.

'And what will the new record be called?' asked Maya.

'Not sure. We still need to come up with a title. Can you think of one?'

She moved her lips comically as she thought of a suggestion.

'Tierra de Campos,' said Animal, pointing to the sign that announced the region we'd just left behind us.

'That's where our surname comes from, isn't it?' asked my daughter, whom I'd witnessed signing her name, with a flourish, as Maya Campos, looking for a personal stamp. Then Maya repeated it. 'Tierra de Campos, it's a nice title.'

'Tierra de Campos?' I said back. 'Could be.'

Animal took the fork in the road. The name Palencia, displayed on a metal sign, reminded me of the centre where Oliva worked. It wouldn't be difficult to find the old seminary – I could spend a day there, ask around for her. Animal gave me a knowing look, as if he knew what was going on in my head at that moment. He raised his fist to bump it against mine. He liked gestures like that, half playground, half gang member; he liked that idea of simple happiness. I brushed my fist against his knuckles. He smiled proudly with a satisfied look on his face.

I remembered the line from the Jorge Guillén poem: 'Friends nothing else, the rest is wilderness'. It dawned on me that the most valuable people in my life are the ones who've pushed me to create my own set of ideals. Fictitious ones, maybe, and yet so beautiful they truly make you want to believe, to cast your lot in with them, sing about them, dream about them – and then miss them terribly when they slip away from you and your whole life goes by trying to get them back.

And why not? That's where it all begins.